No woman [...] desirable, more sensual to the touch, than this delectable redhead. She had been passionate and feisty in the water and Dugan knew she would bring those qualities to her bed. But despite what so many thought, he was a man of principle when it came to women and he did not take advantage of them, even if every molecule in his body commanded him to do so.

"You just hit your head," Dugan said more to himself than to her, and began to rise.

He was about to leave her side, and when he did he would never return. Something inside Adanel refused to let that happen. She reached up behind his neck to stop his retreat and framed his cheek with her other hand. "I know exactly what I am asking. I'm asking you to kiss me."

Dugan held himself immobile, but his heart was pounding loudly, making it clear that her desire was not one-sided. "I won't be able to stop with just a kiss."

"I'm counting on that. . . ."

Books by Michele Sinclair

THE HIGHLANDER'S BRIDE

TO WED A HIGHLANDER

DESIRING THE HIGHLANDER

THE CHRISTMAS KNIGHT

TEMPTING THE HIGHLANDER

A WOMAN MADE FOR PLEASURE

SEDUCING THE HIGHLANDER

A WOMAN MADE FOR SIN

NEVER KISS A HIGHLANDER

THE MOST ELIGIBLE HIGHLANDER
IN SCOTLAND

HOW TO MARRY A HIGHLANDER

HIGHLAND HUNGER
(with Hannah Howell and Jackie Ivie)

Published by Kensington Publishing Corporation

How To
MARRY *A*
HIGHLANDER

MICHELE
SINCLAIR

ZEBRA BOOKS
KENSINGTON PUBLISHING CORP.
www.kensingtonbooks.com

ZEBRA BOOKS are published by

Kensington Publishing Corp.
119 West 40th Street
New York, NY 10018

All Kensington titles, imprints, and distributed lines are available at special quantity discounts for bulk purchases for sales promotion, premiums, fund-raising, educational, or institutional use.

Special book excerpts or customized printings can also be created to fit specific needs. For details, write or phone the office of the Kensington Sales Manager: Attn.: Sales Department. Kensington Publishing Corp., 119 West 40th Street, New York, NY 10018. Phone: 1-800-221-2647.

Zebra and the Z logo Reg. U.S. Pat. & TM Off.

First Printing: April 2019
ISBN-13: 978-1-4201-3884-9
ISBN-10: 1-4201-3884-7

ISBN-13: 978-1-4201-3885-6 (eBook)
ISBN-10: 1-4201-3885-5 (eBook)

10 9 8 7 6 5 4 3 2 1

Printed in the United States of America

In memory of my father,
who very unexpectedly passed away
far too young in April 2016.

Dad, I cannot tell you how much I miss you
and wish you were here.
You are in my thoughts so many times each day
and your words still give me renewed strength
when I have nothing in me left.
You were right.
Family does not have to be made up of those
related by blood, but those who honestly love, accept,
and support you for who you are.
You told me so many times to be around only those
who positively impact one's character and internal mind-set.
The others, regardless of who they are, you just need to let go.
This book is for you, Dad.
You may be gone, but you still come and remind me
of who I am, what is important,
and to do what I need to in order to be happy.
Thank you, and I will always love you.

Chapter One

April 1317, Loch Coire Fionnaraich

"Now *that* is a man," Adanel murmured to herself, brushing a stray lock of her wet, unruly, embarrassingly red hair out of her eyes to get a better look.

Sitting astride his horse, the handsome figure had light brown hair, a strong jawline, and an upper body that would make even the most devout nun go weak in the knees. Whoever this mystery man was, he was as close to visual perfection as Adanel had ever seen. Her large dark brown eyes widened as he stretched his arms high over his head and then out and behind his back. The effort pulled his léine tightly across his chest, leaving no doubt to what it hid—corded muscles, beckoning deliciousness, and most of all trouble. For that was what she would be in if he were to discover her in her current undressed status.

Adanel took one last look at the tempting morsel across the little loch and was about to surreptitiously return to the shore where she had hidden her clothes, quickly slip them on, and sneak back the way she came when a glint of silver caught her eye. A very large sword.

Adanel bit back a groan. Of course, he would not simply be a well-built farmer out for a curious stroll. The Lord's sense of humor would not be satisfied if he were only a scrumptious temptation for her to fantasize about at night. No, the man was a *saighdear*. Her one weakness.

"A soldier? Not fair, God," Adanel whispered. And then with a little more bite, she added, "If I get caught staring, it's your fault for bringing him here, let alone creating such an attraction." *Besides,* she thought to herself, *any Highlander who could wield that large weapon and fill out his léine the way this man did deserved to be ogled.*

She had been around would-be soldiers all her life for most of the men in her father's army did look the part. They were large, brawny, and trounced around carrying scary-looking swords and halberds, but she had spied on them during one of the rare times they had mustered together to train with the handful of mercenaries her father had hired. The sight only proved what she had suspected. They were just large men who could do little more than wave their weapons around in a showy but uncoordinated fashion.

The man across from her, however, was nothing like the ones in her father's army. He had not even touched his sword, yet Adanel suspected that when he did, it was not to boast or to pretend he knew what he was doing. It was to shed blood. Sword, dagger, halberd, or poleax— whatever this man used, he would be deadly.

She had nothing definitive to substantiate her guess, but Adanel's instincts all screamed that she was right. There was something in the way he sat in his saddle, gripped his reins, and studied the area around him. He reminded her of the mercenaries her father often hired. Like them, this *saighdear* was in complete control of his every move. Even the simple stretching of his arms was unconsciously calculated. Such control was perfected only after years of practice, honed and engraved into even the smallest and inconsequential of actions.

Adanel watched spellbound as he adjusted his seat and then swung his leg over to slide off his horse. Without thought, she rested her cheek upon a nearby, partially submerged boulder and sighed. The soldier, whoever he was, was not just incredibly good looking, he was tall—even for a Highlander. She wondered just where her own lanky form would come up to him. His chin? His shoulder? Probably the latter. She could just imagine fitting perfectly against his warmth as he held her tightly to his side.

It had been a long time since she had been held by a man, but that did not mean she had completely forgotten what it was like. Nothing was better at making her long-legged, curvy body feel feminine and attractive than lying against something large and hard. And next to that man . . . Adanel blew out the breath she had been holding. Lying next to him she would feel practically dainty. Unfortunately, that was something she would never know. Lord, why did he have to be the best-looking soldier she had seen in years? Perhaps ever.

Movement across the loch snapped her thoughts from daydreams back to reality. The soldier was bringing his horse closer to the water . . . and therefore closer to her. Worse, she was unable to see where he was going without revealing her current position. Adanel knew she should take the opportunity to sneak away to the shoreline on her side of the loch, but instead she stretched her neck, hoping to continue her gawking.

Nestled high within the Torridon hills next to a massive cliff, the saddle-shaped loch was very small compared to most in the region. One end of the shoreline was comprised of near vertical cliffs from a decades-old landslide, making the water inaccessible as well as frigid from being constantly shaded from the sun's warmth. Only the northern tip of the loch, which was divided into two sections, was free of debris and accessible to trespassing swimmers and mysterious soldiers. On the side Adanel had traversed to access the loch, varying-sized boulders were scattered along the water's edge. Swimming approximately twenty horse lengths directly across the very large boulder Adanel was crouching behind, one could reach the small loch's only other accessible shoreline. That stretch contained fewer rocks and multiple large patches of grass. Until now, Adanel had no idea there was even a path up to the loch via that side. She had thought her narrow, rocky route up to the hidden loch was the only one, but obviously, there was another, much larger path that could accommodate a horse rather than the difficult one she climbed up every week.

Adanel froze when the man suddenly turned and stared intently in her direction as if he could sense he was not alone. The only way he could see her was if he knew exactly where to look, and while he was looking in her direction, it was not directly at her.

Forcing herself to relax, Adanel ducked back down and glanced over her shoulder to see if he might be spying her clothes. Had she left them in the open where he could see them? Adanel did not think so. She had been coming to the loch whenever possible for over a year now, and after one unfortunate afternoon where a bird's waste found her bliaut while she had been swimming, Adanel had been careful to fold all her garments and store them safely under a small ledge. Unfortunately, while that blocked a bird's view of them, it might not from an observer across the loch. As silently as possible, Adanel swam back a couple feet, being careful to remain in the shadow of the boulder so she could check. Upon seeing nothing but gray jagged rocks being lapped by the water, she relaxed and slowly released the breath she had been holding before returning back to the boulder. As far as she could tell, she had left nothing near the shore to indicate another presence. So why did he continue to look her way? A ripple of the water? Was there a shadow she did not realize she was casting?

Tension rose in her again as her mind raced. It only eased when the Highlander shifted his gaze to study the rest of his surroundings. Adanel lay her forehead on the boulder and chastised herself for reading into things and leaping to conclusions instead of just enjoying the view.

She craned her neck once more to take a final look. Now that he was off his horse and standing on the water's edge, he was close enough to make out many more details. *Murt,* the man was *fine.* He had chiseled cheekbones, a strong shaven chin, and thick hair that was too dark to be blond and yet too light to be truly brown. He was too far to actually see the color of his eyes, but with his bone structure, Adanel knew he also had to have dreamy eyes and deep dimples that could snatch a woman's free will with just a glimmer of a smile. But even if she was wrong, he would still remain delectably attractive. Who could resist those powerful arms and large hands? Strong, capable, and without a doubt deadly. If only she had fallen for such a man six years ago. If she had, maybe Daniel would still be alive and she would no longer be living under the tyranny of her father.

With fisted hands on his hips, the Highlander stared at the water. His body was taut as if he sensed something there and needed to be ready to leap into battle. A woman under this man's protection would never have to worry for her safety. And if Adanel were any other woman with any other father she might have called out on the chance he was single and seeking a wife. But she had already been forced to watch one man die for her. She refused to see another.

Daniel had been all things sweet and good, and Adanel had believed him to be her one and only true love. But unlike the Highlander across the loch whose brutal strength could be seen even at a distance, Daniel had looked like what he was—a young, naive, hopeful merchant. She had fallen in love with his easy smile, and his trusting spirit had captured her heart the first time they had met. But what had amazed her the most was that she had captured his. Never did Adanel dream her father would not approve of them marrying. She had honestly believed he would not care or notice her absence. She certainly had no concept of just what her father was capable of to ensure not only that she and Daniel were never together, but that she never dared to fall in love again.

The horse neighed. Taking one last long look at her side of the loch, the man pivoted and walked over to his mount, but instead of getting back on, he pulled free his water bag. Returning to the shore, he knelt down to refill the leather bag. Afterward, he would no doubt disappear the same way he came.

Adanel bit her bottom lip. *Don't leave*, she silently implored. *Just linger for a few more minutes before you vanish, never to be seen again.* She hoped she was wrong, but it was unlikely.

With the exception of the cold winter months, she had been coming to this loch almost every week for nearly a year and not once had she seen anyone or even anything in the area that hinted someone had visited during her absence. The loch's guaranteed solitude was the main reason Adanel came. Constantly surrounded by the noise and stink of grungy dock workers, harbor men, licentious seamen, and overconfident want-to-be soldiers, she needed a weekly reprieve, and this secluded spot gave her the strength to endure another six more days. And while she coveted the peace and privacy the loch typically provided, this Highlander was a feast for any woman's eyes and Adanel was going to enjoy every second of looking at him before he disappeared.

After filling the bag, the soldier put back his waterskin and then, instead of remounting, he closed his eyes and took in a deep breath and held it. His chest expanded and Adanel had the urge to run her fingers across every bulge, from his arms, to his chest, to what she had no doubt were perfect abs, and then on to what was under his tartan. Crinkling her brow, Adanel studied the dark plaid of greens and blues that was accented with bright colors of gold, red, and burgundy.

"*Mo chreach*," she grumbled under her breath. The soldier was a McTiernay. She should not be surprised; after all she *was* on McTiernay lands . . . though just barely. However, multiple nomadic families had made these hills their home and only a handful called themselves McTiernays.

A few years back, the majority of the locals who had been left clanless after years of fighting the English had banded together under McTiernay rule. Most had left this area to live closer to the protection of the closest McTiernay castle, Fàire Creachann, nestled on the edge of Loch Torridon. A few, however, had pledged their allegiance to the McTiernays, who had elected to continue making their living among these hills. Then there was the small handful who had outright declined to move or live under anyone's rule, which included the McTiernays'. The area was technically McTiernay land, but as long as they created no harm, the powerful clan's laird had let them be. Such generosity would not be extended to her.

She was a Mackbaythe, the McTiernays' northern neighbor and enemy.

Her father had made his disgust clear when Cole McTiernay had been named laird of the area. Having lived his entire life in the region and already a laird, he thought he should have been the one to be placed in charge. Rumor was that he had not even been considered or even invited to the talks. As a result, her father had made sure only animosity was shared between their two clans. The last thing she needed was to get caught swimming in the nude on McTiernay lands.

Adanel did not fear the McTiernay soldier; she feared her father. Just the thought of what he might do made her cringe—especially if this Highlander saw her and got the notion to take her back himself. Devoid of any emotion that may have been perceived as kind, her father controlled everything of his with a ruthless, maniacal fist, and her younger brother Eògan longed to prove he was just like him.

It's time, saighdear, Adanel silently urged with a sigh. *Get back on your horse and go back to wherever you came from. Forget this small slice of heaven. I need it far more than you.*

Adanel had discovered the rocky path to the loch a little over a year ago during one of her weekly rides. The escape it afforded was only temporary, but she had grown to need these few hours away from her father and his enjoyment of the misery he liked to create on those around him.

Faden, her uncle and primary guard, had been quite agitated the day they had crossed onto McTiernay lands, but Adanel had felt compelled to ride as hard as she could and had not cared about borders and the potential acrimony her presence could cause. She had just needed to feel free from the confines of her life for a little and the lands belonging to her clan were too small to provide that sense of freedom. Besides, practically no one lived out this way. The northern side of the Torridon hills were cold, rocky, impossible to farm, and provided little grass for cattle to graze on. One needed to seek the valleys to find anyone.

She had been about to turn around and heed Faden's demands that they return back to Mackbaythe lands when a spear of sunlight from the ever-present clouds lit up the entrance to a partially hidden, narrow, rocky path. Adanel had decided God was beckoning her to see what mysteries He had created. Faden had disagreed, and Adanel had almost let him persuade her to leave for she had long learned to suppress any inquisitive thoughts or feelings due to fear of what her father might do if she learned or saw something she oughtn't. But something pressed her to shed her inhibitions and cave to her buried curious spirit.

The path was far too narrow and steep for a horse, so she had climbed. Though not a difficult ascent, it had been farther than she had anticipated, causing Faden to have grumbled ceaselessly. But when she had seen the pristine loch reflecting the clouds in the blue sky, she had been so glad to have persisted in the climb. Adanel felt as if she had found a little piece of heaven God had carved out just for her. Every fiber of her being had wanted to shed her clothes, jump into the waters, and enjoy the tranquility, even if only for a little while.

Of course, Faden had made sure that had not happened with his demands that they return immediately or face consequences. Knowing he was not overstating what might happen, Adanel had acquiesced to leave, but only after Faden agreed to let her come back the next week. And so, she had returned, that week and all the ones that followed for the past year as long as the weather permitted. To Faden's bafflement, the rain almost always abated the morning of their ride.

After weeks of climbing up to the little loch only to confirm that no one or animal was around or even had been near the small water refuge, Faden had elected to stay behind under the excuse of watching after the horses. Adanel fully supported the idea. She loved her uncle and enjoyed his company, but his absence offered her the opportunity to do what she had wanted since she had first spied the loch. Stripping bare, she had dived into the snow-fed waters. Cold and bearable only in the sunlight, the icy water had become the perfect remedy to stave off the sadness that threatened to overtake her sometimes.

Adanel felt a shiver go up her spine. Now, she needed the Highlander to leave for another reason. To stay warm, she had to move or get out of the water. She was starting to shudder keeping herself still with only her shoulders above the surface. Squeezing her eyes shut, Adanel wished with all her might that God would compel the handsome McTiernay to get back on his horse and leave so she could exit the cool waters. Slowly she opened a single eyelid and sighed. The man was still just standing there, hands on his hips, looking around. There was no telling how long he would remain.

Adanel considered her options: freeze to death, continue praying, or call out. The latter was the only one that led to warmth. Unfortunately, it also led to questions of why she was there alone, probable discovery that she was not wearing a stitch of clothing, and worst of all . . . him learning just who she was. The last of which she could not let happen.

Another shiver ran through Adanel's body, and she placed her cheek on a spot on the massive rock that had been warmed by the sun. Lifting her head, she studied the smaller boulder next to it. Maybe she could find a way to climb up on it and somehow slip unseen to the shoreline.

She was just planning her escape when her head jerked at a very unexpected, very unwelcomed sound. Adanel listened, her heart pounding, hoping she was mistaken. A couple of seconds later, her heart stopped altogether upon hearing a splash of an arm hitting the water, followed by another and then another.

Adanel swallowed a groan. The *saighdear* was swimming. *Swimming!* Something *she* should be doing, not him. Adanel should have known the moment she saw the Highlander he would be trouble. All men were. Why would being incredibly good looking and a soldier make this one any different?

She was about to succumb to the urge to sneak a peek and see where he was when the sound of another splash made it unnecessary. The man was on the other side of the enormous boulder she was leaning against. And by the sound of it, he had stopped swimming.

Why? she asked herself, looking toward the heavens. *Why me? Why now? Why him?*

Dismissing the question, Adanel decided she first needed to get out of the freezing water. Trying to make as little noise as possible, she reached out with her foot to use a smaller, submerged rock to stand on. Shivering, she leaned back against the massive warm rock in an attempt to thaw herself, feeling both embarrassed at being openly nude with a man so close and thrilled to be nearly out of the cold water. Now, she just needed to think of a way she could leave unseen.

If she could just stay crouched down as she climbed up and over the smaller boulder that was adjacent to the shore, she might be able to avoid being discovered. Once safely on the beach, she would wait until the Highlander dipped below the surface of the water to run and snatch her clothes. Then, she could leave without him ever knowing she was there.

It was a great plan mostly because it was the only one that offered her a chance of getting her out of her predicament.

Adanel looked up to see where the sun was in the sky. She had perhaps a little over an hour before Faden decided to make the arduous trek and come get her. She could try and wait to learn if this McTiernay soldier was taking a quick dip or was here for a long, leisure swim, but if he decided to swim to this side of the boulder, she was doomed.

Adanel, feeling a little warmer now, began to look around for handholds or footholds she could use to pull herself fully up. She had just found one when once again, her body locked, frozen in shock.

"I know you are there, *ruadh*. I've been watching you."

Adanel stiffened at the sound of the deep baritone voice. *Ruadh,* he had said. There was only one reason the McTiernay would call her the color red. He had seen her . . . or at least her cursed hair. How long had he been watching her? He had stared in her direction for several seconds. The man must have known she was there and had just feigned looking away. Adanel clenched her jaw and shook her head, suspecting that was exactly what had happened. The not-so-noble McTiernay soldier had been toying with her and now expected to have a conversation.

"Arrogant goat," she muttered, uncaring if he heard. When he did not respond, Adanel shouted, "If you knew I was here, then why did you not leave?" She paused, hoping to hear him beg his pardon or at the very least the sounds of him swimming back to his side of the loch.

"I thought you might be as curious as I am as to who else visits this remote place for a swim."

Adanel could hear the smirk on his face in his aggravatingly chipper tone. "I think my hiding makes it more than obvious I am not curious about you at all and prefer to bathe alone."

"Ah, but I caught you staring."

"If you had truly seen me, you would know that I was not staring as you put it, but merely shocked at your unexpected arrival. If I had been looking in your direction, it was just to see who was behind my bad luck of having a lovely afternoon ruined." It was a complete fabrication. She *had* been staring and she *had* been curious, but she had *not* wanted to meet him. Adanel prayed that he took her strongly worded hint to quickly decide to leave.

A satisfied smile curved Dugan's lips. His *ruadh* had spirit. As a commander of the Torridon McTiernays, he found that women usually either fawned all over him, eager to agree to anything he said or suggested, or cowered from him, afraid to learn if all the stories their mother had told them about the battle-worn soldier were true. Most were.

Nearly six years ago, when he had first come to these harsh lands, he had been the leader of a small but deadly group of soldiers who had made a name for themselves fighting in the war for Scotland's freedom. Known for his congenial temperament and deadly arm, Dugan had been one of two possibilities as a potential laird of the lands south of Loch Torridon. Many of the small clans that had littered the area had lost their lairds in battles against the English. The resulting lawlessness had made their small numbers even smaller. Without leadership, they had become nomadic, scavenging cattle and whatever else they could carry, creating problems for the larger clans in the area.

Someone had needed to take control and Dugan was seen as a neutral choice. He was affable, trusted by the local clansmen, wicked with a sword, and most of all—someone whom each nearby powerful laird thought he could manipulate. In the end, however, he had lacked one very important thing, an army.

Dugan had led a small group, but did not have either the financial means or the men Cole McTiernay had. Unsurprisingly, none of the larger clans wanted to shift a significant amount of their men and funds to an unproven leader. Still, they liked him and used their influence to press Cole into naming Dugan as one of his commanders.

Dugan had grudgingly accepted, believing the position was nothing but a temporary consolation prize and that either he or Cole would quickly decide he should move on. But it was not long before he realized that the older lairds had been correct in the decision to choose Cole over him, with or without an army. Leading a band of soldiers was considerably different than overseeing a clan, something Cole had experience doing during the times his eldest brother Conor, the McTiernay chief, traveled.

As weeks turned into months, Dugan had been surprised to find how much he grew to respect the often surly McTiernay as well as his other two commanders. Donald, Cole's best friend and someone he had known and fought alongside for years, had been named the commander of his elite guard. Jaime Ruadh, another McTiernay with whom Cole had a long history, had been placed in charge of Cole's sizable army, making it one of the largest and most fearsome in the Highlands. Dugan had been given the unusual role of liaison between Cole—who was merely rude on his good days—and the rest of the clan.

At first, Dugan had thought the position ludicrous, created in name only as an appeasement for not being named laird. But it was not long before he understood just how important liaison duties were to not just Cole, but to the motley clan as a whole. Outside of the soldiers, if someone had an issue, problem, question, or need, they came to him. His lack of leadership experience had meant he made mistakes, but Cole had proven to be an excellent laird and eventual friend, standing by him and providing input only when needed or asked. Now, years later, Dugan possessed the confidence he once lacked. And hearing this redhead admonish him, he was once again reminded of another reason why he stayed as McTiernay commander—he loved the perks, especially when it came to women. They loved him and he had done his best to make them all feel loved in return.

After six years of riding these hills and visiting the McTiernay farms that spotted the valley near this area, he had thought to have met all the pretty women under his purview. Most—married or not—had made it their mission to meet him. He could not count how many mothers had paraded their daughters in front of him in the hopes that she would be the one to convince him to settle down and make a binding commitment. As a result, Dugan would have wagered there was not a woman around whom he had not met. It certainly had been a long time since he had seen a fresh face. But he had definitely spied one today.

It was rare he got the impulse to make the winding journey up to the little, abandoned loch, but this afternoon he had wanted assurance that he would not be disturbed.

Twice a month, he ventured out to Cole's eastern border to check on the welfare of those who did not want the shelter of the clan's castle stronghold, Fàire Creachann. For the most part, his trips were uneventful. The MacCoinniches were the only nearby clan with any power and size. They were not enemies nor allies; however, both used each other's lands regularly to travel to other Highland regions. Hamish journeyed through their territory to reach his northern home, and unless MacCoinniches wanted to add several days to venture anyplace south of their lands, they had to travel through lands belonging to Conor McTiernay or Rae Schellden, both a close friend and ally of the McTiernays. The three chiefs held a mutually beneficial agreement that extended no further than the free, unhampered use of each other's lands. All knew not to take advantage and no one did.

The only clan that ever gave Cole McTiernay any problems was the Mackbaythes, a tiny clan whose petty laird promoted bullying tactics. They held a wide strip of land that went from the rocky peak of Sgorr Ruadh to the eastern bay of Upper Loch Torridon. The clan would be completely inconsequential except that at its heart was one of the best located ports along Scotland's northwestern shores, Bàgh Fìon.

The Mackbaythe army was small and inadequate, but the clan's power-hungry laird had arranged a strategic marriage in his youth with the MacLeods, a large and very powerful northern seafaring clan. Then, he had established some unknown arrangement with the MacCoinniches allowing them wide use of the port. The combination made the abhorrent laird think he was untouchable and he often liked to strike out against the more vulnerable McTiernay farmers. Cole had decided that the McTiernays were not going to start a war over the loss of a handful of cattle or farm animals each year, no matter how annoying the constant thievery was. Having been in war and knowing its nightmares, Dugan knew Cole was right and, though aggravating, agreed with his decision. Today, however, Dugan had almost changed his mind.

The weather for most of his journey had been wet, windy, and overall unpleasant. His mood, already sour, had deteriorated more so when he had arrived at a farm just in time to catch a Mackbaythe thief in the act. To the outrage of the injured McTiernay farmer, Dugan had let the culprit go, though he had truly given him a fright about ever returning. Then, he had helped the farmer retrieve his livestock to hopefully prevent any retaliation, and in doing so had become particularly filthy.

He finally had left and was on his way to the Allt Bealch Ban River to bathe, when the Finn brothers, Finlay and Finley, had intercepted him and ignored his glaring looks. Both pummeled him with trivial complaints about the trials of living near the border where it was difficult to grow things and hard to survive. After explaining that he could do nothing about the soil, the weather, or their choice of living where there was a lack of protection, Dugan no longer wanted to just bathe; he needed several hours alone. So he had ridden up to the small loch for as it was not easy to reach, it would assuredly be deserted. The peace and quiet would enable him to relax before heading back home.

The loch had not yet been in sight when Dugan first heard the soft murmurs of a woman humming. The melody had a haunting quality and for a moment he had been transfixed by the sound. Intrigued, he had slipped off his horse and snuck up to see just who was enjoying the frigid waters that kept most away.

Loch Coire Fionnaraich was not only hard to get to, it was cold, even in the summer. There were many other more easily accessible and far warmer lochs and rivers to bathe or wash clothes, which is why he normally chose them when in the area. But days like today, he preferred the little loch because its promise of solitude. Not once in six years had he ever seen any evidence that anyone else ever visited his secret retreat.

The moment he spied the redheaded woman Dugan had been riveted. She had been facing away from him with just her bare shoulders out of the water, but it was enough for him to see that she swam as he did—in the nude. It was also enough to confirm that the melodic sounds were made not by an innocent female just outside her youth, but by a woman who looked nearer to his age. That meant she was either married or incredibly homely in either behavior or in the face. Dugan had only two rules when it came to sex and women, and dallying with a married woman broke one of them.

Her humming had caught his ear again as if to remind him that looking did not break either of his rules. So he had and soon afterward cursed himself for doing so.

The woman was breathtakingly beautiful. Tangled waves of copper-colored hair cascaded down her back and floated all around her in the water. He had never seen anything like it. The confused mass encompassed every shade of red from darkest to lightest, made even more vibrant by the pale cream color of her skin. He longed to run his fingers through the fiery locks and have them wrap around his arms and ever-hardening body. If such perfection was as soft as it looked, he would be an addict to its effects.

He had almost gathered enough willpower to break

his stare and return to his mount when she had risen out of the water and turned just enough so that he could see the silhouette of her curvaceous form. He knew instantly that, married or not, she was not a mother. Her perky breasts confirmed her tight stomach had yet to birth any babes. Once again, Dugan had to remind himself that there was no way such perfection had not already been claimed by some man and forced himself to look away.

With a sigh of regret, Dugan had slunk unnoticed back to his horse and mounted, feeling his temporarily forgotten headache return in full force. He had headed back down the mountain unable to control his wandering thoughts. Was her demeanor as fiery as the color of her hair? Or was she the type to yield and cower when confronted? Were her eyes blue like the sky? Or were they as green as grass? Perhaps they were dark with promises of unforetold pleasures. Was she playful or sharp? Intelligent and amusing, or dull and dim-witted?

Dugan had tried unsuccessfully to force his body to relax and answer each question with the negative. But it had been months since he had been with a woman. Every eligible McInernay female who met his criteria he had met long ago. It had not taken long for him to lose interest in those who had initially captured his attention, usually because they had nothing in common. Since then, Dugan had only sought relationships with women who knew how to pleasure a man as well as refrain from excessive talking. Unfortunately, his latest "regular" had come to believe that the longevity of their relationship meant more than it did and he had yet to find a replacement. He had been surprised by her demands, thinking his reputation as a bachelor had been thoroughly rooted. Dugan was never going to commit to anyone—ever.

He had not journeyed far when Dugan stopped and looked back at the trail. Images of the luscious redhead were going to haunt him, especially at night. It would be months before he had a good night of sleep again if he did not at least speak to her and confirm that she was indeed married. If he was lucky and she was not, she just might be what he was looking for, someone unknown, far enough away that they could not be clingy, and best of all, someone who could make these drudging trips to the border worth it.

And so Dugan had returned.

This time, however, he had made his presence known and only pretended to be unaware of her just to see what she would do. A married woman would most assuredly have immediately called out and shooed him away, making it clear that he was not wanted. But his *ruadh* had done the opposite. She had scrambled to hide behind a rock and then boldly stared at him. Such a reaction could mean she was an innocent, afraid of being caught, but in Dugan's experience, a woman that beautiful did not get to her age without having caved to some man's charm and flattery, not to mention her own basic primal desires, at some point.

Her stare had been almost hungry in nature and his resulting arousal had forced him to seek the cold waters of the loch for relief. He was beginning to realize that his brilliant plan had not accounted for the next several days where her image would plague him each time he closed his eyes. Cole's wife, Ellenor, would immediately recognize his distraction and she, with her inhuman sense of knowing when his distress pertained to a woman, would hound him until he admitted all. He desperately needed to learn something off-putting about the woman if he was going to have any control of his thoughts, let alone remain sane. She was beautiful, but was she dim in the mind? Perhaps she was a shrew who thought her beauty entitled her to any whim she might have? If either was the case, he could easily dismiss her mentally, despite the physical attraction.

Dugan had slowly made his way over the large boulder she hid behind, wondering what the woman would do or say when she realized he blocked her path to the shore. The water's temperature was bearable, but one needed to keep moving to stay warm. The place where she had escaped behind did not offer much room to maneuver, especially if her goal was to remain hidden. Soon, his *ruadh* would need to get out of the cold waters and into the sun. How she handled her predicament would tell him if she was a prude, a harridan, or by some miracle an unwed, willing partner open for an afternoon of pleasure. Just the possibility of the latter had him painfully hard again, despite the bitter temperature of the water.

"That you have decided to hide behind this large rock does not compel me to leave. In fact, it does just the opposite," Dugan called out, hoping the cold water would not stop this already refreshing conversation prematurely.

"I don't even *know* you, and yet I am not surprised by your conceited comment."

"Maybe you are hiding as part of a bold ploy to get my attention?" Dugan prodded, grinning with enjoyment. "Women like to play such games to attract a man's interest. And you, *aithinne*, have definitely got me intrigued."

Adanel moistened her lips and dragged in a breath of air. It had been a long time since her temper had caused someone to call her a firebrand. Then again, it had been a long time since she had said or done anything deserving of the title to anyone, let alone a man. Every word she spoke in public was carefully chosen and stated, for showing passion was dangerous. It got one noticed, and that was the last thing she wanted to be at home. But

Adanel was not at home at the present and neither was the man she was speaking to a Mackbaythe. Both facts were incredibly freeing and Adanel suddenly felt like a piece of her that had long been dormant out of a sense of survival had suddenly awoken after a long sleep.

"What a quandary," she said with an overly exerted sigh. "I mean I could emphatically denounce your assertion, but we both know that would only serve to encourage you."

Dugan let go a short laugh of pleasure. "It's as if you have known me for years."

Adanel had to bite her bottom lip to keep from joining him in his laughter. The man was definitely arrogant and needed no encouragement. Somehow that, too, was freeing. "Nay. I don't know you . . . but I have met men like you. You may be surprised to learn that as a soldier, you are not that original."

Dugan crossed his arms. "Hmmm. You openly tease me, so I think I will agree to play your little game."

Adanel's eyes grew large, realizing what she had just started. The Mackbaythes were a small clan, but strategically located on one of the best natural seaports in northwest Scotland. She practically lived on the docks and had been surrounded by a variety of bawdy men all her life. One thing they had in common—their lust of women. Adanel knew she should stop and demand his retreat, and yet she just could not bring herself to do so. At least not yet.

"You are correct. I am a soldier, but I can assure you that I am far from commonplace."

Adanel loudly clucked her tongue. "I wouldn't say you were commonplace, for you are unusually handsome. But then again, your fetching face only makes you even more predictable. Therefore, my initial assessment stands. I find you to be . . . well, banal."

Dugan grinned. Ellenor, and sometimes Donald's wife, Brighid, would tease him, but no other female had ever even tried. That this redheaded beauty thought to do so, despite being less than ten feet away without a stitch on her, was creating incredible warmth in places on his body that should have been shrinking from the coolness of the water. He could not remember the last time he had been so attracted to a woman. With every word spoken, her allure was growing, not dissipating. "I may be many things, but when it comes to women, I can be quite spontaneous."

This time it was Adanel who laughed. "If you weren't so pleasing to look at, I suspect you would be very lonesome. Then again, maybe you will surprise me and prove how unpredictable you are by being a gentleman and leave so that I can get dressed? I need but five minutes and then you can have the loch and its waters completely to yourself."

"I'd rather be predictable than be honorable," Dugan huffed, and a couple of seconds later added with a smile, "Then again, what kind of man would leave a woman all alone without anyone nearby? What if you were to suddenly get in trouble and needed a strong arm to save you?"

Adanel rested her forehead on the rock. She would be tempted to continue verbally sparring with him if she were dressed and looking him in the eye. But she wasn't, and though no longer freezing, she was exposed and uncomfortable and getting more so by the minute standing ankle deep in the cold water. "I have been coming here every week for over a year, so I am sure I will have no need of your heroism."

Dugan could hear that she was starting to get tired and knew she was about to cave. He was not sure why he wanted her to swim by him so much, and he would retreat if she answered his next question in the affirmative. "Does your husband know you're here?"

"Does your *wife* know you're here?" Adanel returned, her tone laced with sarcasm.

"I'm not married."

"I'm not surprised," she groused.

"Does your father know you're here or are you intentionally avoiding helping out on the farm?" Dugan pressed, hoping to learn a bit more about her personality as well as if she was indeed married.

"Clever," Adanel responded. "My father has not cared about my affairs for years," she said, hoping the lack of a definitive answer would nettle the man.

"And if I were to talk to him, would he agree?"

Adanel rolled her eyes. It was encouraging that he assumed she was either a daughter or a wife of a local McTiernay farmer. It was not a leap for him to make those assumptions, but Adanel had no intentions of correcting either of them. She also had no intentions of letting this conversation continue. The last thing she needed was for him to discover exactly who her father was.

"Can you please leave?"

"Aye, when I'm done," Dugan answered, swirling his arms and causing ripples along the water's surface. "I find this loch rather refreshing today."

Adanel took in a deep, steadying breath. It was rare she lost her temper and yet she was seconds away from unleashing years of pent-up anger. "Then can you finish over where your horse is?" she asked through gritted teeth.

"Aye, I could but I don't want to. I like it here. I think it's warmer."

Adanel cursed under her breath. Arguing with a three-year-old was more productive. "It's far sunnier over there," she said, and began to study the rock face in front of her once again. If she could just find a couple of places she could grab a hold of, she could pull herself up and over. Unfortunately, she also needed to continue and distract him long enough by keeping him talking. "Here there are boulders and shade, making the water colder."

"You would think, but I was just over there. I am *definitely* feeling far warmer on this side."

Adanel rolled her eyes. In other circumstances, she might have found him amusing, but being only ankle-deep in the water was no longer keeping the cold at bay. "I don't think you understand. I don't want you here."

"Ah, but I think you do. Remember, I saw you spying on me."

"I've seen better," Adanel mumbled, finding a good place for her hands.

"Liar."

"Boor," she huffed.

"Ouch. I have manners. I could have come around but I have not out of respect for your privacy."

"I doubt there is one woman outside of your mother you hold in high regard."

"Not true. I have no liking of my mother, and there are a couple of women who have my respect."

"Two? Don't they feel lucky," Adanel said gruffly, and then began to pull herself up onto the smaller boulder.

"Ah, but they don't look at me the way you did."

Adanel took a deep breath to keep from grunting from the exertion. "That's because they know you."

"Now, who's being predictable?"

"Women actually don't like arrogant men."

"It's not arrogance to know when a woman appreciates what she sees."

"Well, I looked my fill already and now I just want to get out of this loch."

"I'm not stopping you. You can swim to the shore anytime you please."

"I have no doubt that you are quite familiar with a woman's body. Why do you need to see one more?"

Dugan did not know how to respond. Because the truth was that from what he had glimpsed, her body was not like any other. "Fine, I promise to keep my eyes closed."

"Now who's the liar?" Adanel asked as her foot searched for anything she could use as leverage to push up.

"On my word as a gentleman."

"If you were truly a gentleman, you would have left."

"Only a happily married man would have left a beautiful naked woman alone."

"Why am I not shocked to learn that you are unwed?" Adanel muttered under her breath.

"I'm not married because I choose not to be. What is your excuse?"

"My father," she answered simply, concentrating on the rock in front of her. "And how is it that you are not married? You certainly look and sound old enough to be a husband, and I cannot imagine you are in want for eager partners."

"I have yet to fall in love."

Adanel went a little higher and then stopped. "I have a feeling you don't believe in the concept."

"Not true," Dugan professed with such sincerity, Adanel believed him. "I've seen true love and the happiness it brings."

"So what is wrong then?" Adanel asked, looking for anything that she could grip. One more push and she would be atop the boulder. It was far mossier than she had realized, making the surface frustratingly slick. "Why are you not blissfully wed to the woman of your dreams making little soldiers who go around and antagonize women bathing peacefully in lochs?"

Dugan heard the sarcasm and considered her question. "Maybe it is you who doesn't believe in the concept."

"Not at all," Adanel denied. "I've been deeply in love. Daniel was everything I ever wanted in a man and he was just as crazy about me."

An unexpected jolt of jealousy raced through Dugan. He did not like hearing about how much she loved another man or how her affections were returned. Then, he realized she had said *was*. "What happened?"

Dugan waited several seconds in silence for an answer and was about to end this ruse and check on her when he heard a hard thud and then a splash.

He spun around and watched in horror as her limp body sank beneath the surface.

Adanel slowly lifted her eyelids, trying to remember what happened, where she was, and why she was on warm, soft grass when her last memory was of being cold.

She blinked, but it was bright, so she squeezed her eyes shut. She instinctively tried to lift her hand to block the sun, but her arm was obstructed. The soft touch of a hardened thumb caressing her cheek made her eyes pop back open. This time she saw not the sun, but the McTiernay soldier from the loch.

"Your eyes," she whispered. "I thought they would be green, not blue."

Dugan smiled, relief flooding his veins. When he had heard the sound of her head hitting the rock just before she plunged in the water, his heart had stopped. He had dived in and pulled her out almost immediately, but she had lain limp in his arms and had remained unconscious long after he had gotten her to shore. Her breathing had not been labored, so she had not inhaled much water, and he could not find any blood on her scalp from her fall, but that was not always telling. One never knew about head injuries until the person woke up . . . if they ever did.

And then she had started shaking from the cold. Goose bumps had covered her skin and a wave of guilt overcame him for keeping her out in the cold waters for so long. He had reacted instinctively and draped his body over hers with the sole purpose of warming her as quickly as possible. But now that she was awake, he was the one getting warm and any moment she would realize it.

"And your eyes are also a surprise," he stated. "Large, brown, and so warm and inviting. A true contrast to your fiery hair, *aithinne.*"

Adanel smiled at the compliment. She had never liked her eyes. Long black lashes framed them, which on any other woman would have been an asset. To Adanel, it made her already large eyes even larger. As to their color, it was a dull and commonplace dark brown—her only Mackbaythe feature. Otherwise, she could have passed for her mother and had more than once given a seaman who had just docked a scare, making him think that he had seen her mother's ghost.

Those who knew her mother used to say that Adanel was like her in spirit as well as looks. She wished she could remember, but she had been eight when her mother died and the few memories she had of her were mostly connected to a feeling of being safe, happy, and loved.

Her mother had been twenty-six when she had left this world for the next. The same age Adanel was now. And based on rumors and tidbits she had heard over the years when people did not think she was listening, her mother had been just as miserable as she was. But at least she had two children to love and who had adored her. Adanel had nothing and would continue to have nothing if she did not find a way to escape her father.

"Are you all right? When you fell and did not wake right away I was afraid you might be seriously hurt."

Adanel's brows furrowed in confusion and then she remembered. She once again tried to lift her hand to touch where her head and the rock collided to see if it was swollen, for it did hurt, but her arm was still blocked. She tried to yank it free and looked down, suddenly realizing that he was practically lying on top of her.

"You . . . you're naked!" Her eyes once more darted down and then back up. "I'm naked!"

Her announcement was greeted with a smile, but instead of triumphant arrogance like she would have expected, his eyes reflected only concern and relief. "Aye," he affirmed, smoothing some of her hair off her face. "You were shaking from the cold, and my body heat was the fastest way to get you warm."

Adanel wiggled until Dugan shifted so that she could use her hands. She placed them on his chest and gave a halfhearted push. It was hard to encourage him to move away when her body longed for not less of his touch, but more. She had only seen his chest under his léine, but now, actually feeling him, she realized she had misjudged just how wide and muscular he was. And that his chest was lightly covered with crisp brown hair, which only made his touch even more compelling.

Keeping one leg draped across hers in an effort to keep her from rising, Dugan propped himself on one elbow and reached down to grab her fingers in his large hand. Her elusive, womanly scent was stretching his control. "Aithinne, I'm already finding keeping you warm the most difficult thing I've ever done. You keep wiggling that way, and I won't be just keeping you warm."

Adanel swallowed, realizing what the hard thing was pressed against her hip . . . and it was getting harder. She knew she should feel mortified, and maybe she would have if she and Daniel had never been together intimately. But whatever the reason, nothing—not her nudity, the situation, or his arousal—made her want to pull away.

Just the opposite. She wanted more.

It had been so long since she had attracted the eye of a man. Even longer since she had desired one in return. And right or wrong, she wanted this Highlander. It did not matter that he was a McTiernay and she was a Mackbaythe. It did not matter that they had not even exchanged names. In some ways, that lack of knowledge only increased her desire.

Adanel wanted neither a husband nor even a beau, and yet debating with this soldier had created a spark of womanly awareness in her that was growing in intensity. She wanted more of that feeling. She wanted to be re-minded of what it felt like to be a woman, to be desired and pleasured . . . to feel alive.

Adanel reached up and ran a light finger over his lips. Her head hurt, dirt was in her hair, and her uncle Faden would soon be expecting her return, and yet she could only think of one thing. "Kiss me."

Her request was so soft Dugan almost wondered if he had heard her correctly. But the way she was touching him and the look in her eyes were only repeating the re-quest. And more than anything he wanted to cave to both their desires and do just that. A half hour ago he had been fantasizing about what it would be like to feel her lips move against his and to have her body under-neath him. And the reality far surpassed his fantasy.

No woman had ever been more desirable, more sen-sual to the touch, than this delectable redhead. She had been passionate and feisty in the water, and Dugan knew she would bring those qualities to her bed. And if she had been under him for any other reason than the current one, she would never have had to ask. He would have long since been exploring her mouth and her body. But despite what so many thought, he was a man of principle when it came to women and he did not take advantage of them, even if every molecule in his body commanded him to do so.

"You just hit your head," Dugan said more to himself than to her, and began to rise. Having stayed next to her after she awoke had been a folly. His whole body was painfully tight with desire and he had to immediately separate from her before he no longer possessed the will to resist. "You don't know what you are saying."

He was about to leave her side, and when he did he would never return. Something inside Adanel refused to let that happen. She reached up behind his neck to stop his retreat and framed his cheek with her other hand. "I know exactly what I am asking. I'm asking you to kiss me."

Dugan held himself immobile, but his heart was pounding loudly, making it clear that her desire was not one-sided. "I won't be able to stop with just a kiss."

"I'm counting on that." And then refusing to wait any longer, Adanel pulled him down and the moment his lips fastened to hers she knew she would have no regrets.

Her desire snapped Dugan's control, and when she opened her mouth to him, all he could think about was her taste. She was sweet, ripe, and so incredibly fresh. Even the most exotic fruit had never tasted so exquisitely good. He needed more and instinctively increased his hot assault, dragging her slender form against him.

Adanel was swept up into a world of pure feeling. Her body melted into his, and when she felt the evidence of his desire pressing against her stomach, primal need scorched through her, igniting sensations for which she had no name.

Dugan wanted to take it slow and enjoy every touch, every taste, every reaction he created in her, but he had been celibate for too long. His aggressive body demanded more, but instead of frightening his spirited *aithinne*, she was responding in kind.

His lips moved to the soft, vulnerable line of her throat and pressed warm kisses to the pulse beating frantically beneath her satin skin. He could not remember a time a woman wanted him so passionately, so unreservedly. His body shivered as new waves of desire shot through him, and Dugan knew she felt them when her fingers curled deeper into the flesh of his neck.

Adanel moaned as his teeth grazed down her neck while rough but gentle fingers brushed across her breast. With that simple touch, her body went liquid with intensified need. His palm was filled with her softness, and his thumb moved almost featherlike across the rosy tip, bringing it to a hard peak. Unprepared for the sensations it aroused, Adanel arched her back, silently begging for more.

Dugan was a man unleashed. He wanted to possess every part of this mystery woman. His hands cradled her breasts while his lips trailed hot, openmouthed kisses, down the curve of her throat and to her collarbone before going lower. God help him, he could not stop touching her.

Her nipples had grown painfully hard under his palm and Adanel did not know what to do with the onslaught of sensations. She felt hot everywhere. She did not know her body could feel so much pleasure. Daniel had been her first, her only, and being with him had been beautiful and full of love and wonder. She would always cherish what they had, but this stranger was introducing her to a world in which she knew she would never get enough.

When he took one hard nipple in his mouth, Adanel cried out from the pleasure. She had wanted to feel alive but had not realized that the feeling would be so incredibly addictive. Once with this man would have to last a lifetime and so she was going to revel in every touch, caress, and sensation this Highlander was creating within her. She wanted to never forget a single moment.

Licking one tight nipple, Dugan curled his tongue about it, drew it into his mouth, and then suckled, clasping her tightly as she writhed beneath him, rubbing herself against his hardness. Her movements were unrehearsed and driving him mad with lust. He needed to be inside her more than he could ever remember needing anything.

This encounter was forever going to haunt him so Dugan was determined to ruin her for all other men. When they parted ways, she would never forget him or what their being together was like. So much so, she would be unable to lay with another man. She was his.

Adanel felt herself panting and all he was doing was touching her breasts. She was not sure she could handle much more. He pulled slightly upward, and with a finger traced around the hollow of one bud, "You're so beautiful . . . so very beautiful. . . ." And then, in the next instant, his mouth consumed her once more. His tongue twirled over the first peak, then the next.

Adanel thought she might die from pleasure. Her fingernails dug into his shoulders. His muscles rippled with power, flexing and contracting, symbols of his enormous strength. Touching him and the onslaught of his mouth left her powerless to his tongue and lips. Her body writhed against him, declaring how much she wanted him, how much she needed him.

Between her nails and soft whimpers, Dugan knew he was about to lose control and take her, but he also knew if he did before she was ready, he would never forgive himself. She would know ultimate pleasure, and it would be from his touch.

He gripped her wrists with one hand and lifted them above her head. She strained against the hold, but he ignored her halfhearted protest and leaned down to recommence the flicking and teasing of her nipple with his tongue. His free hand began a new journey as his fingers lightly caressed her stomach and then trailed farther until he met with her core. She gasped, the sound a half cry, half mindless moan created from an overload of sensation.

Adanel closed her eyes as thick, tutored fingers slipped into her most sensitive spot. She could neither move nor think as a rush a pleasure coursed through her. She shuddered. "It's so . . . it's so . . ."

"So what, *aithinne*?"

"So good," Adanel moaned.

Dugan's lips curled in triumph and then he began to move his finger inside her, ever so slightly. He stroked her tight flesh with a careful thumb and watched as she responded to his touch. He had wanted, desired, and had many women in his life and he knew how to bring a lover to fulfillment. But never had the act of simply watching a woman being pleasured aroused him to such a level of need. She had no idea of the blissful, ever-sweet reward she was giving to him, and he was determined that this beautiful woman would receive pleasure in every way possible before he was done.

He bent his head to taste her breast again as he added another finger, stretching her. He pushed deep so that Adanel gasped with pleasure. She was on fire, her body needing, burning, screaming for more. "It is not enough," she panted.

Dugan lifted his head and smiled. Slowly, he withdrew his fingers and let go of her hands. Adanel groaned in protest, but when she felt his hands on her inner thighs, she suddenly realized what was about to happen.

Adanel gasped at the unfamiliar caress and instinctively tried to retreat from the heated touch of his tongue. Her hips bucked against him, but he held them firmly in place. He slipped his finger into her again as he took her in his mouth, his tongue hot, rough, and insistent. Her panic then changed into the most wanton kind of desire.

Her back arched, nails digging into whatever they could find. Adanel shook with pleasure as he traced his tongue back and forth. Her heart beat faster; her breath stuck in her throat.

Dugan moaned as the taste of the sweetest honey filled his mouth. Everything about her was erotic. He was in enormous pain, but he refused to halt his sensual attack until she was satisfied, boneless, and sated. Only then would he crush her to his chest and find heaven within her folds.

He groaned against her, and Adanel could feel the vibration reverberating through her core. Her hips began to rock as increasing pleasure raked through her. Then, with a choking cry, she felt wave after wave of intense pleasure heightened by the relentless caress of his tongue. And yet, it still was not enough.

Reluctantly, Dugan lifted his head. His body was raging at him. He could wait no longer. He had to bury himself deep within her and for her to feel as consumed by him as he was by her.

"I need you," he grunted, his voice husky with desire. "I need you, *aithinne*."

Adanel felt his hard arousal against the junction of her thighs and then him reaching down and carefully opening her to his first thrust. She cried out when he plunged between her thighs, burying himself in the warm softness of her.

Dugan felt as if he was in heaven being burned by a devilish fire. The sudden sensation of heat, damp, and incredible tightness surrounding him almost undid him, but hearing her soft cry, Dugan forced himself to remain still.

She was a sheath of velvet fire, and he had to struggle against his need to keep thrusting, deep and hard. His *aithinne* was not a virgin, but it was obvious that she had not been with a man in a very long time. The tight feel of her around him was driving him mad. He wanted to take her hard and fast, making her cry out his name in bliss, but she was so tight, he did not know if it was possible for him to continue without causing her pain.

But then he could feel her relax as her body accepted his size and length. He eased himself slowly out and then deeply back into her snug passage. Adanel wrapped her legs around him, demanding without words for more. Needing no further encouragement, Dugan started to move within her and soon he could no longer think. The fire inside him raged out of control, searing away caution, reason, and even will. Nothing mattered except being as close to her as he could be.

Adanel let her head fall back as renewed need surged through her. She wanted him inside her, as deeply as she could take him. He was hot and wild, masculine and perfect. She wanted this time to last forever and raised her hips to meet his.

Their bodies came together in perfect union. Dugan watched as her breasts, full and firm, quivered with each hard thrust. He was not going to last much longer.

"*Chruitheachd*," Adanel gasped, unable to bear the sensations any longer. Her body was peaking and going into hard, tight convulsions. He must have known because his arms clenched around her, and he came into her with deep, fierce thrusts that carried her right to the edge. With a soft, choked cry, she surrendered to the glittering storm of sensation that swept over her.

As she cried out her pleasure, Dugan clamped his mouth tightly down over hers, swallowing the sounds of her passion. Her small convulsions squeezed him demandingly, and Dugan could not hold in his own exultant shout as his body surged deeply into hers one last time before rolling to the side to withdraw and release in a hot, deep, hammering surge of waves. Instinctively, he held her to him and then he collapsed breathless, sweat-sheened and utterly shaken.

As the echoes of their release ebbed away, Dugan took a deep breath and slowly exhaled. After waiting a minute to let his heart calm, he leaned over her, and with her face cradled between his hands, kissed her, long, hard, and deep. Then, unable to let her go as he knew he soon would have to, Dugan rolled to lie beside her and pulled her against him.

Adanel nuzzled her face into the crook of his neck. Her hands softly slid back and forth across his chest.

Dugan knew he should stop her sweet caress. Instead, he nuzzled her hair and held her tight as though he never wanted to let go. Her touch . . . his response . . . both felt natural and possessive in a way that normally would send him running. But Dugan was in no hurry to end this moment. If he could, he would prolong it for as long as possible, refusing to examine just why he was suddenly willing to break one of his primary tenets.

Cuddling after sex was fraught with danger. It almost always created a clingy woman, making her feel free to ask for more even though he had made it very clear he did not believe in commitment or relationships. Holding this redhead changed none of that, but she had yet to ask for more, and until she did he was content to stay where he was—locked in her embrace.

"What's your name?" he whispered against her temple before kissing it.

Adanel pushed herself up and placed a soft finger against his lips. "Can't you just be my soldier and I be your *aithinne?* Let's not think about tomorrow. I just want to be here with you, here, now, no more."

Dugan swallowed and then nodded his head. As his beautiful firebrand nestled back into the crook of his arm, he asked himself if there could be a more perfect woman. No wonder he had felt comfortable holding her. Instinctively he must have recognized a kindred spirit. They would part with no commitments or expectations. He should be thrilled. So why did the idea of never seeing her again bother him so much?

Chapter Two

Faden felt the tension running up his arms and back relax as soon as he saw a flash of red. Adanel's hair was the exact same shade as most of the MacLeods', him included. Except for her dark brown eyes, his niece was the spitting image of his eldest sister, Faia.

He had been nine years old when Faia had left their home to marry Laird Mackbaythe, and he had been seventeen when she had passed away. But despite their age difference and time apart, he remembered his sister vividly. She had been the most beautiful and kind person he had ever seen. The complete opposite of his own personality.

Faden was neither kind nor anything close to what passed as attractive to the fairer sex. He had unruly red hair with streaks of gold that belonged on a woman, not a man. His hair was untamable at any length, and he was forced to tie it back, which then made his large ears the focal point of stares and sniggers. His prominent nose was crooked from being broken half a dozen times, and his cheeks looked like carved asymmetrical sculptures that bothered one without knowing why. Only Adanel thought him attractive, claiming that someday a woman's heart would swoon every time she looked into his wayfarer-blue eyes. He doubted it.

It was not unusual to have to wait for Adanel's arrival down the mountain, but he had never had to wait this long. Faden had started to wonder if something was wrong and was considering making the long trek to ensure she was well when he finally spotted her red hair.

When Adanel turned the last corner and beamed him a smile, Faden narrowed his gaze upon seeing her unusually happy expression. He had been tasked with guarding his niece since she was twelve, and only once in nearly fourteen years had he ever seen Adanel so joyful. It was like a warm glow flowed through her being. If he did not know better, he would think Adanel had not been alone all afternoon and had been instead similarly engaged in the same activities he had enjoyed just a few hours ago with a nearby widow.

"Isn't it a little cold for swimming?" he asked, pointing at her wet hair. He debated asking her if she'd been alone, but he knew she had been. Only their footprints were in the area and he could not see Adanel risking another man's life after what had happened to Daniel. It broke Faden's heart that she was forced to keep men at a distance for his niece deserved happiness more than anyone he knew.

"What can I say?" Adanel replied with a shrug of her shoulders. "The sun came out and the cool water beckoned me. I enjoyed it so much that I lost track of time. Why? Worried about me, uncle?"

When Adanel first discovered the loch, Faden had trudged up there with her repeatedly only to sit and do nothing. He could not even really watch her since she was bathing. Then one time on their way to the loch, they had encountered a plain but youngish widow on their weekly outing. She had married one of the men who had chosen to remain independent and cared not that Faden wore a Mackbaythe tartan. Instead, she had made it clear that she would welcome his company if he were interested. She being willing and uncomplicated, Faden had made it clear that he was very interested. She scratched an itch, and their time together gave him something to do when Adanel disappeared to her loch. And so from that week forward, when Adanel went for her adventure, in need of escape, he had gone for his.

"Worried about *us*. We are late," Faden said, and tossed Adanel her horse's reins.

She easily caught the leather strips and hoisted herself onto her mount. "I don't think anyone will notice that we are half an hour later than usual."

Faden scoffed. Adanel intentionally avoided attention and smartly too. Her father, Laird Eòsaph Mackbaythe, enjoyed cruelty and surrounded himself with those who felt similarly. And while the man had never physically harmed his daughter to Faden's knowledge, her father felt no guilt about making her watch as he hurt others. Over the years, Adanel had become an expert at eluding such events, but unfortunately, when certain people came to visit, the laird wanted both his children present. This evening was one of those nights.

"Normally, no one would notice, but tonight your father expects you at dinner," Faden replied, and kicked his horse into a fast trot.

Adanel followed suit. Her smile had faded. "Me? He never wants me there anymore."

It was not exactly true. On rare occasions, her father did demand her attendance, but less and less over the years. When she was young, her presence made him appear like a dutiful parent whenever there were guests. But as she aged, his feasts became a lot more macabre and those who were invited seemed to relish his displays of animal cruelty, having little to no interest in her. So, she had stopped coming, and thankfully her father had not cared.

"He wants you there tonight."

"But I told Kara that I was going to help her prep for tomorrow as two ships are arriving."

The Mackbaythes' lands were not extensive, but they were strategically located. The focal point was Bàgh Fìon, a small port nestled on the eastern edge of Upper Loch Torridon. The inlet was not only protected by mountains, but it was unusually deep, enabling large ships to pull up to a dock to unload and load goods versus ferrying them by rowboat. As a result, Bàgh Fìon was one of a handful of ports that could handle larger ships and the only one along the western Highland shore that was not situated on the open coast and exposed to the turbulent seas between the Isles of Skye and Harris.

The port was defended by three structures. The first and most prominent was Mackbaythe Castle. Strategically located along the southern side of the inlet, it was originally nothing more than a large two-story bastle house, fortified with extremely thick stone walls and a vaulted ceiling. Her grandfather, however, had seen the advantages of a deep bay and, over the course of his lifetime, built the local area into a small but active port. With the profits, he built an L-shaped stone tower house for the laird, his family, and special guests to stay and turned the bastle house into a large great hall. Next to it were the kitchen, a small bakery, a buttery, stables, and even a forge—all the elements of a castle, just without the curtain wall and moat.

Instead, he had built two large peel towers. One was at the center of the port, where it could help oversee and protect those ships coming into the dock. Around it the village had grown, and therefore the tower was known as Baile Tùr—the Village Tower. The bottom and second floors were mostly used for storage and if necessary became bedrooms when the castle was overcrowded. The top floor, however, was hers. She had moved there to be away from her father and closer to her friends in the village, and thankfully, her father had not cared. If anything, he preferred her absence.

The second tower, Daingneach, was on the northern side of the inlet, across from the castle and next to some falls. Some called the tower the Falls but Adanel referred to it as the villagers did—the Fortress. It was the most formidable of the three and where the majority of the Mackbaythe guard, weapons, and the dungeons were kept. Its location gave the best view of incoming ships as well as the perfect setting to shoot at attacking vessels in the bay . . . something that thankfully had not happened in Adanel's lifetime.

Scattered between the towers lived the heart and soul of the Mackbaythe clan, the village. Almost every Mackbaythe worked in and around the docks in some capacity, and her best friend owned the one and only respectable inn. It was also Adanel's refuge for it was the one place she could go and be herself. It was where her mother had been the happiest before she died, and where her father and brother never ventured.

"Kara will have to wait until the morrow, but I'll make sure she knows your absence was due to your father's request. And in case you are thinking about how to get out of attending, don't. You have no choice. You are to be there."

Adanel's brows furrowed. None of her father's friends had paid any attention to her for years. She had been barely seventeen when one of them had made advances and her father had the man severely beaten. After publicly humiliating him and making him crawl on bloody hands and knees all the way out of the castle and through the village, not a single guest of his since had the nerve to even look her way, let alone show any interest. She would have believed herself to be repellent except for Daniel. And he had paid the ultimate price.

"Am I going to learn why I am being summoned after I am there or are you going to tell me why my father suddenly wants me at his table?"

"Willemus and his son Daeron are expected to arrive just before sunset," Faden answered with a sneer, "so you know your father is going to want you to look especially nice."

Adanel blinked. The MacCoinniches were coming, which explained Faden's foul mood. He did not like them. None of the MacLeods did, and the feeling was reciprocated.

Though there were dozens, perhaps hundreds, of small clans littered throughout the western Highlands, only three were of significant size and power. The smallest of the three in size and power were the McTiernays of Torridon. Cole McTiernay had anchored his faction of the McTiernay clan on the southern side of lower Loch Torridon. They had a small port attached to his castle and would have been peaceful neighbors if her father had not made several threats when Cole had been named laird. The villagers whispered that her father had also made several attempts to stir up trouble for the new laird and tried to create rifts between him and the other neighbors. To her knowledge, it had not worked, but the resulting tension and distrust remained today.

The largest in size were the MacCoinniches, whose only disadvantage was being landlocked—something their laird was working to end. They wanted their lands to stretch from the western sea to Scotland's eastern shores at Cromarty Firth.

The second largest clan, but arguably the most powerful, belonged to the MacLeods because they owned the sea. The seafaring clan held the lands hugging the northwestern shores but all their deep ports except for those in Loch Ewe were exposed to rough waters. However, because her father had married Laird MacLeod's eldest daughter, an automatic alliance had been forged. As a result, it was their ships that took and brought most of the goods to and from Mackbaythe docks. That was why Laird MacCoinnich had been forced to work with her father to buy and sell his goods. Otherwise, without the protection of the MacLeods, the Mackbaythes would have disappeared long ago under MacCoinnich rule.

Still, because the feud between the MacLeods and MacCoinniches was well known, Adanel had always been in a little awe that her father had been able to maintain civil dealings with both of them. Then again, it was his connection to both clans that kept her father safe. Each clan knew that any move to take over the port would mean a costly, deadly war.

"Just when did you find out about Laird MacCoinnich's arrival?"

"Just before we left," Faden answered unapologetically. He had almost canceled their ride, but it had been two weeks since their last outing due to poor weather. When the morning rain had gone away leaving warmth and sunshine in its wake, he had not the heart nor desire to disappoint Adanel, not to mention his own physical need to visit his lady friend.

"I'm not sure if I should be angry with you or thank you," Adanel playfully chided him.

"Thank me, of course. If I had told you, we would not

have come today and you seem . . . let's just say especially happy that we did."

"I . . . did enjoy today," Adanel replied just as carefully. "I just hope Father doesn't look for me until after we return."

Faden knew by keeping silent he had put Adanel in a difficult position, but he did not care. He felt no loyalty to either the Mackbaythes or his own clan, the MacLeods. The only one who had his fidelity was Adanel and she had needed today's respite as much as he had.

When Adanel's grandfather built the tower houses, the MacLeods had wanted guaranteed access to the port, but not until his death were they able to strike a deal with his son. Adanel's father had negotiated a small percentage of whatever came through his port as a fee, and in return the MacLeods had unfettered access to the port. To ensure the deal held, Laird MacLeod sent his second child and oldest daughter, Faia, to wed the newest Laird Mackbaythe.

Not long afterward, Faden's father had sent his eldest son as a "guard" for Faia, which Faden later discovered, was in reality the least of his brother's responsibilities. Faden's eldest brother fulfilled his role for two years until the second eldest MacLeod son turned twenty-one and took his place. This happened every two to three years until it had been Faden's turn. He had come with the same instructions as all his brothers had before him.

Adanel had been twelve at the time and her mother had been dead for four years. Her one protector had been her best friend Kara's mother, and she had passed just months before Faden's arrival. His heart had wrenched at seeing Adanel so sad and scared, and he had vowed to do whatever he could to help her. He had promised that when it was his turn to return home, he would not leave her vulnerable.

Unfortunately, being the youngest son meant there had been no one to take his place; therefore, his father had denied his request to return. Later, after Daniel had been brutally executed right in front of Adanel, proving her father to be an unstable monster, Faden had tried again, asking for his father to intervene. His father had sent the same reply: "You have yet to fulfill your duty to me and the MacLeod clan."

That day Faden stopped trying to do his duty, knowing that after nearly three decades, his father asked the impossible. None of his brothers could answer his father's demand, and in his mind, nothing justified abandoning him and his granddaughter.

Adanel sighed. "Well, at least with tonight's company my father will have to keep his cruelty to a minimum. Laird MacCoinnich was not amused during his last visit."

Faden chuckled at the memory. "I expect your father will be wanting to leave a better impression."

"I must admit to being a little surprised that they are returning. Does Laird MacCoinnich have a daughter I don't know about? Then again, I would not wish my brother on even the most horrid of women. It scares me to even think of what would happen to the one who agrees to be his wife."

Faden kept silent, but that did not mean he disagreed. Eògan was four years younger than Adanel, and while both siblings possessed the red hair of their mother, only Adanel possessed her spirit. Eògan looked like a MacLeod, but he was in every way his father's son.

"I wonder why the MacCoinniches are coming here. They left so quickly last time, I thought never to see them again," Adanel pondered aloud.

Faden wondered, too. Young Daeron MacCoinnich believed himself better and cleverer than any soul alive despite being only seventeen. Faden had only met him twice, and on both occasions, he had been surprised at the level of Daeron's intelligence. Unfortunately, the young man's undoubted genius was coupled with an inflated ego that made him ignore unwanted council and rush to incorrect assumptions as well as action. He mistakenly believed that being smarter than those around him meant his needs and desires had priority over all others. Simply put, Daeron was a pompous child in a man's body, and Faden had no use for anyone's arrogance, especially when it was not earned.

"I don't know why they are coming. You'll have to tell me tomorrow."

"You are not coming?" Adanel asked, alarmed by the idea.

Faden rode on refusing to reply, knowing his silence alone answered her question.

Adanel twitched her lips. "As my guard, I could make you come."

"Not even your father could do that."

"I could guilt you into it."

"Don't have any use for that emotion. And you and I both know that as a MacLeod it is best if I am not around."

"Aye," Adanel huffed. "But with no one to help keep me sane, I might accidentally let slip what is really on my mind. I'm half MacLeod, too."

Faden shook his head. "Then I suggest biting your tongue."

Adanel snorted. "If I do that, it will be a bloody mess before the first course is through."

"Do me a favor, Adanel," Faden said, slowing his horse

so that he could look at her. "Avoid young Daeron as much as possible. The MacCoinniches are not to be trifled with, and we have tempted fate enough today just by coming onto McTiernay lands."

"Daeron's only seventeen, Faden. I'm nearly twenty-six. He probably looks at me like everyone else does—as a spinster no one wanted."

Faden shook his head but did not argue with her. "He'll be eighteen come this fall, and boys at that age think themselves just as knowledgeable as the wisest of men. Not until much later do we realize how foolish the notion to be. Be careful of him."

"You worry needlessly. I doubt Daeron will look in my direction. Last time, he was very haughty and only impressed by his own intelligence. The rumor is that he remembers everything he ever sees, hears, or reads."

Faden looked unimpressed. "No matter how clever a man may be, there is always someone smarter. Daeron might remember a bunch of facts, but he doesn't know what to do with them."

Adanel threw her head back and laughed. "You speak as if you believed the rumor were true!"

Faden pursed his lips together. He had overheard the young man speak a few times, and based on the little that he had caught, Daeron MacCoinnich did have an unbelievable memory and possibly could do just as the rumors said. That made him incredibly dangerous and someone to avoid. "Just don't talk to him."

Hearing the seriousness of Faden's tone, a lump of fear began to form in Adanel's stomach. "Do you know something about why they are coming, Faden?"

"Nay, and that bothers me. Powerful leaders like Laird MacCoinnich demand people come to them. Normally, he would never travel to see someone like your father, so something is driving this visit. Pay attention and hope your father does not do something unwise. Laird MacCoinnich has a large army that few can defend themselves against."

Adanel looked straight ahead, not wanting Faden to see her frightened expression for her uncle was right. If Laird MacCoinnich was coming, that meant her father had brought him here. They were making a deal and that could only be for the control of the port. Her home.

Once again, the need to escape her life rushed through her. But to where? The only clan that would not simply return her back to her home was the McTiernays, but they would declare her an enemy. As a Mackbaythe, they would have no reason to see her otherwise.

Adanel blinked. As a *Mackbaythe*, she was an enemy. But what if she wasn't Mackbaythe? What if she could convince a certain McTiernay soldier to handfast with the promise to let him free after the obligatory year? Today proved they were very compatible and if not, she could always live elsewhere. And his actions alone proved he was not committed to anyone. Best of all, a skilled McTiernay soldier was someone her father would not be able to so easily kill or intimidate.

Unfortunately, she had no reason to believe she would ever see him again. Then again, she had mentioned her visit to the loch was a weekly one. If he returned next Tuesday, the idea was not impossible. Thank God, she had never told him her name.

Dugan sifted his fingers through his mystery woman's hair, watching how it played in the sun. "It's beautiful."

"It's red," came a muffled correction against his chest.

"It's red if you mean every shade of red known from

darkest to lightest, all mixed up together. And that, my *aithinne*, is beautiful."

She shifted and raised herself up on one elbow to look down at him. Never had anyone robbed him of breath, but this lady did every time. Even now, with one brow arched in a way that silently called him a liar. But he wasn't lying. He was not even exaggerating. He actually meant every compliment he had ever given her.

"Flattery is something a man typically offers *before* he grabs a woman and kisses her senseless," she said.

Dugan smiled and easily reversed their positions so that he was looking down at her. "I think it was *you* who did the grabbing and me who was kissed senseless."

Her soft laughter filled the air. "I doubt a woman has ever made you senseless, let alone with a kiss."

She was wrong. These past two weeks Dugan had been nothing but senseless when it came to her. To the point he had been practically useless when it came to his duties.

He had been preoccupied before, but that had been due to clan situations, politics, or even a good rivalry during planned Highland games. Never had his mind been so fixated on a woman.

For years, he had unapologetically enjoyed the attentions of many lovely and eager women of all ages. He followed only two rules: they could not be married and no virgins. And while some might have hoped their physical relationship would progress into something more permanent, Dugan had never given them any reason to think it was even a possibility. Commitment was not for him.

To him, marriage was sacred. Honor required vows made between men to be upheld, but those made with a woman and to God were for life. Not only did he not have the capacity for such loyalty, experience had shown him that he did not inspire fidelity in others. In the end, people always chose what was best for themselves regardless of their promises, alliances, or even beliefs.

Though he would have never dreamed it possible when they first met, Cole McTiernay was one of the few men Dugan trusted with his life. The McTiernay laird was abrupt and could even appear cold and heartless at times, but he was fair and one always knew exactly where they stood with him.

Surprisingly, Cole's wife, Ellenor, was also one of the few people Dugan trusted, and if she was not completely besotted with her husband, she might have made him reconsider his opposition to marriage. Then there were Donald and Jaime, Cole's commanders. Both men had been wary of Dugan and he of them, but time had erased their distrust and forged their initially tenuous relationships into surprising but solid friendships.

Never would Dugan have dreamed that he would ever have the strong bond he had with these four McTiernays. They absolutely had had his loyalty. Trust, however, was something very different. He had learned the hard way that there was only one person he could ever completely trust—that was himself.

And that was why he had been useless.

His secretive redhead was stirring primal emotions deep inside him that he had never felt before—unyielding desire mixed with the need to protect, possess, and claim. But his firebrand was determined to remain a mystery, which required a level of trust from him based simply on faith and hope, not history and experience.

The first time Dugan had left her side he had told himself that his anonymous *aithinne* had offered nothing but a fun, unexpected divergence, and he wished her well. Less than an hour later he realized he was already devising plausible excuses to come out this way again the following week.

The excuse he finally had used was an honest one, just incomplete. He had told Cole, Donald, and Jaime that he had missed visiting a couple of homesteads and felt it important that he make sure they were well. Cole had not cared, trusting Dugan to handle his responsibilities. Donald oversaw Cole's personal elite guard, so he had barely shrugged as Dugan's absence really did not impact him. Jaime had merely raised an eyebrow and wiggled it, guessing there was more to visiting the homesteads than Dugan was stating.

Extricating himself this week, however, had not been as easy. He had made the mistake of using the same excuse. And if Cole and Donald did not tell their wives *everything*, he might have been able to continue to use that excuse for the entire summer. But nothing got by Ellenor or Brighid. They both knew that while Dugan did not overly mind going out to the border farms, it was something he did only as necessary as most lived that far out for a reason—they wanted to be left alone. So, when the two women learned he had suddenly changed a routine that he had followed for the past three years for a second time in a two week period, they were all over him, demanding answers.

Dugan had given them nothing, partly because he knew it would drive them insane and partly because for years they had been needling him to settle down and find a wife. They claimed it was because of their love for him, but Dugan suspected they just wanted to increase their female numbers. He had been to enough McTiernay gatherings to see that the McTiernay wives worked in numbers. The more, the scarier.

Last fall, when he broke off his last relationship and did not immediately kindle another, Ellenor had been practically gleeful when she announced that he was finally realizing how empty his way of life was. She had been utterly wrong. The reason why he was alone was the complete opposite of her supposition. His life *was* full. Full of women and their drama and their incessant desire for promises he had no intention of making. He had simply wanted a break. But knowing there would be no convincing Ellenor otherwise, Dugan had let her think what she wanted. But if she and Brighid had even a clue about his current state of mind about this redhead, they would never relent until he was standing at the altar just for a little peace.

In order to help prevent any pangs of guilt about his reasons for leaving again this week, Dugan *had* been seeking out homesteads he had not visited. One in particular—the home of his mystery woman. He had not expected it to be so hard to find. Adanel was easy to describe and one would remember seeing her, even if some time ago. And yet despite a very concerted effort, Dugan could not find a soul who knew anything about a redhead, daughter, or wife. No one had red hair. There was only one unwed female past the normal marrying age, and he had known about her for years.

"Does your entire family have hair this color?" he asked, fingering it once again.

She smiled up at him. "On my mother's side. I inherited it from her, but she died when I was young."

Last week, Dugan had tried multiple ways—most of which were mutually delightful—to persuade his *aithinne* into revealing her name. She had been surprisingly resistant, insisting that she had no desire in sharing hers or learning his. She claimed it would ruin the mystery, which could affect the pleasure they found in each other's arms. At first, Dugan thought it was her way of remaining a challenge in order to keep his interest, but he now wondered if there was another reason she wanted her identity to remain a secret—one that he intended to discover. And when he did, he would prove to her that it changed nothing. He had even tried to follow her as she left the little loch, for she did not use the same path he did. He had learned very little, but he was not giving up. For it was not as if he planned to expose her secrets; he just wanted to learn them. Somehow this woman had slipped under his defenses, and as a result, he felt compelled to learn everything about her. Until he did, his *aithinne* would plague not just his dreams, but his every waking thought.

"I'm sorry," he murmured, letting go of the lock to lightly caress her cheek with the tip of his finger. "It sounds like you miss her a great deal."

"Every day," she replied, staring at a low, but fast-moving cloud in the sky. Then, with a deep breath, she pasted a smile on her face. "Do you enjoy being a soldier?"

Dugan bit back a grin at the sudden change of not only topic, but the person of focus. "I do. It's the only thing I've ever been good at."

Her brows furrowed in disbelief. Then, with a mocking chuckle, she said, "I think there is a lot more to you than being able to effectively wield a blade. And deep down, I think you agree."

"Wouldn't matter if I did or did not, because a soldier is all I'll ever be."

"But you lead men."

Dugan studied her fathomless brown eyes and saw that she had spoken in earnest. He wondered just how she came up with that conclusion because he knew that he had never said anything about being a commander. It was clear by now that she enjoyed being with him, but a little piece of him feared that things might change if she found out he was in a position of power. Would she make demands? Suddenly seek a commitment? It was a slightly paranoid reaction, but after years of having that happen repeatedly, it was a justified paranoia. But based on her comment, she already knew. "And just why do you believe that?"

She blinked. "Well, I guess I don't *know* it to be certain," she stated readily with a shrug. "It's just . . . I don't know. I just knew from the first time I saw you. Soldiers act differently from other clansmen. Soldiers who have fought in battles and faced death act very differently than those who have not, and men who lead other soldiers also have distinct qualities that stand out."

"How so?" Dugan demanded, making it clear he wanted to know and was not going to let the subject drop.

His *aithinne* gave him a withering look. "First of all, men who lead are far more arrogant," she said, and sat up, pushing her hair back. "You know exactly of what I speak as you can distinguish the difference as well as I. As for how *I* know? Well, I'm not a young lass. This part of Scotland has changed much over the years, and I have witnessed it. People change when they see death. They change more when they cause it, and change even more when they order others into situations that could result in the loss of their lives."

Dugan blew out a breath and urged her to lie down. "Arrogant? I'm not arrogant."

With a swat on his arm, she let herself be pulled back down. "Aye, you are and on just about everything."

"*Everything?*"

She laughed, feeling the momentary tension slip away. "Aye, *everything*. And if you are half as good at leading your men as you are at making love, then you should be a laird."

Dugan almost blurted that he nearly had been one, but bit it back. If his *aithinne* was not going to reveal key pieces of her identity to him, he would not to her. Besides, she saw too much of him as it was.

His thumb caressed the inside of her palm and the small calluses that revealed she worked. "You get these on the farm?"

She scoffed. "I wish as I enjoy gardening, but my father would never allow it."

Dugan felt her tense as if she realized she had just said too much. He could feel her about to flee and rubbed the palm again. The calluses were not thick or hard, but they were there, so she definitely worked and consistently. "Are you close with your father?"

She bit her bottom lip in thought, and it made him want to lean down and pull the plump flesh into his own mouth and suckle. But before he could act, she stated, "My father and I have little in common, and we actively avoid each other's company whenever possible."

Dugan stared down into her deep brown eyes. A raw, honest emotion had flashed their dark depths for a moment. Fear? Regret? He was not sure, but it might explain why no one admitted to knowing her. "You don't like your father?"

She shifted as if uncomfortable. "I despise him, so can we talk of something else?"

Dugan did not want to as he was finally learning something that might tell him more about her, but it was clear that he was going to learn nothing more of her family today. "So how do you know widow Nell?"

This time the emotion that flashed in her eyes was unmistakable. Anger. *"If you follow me again, I will stop coming here."*

He was a little shocked by her reaction, but that did not make him repentant. "I only wanted to make sure you were safe."

"No, you wanted to know where I lived," she stated crisply.

Dugan's jaw tightened at the accusation. She was right.

He had followed her and stared at the small cottage she had entered for nearly half an hour before turning around and returning back home. All knew Nell lived alone. Finley and Finlay often brought her meat and would have let him know if she needed anything even though she was not a McTiernay. The Highlanders in these hills were good about taking care of their own, and he thought that might have been what was going on with his redhead. "I *do* want to know you are safe."

"I am. When I am visiting you, my uncle visits Nell. Neither of us asks questions about what the other is doing during our outings. *We respect each other's privacy.*"

Dugan raised his brows and blinked, taking in all that she said. "You have an uncle," he repeated under his breath.

"You seemed surprised."

Dugan shifted his weight so that he was on his side. He *was* surprised. For some reason, he thought their afternoon encounters to be completely unknown to anyone but her and him. That she had an uncle who was not only aware, but indirectly involved in supporting their clandestine meetings was somewhat disconcerting. If her uncle could know about him, why could he not know about her uncle?

"You can trust me, *aithinne.*"

"It is not about trust," she whispered as she closed her eyes. They remained shut for a long moment before she reopened them. And he saw no coyness, no playfulness, no goading in their dark depths. Only an urgency for him to understand that she was not playing a game. The woman was being earnest. She *really* wanted to keep her identity a secret.

"Aye, it is about trust," Dugan stated, his deep voice soft but serious. "And I'm beginning to think that only if

I learn and keep your secrets will you finally believe that you can trust me."

Her hand reached up and cupped his cheek. Sadness enveloped her features. "Each time we leave here, you return to your world and I return to mine. If anyone in mine were to ever learn about you . . . and me, I would be forbidden to ever come near this place again. And I'm not sure I could handle that. I want you. I desire you, but I *need* my freedom."

Dugan finally understood. His pursuit was putting something at risk that was far beyond just him and her. Who would take away her freedom? She avoided her father . . . and did she say *forbid*? The word reminded him of a priest from his youth. *A priest* . . . Dugan almost said aloud as understanding dawned on him.

Could this beautiful woman be a nun . . . or something very close?

There *was* a small priory of Culdees somewhere near here. The Culdees were a strange lot compared to most religious communities. They never took monastic vows so technically none of them were nuns or monks, but they did live in a monastic fashion, devoting their lives to religion and supporting those sick or in need. He had only visited the priory once, and it had been several years ago. The community kept to themselves and made it clear that while they accepted Cole's authority, they wished to be left alone and would reach out should they ever need assistance. Out of respect, Dugan had not been back.

His firebrand had to be a Culdee. It was the only thing that made sense. None of the homesteaders probably had any interaction with them, which explained why no one had seen her. And it was not like she was the first nun to seek physical comfort in the arms of a man. However, it seemed that tight-knit community was far stricter than his first impression. It was possible they would evict her should they discover just why her weekly outings had become far more pleasurable.

If that happened, she would be cast out and then become his responsibility—something he was not remotely ready to consider. He had enjoyed the last two weeks immensely, but that did not mean he wanted anything more. His desire to learn her identity was out of curiosity. He simply wanted to know who she was, and now that he knew, their relationship could continue to be just what it was—a deeply satisfying encounter between two adults.

Dugan rested his forehead against hers. "I understand as I need my freedom. So no more following, no more schemes to get you to reveal more. It is as you said. We have no need for names and calling you *aithinne* will suffice." *For now,* he added to himself.

Visible relief flooded her every pore and once again a smile took over her mouth. "Then stop wasting time and kiss me."

Dugan grinned. "You know, I won't be able to stop with just a kiss."

Her whole face lit up. "I'm counting on that."

His lips met hers. Nothing felt or tasted as good as this woman. And somewhere inside him the embers of possibly wanting something more began to burn.

Adanel waited until just after his head emerged to take a deep breath and slammed her hand against the surface of the water, creating an excellently placed splash. Dugan sputtered at the unexpected assault but recovered fast. Adanel yelped seeing his expression and immediately dove under the water as he wiped his eyes in preparation for revenge. She did not get far before a firm hand circled her ankle and yanked her toward him. She fought as best she could but her body, like it did every time she was in her soldier's arms for the past four months, betrayed her. Maybe it was his sensual warmth that called to her femininity. Maybe it was his strength and the feeling that no one would ever be able to hurt her while she was in his arms, but whatever it was, she always succumbed quickly.

"I got you," he murmured, and pulled her back closer to his chest. "You can't get away. I won't let you. Not now. Not ever."

Adanel did not argue, loving the way his arms felt around her middle. Whether his meaning was literal or figurative, he did indeed have her. Heart, body, and soul. Still, his audacious claim had to be countered. "Only because I let you have me."

"Nay. I'm stronger."

"Yet to be proven, and we both know that I'm faster," she said proudly. Two weeks ago, they had a swimming contest, and she had won handily.

"Hmmm," he hummed, and she could feel him smiling as he trailed kisses along her shoulder. "Then you must have wanted me to catch you. But why, I wonder?"

Adanel twisted around in his embrace so that she faced him. "Use your imagination," she purred, and leaned back so that she floated in the water.

As he twirled her about, Adanel closed her eyes, enjoying the feel of the water through her hair and the warm sun on her face. Adanel could not remember feeling as happy as she had these past few months.

She felt warm lips at the hollow of her throat. Despite having recently satiated their passions, Adanel felt her body stir and she lifted her head. His blue eyes studied her for a second, and then without a word, he

devoured her lips in a desperate claiming to which she
submitted willingly, eagerly.

When he finally ended the kiss, he said, "I think I'm
becoming addicted to you. You're worse for me than ale."

"You don't like ale?" she giggled. She did not know of
a single man who did not enjoy a large mug of ale.

"Aye, but it doesn't like me in large quantities. I tend
to do and say things I regret," Dugan admitted.

Drunk men were not something she was unfamiliar
with, but just what kind of drunk was her soldier? Angry?
Violent? Ridiculous? "Hmmm," she said, running her
fingers up and down his bicep. "Ale can make a man
fight a friend."

He chuckled and Adanel could see from his expression that he knew exactly what she was asking. "Nay, I
wish it were fighting. Far less embarrassing than an-
nouncing every thought and emotion I have."

Adanel's fingers stopped, and she knew her mouth
was ajar. Then she broke out into peals of laughter. "How
I wish I could see that!"

"Nay, you would take advantage of my defenseless
state and leave me with no secrets of my own."

"How else am I to know how you truly think or feel?"

Suddenly the lower half of her body was pressed
against his own, and despite the loch's cold waters, his
desire was unmistakable. "No need for ale. I think only
about you, and when I am not with you I feel miserable
and am in constant pain."

"That is not what I meant," she said with a playful
huff, and pushed against his chest.

He loosened his grip but did not let her go. "And just
what would you like to know?"

If I am special, Adanel thought. And though she desperately wanted to know what he would say, she could
not bring herself to ask. "How I compare," she finally
answered. "For I know you have had many women."

"None since I met you," he replied honestly. Then leaning down, he whispered into her ear, "And aye, I've had women, but you, too, were no maiden when we met."

"True, but it was only one time and long ago."

"One time," he repeated, realizing what that meant. She may not have been a virgin, but his *aithinne* had been close to it. "I must admit that I have wondered how it is you are not married."

Adanel stiffened. "I could ask the same of you."

"The reason is simple. I never asked anyone, but I cannot believe you've never had a proposal. Just how old are you?"

Adanel gave him a firm push, and he let her go. She knew he was not trying to be cruel, but his words were angering her nonetheless. She moved back a couple of feet so that she could stand on the pebbly lake bed and not tread water. She leveled him with an icy look and answered, "In a month, I shall be six and twenty, and you are right. Years ago, I was engaged to be married."

His gaze did not falter under her stare. "Daniel," he whispered under his breath. She was surprised that he had remembered the one time she had mentioned her first love's name. "What happened?"

Adanel's jaw tightened, and she lifted her chin. "My father had him killed right in front of me for daring to fall in love without his permission,"

This time he flinched. "Your father wants you to stay with him that much? He would actually *kill* a man to prevent you from leaving his side?"

"My father couldn't care less about me, but if I were to marry and leave, that would strip him of some of his control. And *that* is unacceptable."

She had shocked him. Adanel could see the revulsion on his face. And if that small amount of truth had him reacting in such a way, there was no way she could tell him everything.

Adanel, near tears, turned away and was about to go to shore and get dressed when she felt a hand on her shoulder stopping her. Without a word, he pulled her around and kissed her with so much tenderness it felt like her heart was swelling in her chest, nearly choking her. When he finally ended the embrace, it was a long while before she opened her eyes.

Adanel rested her cheek against his chest, wishing once again these stolen moments with him would never end. She was losing her heart to this man, and unless he was an incredible liar, her McTiernay soldier felt the same about her despite what she had just told him.

Falling in love had never been her plan. She was just supposed to get him to like and care for her enough to help her. Ideally, they would handfast for a year to ensure her father accepted she was no longer under his control, but now that idea was no longer palatable. She wanted her Highlander forever, and it was long since passed the time she should have told him the truth about who she was. Every time they met, she became more afraid to do so.

Each week, he captured another piece of her soul, and if he cared about her the same way she felt about him, soon these weekly rendezvous would no longer be enough. He would ask for more, and more than anything Adanel wanted to spend her life with him, but before she could, she would have to tell him who she was. And when she did, Adanel prayed he would listen to her reasons and understand that it was fear of losing him that prevented her from saying something sooner.

Each week she rode out, promising herself that today she would open up and explain. And each week, they would kiss, and the moment their lips met she could not bring herself to risk losing him with the truth quite yet. Eventually, there would be no more chances to delay, and when that time came, he would be angry, he would yell, but he would also come to understand why. Their love for each other *would* prevail. But would love protect him from her father? It did not before, but what she had felt for Daniel was nothing compared to her feelings now.

"How much time do you have left?" he whispered against her hair.

Adanel looked at the sky without lifting her head. "We still have a few more minutes," she answered, needing to feel him, to be wanted and loved.

She felt his arm tuck underneath her knees as he carried her out of the water and onto the shore. He laid her down on the soft grass and slowly trailed a finger down her side. His blue eyes sought her brown ones. *"Aithinne?"*

Adanel said not a word and just opened her arms. He rolled to pull her under him, and they groaned in mutual ecstasy when she opened to take him in.

They had been meeting almost weekly for nearly four months. Twice, they had had to endure a prolonged separation due to poor weather that included fierce storms and lightning. But most weeks, fate had been unusually kind with sunny weather and little rain. And each time they saw each other, it felt as if it had been months, not seven days.

Often, they had loved long and hard, neither wanting to waste a moment, but right now the loving was soft and slow, each wanting to draw out the moment and make it last forever.

"My *aithinne*," Adanel heard him say as he began to thrust with more speed, hard and deep. She could only moan.

"You feel so beautiful, so perfect." How he could speak Adanel did not know. She could barely think. Her hands roamed his body, scoring her nails along his back as she tightened her legs around his hips, claiming him as hers.

"Let go, *ruadh*, I've got you," he demanded. Adanel's large eyes met his darkening blue ones as her body searched for its release. He pressed against her most sensitive part, and pleasure took over. With one final thrust, he shouted "*Chruitheachd!*" as they jointly found heaven.

Adanel lay there for what felt like hours, breathing deeply with him at her side, in a similar state. Every time it got only better. She would have thought it impossible, and yet, it was not.

His large hand curled around her side and pulled her closer to him. He took a deep breath, inhaling the scent of her hair, and then exhaled. "When I'm away from you I can't sleep. I'm not hungry. I can't concentrate. I see you in my dreams. I relive moments like these, and I almost wonder if I've made you up, because it is so good. And then when I actually have you, touch you, I realize that my dreams paled in comparison. I'm trying to give you what you want, letting you dictate the terms, but I'm not sure how much longer I can last."

Adanel did not move. He had not used the word *love*, but that was what he was saying. She held his heart just as he held hers.

Adanel opened her mouth to speak but the words would not come out. She knew she should open up and finally be completely honest with him, but she could feel the panic once again begin to well within her. She needed time to think, to find the right words that would somehow keep him listening until she was done. He needed to believe that she felt the same as well as understand the threat her father posed.

With a deep, steadying breath, Adanel stroked his arm. "I'm scared," she finally admitted.

"Of me or this?"

"What is this?" she asked, turning her head to look at him.

He stared at her for a long moment, far too long if he was going to ask her to marry him. Something was holding him back as well, and she knew what it was—her. He was waiting on her to believe in him, and her time to do so was running out.

"Next time, *aithinne*," he said in a breathy but serious tone. "You have this last week, and then we are going to talk only truths between us and you will see that you can trust me."

His blue gaze was steady and unyielding, waiting for a response. Adanel swallowed. There was a hardness in them as well. Trusting him was the only way for her to find the once seemingly impossible future she had always wanted. It also carried the very real possibility of his death and a pain and loss unlike any she had ever known. And yet, finding one's soul mate was a gift from God, and she had to have faith that such a gift could overcome any obstacle.

At last Adanel nodded, but with a gaze just as serious and steady as the one he had given her. "And when you hear my truth, you must give me your vow to listen to it fully. Only then will your heart understand and believe what I say is true."

Dugan's eyes bored into hers. "My decisions are my own as are yours. No one else can carry the burden of their weight. But I will not make them in ignorance," he promised, closing his eyes. He rested his forehead against hers. "And neither will you."

Adanel nodded and immediately, he claimed her lips in such a way that ensured she was ruined for anyone else.

Chapter Three

Dugan finished prepping his horse and was about to mount the animal and begin the long ride back to Fàire Creachann when he paused and looked back across the small loch where he had spent the afternoon with the woman who had stolen his heart. It was empty now. She had quickly dressed and dashed away like she did most weeks, mumbling about being late to meet her uncle. He really needed to meet the man.

Murt, he needed to meet her entire family. And he would. Soon.

Deep down, Dugan knew that he had done what he had sworn never to do—he had fallen in love. Fact was, he had been falling for her since the day they met. Too often he had found himself thinking and feeling things Cole and Donald professed about their wives that had previously been a mystery. He had not wanted to be in love, but it seemed he was in it regardless, and unable—not to mention unwilling—to break free of its grasp. Ellenor had been right. Once he found the right woman, his wandering days would not only be over, but he would not miss them.

He had only known his *aithinne* for a few months but

that did not seem to matter. Her refusal to pretend shame or any other emotion had intrigued him the first time they had met. Her dry wit, gorgeous body, mass of untamable red hair kept him returning for more. And the more he learned, the more he craved to know. She created an unquenchable thirst in him that he never wanted to satiate.

Her secrecy and evasiveness about her home life were inconsequential compared to what he did know about her. And in truth, he had been almost as secretive. She did not know he was one of Cole's commanders. And while he had told her a little of his past—the battles he had fought and the friends he had made before joining the McTiernays, he had said nothing about his own family and reasons behind his inability to trust even his friends. And yet, he trusted her. Maybe it was because she had gotten to know him, not his past.

He would have asked her to marry him this week, but he had felt her stiffen and could feel her need to mentally and emotionally prepare for their conversation. If he was right, she also needed to prepare to never come home. The next time they met, she would never leave his arms again . . . which was another good reason that he offered her a week. He needed time to prepare as well.

First, he had to confer with Cole and let him know what was going on just in case an impromptu wedding next week created an issue with some locals. Then he needed to send word for Father Lanaghly to come and open the church. He also wanted to speak with Cole's wife as well as Donald's. Unless Ellenor and Brighid understood that this time was different, they would feel the need to "protect" his *aithinne* from a broken heart by detailing his past. If, however, they knew his heart was true, both women would do just the opposite, for not a fortnight had passed in the last seven years without at least one of them making a comment that he needed to settle down.

Dugan smiled to himself and swung a leg over his mount. He almost would like to see Ellenor try and persuade his *aithinne* against him. He may not know her name or where she lived, but he knew *her*. His firebrand would not let anyone influence her opinion—not even him. And if their union created issues with someone in the clan, then that was for Cole McTiernay to deal with. Lord knows Cole had created enough challenges when he had wed Ellenor, her being English. Whatever secret his firebrand had about her identity, at least she was Scottish!

Dugan squeezed the reins in anticipation. One more week and then she would be his. He knew she was afraid and knew just as certainly that she had no reason to be. It did not matter what she had to say. He might be asking her to run away from the church and her vows. She could even say that she had been married before, and he would still want her for his own. Nothing would dissuade him now that he had made up his mind.

Dugan glanced back one last time. *Why wait?* he asked himself. What was one more week going to change? He did not *need* to confer with Cole or anyone. Ellenor and Brighid had probably already deciphered his feelings and reason behind his weekly trips long before he had. So why should they put themselves through one more week of torment? He knew how he felt about her, and unless she was a remarkable liar her feelings for him were the same. If she needed to face something or someone at home to be with him, she would not do it alone. They would do it together. Today.

Dugan urged his horse down the mountain and headed to the opening he knew she used to reach the loch. If he was lucky, he would get there before her uncle arrived to take her back home. It was long past time they met.

Dugan sighed in relief when he saw the two figures in the distance. They were riding away from him heading north, but not urgently. Dugan gave his horse a sharp kick, quickening the pace. He was about to shout, get her attention, and wave for her to stop when he abruptly pulled back his own reins.

He sat there staring at the truth she had refused to tell him. The bright blue and red tartan tossed over her shoulders was unmistakable. She was a Mackbaythe. *Ruadh.* He should have known. Both of Laird Mackbaythe's children had the fiery red hair of their MacLeod mother.

Everyone knew her father lied and schemed, and it seemed his daughter was no different. Week after week they had been together, growing closer. If she were truly in trouble she knew weeks—nay, months—ago that she could have told him what was going on and he would have offered her help. But she had remained silent. For what reason? The only one plausible was that she had wanted him to fall under her spell. And he nearly had.

He took one last look at her and the man riding beside her before turning around. Uncle? Hardly. That *guard* was probably under orders to remain hidden and ensure Dugan and she were always alone, giving her time to work her charms.

Of all the foolish blunders he had committed in his lifetime, this one was the worst of all. He *never* trusted anyone, and this was why. People lied. They would lie out of fear, to protect themselves, to protect others. There were countless reasons why people failed to tell the truth, but he was looking at the most common of reasons— greed. Mackbaythes always wanted more. More control, more land, more power, more money. The woman who had thought to steal his heart no doubt wanted all those. It was at the core of what a Mackbaythe was.

Dugan's heart grew cold wondering what she and her father said about him during the days they were apart. Did she laugh or call him a fool? All those comments about him being a soldier when she must have known exactly who he was. Loch Coire Fionnaraich never was visited by anyone. What a coup it must have been to arrive before him and catch his eye. All knew her father made alliances through marriage. Did they think that a marriage to him would grant them McTiernay privileges or worse, get Cole to let down his guard? Whatever their ultimate plan was, it had just failed.

Dugan was tempted to play the fool for one more week to discover just what she intended now that she believed him completely under her spell. But he would rather leave her sputtering and alone wondering how she had so horribly miscalculated her effect on him.

Dugan kicked his horse in the flanks and headed back home. He would not come this way again. Jaime could check on the farms and see to border clansmen needs. When he couldn't, then Donald and the elite guard could journey this way. Regardless of whoever came out, it would not be him.

Ellenor would have questions, but she would not ask them. Brighid would cajole Donald into pressing him for answers, but he would learn nothing.

The only peace Dugan had to cling to was that no one knew it had been a Mackbaythe who had almost captured his heart.

Adanel blinked, glad her back was to her best friend as she placed the last log in the small fireplace. She had just finished helping to clean the last room of the small inn and was physically drained, so she knew she had to have heard her friend wrong. Pasting on a smile that she hoped was encouraging, not horror-filled, Adanel prompted, "Say that again, Kara?"

"We *finally* had a conversation! Not mumbled courtesies we usually exchange. He did not ask inane questions about the weather or my health, and for once he did not inquire about you! I'm telling you, it was a *real* conversation. After twelve years, Fearan is finally seeing me as a woman, not some young orphan that needs protecting. And before you shake your head at me, Adanel, I am *not* embellishing what happened. He spoke *with* me. Not *to* me. I was there . . . you weren't. It happened. It really and truly did."

Kara's bubbly excitement could not be contained. Her thick, dark, wavy brown hair bounced around her hips and her sky-blue eyes were sparkling with joy. Even the freckles along her nose seemed to dance with merriment.

Adanel had no wish to stomp on her best friend's heart, but this was not the first time Kara had made such a claim. No matter how much Adanel wished otherwise, she could not see Fearan and Kara ever being a couple. And it was incredibly sad because nothing lit up her friend's face like the mention of Fearan. If only he could see her now, maybe then he would realize just what he could have if he gave them a chance.

Kara was everything a man wanted in a woman. She was neither too tall nor too short. She had perfect curves that drew a man's eye without being the object of ridicule or snide remarks. And if that were not enough, Kara also had a melodic voice that conveyed so much optimism and hope, it was nearly impossible to be in a bad mood around her. Add clever, a hard worker, and her loyalty, and *any* man would be lucky to capture Kara's heart. And several had tried, but her friend would not be swayed. Kara did not care that she was six and twenty and the topic of some of the more tiresome gossips around the port. She wanted Fearan and no other.

Adanel knew this and had given up long ago on trying to persuade her friend to choose someone closer to her age. She had also given up trying to convince Kara that Fearan did not care for her that way. More than a dozen years older, Fearan had never shown any interest in anyone—including Kara. Not once had Adanel ever heard him hinting at his feeling anything other than neighborly for someone else.

"I believe you did indeed speak and have a conversation, but do you honestly think that after all this time that implies interest?" Adanel posed cautiously.

"Fearan is not just shy, Adanel, but *incredibly* shy. And he thought he was too old, something I very quickly made clear that he was completely wrong about."

Adanel's eyes widened, imagining just how her bold friend had gone about reassuring Fearan she was perfect for him. Rising to her feet, she went over and helped Kara to make the bed.

The chore was one of many that, if her father knew she helped Kara with, he would ban her from the small inn. It had nothing to do with the work. He could care less how much she toiled, but he had much to say about anything concerning his reputation. When certain men came to visit, he would dress her up and parade her around as if she were a much sought after yet unattainable prize. How her value would drop if it were widely known that she often helped wash linens, clean fireplaces, haul water, and sweep floors. The only thing she was not allowed to do was cook. Everything her friend made was delicious, and the only time it was not was when Adanel tried to help.

Adanel tucked in her side of the bed. "Last one, right?"

Kara nodded her head. "Only two seamen were here last night, and both left on their ship this morning. But Fearan told me another ship would be in before the sun set," she said smugly, as if the information proved her prior claim. "*And* that he would stop by tonight to talk with the inn's guard. He even said that he should speak with Nigel about adding another one. He's worried about me with men staying here."

Adanel raised her brows at that bit of information. Maybe it was possible Fearan had shown Kara more than just the casual interest of a friend.

The inn was not a large one, but it was the only one at the port that was clean, quiet, and not geared toward providing female company. Kara's grandfather had started the business of taking care of seamen who wanted a clean bed and decent meal cooked over a fire versus a constantly swaying hammock and dried beef. Her mother and father had taken over, and upon their deaths, Kara and her brother Nigel had been running things.

Unfortunately, Adanel's father was a greedy laird and not a good one, with no interest in the welfare of his clansmen. In his mind, he was the reason the port was active, which enabled his clansmen to earn a living and provide for their families. That the Mackbaythe clansmen owed *him*. Therefore, he periodically sent his guard to do random search and seizures of anything that looked valuable. As a result, to protect themselves, homes, and businesses against such intrusions, many families made sure at least one member of their family joined his guard. The aberrant symbiotic relationship ensured Laird Mackbaythe had an army large enough to guard the port and himself, and though he gave them little training and most held no loyalty for their laird, they did their job in order to protect their families and businesses.

"Nigel has always ensured you and the inn were safe," Adanel responded.

"My baby brother assured me he has a trusted guard watching the inn every night, but you and I both know that people listen to and fear Fearan more than any Mackbaythe guard."

Adanel nodded for Kara was right. Even her father avoided angering the port master. The man was a natural leader, and no one was better at ensuring ships got in and out of port and their goods on and off ships quickly without issue. Unfortunately for Adanel's father, Fearan was also honest. A fact the laird had been able to circumvent by appointing a dockmaster to oversee all the goods in storage who was much more amenable to corruption. Fearan was aware of that fact, but he was smart enough to stay out of it.

Adanel sat down on the bed she had just helped to make and studied her friend. "Kara, you've been in love with Fearan for ten years now—"

"Twelve," Kara corrected, sitting down on the other side of the bed.

"Fine, twelve years. And while it is noteworthy that Fearan has taken an interest in your welfare, I think he is just making sure you are doing well now that Nigel has been reassigned to the Fortress. Without your brother around, could it be that Fearan just wants to make sure everyone knows that this inn and you are still protected? I mean he did do the same thing right after your mother died."

Kara sighed and picked at a loose string on the blanket. She had been thirteen years old when Fearan had first stepped into their lives. Nigel was a year younger than her and the two had been barely making it until Fearan had come in to help. It had been his idea to not offer breakfast or lunch anymore. Kara and Nigel would work in the morning, keep the rooms clean, and in the afternoon, she would make dinner. Fearan had worked with Nigel, teaching him how to haggle and get meat and goods for the inn. Whenever Adanel could, she, too, helped, which became almost daily after Nigel had been compelled to join her father's army.

Both Kara and the inn had survived, even thrived, and that would not have happened without Fearan. Kara had known it, and since his first visit, she had been utterly besotted with the man.

Fearan's appeal was a mystery to Adanel. The port master was brilliant and kind, with warm brown eyes that made one trust him, but he had graying black hair and a gut despite being a huge man. He rarely smiled, and his mind was always going in multiple directions, never slowing. His speaking voice was both gruff and loud, a definite benefit to being a port master. When he actually did intentionally yell, the sound boomed and hurt the ears. But the thing that probably kept most women from throwing themselves at him and the power he held was that he was hairy. Very hairy and all over. But it never once bothered Kara, and she scolded Adanel once for shivering at the thought of being naked with such a man.

"I knew you would not believe me," Kara said, unfazed, "but if you had been here, you would have seen that he sees me differently now, Adanel, truly you would have. And it is all because of my idea."

Adanel rolled her eyes and flopped back on the bed. "If that is true, and he learns what you did and how it was all a trick . . ."

Kara giggled and dropped down beside Adanel. "He already knows. Fearan knew it the whole time."

Adanel pulled up so that she was leaning on her elbows. "Wait. Fearan *told* you this?"

"Aye. He said that I should never try to make him jealous again. That it was no longer necessary. Then he made me promise to save a dinner plate for him."

Adanel flipped over to her side. "*No longer* necessary?"

"Aye, I told you it would work. Fearan just needed to realize what he would feel seeing me in the arms of another man. And he did not like it *at all*," she giggled. "Stay for dinner, and you will see for yourself."

Adanel reached out and clasped her best friend's hand in her own. "I wish I could, but I have been told the MacCoinniches are visiting *again*, which means I must ready myself for my father will demand that I dine with them."

Kara wrinkled her nose. "This is the fourth visit in as many months. I wonder why."

Adanel shrugged. "I have no idea. They discuss nothing really, and I find the night extremely tedious and annoying. Laird MacCoinnich's son stares at me the entire time while his father just sits there in obvious boredom listening to my father speak nonsense about how powerful we are becoming and how their alliance is mutually beneficial. Trust me, I would rather be here seeing for myself that Fearan has finally woken up and realized how lucky he is that you want him and no other."

Kara sat up, beaming once more. "He *is* lucky, isn't he? Thank God, he is finally realizing it. Before the year is out, he will be mine. You will see," she said, sliding off the bed and spinning around.

Adanel felt a tear of joy escape. For three days now, she had not known what she was going to do if next week went the way she hoped. Once she explained everything,

Adanel had little doubt that her soldier would insist on whisking her away from her life, never to return. Even if he decided being married to a Mackbaythe was not what he wanted, he would at least ensure she was safe. She knew that after he had told her about the battles he had fought and the group of friends with whom he had been close before joining the McTiernays. Her soldier was arrogant and far too good looking, but he was also honorable and protected those he cared about. And she would stake everything that he loved her as much as she loved him.

The only worry she had was that it meant abandoning Kara.

Their mothers had met when she and Kara had been barely a year old. Feeling the pull of kinship, they had bonded and soon became the closest of friends. This friendship instilled an even tighter bond between their daughters. Adanel did not think of Kara as a friend, but as a sister. Even her brother Nigel was more like family than her own brother had ever been. Eògan rarely acknowledged her existence, a fact of which Adanel was grateful.

For years, she, Kara, and Nigel were all each other had. Adanel had been racking her brain to try and find a way to bring her friend with her. But even if she had, it would have been pointless. Kara would never go anywhere without Nigel and talking him into going would have been highly unlikely. The inn was his home, as was the port and the people around it. And even if by some miracle, Adanel and Kara could convince him to leave, there was no guarantee her McTiernay soldier would welcome either of them or guarantee their safety. The Mackbaythes were not just disliked by their southern neighbor, but despised and most of all distrusted. Because

Nigel was a Mackbaythe soldier, there was a chance someone might assume he was a spy and execute him.

But if what Kara was telling her was true, then all her fears and worry were for naught. Her best friend would be fine. Fearan would ensure she was safe and happy.

Seeing Adanel's tears, Kara sat back down. "Don't cry, Adanel," she said, her voice full of concern. "If anything, it will be better now. Your father listens to Fearan. Maybe he can convince him to let you go and have a life."

Adanel shook her head and wiped her eyes. "I don't need help. Honest. I don't. And you know that my father has his reasons for not letting me go. He likes to dangle the possibility of a marriage to me as leverage. What I fear is that one day soon he will realize that I am too old to be considered a prize. A few months ago, I almost believed that had already happened."

Kara stood up once again and stared at Adanel. "A few *months* ago?" she asked, her tone accusatory.

Adanel bit her bottom lip. "The good news is that come this Tuesday it no longer matters," she said with a sly smile.

Kara stared at her wide eyed for several seconds. When Adanel returned the stare and gave her a small apologetic shrug, Kara clapped her hands and let out a squeal. "I *knew* it!" she yelped. "I *knew* there was more to your weekly rides than a need to just escape this place and your father. You met someone! And you *like* him," she said, grinning and nodding at the same time. "More importantly, he likes you." Then Kara slapped her hand against her forehead. "*Mo chreach!* What is your father going to do when he finds out?"

Adanel's eyes grew wide, and she started shaking her head back and forth. "He can't know. You cannot say a thing, Kara, not to Nigel or anyone. I'm not even telling Faden. By the time my father finds out, I need to be under the protection of the McTiernay army. Or at least that is my hope."

Kara wrinkled her nose. "The McTiernays? How did you manage that? They don't like us and with good reason. And knowing that your father is our laird is going to make your situation even more—" Kara paused, seeing Adanel fidget. Her eyes grew large as she accurately guessed why. "*He doesn't know?*" she hissed. "*Murt,* Adanel, it is going to be Daniel all over again!"

"Nay, it won't," Adanel countered vehemently, and squared her shoulders. "Daniel was young, inexperienced, and a merchant. My McTiernay is a soldier and not only can but will protect me."

Kara swung her arm open. "Every man in your father's army would say the same thing. That does not make it true."

"But unlike them, he has the scars of war and has seen plenty of battles. He would not be scared by my father or any of his men, including his hired mercenaries."

"Hmmm. A soldier *and* a McTiernay. Smart thinking to seek out someone like him for help. But how did you convince him to take you with him next week?"

"I haven't. As you guessed, we have been meeting each week and well . . . I fell in love. And based on what he told me when we parted this last time, he has too. I think he is going to ask me to marry him."

Shock overtook Kara. "Let's hope his impulse is to whisk you away to safety and not confront your father to defend your honor or something stupid. Thankfully you chose someone who can defend himself if necessary."

"First, I did not *choose* him. We stumbled upon each other at Loch Coire Fionnaraich. And while I admit that his being a McTiernay soldier was the reason he first caught my eye, something soon changed. I realized that with him I was comfortable being just me."

Kara's hand flew to her chest, and she pretended to be injured. "Well, I just want you to know that I have never been comfortable with you either."

Adanel gripped the pillow behind her and chucked it at her friend, hitting her in the face. "He makes me laugh, I mock him, and then he just responds in kind. We tease each other, and despite his arrogance"—she paused and nodded with a slight grimace—"aye, arrogance, but I actually like it. Self-confidence is incredibly . . . stimulating, though I would never let him know I think that."

"And despite this arrogance that you secretly like . . ." Kara prompted, wanting Adanel to finish her thought.

Adanel wiggled her brows and grinned. "He is incredibly attractive. Oh, Kara," she said, her cheeks growing redder by the second, "he has a ruggedness about him that is so alluring. It's hard to describe, but basically he is the most intensely, overwhelmingly male man I have ever met," she said, throwing her hands up in the air. "Unfortunately, he *knows* it."

"Hence the arrogance."

"I have no doubt his ego has been stroked by many women over the years."

"Sweetie," Kara said with some hesitancy, "men like that don't marry women. They play with them."

"I would have agreed a couple of months ago, maybe even a couple of weeks. I mean he oozes confidence, so much that it can be annoying. And then I usually end up mocking him, which based on his reactions, is something to which he is unaccustomed. But instead of getting mad, he teases me in return. It becomes a contest of wits. We share all our opinions and thoughts, and argue—"

"—wait, argue?"

"Aye, argue. All the time. He actually *likes* the feisty side of my personality. He calls me his firebrand."

Kara stared at her with her mouth open.

"What?" Adanel prompted. "You are making me nervous."

"That's because you love him."

"Well, I *do* plan on leaving with him next week. My only hesitation in doing so was you, but if you and Fearan are truly—"

Kara waved her hand, stopping her from finishing her sentence. "I said you *love* this McTiernay. This is not just about him being good looking, stimulating, arrogant, or even a soldier who can protect you. You. Are. In. Love. It's all over your face when you talk about him. You're practically glowing."

Adanel wanted to deny it. It was easier to lie to herself than to Kara. And her friend would not judge her. They wanted the same things for each other—love and happiness.

"I am in love, Kara. And I think he loves me in return, but I am so afraid that I am going to lose him." She looked up, tears starting to form once again. "He doesn't know who I am. He doesn't even know I am a Mackbaythe. All he knows is that I hate my father."

Kara went over and sat down, covering Adanel's hands with her own. "You need to tell him *everything*, Adanel. No more waiting and no more secrets. If he loves you, he will accept you despite who your father is, but he won't regardless of his feelings if he thinks you are lying to him."

"But I haven't lied."

"That is good. Because all I know is that if Fearan thought I was intentionally misleading him, I doubt that—"

Kara's last words were cut off by someone unexpectedly opening the door. Adanel fought off a groan seeing

Faden. "*Halò*, is it time to leave already? Are you *sure* I have to come? I'm telling you Laird MacCoinnich cares not if I am present."

Faden nodded. "Your father told me to tell you he wanted you to look especially nice tonight. There is to be an announcement."

A feeling of dread washed over Adanel. Her father's announcements were never good. And the fact that she was to be paraded as the unattainable bride once more in front of the MacCoinniches was worrisome. One did not tease powerful lairds or their sons. Thank God, this was going to be the last time she would have to endure such an evening.

Kara reached out and grabbed her hand and gave it a squeeze. "Four more days," she whispered.

Adanel returned the grip. It was going to be the longest four days of her life.

Chapter Four

Dugan shot straight up, and immediately his hand reached for his sword. His body was locked, and his jaw froze as he tried to ascertain what it was that had awoken him. He looked around the crowded area, and he could see from the moon's light everyone was asleep. Something had startled him out of a dead sleep. He vaguely thought it had been someone running by him, but he was not sure. He had just fallen asleep, tired from all the Highland games that had been taking place over the weeks leading up to Conan's wedding.

It had been something for the men to do, and Dugan had participated every day, giving all that he had until he was worn out with exhaustion. It was the only way he could sleep.

Dugan forced his body to relax. Lying back down, he stared at the night sky. Conan had gotten married just a few hours ago. The one McTiernay—hell, the one *Highlander*—no one thought would ever wed, Conan included, had actually said vows. He had even meant them.

Incredibly, the man had met a woman who had accepted him, loved him, and was his equal in every way. And what did Conan do? He had asked her to marry him. She had said yes, and now they were blissfully happy.

No one had believed it to be possible. Practically every Highlander in Scotland who was ever an ally or friend to the McTiernays had demanded to be present at the wedding. Dugan had never seen so many clans gathered in one area outside of battle. He almost expected Conan to back out from the pressure, but the man—in front of everyone—had proudly, without hesitation, claimed Mhàiri as his and only his for the rest of their lives.

Every fiber of Dugan's being had been and still was jealous. For that should have been him.

Almost a year ago, he had met the woman God had created just for him. He had known it eight months ago when he turned his back on her, and he still knew it today. There was no one else for him. Unfortunately, he could never proudly claim his *aithinne* as his own. To her, he was nothing but a fool who had narrowly escaped her clutches.

He was in limbo. He could not go back to his prior life of just enjoying a woman's body. Neither did he know how to move forward. But he was going to find a way, because he could not continue thinking about her all the time.

Dugan sighed and wondered if she thought about him at all. Had his *aithinne* continued to visit the loch each week on the chance he might appear? Did she have any regrets? Did she miss him at all? Did memories of their being together haunt her like they did him? Had she already moved on to someone else? He squeezed his eyes shut and rubbed his face. *Murt*, these thoughts, they needed to *end*.

Dugan took a deep breath and tried once again to find

sleep. He had just closed his eyes when they shot wide open, this time from sounds. No, not sounds. Screams.

They were screams of terror. Screams filled with agony and anguish of the most intense kind. Etched in every note. He could *feel* these screams, and they terrified him as to what they could mean.

Without thought, Dugan grabbed his sword and started running toward the sound. He knocked over bowls, crushed blankets, and kicked several legs and feet, but he barely noticed. The sounds of grief were tearing at him.

Like most soldiers who were sleeping outdoors, he did not sleep nude as was his preference when a bed was available. Tonight, he had collapsed on his blanket exhausted and was therefore still dressed, tartan, shoes, and all. But even if he were in the buff, he would have been running toward the screams that were getting louder with each step. Agony like that did not care about clothes. It could not see. It only felt, and by the tone, the pain was so deep there was no end.

Heads were starting to emerge out of the tents, their sleep-filled expressions starting to be replaced with concern and then alarm. Dugan saw out of the corner of his eye that others were running as well. Many of the soldiers were dressed like him, ready for battle; some were only in a léine, but all of them had their swords in their hands, prepared for fight.

All except one man. He was running in the opposite direction of the screams.

Dugan slowed down for a second and watched the tall, thin figure. There was something about him that he recognized, but before he could figure out what it was, the man had disappeared into the night. Dugan's instinct said to follow him, but then the intensity of the cries became worse. And they were coming from nearby.

Dugan's head darted around as he saw another man dash by him, heading toward the sounds. He was surprisingly spry and agile for being an old man, and Dugan recognized him as Laird MacInnes, Laurel's grandfather and the McTiernay brothers' godfather.

Dugan turned to follow, catching up to the older laird. "Do you know who? Where?"

MacInnes pointed to a tent that was set apart. "I know that scream," he huffed. "It's Laurel."

Dugan's eyes widened and he sprinted ahead, arriving at the same time a couple other soldiers did. One of them was Loman, who, along with Seamus and several other of the elite guard kicked out of the castle, had been sleeping outside with most of the soldiers.

Loman did not even ask. He yanked up the flap and entered, followed by Dugan, MacInnes, and a growing number of men.

Dugan had fought bloody fights. He had been in many gruesome battles. He had killed men countless times and seen even more killed. He hated it. Loathed it. Knew sometimes it was a necessary evil, but not once had he almost physically become ill at the sight. But what he saw had him green and shaking.

Conor, Cole's eldest brother and chief of the entire McTiernay clan, was lying lifeless in a pool of his own blood, which was draining from a dagger that was still protruding from the middle of his chest. His head was in Laurel's lap, and her hands were covered in blood, clutching him. She was screaming, begging him to stay with her.

Realizing she was no longer alone, Laurel looked up, her face one of absolute terror that she was about to lose the man who was her very heart and soul. "He . . . he . . . came in. Said that Conan McTiernay could not be allowed to live. That Adanel was pledged to another. And

then, then he plunged the . . . the . . ." Then she looked
down and started yelling at Conor. "Don't you dare
die on me! Don't you dare! Don't you leave me!" she
screamed once again.

Then with a sob and a wail, she began to beg. "Please.
Please. Please, Conor. Don't leave me. I need you. I need
you. Please. Please. Oh, God. Please. Please don't take
him. He's mine."

People began to move around Dugan in an effort to
get to Laurel and Conor. With so many of the visiting
ladies being in varying stages of pregnancy, multiple
midwives were around, and some were well versed in a
variety of medicines. Dugan stepped back out of the tent
to give them room and looked in the direction the dis-
appearing figure had gone. He had been heading north,
away from camp and in the opposite direction of
McTiernay Castle. He had not been seeking help. He
had been running away.

Dugan looked back at the tent. It was now full of
people. He could still hear Laurel crying. Someone was
saying they were going to take out the knife and to be
prepared. Dugan just stared at the opening, his mind
churning. Why would anyone stab Conor? How had they
even found him in this sea of tents? His eyes narrowed as
he studied the entrance. It was decorated with flowers
because it was not Conor's tent . . . it was *Conan's*. It had
been intended for today's bride and groom.

Dugan's thoughts began to race. "*Conan* had to die,"
Laurel had said. Conor had not been the intended
victim. He had simply been stabbed by a man who had
been seeking to end his younger brother Conan's life.

Gasps were coming from inside the tent, and Laurel's
cries renewed. People were shouting, but Dugan was
blocking out all the sounds. He started to move in the
direction where he had seen the figure running. Why was

he familiar? Dugan stopped. The man was not familiar. He had never seen him before. . . . It was the hair he recognized. It was flame red—the same color as hers.

Dugan closed his eyes and gripped his sword, disbelieving his conclusions but knowing they were right. Last fall, soon after Dugan had discovered the truth about his *aithinne*, Conan had been attacked by two men. One he had killed, the other had gotten away. Conan had not recognized either man, but he had been able to describe the one that escaped—red hair, tall, and very thin. The exact description of the man Dugan had just seen running away.

"*Adanel,*" Laurel had said. "*Adanel was pledged to another.*" Until now, he had not known her name. Soon, she would know his. For after tonight, there was no place she, her brother, or her father could escape.

He was coming for them. And when he arrived, he was going to be lethal.

The Mackbaythes would pay with their lives for what they did to Conor.

Dugan studied the scraggly, reed-like figure just below him as he stopped to rest and get a drink. The sun was setting, and Dugan would need to make his move before his quarry started moving again. The soon-to-be-dead man looked nervous and kept glancing back to see if there was any sign that he was being followed, but the fool failed to ever once look up.

For the past two hours, the man had been working his way through a mountainous section of the south edge of the Torridon mountains, and Dugan had taken advantage of the terrain to follow him.

Conor's attacker was wearing a Mackbaythe plaid, and as he suspected, the color of his hair definitely indicated he was related to Adanel. Younger brother, Dugan guessed. He knew very little about the Mackbaythes, only that there was a son and a daughter who had inherited the red hair of their MacLeod mother. And if Adanel was the daughter, the man he was tracking had to be the son. He was no longer a boy, but his frame had yet to fill out into a man's, which made it hard to tell just how old he was. But he was definitely younger than Adanel.

The man went to his horse and, to Dugan's surprise, he started to whistle a happy tune as he freed the saddle and placed it on the ground. The *gloichd* was going to make camp. Only a fool would stop so soon after committing murder.

The only reason Dugan was alone on this trek was because he had ordered it so. If he had not, McTiernay allies and soldiers would have been up this way, chasing down every possible lead, including the tracks Mackbaythe left behind. And while the unusually thin man had moved surprisingly fast, his tracks had been easy to follow. Dugan had caught up to him by the afternoon despite his having an almost two hours' head start.

When Dugan had put all the pieces together, guilt had plagued him. Instinct said that his relationship with Adanel was related to the attack. Perhaps it was retaliation for spurning Adanel, maybe it was something else, but what happened was because of him and therefore, Dugan refused to let anyone else lay chase. They could hunt down any other leads, but Dugan knew the young Mackbaythe had been the one to stab Conor. He also knew that the McTiernay brothers would want to deliver their revenge personally. Dugan intended to see that that happened.

"I will take care of Adanel and her brother—" Dugan had told Donald as he prepped his horse to ride north.

"If you are right, that is not for you to do. Cole is going to want to be the one exacting revenge for his brother," Donald had told him brusquely, his brown eyes dark with fury. Cole's commander had been at the castle and was still reeling from the news. The McTiernay brothers were convening even as they spoke, and the whole hillside was awake with activity even though the sun was not to rise for several more hours. "He will demand to come with you."

"It won't be just Cole wanting revenge. It will be all of them and they shall have it. Let Cole know that they will soon have the mastermind behind this attack, and he is going to walk right into their hands," Dugan sneered, tightening the cinch on his saddle. "And if I am wrong, I will get you word right away, but Donald . . ." He waited until the large commander lifted his chin to look him in the eye. "I'm not wrong."

"Then take someone with you so you can send back word."

"They will only slow me down, and I am going to do this my way. I was played the fool by them once, Donald. I brought this here. I did not do so knowingly, but I was the one who spurned Mackbaythe's daughter, and this is the result. I will see this through, and I vow to give the McTiernays their revenge. I need you to trust me to do this."

Donald pressed his lips together. After weeks of enduring Dugan's surly attitude the previous summer, he and Jaime confronted their friend, demanding an explanation. Dugan had refused to go into details, but he had trusted them enough to say that Mackbaythe's daughter had nearly played him for a fool. That relationship, what happened to Conan in the fall, and tonight's attack all reeked of a Mackbaythe plot.

Donald finally gave Dugan a single nod. "I will explain to the others and make sure they understand. We will

continue to look for other possibilities, but I doubt we
will find any other tracks but the ones you are following."

"One week," Dugan said, sliding his foot into the stir-
rup and hauling himself up onto his mount. "Tell our
allies to send for more troops. No one likes the Mackbaythes, but they have ties to both the MacCoinniches
and the MacLeods. If either clan feels their interests are
in jeopardy, they may decide to join him."

"Let them," Donald snickered. "It will change nothing."

Dugan leaned back against the waist-high boulder
and waited for Eògan Mackbaythe to wake. The man was
even scrawnier up close, and it had made it more difficult tying him to the tree. He had not cooperated and
flopped around so viciously trying to get out of Dugan's
grasp that Eògan had hit his own head against the trunk
and knocked himself out.

Dugan sighed. Only one more day until they reached
Mackbaythe lands. Then Eògan would learn that all of
his fighting had been for naught.

It had been easy to catch the man, and Eògan had surrendered almost immediately, begging for his life. At first,
he pretended to know nothing about the attack, but after
being tied up and draped across the back of Dugan's
horse for half a day, Eògan admitted his crimes. Then he
had gone on a verbal rampage about who he was, who
his father was, and the painful death awaiting Dugan in
the near future once his father learned how he was
being treated. When that got no response, Eògan had
tried screaming, which had quickly gotten him gagged.

A low moan reached Dugan's ears. Seeing Eògan was
starting to look around, Dugan tossed him a chunk of
cooked fox. He had been fortunate to find and kill the
wily animal rather quickly when he had gone in search

of food. The fox had not been large, but the meat it provided was enough to feed two men for the night.

Large brown eyes the exact same shade as Adanel's stared at the piece of meat. Eògan began to squirm once more, testing the knots on his wrists and ignoring the food. Dugan shrugged and continued eating. He had tied Eògan in a way that gave him just enough maneuverability to feed himself, because Dugan knew he was not going to do it. The man would starve before that happened, but it sounded like he was going to whine a lot before he did.

Eògan began twisting back and forth in frustration. The rope securing him went around a very large oak tree. Each end was tied to a wrist. If he stretched his left hand out, it pulled his right arm back, but it gave him just enough slack to lean down and pick up the leg bone with the tips of his fingers. Rather than eating, however, Eògan was attempting to wear down the rope. "You do that," Dugan warned, "then you make keeping you alive more trouble than it's worth."

Eògan stopped immediately. Fear filled his eyes. "You won't kill me."

"Aye, I would, and if you won't eat that meat, then I will," Dugan said, gesturing toward the fox right next to Eògan's thigh. It was soiled, but Dugan had eaten plenty of filthy meals during war. Dirt didn't kill men. Starvation did.

Hatred churned in every facet of Eògan's face, but after a couple of minutes, he reached down and picked up the leg bone. Within minutes, he had devoured it. Dugan then threw him a leather bag of water. Immediately, Eògan took the waterskin and, using his teeth, pulled out the plug and drank until the bag was empty. He then leaned back against the tree and looked around.

The moon was out and the firelight was casting shadows everywhere, but Dugan was still surprised when Eògan sat up as if he saw something he recognized.

"We are heading north, not south."

"Aye."

Eògan's brows furrowed, and he again studied his surroundings, verifying where they were, which was obviously not where he expected to be. "We are almost to Mackbaythe lands."

"Aye."

"I thought you would have brought me back to the McTiernays."

"Then you thought wrong." Eògan's life would have ended bringing him to the McTiernay brothers, but the act of killing him would have served little purpose. And in cases of revenge, death needed to serve a purpose. Dugan learned that from the McTiernays, and that was the primary reason behind Donald letting him go.

"Whoever you are, you better let me go or you are a dead man," Eògan once again declared.

Dugan snorted and picked up the last of the cooked meat. Eògan truly believed that despite being the one tied to a tree. The man was either stupid or a fool. Probably both. "I doubt it."

"When my father learns of what you are doing to me, he is going to be angry and will get enormous pleasure taking his anger out on you in very cruel and painful ways."

Dugan shrugged. "He's welcome to try."

Eògan's breathing became more rapid and shallow. Dugan could see that his nonchalant response scared him. Most feared Laird Mackbaythe and for good reason. The man was evil. Those who did not were usually colder and even more immoral.

"You're Cole McTiernay's man. I've seen you riding along the borders a couple of times." Dugan nodded, confirming the guess. Eògan cackled, relief flooding through him. His father would make mincemeat of this McTiernay just like he did anyone who defied him. "I never would have guessed a high and mighty McTiernay commander would be anything like me."

Dugan finished gnawing on the leg and threw the bone into the fire.

"Does Cole McTiernay realize he has a traitor in his midst? Do his brothers believe it was *you* who attacked them?" Eògan pressed when Dugan did not respond to his barb. "Maybe you are running from your own death and think to use me to get my father to offer you refuge?"

Dugan shifted his weight and leaned back against the boulder. He learned long ago that the best way to get a man to talk was to pretend to be uninterested in anything they had to say.

"Or is this some scheme to infiltrate *my* clan? Because if it is, you will fail. My father will never accept a McTiernay. He will carve you into bits. The only chance you have is to let me go. If you do, I'll save your life in return."

"I don't believe you have that kind of power," Dugan said with a yawn, and then closed his eyes, pretending to relax.

"I do, but only if you let me go now," Eògan shouted. "Because if my father catches you, nothing you say or do is going to convince him to let you live. He hates McTiernays. He hates them so much he ordered me to kill their precious Conan."

"Conan's not dead," Dugan stated. Keeping his eyes closed, he listened as Eògan continued to squirm.

"My blade in his chest says otherwise."

"It was in *a* chest. Just not Conan's."

There was a long pause as Eògan digested that information. "Then who did I stab?"

Dugan opened his eyes and then moved to stand up. He went to check on his horse and get his plaid and saddle. He set the saddle down and laid the blanket out in front of it, close to the fire.

"Who did I kill?" Eògan's voice was an octave higher and full of panic.

Dugan went behind the tree and wedged two chunks of wood between the trunk and the rope, removing any slack and preventing any movement that might fray it. Then, he went back over to the fire and stretched out on the plaid, getting ready to settle for the night.

"Tell me!"

Dugan closed his eyes and took deep breaths, focusing on the sounds of the wood crackling in the fire. The last thing he heard was Eògan screeching, *"Who did I kill?"*

Chapter Five

"So tell me what happened next," Adanel asked, looking at Nigel expectantly. "I want to hear everything. Every detail, every word spoken, every vow. I need to know all that you can tell me about Kara's wedding."

Nigel threw his hands in the air. "I told you everything I know. She was pretty. Fearan seemed more nervous than she was. She missed you being there, of course. The food was good. People clapped, and everyone seemed happy. That's about it."

Adanel threw a pillow at him. "Some brother you are. No details at all."

She had known Nigel since they were children, and he felt more of a younger brother to her than Eògan did. Nigel had brown hair that was neither dark nor light and usually hung down to his shoulders, and even when it was clean, it was stringy. Because he was so tall and thin, his clothes were baggy and hid the true nature of his form. And while a lack of muscular bulk usually meant lack of strength, Nigel was the opposite of frail. If one paused and truly studied his forearms and calves with an unbiased eye, they would see both were well developed, hinting at the fact that Nigel was far stronger than he initially appeared.

He was also smarter, funnier, and far kinder than one would guess. Where her own brother, Eògan, was cruel, Nigel had an instinctive protective streak. Being only a year younger than her and Kara, the three of them had been very close growing up, and their bond had only gotten stronger after the passing of their parents.

Nigel threw the pillow back. "I *am* a perfect brother. And if you want girly details, then you will have to talk to Kara." Realizing what he had just said, Nigel's eyes went wide with guilt. "Oh, God, Adanel, I'm so sorry. You will get out of here soon and see Kara again. You will."

Adanel shook her head, fighting back tears. "You and I both know that is not going to happen. And if I do somehow get out, I'll have to disappear. I would never see you nor anyone from here ever again. And that includes Kara. That is the way it needs to be if she is to remain safe."

"You *will* get out. We have a plan, and it's a good one. We only need to be patient just a little while longer and wait for the right time. But it's going to be soon. Real soon. I promise."

Adanel nodded. They actually did have a plan—one to which she had only recently agreed. But after her father had told her about Conan's refusal to marry her and that he had no care for the babe she carried, she had finally succumbed to Nigel's insane idea of an escape. It was risky and posed a high chance of her dying, but that was better than her other choice. Adanel was *not* going to marry Daeron MacCoinnich. Ever. Something she had tried to explain to her father months ago.

"You need to eat," Nigel said, and pointed to the food he had brought.

For months, he had been sneaking in food Kara had

prepared. How Adanel missed talking with her best friend. If only she and Kara had had their last conversation a week earlier.

The same day Kara had pressed her to tell her McTiernay soldier the truth the next time they met, her life had come to a complete halt. She had been summoned to prepare for a special dinner with the MacCoinniches only to discover that what made it so special was the announcement that she and Daeron were betrothed.

Adanel had been eight years old when her mother died, and her father had actually threatened to kill her as well, stating Adanel's independent spirit made her more trouble than she was worth. But before he had done so, her father had remembered just how useful marriage alliances could be. He had married a MacLeod and that had kept that powerful clan away. If Adanel were to marry Laird MacCoinnich's newly born son, Daeron, it could prove to be mutually beneficial. MacCoinnich would have guaranteed access to a port and the western seas—very important to a landlocked clan—and it would give her father a powerful ally to crush any enemy.

The deal had been struck. The plan had worked for years with only a few minor obstacles, one of which had nearly been a disaster. Adanel had almost run off to marry some lovesick merchant, which would have not only ended her father's ability to influence one of the most powerful clans in the Highlands, but it would most likely have gotten him killed. To ensure Adanel never even considered another man again, her father had slaughtered her betrothed right in front of her, promising to do the same to any man who came near her.

It had worked. Time passed, and when Daeron had turned eighteen, he had come to claim his bride. Adanel, however, wanted nothing to do with the young man.

Daeron was not bad-looking for someone so young—in fact just the opposite. He was exceedingly brilliant, with the ability to recall anything she or anyone else had ever said. But that ability also made him frightening for he never forgot anything. Not any mistake, not any promise, not any slight—nothing. There was no flexibility with him, and he resented any compromise he had to make. Her father was cruel, but at least he ignored her. Life with Daeron would be the opposite. He would rule her completely, and eventual death would be her only escape.

So Adanel had done the only thing she could think of to give her McTiernay soldier time to find and save her. She told her father that night that she could not marry Daeron. She was pregnant with a McTiernay babe. Adanel knew she had been taking a chance, but she had faith that whoever her McTiernay soldier was, he loved her as deeply as she loved him. When she did not come to the loch, he would come looking for her. Eventually, his search would bring him here, and she would be rescued. She just needed to give him time.

Her father had exploded, demanding to know the McTiernay's name. Adanel feared he wanted to kill him and was glad she could tell him nothing. He had then looked to Faden for answers, and when her uncle could not offer any, her father had imprisoned him in the dungeons of the Fortress, the most secure of the three towers. She had not seen her uncle since.

The only thing that had saved Adanel from a forced abortion had been the death of her mother. She had died trying to abort her third child. Both her children looked like her, but only Adanel had gotten her kind heart. Eògan was like his father in nature, which his father had honed from his birth to continue his legacy.

Adanel's mother had never intended to die, but she could not conceive of bringing another son into the world only to grow up under the cruel direction of their father. Juniper berries were known to end pregnancies, and while they rarely killed, they had caused her mother to start bleeding when she miscarried. The blood had not stopped flowing until her heart had stopped beating.

If not for her mother and how she died, Adanel had no doubt that her father would have forced an abortion on her. But he had been afraid to risk it. Adanel was only useful to him alive. So, her father had decreed her to be sequestered away in her room until the babe was born and told the MacCoinniches some story about Adanel wanting a spring wedding and needing the winter to prepare. Adanel could only imagine how unhappy they were, but they had left.

Her father, however, had only just begun.

He wanted to find the McTiernay who impregnated her and kill him. He had questioned everyone who had ever seen her ride and finally learned about her and Faden's weekly route to the small loch. Faden had told someone of their weekly escapes a year before she had ever met the McTiernay, never dreaming that such information would someday need to remain a secret. And so, her father had sent Eògan and one of his meanest mercenaries to discover her McTiernay lover's identity and to kill him.

Eògan had failed, but swore it was because he had learned she had not just been sleeping with any McTiernay, but one of *the* McTiernays. There were seven brothers, and Adanel had been with Conan, known to be extremely smart, arrogant, and incredibly good looking.

Adanel had been shocked. She knew very little of the McTiernay brothers, but news that she had fallen for one of them had renewed her hope. The McTiernays were powerful and smart, and when her Conan finally learned of her situation, she was positive he would find a way to rescue her.

That hope died the day her father had told her about her brother's attempt to forge an alliance using her pregnancy as insurance. It had failed. Conan had flat out refused to marry her. He denied even knowing her, let alone admitting the possibility the babe she was carrying was his. Adanel had almost given up hope then and would have lost the will to live if not for her two guards—Nigel and Brùid.

Brùid was bald, had deep-set green eyes, and wore a perpetual solemn expression. But people rarely saw those characteristics. All they could see was his size for he was a giant among even very large men. His enormous height and girth made him an oddity and feared by most clansmen. Treated as an outcast for most of his life, Brùid had lived in the forest a few miles north of the port away from the jeers and false accusations that he was robbing others of their share of the food. As a result, he was used to being alone and rarely spoke. Many mistakenly misinterpreted that to mean Brùid was dumb, her father included, but Adanel had instinctively known they could not be more wrong the first time she saw him.

The night her engagement was to be announced, her father had ordered for Brùid to be found and brought forward to be used as entertainment. Unable to watch what her father had planned, Adanel had intervened. Guarding her was supposed to be a punishment, and it would have been for anyone else standing alone with only her to see and talk to day after day, but Brùid was not any man, and over the months, the two of them had formed a tight bond. Adanel trusted him so much that he was the one person to whom she had told everything. Nigel and Kara knew the facts, but it was Brùid to whom she had confided her pain.

Brùid had vowed to get her out of there before the spring when she was due to give birth. It had taken time, but he, Nigel, and Kara had finally come up with a way to make that happen. Their plan was dangerous. It needed perfect timing. But when everything was in place, Adanel would go into labor, and if it all worked out the way it should, she would die.

"I need to get out of here, Nigel," Adanel whispered, looking out her window. "I'm not sure I can wait much longer before having this baby," she said, waving a hand at her large stomach.

Thankfully, her father had sequestered her to her chambers in Baile Tùr. He thought it to be torture keeping her in the Village Tower where she could see people and her friends but never interact with them. Only her guards and recently a midwife were allowed to see or speak to her.

"We are just waiting on the *Destiny's Fortune*. We will leave the night it arrives," Nigel stated, keeping his voice low just in case someone was lurking outside the door.

"I know," Adanel stated softly.

Both stiffened when the door opened, but relaxed upon seeing Brùid. Then the tension grew to exponential levels when her father stepped into the room, barely able to remain upright. His stringy brown hair looked greasy, and his brown eyes looked both gleeful and manic. It scared her when he was in this much of a drunken state for he was capable of anything.

Adanel instinctively grabbed her stomach. She knew her pregnancy was the only thing keeping her safe and prayed nothing had changed.

Laird Mackbaythe waved his finger at her. "That bastard will soon be born, and *you* will finally be useful. But just in case you've kept hope that your McTiernay might change his mind, I thought I'd tell you that he just got married. Supposedly found the love of his life," he slurred.

Adanel had not thought any more news of Conan could hurt her further, but she had been wrong. Whatever they had shared last spring and summer had not been love. It could not have been. Such feelings did not fade away only to be replaced so quickly. Her hopes and dreams had been a foolish fantasy.

"*And*," her father continued with a hiccup, "he is now dead." He smiled a sick grin of triumph. "I sent your brother Eògan to kill him on his wedding night. I thought it only fitting. If he isn't to marry you, *my* daughter, pregnant with *his* child, then he shouldn't be able to marry anyone. We just received news. A McTiernay was stabbed and left in the arms of his wailing wife. Your Conan is *dead*." His face was pinched as he sputtered the last words with a sneer. Then, not giving her a chance to say anything or ask questions, her father spun around and left her to her pain, cackling as he went down the stairwell.

Adanel lost the ability to stand and dropped to her bed. She found it hard to breathe. She should have known her father would have figured out a way to have his revenge. Part of her wanted to cry out in denial, the other part of her was numb.

For the second time, her father had killed the man she loved. This time, however, she was not sure she would recover.

"This is your fault!" Eògan screeched at Dugan as urine trickled down his leg.

He was once again tied to a tree, but after rubbing his

back raw, he had wiggled his way to a standing position. He had been demanding for the past hour to be freed so he could relieve himself, but Dugan had not felt inclined.

Dugan looked at him just long enough to see the front of Eògan's plaid grow dark and wet. Dugan shrugged and returned his attention to the fire. It had rained most of yesterday, making it cold and miserable until the clouds finally parted sometime during the night. He glanced up and sniffed the morning air. The humidity had dropped, and based on the near cloudless sky, it was going to stay dry for a while.

Fat from a small rabbit dripped onto the flames and sizzled. Dugan took in another deep breath. He was hungry and wanted to eat well as he was not sure what the rest of the day would bring. Last night's meal had been dried beef due to the rain, and he had given none to Eògan. The man had whined as expected and made more threats, but Dugan had pretended to ignore him.

"You will pay for this!"

It had been hard to not gag him. Fear, cold, and hunger had worn away at Eògan, and all night he had been spouting nonsense. But periodically, he rambled on about something that was potentially useful.

Dugan had been right about Mackbaythe's ties with the MacCoinniches; however, Laird Mackbaythe was not at all close with his wife's family, the MacLeods. Mackbaythe only had about a hundred men, which could be less if Eògan was exaggerating. Laird Mackbaythe's army was full of untrained clansmen, but supplemented by mercenaries, who were loyal to the Mackbaythe purse. That bit was not exactly new information, but it proved that Eògan's ramblings were at least partially honest.

Dugan pulled the rabbit off the stick and took a bite, savoring the meat.

"What about me?" Eògan yelped, no longer snubbing any food that came his way.

Dugan continued to ignore him, making it clear he was still not inclined to share.

Eògan took a deep breath, licked his lips, and decided to try another tactic as ranting was working to his disadvantage. "So, um, how much longer are we going to stay here?"

Dugan grunted. He had made camp just on the McTiernay side of their bordering lands almost two days ago. Bad weather had rolled in, and he had wanted to be sure enough time had passed for Laird Mackbaythe to learn of Conor's death. He wanted the man to have no doubt as to why his son's body was being returned to him.

"We leave today."

Eògan jerked up with new life and eagerness, believing his captivity would soon end. "My father has lots of money. More than anyone knows. He skims it from both the MacLeods and the MacCoinniches. I know where he hides it. I could get it. You could use it to bribe my father or do and go wherever you want."

"Don't want your coin," Dugan said between bites. "Don't want to bribe your father."

"Then what do you want?" Eògan wailed, desperation mixed with fear in his tone.

"Nothing. You've told me all I wanted to know."

"Then why not untie me and let me go?"

Dugan put down the rabbit, turned to look at Eògan, and smiled. "I need you to deliver a message."

"I can do that," Eògan said, nodding. "Just give me some food, and I'll tell my father whatever you want me to say."

Dugan's smile grew. He had no doubt that Eògan would relay everything said and done over the past few days if given the chance. "It's not that kind of message."

Eògan blinked. "You think to use me as bait? To draw my father away from the protection of his guard and into a trap? It won't work. I won't cooperate."

Dugan shrugged. "Dead men rarely do."

Blood drained from Eògan's face, and he began to shake his head vigorously back and forth in denial. "If . . . if you were going to kill me, you would have done it days ago."

"Dead men smell and attract flies."

Eògan stood still as comprehension dawned on him. His days had been numbered from the moment he had stabbed the man he had thought was Conan McTiernay. "So who did I kill?"

Dugan's blue eyes bored into Eògan's brown ones. "Conor, chief of the McTiernays."

Eògan's legs gave out, and he slumped to the earth, uncaring of the excrement he sat in. "Then I truly am a dead man," he whispered.

"Aye."

Dugan kicked dirt onto the fire, dousing the flames. He then got his plaid, which he had laid in the sun to dry, and shook it out. He had had some protection from the rain under a makeshift shelter he had built, but the plaid had gotten soaked. It was finally dry enough to use under the saddle.

Dugan had just finished tightening the cinch strap when he saw that Eògan had once again gotten to his feet. The man looked and smelled awful. Maybe it had not been such a good idea to force the man to relieve himself where he was tied.

A crazed look overtook Eògan, and Dugan prepped himself for one last rant. "You think by killing me you will have revenge?"

Dugan crossed his arms and tried to look bored. "If I

thought that, then your guts would have already seen the
end of a McTiernay sword. You are to deliver a message."

Eògan cackled, the idea of his imminent death causing him to become unhinged. "Well, my body will be a
message that my father will respond to in kind. For if you
kill me, my father won't give the McTiernay babe Adanel
carries away. He'll slice its head off the moment it's born.
Tell Conan his *son* is going to *die* before he takes his
first breath."

Dugan stood frozen into place. "Adanel's pregnant."

Eògan threw his head back and laughed at the glory
of knowing he had one last bargaining chip. If he had
only realized it two days ago. "Aye. She's pregnant with
Conan's bairn. She's due any day. *That's* the reason my
father wanted him dead. He tried to get Conan to marry
her using the babe as leverage, but the damn McTiernay
refused, stating he would never marry anyone regardless
of the circumstances. Liar. For just a few months later, we
get news that there is going to be a wedding. Conan,
famed McTiernay bachelor, has finally found love. My
father decided to send *him* a message. Granted it was a
different one than he intended, but I wonder, how will
Conan live knowing he is responsible for the death of
not only his brother, but his firstborn son?"

Dugan felt like he had been kicked in the stomach.
Adanel was pregnant? If she was due any day, it was most
likely his. It was possible that he had not been her only
lover, but Dugan remembered the first time they were together, and it had been a very long time since she had
lain with a man. Though hard to believe, Adanel was
almost assuredly carrying *his* child.

"Why do you think it's Conan's?"

"Found him at their meeting spot in the fall."

Dugan's jaw tensed at the memory. He had already

made the connection, but now he knew *why* Conan had been attacked. Last October, Conan had been riding north on Father Lanaghly's behest to help a woman living at a priory—the same priory Dugan had thought to be where Adanel lived. He remembered Conan arriving at Fàire Creachann fuming about two men attacking him. One was a mercenary he had killed and brought back with him, but the other—a tall, skinny redheaded man—had escaped. That man had been Eògan, and he had run home and told all that Conan was the father of Adanel's child.

It made sense. *Murt*, even Adanel probably thought Conan was the father for Dugan had never told her his name. Then again, everyone knew McTiernays had dark brown hair and bright blue eyes. His eyes were blue, but had the hue of a sea storm, and his hair was the color of a sandy beach. He could never be mistaken for one of the McTiernay brothers. So, ensnaring a McTiernay commander was not good enough for Adanel, and she had decided to pursue ways to ensnare one of the brothers.

"You may kill me but I have a message for you to deliver to Conan. Adanel is promised to Daeron MacCoinnich." Dugan's jaw shifted, but Eògan saw it. "That's right. He's the son of Laird MacCoinnich—a man who has no fear of you McTiernays. My father *will* avenge my death by telling Daeron about what Conan did to his bride. His father will join mine, and then *all* you McTiernays will pay. We will take your lands. We will take your lives. And that will include yours."

Dugan twisted and pulled free his sword from its sheath. He then slowly walked up to Eògan. Adanel's pregnancy meant that some of his plans changed but only in the way that tomorrow morning Laird Mackbaythe would get two messages, not one.

Dugan stood in front of Eògan and gave him a smile that was as cold as his gaze. "Conan was not Adanel's lover," he whispered. "She was mine."

That was the last thing Eògan heard before death claimed him.

Chapter Six

Dugan pulled on his reins and looked back at the horse tethered to his saddle. Eògan's dead body was still draped across its back. Dugan had thrown the man's plaid over him to keep the flies away, but the ends had loosened slightly as the body had stiffened in the past few hours.

Dugan slid down and re-secured it around the head and face. Eògan needed to be recognizable. Dugan then tied both horses' reins to a nearby prickly bush next to a small stream.

Pulling out his sword from where it was hooked to his saddle, Dugan attached it to his belt and began making his way to a small cottage isolated at the edge of Mackbaythe lands. Smoke was coming out of the chimney, indicating that someone was home. Dugan hoped it was the same person he had spied over a year ago when he had ventured this way after a particularly ambitious raid of a McTiernay farm.

He had almost called out then, but at the last second changed his mind. Garrett knew where he was and had never sought him out. It was understandable as he was working as a mercenary for the Mackbaythes, and Dugan was a commander for the McTiernays. No one would believe that they had at one time been very close, but since those days, many years ago, they had forged different lives.

Unfortunately, they had not parted on friendly terms when Garrett had left the small group Dugan had led that had formed initially out of survival. Their numbers had not been many, but they had stayed together out of respect for each other's fighting skills as well as a sense of loyalty, for they all had saved each other's lives many times in the course of battle. He and Garrett might have shared harsh words the day Garrett had walked away, but Dugan hoped the respect they had for each other still remained to this day. With Adanel pregnant with his child, he was depending on it.

Garrett was by far the most complex man Dugan had ever met. He was also one of the most cunning, crafty, wily, and unnaturally skillful Lowlanders he had ever seen fight. And there was no one else he trusted more to have his back in battle. Deep down, Dugan knew Cole or any of the other McTiernays would be there for him just as he would for them, but that had never been truly tested in a battle to the death. These past few years, no one had challenged the McTiernay army in such a way that could offer such proof. All McTiernay soldiers were sent off to fight and support King Robert for a few years to ensure they had actual battle experience, but knowing that and actually fighting beside a man were very different things. As such, the things that were said those many years ago mattered not. Dugan knew if a fight were to happen right now, he would defend Garrett until his dying breath and was betting the life of his unborn son that the man would do the same for him.

Garrett had an unusual code of honor. He was a mercenary for whom fighting, blood, and death were as commonplace as taking a bath. He had no qualms about getting paid to kill another man who was stupid enough to raise a sword against him, and yet Garrett could not stand bullies. He'd crush a windpipe of someone carelessly hurting a child—and liars? He *really* could not abide liars. He would give a scar to a man for nothing but a little, seemingly harmless fib, so it was beyond odd that he had taken up with Mackbaythe as one of his mercenaries. The pay was rumored to be uncommonly good; however, Dugan suspected Garrett stayed for personal reasons. Nothing else made sense. Then again, one of the last things Garrett had said to him was that he was far too naive for his own good. That real life did not cater to the fair just because Dugan wished it to.

Dugan had taken the comment as an insult. He had seen the harshness life had to offer, held men as they died, and as for unfairness, its painful claws had dug into him so deep as a young man that it would always affect him in almost everything he did. He had led men, kept them alive, and refused to let the pressures of survival ruin how he treated people. Garrett had disagreed, and when Dugan had been considered for the lairdship that had eventually gone to Cole, Garrett had told him outright that he was not prepared for such responsibility. To stand by him and support his petition would be akin to lying to all the clansmen who needed a leader, not a friend, to protect and guide them. He would have none of it and had been the first to leave their small band.

It had taken years for Dugan to realize that Garrett had been partially right. He had not been ready to lead a clan, but the man had been holding to a grudge with a fierce grip for as long as Dugan knew him. And if Garrett were a mercenary, that had not changed . . . which right now, worked to Dugan's advantage.

Garrett's choice of profession was the key to his plan.

Originally, Dugan had intended to leave Eògan's body
with a provocative message and be long gone before
Laird Mackbaythe was notified about his son, but that
changed with Eògan's revelation about Adanel. Her
being pregnant changed everything. Dugan had to know
if it was his child. If it was, he was going to do everything
in his power to protect it from the Mackbaythes—and
that included his mother. But to do either of those things,
he had to get close enough to speak to her and then be
able to spirit her away. That meant he needed a man on
the inside.

If his Garrett was anything like what Dugan remembered, he would offer his help. If not, then his old friend
would soon learn that Dugan was not only no longer
naive, he was now far deadlier with a sword.

Garrett spotted Dugan long before he had slid off his
horse and started walking toward his home. He had
always liked the man, for it was hard not to. Dugan radiated charm, which he had always applied liberally to any
decent-looking woman welcoming attention. If rumors
were correct, that had not changed. But his respect for
Dugan grew after he had decided to accept the decision
of Cole's lairdship as well as agree to becoming his commander. That took a different kind of courage, and it
was the kind Garrett respected the most. Dugan was also
one of the few men he had come across in his life who
was openly honest and judged people for their actions,
not their appearance.

Like Dugan, Garrett was a Lowlander by birth. He was
neither tall nor short. His girth was that of a muscular
man, but not notable enough to stand out or cause
questions. His brown hair and hazel eyes were also unex-
ceptional, enabling him to blend in with a crowd rather

than stand out. None of these features did he try to change. Instead, Garrett embraced his mundane characteristics and honed them, until they had become a weapon. Men who overlooked him, or worse underestimated him, made a deadly mistake.

Only a few had ever tried to see beyond his seemingly ordinary surface, and even fewer had succeeded. Dugan was the only one who had correctly deciphered his background upon their first meeting.

Garrett acted and spoke like a true Highlander, and almost all who met him assumed he had lived and grown up among Scotland's wild, ferocious mountains. Never did they guess that he was the banished eldest son of a small Lowland clan from the southwestern area of Scotland where the Stewarts and Fergusons ruled with iron fists. Dugan—though he had never revealed how—had seen through his veneer, but had never questioned him about it.

The man had always known when to push and when to let something be. And for the past few years, Dugan had chosen to leave Garrett alone. But with him marching up to his home with a sword at his side and a dead body lying across one of his horses, it looked like that was about to change.

Garrett opened the door and stood at the entrance with crossed arms. He wondered what Dugan thought about him working for Laird Mackbaythe, a man known to be both corrupt and deceitful. Garrett hated liars. He hated being deceived. But everyone knew exactly the kind of man Laird Mackbaythe was, so one expected him to try and cheat and lie. Anyone who did otherwise was a fool.

Garrett hated dishonesty, but he also hated tyrants, and Mackbaythe hired a lot of them to ensure his lands were protected and nothing untoward happened to any goods making their way to and from MacCoinnich lands and the Mackbaythe port. The mercenaries did as they were paid, but they also would have taken advantage of the local clansmen, knowing their laird would never interfere. Garrett had stealthily gotten himself hired and then used his skills to be placed in charge of all the hired soldiers. He lived out by the border so that he could ignore Mackbaythe's insanity, which infested the castle. But that insanity seemed to be encroaching farther and farther away from port. Garrett suspected it would soon be time for him to move on.

"*Seòlta duine.*"

Garrett raised a brow at the old nickname. He had not felt like a clever man for a long time. "McTiernay."

Dugan's jaw twitched, but then he held out his arm. Garrett grabbed it and embraced a man he had thought might never speak to him again. He was glad he was wrong.

"Nice bit of land," Dugan said, looking over his shoulder. The cottage was nestled in a valley, and it was on the direct route to the port. The mountains also protected the area, making it good for grazing cattle and horses as there was a lot of grass. "Never saw you as a farmer."

"You know what I am," Garrett replied.

Dugan arched a single brow. "I could have been wrong, but I did hear that Mackbaythe pays well and that he's paying a lot of men."

Garrett raised his hand to shelter his eyes from the sun. "He's a fool. One cannot buy loyalty. But it can be earned from what I hear," he said, giving a quick glance down to Dugan's plaid.

"Aye. Things happened the way they should have."

That simple statement was enough for Garrett to confirm that Dugan was loyal to the McTiernays and not just Cole's commander because of a lack of options. "I was sorry to hear about Leith."

Dugan took in a deep breath as the memory of his best friend's betrayal hit him. It still hurt, though less each time. "Each man makes his own choices. Leith chose the ones that led to his death."

Garrett placed his fists on his hips, hearing the implication. Dugan was not just talking about Leith, he was talking about him. Whatever made Dugan appear before him today was serious, and he was warning Garrett that he was about to face one of those "life choices." "Tell me why you are here, and *I* will make mine."

"Mackbaythe declared war on the McTiernays earlier this week."

Surprise forced Garrett to remain completely still. If it were another man bringing this news, he might wonder if there was some exaggeration in the statement, but Dugan knew war. And those who lived with war for as long as they had did not use the term lightly.

"Well, that explains a lot. MacCoinnich arrived yesterday, and his army is camped just in the next valley over. They came supposedly to ensure Mackbaythe doesn't delay his daughter's wedding once again to his son Daeron. I'm thinking their presence serves a dual purpose. Mackbaythe wanted protection. So, if you are here to seek his throat, you would die before you even got close. It would take an army and a lot of bloodshed to reach that man."

Dugan's lips curved into a sickly smile. "I don't want to kill him, Garrett. I'm here to return his son." Using his thumb, Dugan pointed over his shoulder to where he left his horses tethered. "I'm thinking you might know of a man who could serve as a McTiernay messenger."

Garrett rubbed his face with his hand, and then shook his head. He had no idea what foolish thing Eògan did to earn death by a McTiernay sword, but that he ended up in such a way was no surprise. The worthless *gealtaire* was always picking battles thinking that being Eòsaph Mackbaythe's son ensured he would win. His baseless arrogance only ensured his having a short life.

Garrett took a couple steps outside and squatted down. Using a stick, he began to draw a map in the dirt. "I suggest Alwyn. He's a farmer and lives over the next ridge. He hates Mackbaythe enough to deliver the body but is smart enough to disappear before orders are given to kill the messenger." He drew an *X*. "Leave the body there after sunset."

Dugan nodded. "That's not the only thing I came for."

Garrett stood back up, brushing the dirt off his hands, and then sighed, realizing that whatever Eògan had done was serious enough to not end with his death. McTiernays were waging war and, like good strategists, they wanted to wage it where it was advantageous to them. "Mackbaythe *will* retaliate, but I doubt there is much you can do to influence when that will happen. He's . . . too busy appeasing the MacCoinniches right now. Eventually he'll avenge Eògan's death, but the man's smart enough to wait. He won't come until he believes he is at his strongest, and the McTiernays are at their weakest."

"He won't wait if I have Adanel."

A puzzled look overcame Garrett's expression. He had never spoken to Mackbaythe's daughter and had only seen her a few times. She was undeniably beautiful, and rumors were that she was kind and completely unlike her father. "I have not seen Lady Adanel in months. She took it very hard when her father locked up her uncle for supposedly failing as her guard. Since then, she has kept to herself in her tower in preparation for her wedding."

Dugan's fingers flexed before tightly gripping the handle of his sword. "There will be no wedding," he declared, his tone allowing no room for misinterpretation, argument, or debate.

Garrett's brows shot up. "You intend to forcibly take Adanel back with you?"

Dugan gave a single sharp nod.

The anger rolling off Dugan was almost palpable. What possibly could Lady Adanel have done? Garrett slowly inhaled and then blew out the breath. Whatever it was, the situation was far more complicated than he had assumed. "And just why do *you* want Adanel?"

Dugan stared at him for a long moment, clearly unused to having to explain himself. He was no longer the young man Garrett had known. The days of him being eager to please and make all those around him feel in accord were gone. He was now a very angry, very determined McTiernay commander. "She's pregnant with my child, but she's claiming it to be Conan McTiernay's."

Garrett's jaw dropped, understanding what that meant. If what Dugan said was true, there was no talking him out of getting her. There would be no compromise, discussion, or delay. Dugan *was* going after the woman. The question in front of Garrett now was that of his involvement.

Garrett rocked back on his heels as he thought about the multiple implications of Dugan's declaration. "If what you are saying is true, then Adanel has not spent all this time in her room out of *choice*. She's being held there by her father . . . which does explain why no one has seen her. The woman rode all the time and then just, well, stopped."

It also explained why the young man who was reportedly very close friends with her had suddenly stopped coming to him for training after he had been reassigned to guard duty. Someone had told them that Adanel allowed only two guards, her childhood friend and some Goliath of which everyone was afraid.

"With Eògan's death *and* Adanel gone, Mackbaythe would definitely follow. But so would MacCoinnich as his son thinks Adanel is going to be marrying him any day. Though I'm not sure how *that* is to work with her being pregnant."

"Supposedly, MacCoinnich is unaware. They were to wed soon after my bairn took his first and last breath."

Garrett's eyes narrowed. "Mackbaythe is a sick bastard, and I have no doubt what you say is true. He's an experienced liar and could easily fabricate some twisted story to ensure MacCoinnich became similarly enraged. And don't underestimate MacCoinnich. That man's army is not just large, but skilled."

"Let MacCoinnich come. It won't be just the McTiernays he's facing." Dugan went on to explain Eògan's attacks last fall on Conan and recently on Conor.

Garrett's stomach rolled. Dugan was right. If Mackbaythe did *not* follow Dugan, the wrath of the McTiernays would soon be upon this small clan. If that happened, Garrett had no intentions of being here when they arrived. Any man who picked up a sword in defense of Mackbaythe was a dead one, and he would never use his sword to protect a man who sent his son to perform such a monstrous, cowardly act. Dugan *had* to successfully abduct Adanel in order to get her father to follow him. Not just to save his child, but to save the lives of all the Mackbaythe clansmen who were innocent of their laird's crimes.

Garrett made his mind up. "I think there might be a way to get Adanel and be off Mackbaythe lands before anyone suspects something is amiss. But there will be conditions."

Dugan held his gaze steady for several seconds before

asking, "And just what, *seòlta duine,* sacrifice must I make to realize this plan?"

Garrett crossed his arms. "It won't be just Adanel coming with you. I'll need the help of Tybalt. He assigns the duties of every mercenary soldier and guard Mackbaythe has. He has no loyalty to the laird, and his life will be in jeopardy if he helps you. He, plus Adanel's two guards—who are loyal to her not her father—as well as I will need safe passage to and while they are in McTiernay lands. Can you guarantee that?"

Without hesitation, Dugan nodded. "None of you will be harmed as long as you do nothing to protect or interfere when we McTiernays dispense our justice."

Garrett wanted more assurances. He wanted guarantees that they would be treated well, but unharmed was the best he was going to get. Dugan was far too angry to ask for more. And if they stayed, they were inviting bloodshed not just for the guards and soldiers who signed up for such duty, but every man and woman around the area. Very few Mackbaythes had any respect for their laird. They would be fighting for principle, which in Garrett's experience was not a good enough reason if pointless in the end.

"You'll need to keep your 'message' away from the flies and birds for one more day. It will take that long for me to put things in place," Garrett stated, squatting back down to draw another map in the dirt. "When all is ready, I'll have what we will need to get you and Adanel away without being seen. Meet me here just after sundown tomorrow."

"What did you tell this McTiernay about me?"

Garrett briefly glanced down at Tybalt, grunted, and

returned his gaze to the darkness. "Only what he needed to know. That you are the scheduler."

Tybalt snorted but said nothing else. It was rare he was self-conscious about his height, but those who did not know him always judged him incapable immediately upon seeing him. Garrett's plan did not include enough time to convince a Highlander that he was far more than he appeared.

"You should have told me about Lady Adanel," Garrett hissed.

"Why? What could you have done?"

Garrett shrugged, but he would have figured out something. It rankled that no one who knew of Adanel's imprisonment had thought to tell him. But being kept in the dark of such things came with being a mercenary. Being loyal to nothing but coin meant no one was loyal to you. And for the first time in a long time, Garrett was not comfortable with the life he was living.

"Does Lady Adanel understand the plan?"

Tybalt puckered his lips before answering. "She knows that the plan to escape from her imprisonment is to happen tonight."

Garrett bit back an expletive. There was no telling how the woman was going to react upon seeing Dugan. They needed her awake, not passed out in a fit, and they certainly did not need her screaming. His thoughts were interrupted when Tybalt lightly elbowed him to get his attention.

"That him?"

Garrett nodded.

Tybalt watched the dark figure of a Highlander emerge from the shadows. Damn Highlanders. Tybalt doubted the top of his head reached this McTiernay's shoulders. At least the man was wearing a Mackbaythe plaid and looked the part he was supposed to play.

Tybalt was one of the few who knew by sight every single Mackbaythe guard and mercenary. For everyone else who saw the McTiernay walking toward them, he would be just someone new to be ignored and instantly forgotten. Then again, with each step Dugan McTiernay took, Tybalt was less sure about the man's ability to remain incognito.

Appearance alone made it clear that he was a large, deadly Highlander, but his walk made him stand out. With the exception of maybe Garrett, no one around here carried himself with a commanding air of self-confidence born not from deference, but from knowledge of their own abilities and power. Such men could be terrifying or inspiring, and Tybalt had just put not only his life, but those of Lady Adanel and her guards into the hands of such a man.

"This your scheduler?" Dugan asked as he approached.

Immediately, Tybalt felt the Highlander's gaze slide down and up his small frame. He hated being reminded of how short he was with such sweeping looks. Even most Highland women were taller than him.

Dugan stopped a few feet away. He was close enough for the three of them to have a private conversation, but not so close that Tybalt felt physically smothered. As a result, Tybalt found himself both surprised and cautiously encouraged. Most soldiers tended to stand where he had to not just angle his head, but tilt it way back to look them in the eye.

"I'm Tybalt."

Dugan used his chin to point at the sword hanging at Tybalt's side. "You just wear that or do you know how to use it?"

Tybalt blinked. At thirty-two years of age, that was the first time anyone had ever asked, even indirectly, if he had earned the right to be called a soldier. His smaller size made it impossible to have the physical strength of most Highland warriors, so most just assumed the sword to be merely symbol and nothing more. "I earned mine the same way you earned yours," Tybalt replied.

If Dugan doubted the assertion, it did not show. His deep-set blue eyes did not once waver as Tybalt returned the steady gaze with one of his own.

No true soldier lived to be as old as he was without being able to live up to his station. Tybalt had scars that proved he had earned his right to be called a warrior, and Dugan was the first in a long time to recognize the possibility without first seeing them or making him prove he could do more than most with a blade. Soldiers always underestimated him, his skills, and his speed.

Dugan looked at Garrett. "Alwyn will see my 'message' next time he visits his barn in the morning. All in place here?"

Garrett nodded and then threw Dugan a large cape before gesturing to a small, inconsequential building wedged in between two larger ones. "We enter and leave there."

"That's where the escape tunnel leads?" Dugan asked, taking a look at how close it was to the Village Tower where Adanel was being held.

"Aye," Tybalt stated. "None of the escape tunnels are very long. This one only extends about a hundred feet, exiting into one of the busiest areas of the village. Fortunately, they are regularly used and so seeing guards enter and exit will not raise suspicions. As long as her ladyship immediately blends in with those around her, no one will think twice about it, let alone assume it is her."

Garrett pointed to the hooded cape Dugan was holding. "Make sure her hair is completely covered, otherwise someone *will* notice, especially as she has not been seen in some time."

Dugan nodded and then pointed to the tower. Two figures could be seen standing as guards up on top. "What about them?"

Tybalt snorted. "I assigned two of Mackbaythe's laziest men to guard the tower tonight with the promise they will have the next two nights off. By now, they are either drunk or close to it, and almost assuredly unaware and uncaring of what is going on around them," he added with a sly smile. "There are going to be several guards roaming the streets tonight, but they are off duty, and therefore their focus will be solely on what interests them. The only ones you have to worry about are *his* men," he said, pointing to Garrett.

Garrett looked unconcerned. "I've assigned my men to oversee the valley and ensure no MacCoinnich soldier ventures to where he shouldn't."

Dugan raised a brow. "Will your men ride with Mackbaythe?"

Garrett pursed his lips together and then gave a shrug. "Most of the mercenaries Mackbaythe hires can be deadly. They are not inclined to drink and aware of their surroundings at all times, which is why they are alive and I use them. But their numbers are not as many as Mackbaythe claims, and they have allegiance only to themselves. My guess is about a third will decide it is time to move on when they discover Mackbaythe is marching to war. Half of those that remain have been itching for a fight, so it will take little to persuade them to join Mackbaythe's cause. That will leave about another dozen, who will join simply because they will demand lots of coin and get it. Where Mackbaythe gets his money I know not, but he does seem to have a great deal of it."

"The port that profitable?" Dugan asked incredulously. Cole was successful, but it was costly to run a castle and maintain an army. But a mercenary army, even a small one, was significantly more expensive.

Garrett threw a hand up in the air, his expression one of mutual puzzlement. "He ships almost all goods MacCoinnich sells, and he has some lucrative deal he made years ago with the MacLeods."

Tybalt grunted. "Mackbaythe's corrupt. He steals from both MacLeod and MacCoinnich. They know it, and they even expect it, but he'd have been dead long ago if they knew how much."

"Do you?" Dugan asked.

Tybalt shook his head. "I've just run the figures. I know every man and woman in these parts. The port is busy, but not large enough to generate the coin Mackbaythe disperses. He has no steward, and separation of duties between the port- and dockmaster ensures that no one person knows enough of anything to threaten him with exposure."

Dugan's eyes went to Garrett, who just gave him a look that said that there was more than one reason he had wanted Tybalt to join them.

"What about the guards at the tunnel and tower exits?"

"They are clear now," Tybalt answered, "and Garrett will make sure that no one enters while you fetch her ladyship. Brùid and I will take care of any guards who opted not to go out on their free night."

Built for both habitation and defense, the towers were where some of Mackbaythe's most prized men—either for their bloodlust or their ability—were allowed to sleep. Tybalt assigned the maniacal ones to the main castle and the most deadly to the Fortress overseeing the ships entering and leaving the harbor. The ones he trusted, as well as himself, he assigned to the Village Tower where Lady Adanel was kept, on the top floor. He also stored the majority of the weapons there.

This made the effort of getting Adanel out both easier and more complex. Fewer men, but they would be harder to contain. Hopefully, most had already taken advantage of their unexpected time off and were out of the tower seeking carnal pleasure. With Brùid and his giant size and strength, Tybalt did not foresee any lingering guards as being a serious problem. "Nigel is with Lady Adanel, waiting for you. He will help convince her to come with you."

Dugan ran his tongue along his teeth. "She has no choice."

Tybalt's bushy brows shot up in alarm. "Garrett promised her ladyship would be safe with you."

Anger flickered in Dugan's eyes. "She carries *my* child. You can be assured that she is in no physical danger from me and that I will ensure she is protected."

"Even after the babe is born?" Tybalt questioned. He did not know Lady Adanel well, but he had made promises and did not like the cold look in Dugan's eyes.

"As long as she does nothing to impede the McTiernays' revenge on her father or cause harm to the child, she has no reason to fear me or any other McTiernay."

Tybalt swallowed. Her ladyship was carrying a *McTiernay* babe? No wonder the laird had kept postponing such an advantageous wedding.

Tybalt nodded and was about to turn and head down the street when Dugan's hand reached out and gestured for him to wait. "Now I have a question. Just why are you so eager to help a McTiernay you don't know and betray your own?"

It was a fair question, and Tybalt was a little surprised Dugan had not asked it right away. Then again, if he had, he would have had nothing but intuition to judge the answer. It took surprisingly little conversation to gauge the measure of a man, and Tybalt knew that the words he was about to speak would seal his fate.

"Three reasons. Several months ago, Brùid, one of Lady Adanel's guards, came up to me and asked if I could help her disappear. I thought the request both strange and unwise at the time for anyone who knows Laird Mackbaythe knows what that means if caught. I naturally refused to help with what was in my mind Brùid and Lady Adanel's execution. Brùid then asked if I could somehow assign Nigel as her ladyship's second guard, ensuring that either he or Nigel was always with her. I agreed for I always liked her ladyship and knew that she and Nigel were close. Brùid last made me promise that if I ever learned of a way that Lady Adanel could safely escape, I would do everything in my power to make that happen. I said I would knowing that what was being asked was impossible. Even if I could think of a way to sneak her out, there was nowhere for her to go. Then last night Garrett approached me with a plan that involved a McTiernay soldier who could ensure she would be safe and protected. *You* are allowing me to fulfill that promise."

Dugan looked unmoved, "And the other two reasons?"

Tybalt pursed his lips, hesitating before saying his thoughts out loud. "Eògan. If I help you, not only are the lives of Lady Adanel, myself, and her two guards saved, but those of all the men, women, and families around you." Tybalt narrowed his eyes and Tybalt's voice dropped. "My helping you will ensure the fight is not *here*, but on *your* land, risking McTiernay people. And last, if you succeed, for the first time in two generations, the Mackbaythes will be free of tyranny and have a chance to regain their pride."

Chapter Seven

Adanel paced in her room, praying Nigel would return soon. He had gone to get the midwife, but that was hours ago.

A new ship had come into the port, and since Nigel said she was escaping tonight, it had to be the *Destiny's Fortune.* Thank God, because she was out of time. The MacCoinniches had arrived two days ago, and soon they would demand to see her. Whether she was pregnant or not, her father would be forced to oblige. She had only been able to delay doing so this evening by claiming that she felt a growing aching in her lower back—the first sign she was going into labor. But she could only be in labor for so long before she produced either a child or was claimed by death. By tomorrow morning, her father needed to believe that she was the latter.

The midwife was bringing the berries from one of the more dangerous nightshade plants. Most shied away from it as it was unpredictable and potentially a deadly poison. However, taken in the right amount, the fruit was also used as a sedative for major injuries and surgery. When used, it made one appear dead. The midwife Nigel secured was supposedly knowledgeable in its use, having used it once on her son when stitching him after his being forced to participate in one of her father's torture-filled entertainment nights. He was not a large man and had no training, and therefore he had not been able to adequately defend himself. If his mother had not a talent for healing herbs and medicines, he would have perished. Tybalt had stationed the man safely away from the castle, and in return, his mother was to serve as midwife. When the time was right, she would proclaim Adanel dead from labor complications.

At the sound of the door opening, Adanel spun her head around. "Nigel, thank God! Did you . . ." She froze midsentence. A man she had never thought to see again was standing right in front of her. "Conan," she whispered in shock.

Her McTiernay soldier was standing before her. She could recall every detail of his face and body vividly. Nightly dreams of him saving her had turned into nightmares. In some, he just denounced their love, in others, she ranted and railed at him for not listening to his heart, but more frequently, she was forced to watch him marry his new wife and profess his love to her. Regardless of the dream, her McTiernay soldier was there looking exactly as he had the day he left her. The man standing before her did not.

His hair was the same sandy brown, his chest was still broad and muscular, and he still held himself in that semi-arrogant way that hinted of his inexorable self-confidence, but at the same time commanded respect and obedience. It was smaller things, such as his facial features, that time had altered. The lines around his eyes and mouth were etched a little deeper. The angles on his cheeks look sharper, and there was at least two days of stubble on his chin. But it was his once warm blue eyes that had changed the most. No longer inviting, they looked like dark, angry thunderclouds—dangerous, cold, and able to deal deadly violence to victims in its path.

"Sorry to disappoint you, *my lady*, but I never have been Conan. Your plan to ensnare one of the famous McTiernay brothers failed."

Adanel blinked. The hostility in his tone matched the arctic coldness of his gaze. "But my father said that . . ."

"Your beloved father did try to kill Conan, *twice*. Once last fall and once on his wedding night. You'll be disappointed to learn he failed both times."

Adanel sank onto the bed, barely registering what he had just said. All she could think was that her McTiernay soldier had survived her father's campaign to see him dead. "You're alive," she whispered. "You're alive, and you're here."

Tears started to form and race down her cheeks. "I had given up hope that you would come. When my father said that Eògan had killed you . . ."

"Eògan did not kill me, nor Conan. He stabbed Conor, *chief* of the McTiernays."

Adanel stared wide-eyed at him as the weight and full meaning of what he was telling her sank in. "*Mo chreach-sa a thàinig!*" she barely choked, grabbing her neck. Eògan had killed the McTiernay *chief*? Large clans like the McTiernays had several chieftains. She knew that Cole was the chieftain of the McTiernays of Torridon and heard there were two others. But Conor was the McTiernay chief and in charge of their entire clan. There would have been retribution for killing Conan, his younger brother, but if Eògan had killed the McTiernay chief, the Mackbaythe clan was about to be erased from existence.

"Go ahead and pray to God, but it will change nothing."

"If you are not Conan, then who are you? And are

you here to kill me?" she asked softly, looking up into his glittering eyes.

"I'm Dugan, and I am who I always was, nothing more than one of the McTiernay commanders of Torridon. And nay, you will not die until after my child is born," he stated, using his chin to point to her stomach. "It is mine, isn't it?"

Adanel's hand flew to her middle. She swallowed and said defensively, "I've only lain with you."

Dugan scoffed. "Then rise. We are leaving. Now." He turned to reopen the door.

"Dugan," she said softly, remaining seated. "Why did you not come for me earlier? Why now?"

He spun around and took a menacing step forward. "I may have acted the fool last summer, but I am not so dull as you might think. What happened last fall when you discovered you were pregnant with my bairn? Were you ever going to tell me or was that your plan all along? Entice a McTiernay into your bed and then capture a McTiernay brother by claiming *my bairn* was his? Did you think Conan so obtuse he would forget the women with whom he slept?"

Adanel jumped to her feet, the shock at seeing Dugan having been replaced by a seething anger of her own. "*I* did no such thing! And if anyone has been the fool, it has been me. For I have been *here*, locked in this tower, waiting for you to rescue me! My father is the one who told me your name was Conan and that he found you lurking around our loch. So of *course*, I assumed he was talking of you. And it was *my father* who tried to create an alliance through marriage. How could you for a moment think that *I* had anything to do with his plans?" Adanel demanded. "You know me. You *know* the animosity I feel toward my father. I despise everything about him."

"Which I guess made me quite convenient. Or are you

going to deny that you saw me not as a man, but as a means of escape?"

Adanel stood with her mouth agape, unable to deny the accusation. For a short while, she *had* thought of him as a tool to be used . . . but only for a brief period. She had fallen in love with Dugan and had thought those feelings had been reciprocated.

"And now I have recently learned that you have finally seduced yet *another* to the altar," Dugan sneered. "Daeron MacCoinnich is more boy than man and you can have him, *after* you deliver my son."

Mortified that Dugan thought so little of her, Adanel lifted her chin and moved to press a finger into his chest. "*You* are taking *nothing* away from me. And I was never going to marry Daeron. I had plans tonight to escape, and I will be doing just that *without your help*."

"Uh, Adanel?" came a hesitant voice at the door.

"What, Nigel?!" she snapped.

"Um, this very large, very angry McTiernay *is* the means of your escape, and while getting all of us out of here without anyone noticing may sound easy to you, I can assure you it is not. And it won't even be hard very soon. It will be impossible if you both don't stop arguing so we can leave." Nigel looked at Dugan. "The way is secure for now. All the guards that had not left the tower have been tied up. Brùid is gagging them now to keep them from calling for help when they awake."

Adanel took a step back, shaking her head. "Nigel, I'm not going anywhere with him. Did you hear what this . . . this *man* accused me of?"

"My name is *Dugan*."

"I no longer care what it is!" She looked back at Nigel. "He thinks that I—"

"Does it really matter what he thinks?" Nigel asked,

his hands on his hips. He bobbed his head toward the hallway. "The man is offering you *a way to escape*."

Adanel waved a finger. "But the midwife . . . the nightshade berries . . . "

"That plan is far more dangerous than a McTiernay protecting your hide and giving us a safe place to go when the hell your brother stirred up comes this way. Plus, you leaving encourages your father to do so as well."

Adanel's jaw dropped. "I'm being used as *bait*?"

Nigel nodded. "Would you rather be used by your father as *leverage*?"

"Nay, but this . . . this *man*"—she waved her hand at Dugan, refusing to say his name—"hates me!"

"And by the look on your face, you hate him too. This makes you two even. And yet he is still offering you a means to both escape *and* live. You can fight about the rest later. *We need to go*."

Dugan crossed his arms and grunted. "*You* hate *me*?" he snorted rhetorically. "I'm not the one who lied and tried to make you believe I was something I'm not."

"I did *not* lie to you. I did *not* give you a fake name, and I *never* said to which clan I belonged. In fact, everything I ever said about myself was true. It was *you* who constantly leapt to conclusions and assumed they were true."

"Twist this however you want, but it does not change the truth. You are the one who used *me*. Whether for your father or for yourself, I was nothing but a means to an end. Your mistake was that I found out in time."

"The only mistake I made was thinking that I loved you!"

"I highly doubt you know the concept of either love *or* honesty!"

Adanel threw her hands up in the air. "Well, then how about this for honesty? You did not want to know the truth, *Dugan*. You were afraid of what was happening between us and ran away instead of confronting me like a real man would do. You wanted an excuse, and now you feel morally superior because you think you actually found one. I know that because even now, with all the horrible things my father and brother just did to your clan, you refuse to acknowledge that I might have had a good reason for not just keeping my identity a secret but needing a means of escape!" She shoved his chest in frustration. When Dugan did not move, her frustration grew to the point she was shaking. "I should be the one angry and guess what? *I am!*"

The sound of furniture scraping caused both their heads to turn toward Nigel. He casually gave them a wave to continue as he sat down and stretched out his legs in front of him. "Don't mind me. The plan was to leave before anyone noticed or heard us." Nigel tapped the sword on his hip. "Lucky for both of you, I'm pretty good with this thing. So, keep arguing. It's no problem."

The door opened once more, and the second of Adanel's two guards entered. Nearing seven feet in height, Brùid towered over most men, including Dugan. Massive and menacing, his shaven head and piercing green eyes made him look even more so. His extra-large, extra-long kilt stretched over his muscular thighs, barely covering what Adanel never wanted to see. If it matched the rest of him, she was not sure a woman had been made for such a man. But if there was one, she would be the luckiest in the world, for Adanel had seen Brùid move. Smooth and graceful, his every movement was under complete control. If Brùid brought those skills into the bedroom, the right woman would live in bliss.

Ignoring Adanel, Brùid looked at Dugan. "Tower's clear." Then to Nigel, he asked, "What's going on? You were supposed to get them and bring them back down."

Nigel shrugged his shoulders and linked his fingers

behind his head. "Tried, but they'd rather argue. I'm willing to go, big boy. It's these two who are not interested."

Brùid rolled his eyes. "You are useless."

Nigel gave him a large, toothy grin. "And you really are a big boy," he said with a wink, knowing how much the pet name irritated his large friend.

Brùid could probably break his bones with just his pinky, but Nigel had never been scared of the man. Brùid looked every bit like the fiercest of soldiers, and his enormous size had forced him to be in complete control of his every step and move. Everyone assumed he was what he appeared—a very deadly, competent soldier. Truth was the man had never learned how to wield any weapon, let alone a sword. He had trapped his prey when he lived on his own, but when it came to battle, size did not equal experience.

"I could squash you like a bug," Brùid mumbled. "Probably should. Adanel wouldn't even notice."

"Ah, but my sister would," Nigel countered, and stood up. "Kara loves me. So does Adanel. That makes me exempt from all threats of dismemberment and death." Nigel cocked his head and said, "Well, maybe not threats. Besides, deep down, you know you would miss me. Admit it, big boy, you and I are family. Why, we are practically best friends."

Brùid visibly shuddered. He actually did want to kill Nigel most of the time. The overly cheerful man drove him insane, teasing him with childish names, torturing him with his endless prattle, and persecuting him with his insistence that they were the best of friends. The man was delusional. If it was not for Adanel, Brùid would have forced Tybalt to reassign Nigel as far away from him as possible.

Unfortunately, Adanel did love him. And as Kara's younger brother, Nigel was the means for the two friends to communicate. And then there was the niggling point that Nigel had kept secret that Brùid knew nothing about fighting. Instead, Nigel had been helping as best he could to train him when there was no one around. So maybe Nigel was not completely useless. But he *was* completely annoying.

Nigel took a step closer and used his shoulder to nudge Brùid. "Admit it, big boy, you love me and are thrilled that I am coming with you to keep these two in line."

Adanel yelped in delight hearing that news. "You both are coming with me?" The plan had been for her to board the *Destiny's Fortune* and stay hidden until the ship had reached its next port. Kara's husband, Fearan, knew the captain well and planned to convince him to offer her safe passage to a place south, far away from the possibility of her father learning of her deceit. If Brùid or Nigel had left with her, her death would have been questioned, for all knew neither man would have willingly left her side. That knowledge was one of the keys to their plan's success. The only problem was that *Destiny's Fortune* was overdue for an appearance.

Brùid raised a single brow. "I am your guard, my lady. I promised to stay by your side the night we met, and I will remain true to that promise until I die."

Adanel flew across the room and hugged Brùid with all her might. The night her father had told her she was to marry Daeron, her brother Eògan had decided there should be entertainment that befitted such an announcement. He had dragged in Brùid and asked the crowd to wager how many men it would take to kill the beast. Adanel had never seen Brùid before, but she had heard tales of a man who lived in the hills and was larger than any other who had ever lived. Eògan must have captured him and waited until such an opportunity to reveal his find.

Without thought, Adanel had run and stood in front

of Brùid, declaring that to kill him, they would first need to kill her.

Brùid curled his large arms around her and gave her a gentle squeeze at the memory. He would have perished that night and might have gone willingly. All his life he had been feared. Even his own family had cast him out at an early age, stating he always consumed more than his share and cost more than the help his strength provided. Some thought being a guard to a woman locked in a tower boring, lonely, and borderline torture. But Brùid knew differently. Torture was having your family turn their back on you. Adanel had been the first to stand up in his defense, and in that moment Brùid had vowed to keep her safe until his death.

After jumping in to stop the attack, Adanel had been forcibly removed from his side and tied to her chair to keep from interfering again. The attack had been halted a second time by Laird MacCoinnich, who mumbled something Brùid had not been able to hear. But moments later, to the surprise of all, Laird Mackbaythe announced that he was to be Adanel's new guard. Later that night, Brùid had learned he was replacing her uncle Faden, who had been dragged to the dungeons for failing in his duty.

Nigel twisted his head to glance back at Dugan, who was now glaring at Brùid and his embrace of Adanel. "Don't worry, *chomanndair*, her affections for him are the same brotherly ones that she has for me."

Adanel let go and went to hug Nigel. "I can't believe you both are coming."

"Of course, we are. Kara would kill me if I was not around to make sure big boy here did his job right. I'm the trained soldier, remember? I'm the deadly one. He's just . . . big." Nigel grinned at Brùid, who snarled at him.

"None of us are going anywhere if you don't stop fondling every man you see," Dugan spat out.

Adanel's spine stiffened, and she stepped back from Nigel. "Not every man. Nothing could make me come near you ever again," she hissed.

"Thank God for that. Here." Dugan threw her the hooded cape. "Put that on and make sure you hide your hair."

Adanel looked at it and recognized it to be Kara's. She looked at Nigel. "Does she know? I cannot just leave without saying good-bye."

All playfulness gone, Nigel said firmly, "Not only can you do just that, you *will*. Fearan will protect Kara from your father, but he can't do that if you two are found together."

"But what about you? She will never see you again."

"How did I ever think you were intelligent?" Dugan scoffed, rolling his eyes. "Right now, I have half a mind to tell you to stay and die, but that is *my* child you are carrying. So even if I have to throw you over my shoulder, you are coming. And there will be no stops along the way to say your good-byes and catch up with friends."

Adanel narrowed her eyes and wrinkled her nose at his sarcasm. "I was not—"

"What in *an ifrinn* is taking you so long? At this rate, we will still be here at sunrise!" All turned to see an impatient and unhappy Tybalt standing at the door.

"Tybalt?" Adanel said, stunned to see him. "You are going as well?"

"Not unless, my lady, you put that cape on and follow me. If you have something to say, do it later. We should have been gone by now."

Adanel nodded and tossed the cloak around her shoulders. Stuffing her hair back under the hood, she looked at Brùid. "Is Faden joining us downstairs?"

Brùid looked back at her, his green eyes telling her what he would not say.

She looked at Tybalt and then Nigel. "You know I am not leaving him locked in the Fortress." She turned to Dugan. "He's my uncle, the one who made it so that I could see you. He protected me from my father for years, and if I am gone, there is no telling what my father might do to him. He's alive because he's a MacLeod, but my father knows what he means to me. The first thing he will do upon discovering my disappearance is kill him. I cannot let that happen. I would rather marry Dacron MacCoinnich than be the reason why something ever happened to Faden."

Fear filled Adanel's eyes, and Dugan knew that she was not just being obstinate. She was in earnest. Adanel loved this uncle of hers and would not cooperate if it meant his death. He looked at Tybalt. "Can you get him without being caught?"

Tybalt took a deep breath and exhaled. For the first time in his life, he was being asked to do something like any other soldier. Garrett had come to him because he was smart and had no affection for the laird, but mostly because he was the one who gave out guard duty assignments. Dugan was not just asking, but trusting *him* to do something any other man would have asked Brùid, Nigel, or Garrett to handle. But Dugan recognized none of those men could do what he could.

Tybalt knew every soldier, and every soldier knew him. He also made them feel uncomfortable. It was not just his height, but that he had beaten most of them at one time or another during training. Initially, the soldiers had allowed him to train with them, thinking he would be a bit of sport to play with, and were surprised when it was they who landed on the ground with a metal tip to their chest. Smart and capable, Tybalt had quickly created the position as scheduler. It had kept him from having to serve with or under any of them, which none would have tolerated, as well as relieved them of a much hated chore. It was this hate for him and what he represented that would enable him to get in the Fortress Tower.

Once word spread that Tybalt was inside the Fortress, the men would become scarce. Most would leave rather than be alone with him. This would allow Tybalt to visit Faden, free him, and then exit through the escape tunnel with no one knowing. But even if they did come across someone, the two of them had the skills needed to ensure no tongues could tell any stories about what they had seen.

Tybalt finally nodded. "Aye, I can get him, but don't wait for us. We will catch up to you."

Tybalt turned and headed down the stairway. Nigel and Brùid followed to ensure the way was still clear. Dugan then looked at Adanel and pointed at the door.

Adanel was about to leave when she threw up her hands. "My bag!" She spun around, dropped to her knees, and started searching under her bed with the same agility she had shown last summer. "Got it!" she chirped, sliding the unwieldy bag out into the open. Then with one hand holding her stomach as she got up, Adanel stated, "*Now* we can leave."

Dugan furrowed his brows at the dusty, lumpy object. "We are not taking that."

Adanel reached down and picked up the hefty satchel. "Aye, we are. I packed this the day after my father locked me in this room, thinking that at any moment you would come and rescue me. Well, you are eight months late so the least you can do is let me take some of my things."

"You shouldn't be carrying anything so close to your time."

Adanel waggled her eyebrows and then threw the bag at him with much more force than he thought a woman could muster who was so near the end of her term. "You're right. You carry it, but it *is* coming with me."

Adanel then re-tucked her hair under the hood of the cloak, ensured no stray pieces were visible, and brushed passed him into the hall.

Dugan watched Adanel descend down the staircase. She was a deceiver, a manipulator, and a sorceress with the power to make a man's head spin just with a look. Unfortunately, she was also every bit what he had named her so many months ago—*aithinne.*

His very own firebrand.

"Well, somebody needs to do something," Nigel said, staring directly at Faden.

Faden waved a hand and leaned back against his saddle. "Look at someone else. I'm staying out of it."

After traveling nonstop through last night and for most of the day, they had finally stopped for more than just a short water break. By now it was clear no one was following them. While their small group's speed had been steady, it had not been nearly fast enough to avoid any men ordered to chase them down. Dugan had suspected there would be none, and Faden was slightly surprised that the McTiernay commander had been right.

Either Mackbaythe realized that a small attack posed a risk to Adanel or, probably more likely, he knew it would have only delayed, if not prevented, him from getting what he really wanted—the McTiernays. The slaughter of a few betrayers and a single McTiernay commander was not adequate retribution for Eògan's death and the abduction of his daughter. Mackbaythe would want to see all McTiernays suffer and seek every possible means to make that happen, including persuading Laird MacCoinnich to go to war. After all, it was a McTiernay who had stolen his son Daeron's bride.

Nigel rolled his eyes before turning them to the small group. Brùid ignored him and continued cooking his third rabbit. Garrett and Tybalt just stared back. "Not me," Garrett finally said.

"Come on! It's clear to anyone with eyes and ears that they still like each other," Nigel argued.

Tybalt snorted. "I don't know where you get that notion. I have not heard either of them speak a single word to the other. If that is how a woman and man in love look, then I'm glad I'm single and I pray I never get close to an altar."

"If a woman was that passionate, even in anger, about you, you would drag her to the nearest priest as fast as you could. Any of us would."

Garrett waved a bone in the direction of Dugan. "My friend over there is seriously angry. He feels used, and that is something *no* man ever likes to feel. Dugan is not likely to calm anytime soon and talking to him before then is pointless."

"Lady Adanel is just as angry as your friend," Brùid said in her defense. "And she feels just as betrayed."

"Maybe, but their issues are not ones a few eloquent words can resolve."

Faden bobbed his head in agreement. "Those two are going to have to work it out on their own. Like I said before, I'm staying out of it."

Nigel was not satisfied. "I've known Adanel all my life, and she is incredibly *stubborn*. But she can be reasoned with, and Dugan, when not talking about Adanel, seems to be fairly rational. I'm not saying we should be doing the talking. I'm saying we need to help them confront each other." He kicked Brùid in the leg to get his attention. "*There is a lot that needs to be said*," he stated pointedly. "You know it. And you also know you would have never agreed to taking her out of there if you did not think Dugan was good for her."

Brùid gave a small shake to his head. "Anything was better than where she was. And I'm not speaking for Lady Adanel, *and neither should you*," he said, shoving Nigel's leg away.

Undeterred, Nigel then looked to Faden. "Brùid didn't see her last summer. You did. She practically bubbled with joy. Adanel has never been that happy, even after she had met Daniel. This *chomanndair*"—he paused and tilted his head in Dugan's direction—"made her come alive. Kara and I were so relieved. She was wasting away with nothing to live for."

"Better not let Dugan hear you call him *commander* that way," Garrett cautioned. "Could be the last thing you say."

Nigel rolled his eyes. "That's not my point."

Tybalt stood up and said, "Do you have one? Because for someone who talks nonstop, you never really say anything."

"Tell me about it," Brùid muttered.

"*My point is* that the same thing is going to happen again if one of us doesn't do something. Adanel needs to believe she can be happy again."

Faden shifted to a more comfortable position and closed his eyes. "Hate to agree, but Nigel's right about Adanel."

"See! Even Faden believes she loves Dugan."

Faden popped open one eye. "I never said that. But Adanel's running on anger right now. Once that goes and she realizes what's happened, she is going to retreat back into her shell."

"That's because she doesn't think she has anything to live for. But she does. She has Dugan, and he has her. They just need someone to do *something* to remind them."

Brùid pulled the rabbit off the stick and popped a piece of meat into his mouth. "But he acts as though he hates her," he mumbled between chews.

"That just means Nigel's right," Garrett said. "If she hadn't crawled under his skin, he would not care. The man has had plenty of experience with dismissing women who have liked him. Him caring for one? That's new territory, which is probably why he ran away instead of confronting her about what she did."

Nigel sighed. "I think they would be good for each other."

"I agree," Garrett mumbled.

Tybalt snapped his blanket in the air and let it settle down on the ground. "Why's that?"

Garrett tilted his head and stared at the star-filled sky. The weather had held out this long. They just needed it to last a little while longer. "I don't know. Just watching them fight in the tower made me remember my parents. They loved each other, but they'd argue like that, with lots of emotion. I hope to find that someday."

"Someone to argue with?" Tybalt asked as he lay down.

"Nay. Someone passionate who is willing to challenge me and love me at the same time."

Silence was the reply, but Nigel knew not one man in their small group disagreed.

Somebody really should do something, he thought. Unfortunately, he had no clue what that something should be.

* * *

"Hey, *chomanndair*, want us to ride on ahead and make sure there's nothing unexpected?"

Dugan looked up to answer Nigel and tell him to stop calling him *commander*. While most of his men called him by his rank, Nigel was not someone under his leadership, so it came off somewhat sarcastic. But before he could say anything, he saw everyone but Adanel was on their horse waiting on him to ride out.

With a sigh, he gave a nod and waved them on. He then went to get Adanel's horse only to learn that somebody had already prepped it for her. He had not expected the group to be so eager to get to their destination. Less than an hour ago, he had been the one ordering everyone to get up and be ready to leave at first light.

Donald had given him a week to return, but with all the delays, he would not be back until two days after his expected arrival. The McTiernay brothers would send riders north and find them on their way, but Dugan wanted to be as close to McTiernay lands as possible when that happened. The unrest caused by his absence had to be growing daily. The sooner he could focus the collective anger and give both the McTiernay brothers and their allies assurances that Conor's death would be avenged, the better.

Dugan had waited as long as possible before waking Adanel. She had not said a word. She had barely acknowledged him. She had just slowly gotten up to wash her face and relieve herself. He had felt guilty about rousing her so soon after pushing the group so hard and wished he could have given her more time to sit and eat before making her get back on the saddle. After seeing Ellenor and Brighid go through multiple pregnancies, he knew that women, especially near the end, needed a tremendous amount of sleep. And when they were not asleep, discomfort was a constant companion. Adanel, however, had endured beyond what he expected possible yesterday. Dugan doubted Ellenor or Brighid would have been able to ride silently without so much as a whimper.

They had ridden for nearly eighteen hours before he put in enough time and distance to feel somewhat safe. He had not expected Mackbaythe to send any men after them. It would have taken a dozen of his most skilled mercenaries to have had a chance fighting against him, Garrett, Faden, and Tybalt. Nigel and Brùid, on the other hand, would have fought and died. He had seen both men go against a couple unarmed soldiers in the tower and, until they received significant training, they would not be a match against even a novice McTiernay. And yet, they had potential. Brùid did not lumber, despite his size. His movements were controlled and deliberate, just untrained. Nigel was a victim of Mackbaythe's choice to hire mercenaries instead of investing into a good commander. And yet, Dugan felt that Adanel had been fortunate to have them as her guards.

He doubted anyone else would have been as protective of her. At least they were willing to die for her if necessary, and both had made it clear they were unhappy with him for pushing Adanel for as long and as hard as he had.

Dugan had not liked it any better than they had, but he was glad for every mile Adanel had persevered. He had not said a word to her, nor she to him, but he had been watching her carefully. When he realized that her fatigue had finally taken over, he had ordered Faden to carry her until they reached a protected area Dugan knew their small group could defend.

Once they stopped to make camp, Adanel had offered no complaint about the long ride. She had only stretched her back and limbs. Not once had she shown signs of her stomach bothering her or any cramping. The only pain she displayed was in how she walked, making it clear it had been some time since she had been in a saddle. If Adanel had been facing away from him, he would have never even known she was with child.

In the past month, Dugan had been around what felt like hundreds of pregnant women. Normally, women who were expecting never traveled. Husbands feared for their wives and the wives feared for their unborn children. But Conan's wedding was something no one had been willing to miss. So every woman married to a McTiernay brother or ally came—and too many of them were with child.

Like them, Adanel's stomach was round and protruded, but unlike those expectant mothers, the rest of Adanel remained unchanged. There was no puffiness around her eyes, and her face and limbs still seem slender, not swollen and stiff. She looked just as he remembered, stunningly beautiful. So much so that he had to remind himself repeatedly of just how she had played him for a fool.

Adanel emerged from some bushes and looked around. "Where is everyone?"

"They rode ahead. Are you ready, or do you need more time?"

Adanel licked her lips and looked as if she wanted to say something, but instead shook her head. "I'm ready," she stated, and then went to her horse, tied her bag to the back of the saddle, and unhooked the reins.

Dugan walked toward her with the intent of helping her mount, but before he got to her side, Adanel had put her foot in the stirrups and was easily pulling herself astride the animal. The reins, however, had slipped from her grasp. She reached over to get them, seriously squishing her stomach in the effort.

Dugan jogged over and, upon picking them up to hand them to her, he discovered the leather straps had been significantly shortened. No one could have held on to them when mounting.

"Who would do this?" he mumbled out loud, more to himself than to her, and began to fix the knot around where the reins attached to the horse's bit. "Nigel probably. Does he *want* you to go into labor?" he asked aloud, thinking about the saddle horn and how it poked into her stomach.

Adanel swallowed, her eyes wide when Dugan handed her the leather strips. "I, um, thank you."

Dugan gave her a single nod of acknowledgment, and then went to get something from his own horse. "Here," he said, pressing a small wrapped bundle into her hand. It was meat from the previous night.

Adanel was again speechless, barely managing another small thank-you. This time Dugan ignored it and went to mount his own horse.

After a half hour, it was clear the group was much farther ahead than Dugan had anticipated. The day before, with the exceptions of Nigel's periodic need to sing or needle Brùid, the six of them had ridden with little need for conversation. Dugan had welcomed the silence and found it comforting. Now, with just the two of them riding together, the quiet was near intolerable.

After months of repressing all emotions associated with Adanel, they were suddenly boiling back up to the surface. Conor's death, her promise to wed another, all her lies and manipulations—nothing he thought of was helping. He still wanted Adanel. He missed her voice. He longed to see her smile and hear her laughter. Once again, every fiber of his being ached to touch her and be touched in return.

Before Adanel, Dugan had never allowed himself to be ruled by his emotions, especially when it came to women. The pursuit of pleasure had been predictable. He knew how he would feel before, during, and after a relationship. Only slight subtleties ever varied from what was expected and what actually occurred. But Adanel had been different from the moment he had first spied her.

Dugan forced himself to look forward but was unable to suppress his sigh. Today was going to be a long, miserable day.

Unable to take the strain of not speaking her thoughts any longer, Adanel said, "Despite what you believe, I am sorry about what Eògan did to your chief. I had no idea what my father had planned until it was too late."

"So you knew," Dugan accused, with a sharp bite to his tone.

Adanel squeezed the reins and then forced her hands to relax. "Two mornings ago, my father came to my room to gloat about a McTiernay Eògan had killed. He assumed it had been Conan, and therefore so did I. I don't think my father realizes just who Eògan really attacked. I'm not even sure my brother does."

"Eògan knew exactly who it was he killed before I ended his despicable excuse for a life."

"Ended?" Adanel repeated softly, realizing what that meant. She would never have to worry about him again. Only her father.

Dugan pivoted on his saddle to look at her. "What did you think would happen? Or are you saddened that your beloved brother will never again be able to plot and enact more violence against the McTiernays at the behest of your father?"

"Beloved?" Adanel said, her face and voice full of disgust at the idea that anyone would think she and Eògan had ever been close. "I hope he died screaming. He was cruel and vindictive just like our father."

Her answer stunned Dugan for a moment, but anger won over rational thought. "From what I can tell, everyone in your family is an expert on cruelty."

Adanel felt like Dugan had kicked her in the chest. He truly believed her to be like her brother and father simply because she had withheld her identity.

"I wonder if Daeron MacCoinnich knows that the woman he's going to marry is heartless."

The guilt Adanel had been feeling was rapidly replaced with anger. "Oh, I have a heart." She almost added that he had broken it months ago, but just pressed her lips tightly together.

"And it belongs to no one but yourself. Tell me the real reason you were marrying that MacCoinnich boy. I mean it seems that over the past year, you keep increasing your sites. First there was me, a mere commander, then Conan—the younger brother of a powerful laird, and now Daeron, the next in line to be the MacCoinnich chief."

"I guess you should consider yourself lucky that you ran away."

"I did not *run* away. I got wise to who you were and *decided* never to see you again."

"Ah, well, I'll believe that when you stop accusing me of going after Conan when you *know* that I had no more idea of who you were than you did of me. My father's men found a McTiernay at our loch who announced himself as Conan. Even I assumed that my brother had been talking to *you*."

"I don't look anything like the McTiernays."

"And how would I know that?" Adanel practically screamed.

"Because everyone knows!" Dugan yelled back.

Everyone knew what the McTiernays looked like because the seven brothers had been attracting the opposite sex since they were youths. Thankfully, all but the youngest McTiernay was now happily married and no longer stealing the most eligible women around.

Dugan narrowed his eyes on Adanel. "Then why did your brother visit the McTiernays this past winter in an attempt to threaten Conan into marrying you, using *my* child as leverage?"

"Probably because my father told him to! *Not* because of me!" Adanel huffed. "I cannot be held accountable for their actions, but I can hold *you* accountable for *yours.*"

"Mine?" Dugan choked.

Adanel pulled back the reins to stop her horse. "I told you that I despised my father, that he controlled my life and my need for escape. You, on the other hand, were the one who deceived *me.*"

Dugan halted his mount and faced her. "I never once deceived you. You knew I was a McTiernay, and you yourself said that I was not just a soldier, but a leader. *Murt*, my schedule alone, meeting with you repeatedly for hours during the week, proved what I was. *You*, not your father, planned to take advantage of what I could offer."

"And you believe I made you out to be a fool?" Adanel asked, with a self-derisive chuckle. "Well, you definitely made me into one. My wicked plans to snare me a McTiernay husband needed remarkable forethought for when we met *I was already at the loch*," she sneered derisively. "You know, I was so dazzled by you. There I was, swimming all by myself when a gorgeous man with a sense of humor ventures to a place *no one* ever goes. But you were so witty and so charming, oozing with experience in knowing how to get women where you wanted them. I nearly drowned trying to get away from you. But then I awoke naked and pinned underneath you, exactly where you probably wanted me from the moment you opened your mouth. And idiot that I was, I thought *why not?* My father's leash had been so tight for so long, and I wanted something for myself. I wanted *you.* You ran away from me in the end, but I should have been the one running from you in the beginning because that first time we were together made me realize that I had been frozen for years. I had been alive but not living, and suddenly I wanted more. I wanted to *live.* So very badly. So, *aye,* I did hope that you would return each week and that eventually our time together would be enough to convince you to take me away, but I made a huge mistake. I fell in love with you, and actually thought that you cared for me in return."

Adanel glared at him, all the anger and hurt she felt pouring out of the dark depths of her eyes. She gritted her teeth and ground out, "I cannot believe that I waited for *months* for you to come find and save me! And what is worse, even if you had known that my father had locked me away, you would have done nothing because it was *you who deceived me.* You are not the man I thought you were."

Dugan's heart was pounding. Adanel was twisting events to her favor. He had spent the past winter in more agony than he had ever experienced. Even Leith's betrayal had not wounded him so deeply. And nothing Adanel just said could remove any of the pain she had caused. He had become dependent on it. Needed it to feed his anger. And yet, hearing Adanel say that what occurred between them had not been all a farce soothed a piece of his fractured soul that he had thought to be broken forever.

Summoning what he had left of his control, Dugan stilled his rampant thoughts and willed his heartbeat to a slow and even tempo. He focused on the most incredible portion of her outburst—her claim to have fallen in love with him.

Adanel let go a frustrated growl. "All that and you have nothing to say." Through gritted teeth she continued. "You are just determined to think the worst of me, to bend everything into the most evil, most vile way it can be viewed, and examine me through that lens. Go ahead because whatever I felt for you died and like everything else connected with us, it was a long, painful death."

The air vibrated with tension as emotions warred within Dugan's body. The very moment he started to let his guard down, to believe that just maybe Adanel had not been playing him false, she had found a way to rip him anew. Never again. The tatters of his own heart proved that love did not die so quickly or because one willed it to. "By your tale, you fell quick enough for me," he stated in a clipped, icy tone. "I have little doubt that you will just as quickly fall for that mooncalf MacCoinnich you've ensnared."

Adanel's back straightened, and her features grew taut with a level of anger she had not known she could feel. "I just hope he's honorable and understands that love is not about lust, but faith and trust. Neither of which you felt for me." Not giving him time to rebut her assertion, she added, "Then again, I should not despair. With my brother dead and father soon to join him, I'll be free for the first time in my life. Free to meet someone and be openly happy without any fear. Who knows? Maybe my soul mate resides with the McTiernays and I am but a day away from meeting him."

Dugan felt the blow as if her words had formed actual fists. He dismissed the nagging thought that he was the reason Adanel was making such threats. That he had pushed her to this point and could blame no one but himself. But Dugan also knew what she said was a very real possibility. Now that all but one of the McTiernays were happily married, their guards were hoping to find success with women. Loman was definitely on the prowl and so was Donnan and Sean. One look at Adanel and any number of Conor, Cole, or even Hamish's men would seek her out.

The image of her with another man was too much, and Dugan lashed out. "You're a Mackbaythe. Do you really think another man would look in your direction, let alone speak to you, all while you are pregnant with my son?"

Adanel's eyes flashed with a sudden shower of angry sparks. She began to unlace the belt to her bliaut and, with a look of defiance, she reached up inside her gown. With two strong tugs, she pulled out a large pillow and threw it at him. "There's your son. Now I am truly free. Free of torture, pain, loss, and of ever having to deal with you again!"

"Aye, that went *really* well," Faden said sarcastically as he watched Adanel and Dugan silently urge their horses ahead.

"I told you they should talk only after he had calmed down," added Garrett once they were no longer in earshot.

Brùid used his thumb to gesture to Nigel. "But according to him, they are good for one another."

Nigel glared at Brùid. "At least they were talking."

"The only good thing that came out of that discussion

is Dugan finally knowing the truth about that damn pillow," Brùid mumbled.

"Aye," Nigel agreed. "I told her that it took more than bigger pillows over time to pull off being pregnant."

Faden, Tybalt, and Garrett glared at both the guards. "And just when were you going to tell us?" Tybalt growled.

Faden leaned over to punch Nigel in the jaw, who leaned out of reach just in the nick of time, causing him to miss. "I damn near panicked the *entire ride* yesterday that at any moment Adanel would stop and go into labor!"

Nigel winced out of guilt and then, unable to help himself, began to laugh. "I'm sorry!" he yelped as Faden lunged for him again. He quickly clamored up on his horse, and just before he gave his mount a kick, he let go one more cackle. "But you have to admit the idea of big boy here playing midwife is hysterical."

And with another hoot, he rode out of sight leaving a large, bald giant red and fuming.

Chapter Eight

Adanel sat with her back straight and chin up, and slowly returned the stare of each laird scattered around the throng packing the McTiernay great hall.

A team of a dozen McTiernay and allied soldiers had caught up with Dugan less than a day's ride out and escorted all of them to McTiernay Castle where their small group was quickly disbanded. The only thing Dugan had said or done was issue orders that none of them were to be physically harmed.

She had been led to a small but comfortable room in one of the towers and locked inside. For three days, she had been sequestered there with only a deep ravine as a view. The handful of souls she had seen were the servants who periodically stopped by just long enough to give her food and drink, and empty her chamber pot. Few spoke directly to her though all said volumes with their eyes. They did not trust her, and she could not blame them. Her father had killed their beloved laird, and war was nearly upon them because of her family.

Then without warning, a bath, or even her bag to change her clothes, she was ordered to appear in the great hall and answer questions. Adanel had expected to meet with Dugan as well as most of the McTiernay brothers, including the infamous Conan who had unknowingly made her life a living hell. What actually greeted her had her staggering backward. The room was *filled* when angry men, and they were not just wearing McTiernay plaids. Conor McTiernay did not have a handful of associations with nearby clans as her father did. The man had allies—a plethora of them—and she had become the object of their hate.

Adanel closed her eyes and reopened them. Needing to block out all the not-so-quiet whispers aimed in her direction, she focused on the room itself. The hall was much larger than she imagined it would be and far grander than that of her father's. The rush-covered floor was made of timber, and the V-shaped ceiling had been made even more elaborate with the addition of stone vault ribs. Across from her, against the east wall, was a massive canopied fireplace, and located in front of it was the high table where five of the McTiernay brothers sat along with their closest allies and commanders. Included among them was Dugan. They along with dozens of other lairds and their commanders filled the hall, each glowering at her, waiting for her to whither under their questions and stares.

Behind her was a wooden partition that screened the service area, which by the scent coming through, connected directly to the kitchens. To her right were large doors next to a series of arched windows that faced the courtyard, where she could see a huge crowd had gathered to stare at the proceedings. They had been there for hours, watching and waiting. But for what? Her to break down? Her to be sentenced to death? Adanel no longer knew.

To her left, on the north wall, was a large window that let in the sun. During feasts and parties, with the decorated walls of weaponry and tapestries, the great hall would have had a warm, inviting feel. Right now, it felt more like a dungeon, cold and decidedly unfriendly.

When the questioning had started, her goal had been to be completely open and honest about everything she knew. Now, Adanel was hungry, tired, and no longer felt like cooperating with anyone. She was beginning to think that the McTiernays were no different than her father. They took delight in being cruel and lacked compassion.

"I am done repeating myself." Startled, the man she had interrupted just stood there with his mouth open. "You obviously are not interested in what I have to say, do not believe it, or simply are too dense to understand the truth when you hear it," Adanel stated with an unapologetic sneer, finally letting her frustration come out.

"Watch your tongue," came a dark warning on her left.

"Why?" Adanel challenged, swiveling her head to meet the glare with one of her own. "Are you waiting for me to say something different? To state a new piece of information that will implicate me in some dastardly plan that will enable you to kill me and wipe out my clan without the guilt of knowing you'll be killing innocents? I cannot provide that. My father deserves to endure the pain of multiple deaths and so do a small number of his loyal men. *My* guards and *my* people, however, are not to be blamed for his actions. But after hours of sitting here and answering your questions I can see you McTiernays are all alike. You leap to the worst conclusions when others could have been just as easily made." She stared at Dugan, who had sat in silence the entire time of her interrogation.

Adanel found it sickening that people who did not know her, never met her, who never even held a conversation with her could leap to the vilest presumptions of her character. Armed with a few facts, they had filled in the rest with conjecture and lies. But what made her truly ill, hurt her beyond what words could convey, was Dugan's lack of reaction.

He had the power to stop their accusations or at the very least he could have stood up and defended her where he *knew* they were wrong. Despite all the angry words they had exchanged, he knew she had been locked away. He knew she despised her father and brother. And deep down, he knew that everything she had told him had been the truth. But instead of saying one word of support, he had sat still with his mouth shut, refusing any support. As a result, all thought he agreed with their accusations and insinuations. He knew that as well and still, he had said nothing.

Adanel issued Dugan a final disgusted look and then shifted her gaze to the McTiernay brothers next to him. "It is clear to me that you have done the same. Nothing I say will change your opinions of me, my motivations, or my actions. So, spend your time berating me with your scowls and pointless questions. But while you do, let me remind you that my father *is* on his way, and he will not be coming alone."

"Do not dare to presume you are in a position to make threats here. You've lied about your identity to Dugan for months and falsified your pregnancy for even longer. It is not a leap for us to think you lie still. So do not dare to condescend to us, you . . . you . . ."

"*Lady Adanel*, I believe, is tired, as am I, Laird Crawford," came a new voice off to the side.

Adanel blinked. Not only had someone spoken her name with respect, but in doing so they had just verbally slapped the laird who was almost certainly planning to insult her.

For hours, Adanel had endured nothing but attacks and questions from men. While she had seen a few females lurking in the back when she had first entered the hall, none had spoken, until now. Whoever she was, the woman had clout for the man who had been about to call her a string of names and accuse her of new crimes had suddenly gone silent.

Adanel twisted in her chair to see who had come to her defense and her eyes fell on one of the most beautiful women she had ever seen. Long, wavy, pale gold hair with strawberry highlights fell around her delicate frame. Her dark blue-gray eyes swirled with displeasure and looked out of place on her heart-shaped face. The woman was ethereal and yet radiated power and confidence. Adanel had only ever wished to be just like her mother, but seeing this woman hold the attention and respect of a room full of powerful men, she longed for a little bit of her ability as well.

"May I point out, gentlemen, that Lady Adanel has not changed her story once since you have begun. I have listened carefully to all she has said and not once have I caught two conflicting points. I've heard nothing that hinted there are any more layers to her knowledge regarding the size of her father's impending army, his fighting strategies, or even the time and date of his arrival. I doubt further questioning will bring you any peace of mind as to her true intentions."

"Laurel . . ." The tone was both cautionary and scornful.

Adanel swiveled her head to see who spoke. It had been Colin, whom she had learned was the second eldest of Conor's seven brothers. All but Conor and the youngest McTiernay were present, and all of them exuded strength, power, and significant levels of hostility.

"Enough, Colin, and remember who I am and just where you are sitting," Laurel said crisply, making it clear that her word was law. Suddenly Adanel knew exactly who she was. Conor's widow.

Standing up, Laurel looked around the room. "Lairds, commanders, you have received much information and that needs deliberation. I will take Lady Adanel now so that you may begin." She then snapped her fingers, and a servant rushed over. "Have you done as I asked?" Seeing the nod, she said, "Then tell Fiona that she can start sending in the food. I think a little good food and ale will help cool some tempers."

Laurel then looked at Adanel and, with a small wave of her wrist, instructed her to follow. Having little choice, Adanel rose and followed her out the doors, across the bailey, through the self-parting crowd, and to the largest tower she had ever seen.

Seven stories high, the tower was accessed via a large doorway that mirrored the shape of the hall's arched windows. As they crossed the portico, a guard stationed in the small chamber to the right of the door straightened to attention. Seeing that the sentry post was manned sent a shiver up Adanel's spine. It was a small reminder of just how large the McTiernay army was. Everything was guarded and protected.

Adanel's first thought was that she was being led to a large prison-like structure to await her fate, but as they went up the stairs she could see inside a few of the rooms where the doors had remained open. This tower held no dungeon. This large structure was the laird's keep, and these rooms belonged to his wife and their family. Adanel never felt more like an intruder or out of place.

On the fourth floor, they went down a narrow hall where Laurel stopped in front of a somewhat small door between two larger ones. Having a similar setup in the Mackbaythe's main tower keep, Adanel knew the door in the middle led to a chambermaid's room, so she could sleep nearby in case she was needed.

"Lady McTiernay? Am I correct in believing that is who you are?" Adanel asked hesitantly.

Laurel glanced over her shoulder, narrowed her gaze, and said, "Aye, but you may call me Laurel."

Adanel swallowed a cough. Calling this powerful woman by her name as if they were friends, not enemies, was the last thing Adanel was going to do. "Lady McTiernay, I don't understand why you have brought me here."

Again, Laurel looked back and studied her with a pensive expression. There was no warmth in her look or demeanor, but neither was there hatred. Instead, Adanel felt cool detachment coupled with reserved judgment.

Unhooking the door's latch, Laurel set aside her most immediate fears. "As I said, call me Laurel. Using titles adds an air of formality that I wish to put aside for now. I want us to have a frank conversation, which is best done using our names."

"You want to have a conversation? With me?"

"Aye," Laurel answered, and gave a firm yank on the handle, opening the door. She waved Adanel inside.

"In a servant's quarters?"

Laurel nodded and took the one lit candle and began to light the half a dozen others around the room. "I don't want to be interrupted, and it's the only place where we won't be found before I am ready." She pointed to a plate of food on the small table next to the bed. "Are you hungry?" she asked before pouring ale into two mugs and handing her one. "You have to be parched after the horrific afternoon those men put you through."

Adanel stood stunned holding the cup. She was not

sure what was going on and felt very much like a sheep being led to its slaughter with a bit of kindness, some fresh food, and a mug of ale. Any moment, Lady McTiernay was going to pounce and declare Adanel to be part of her father's plan and should pay for her brother's crimes.

Adanel put the mug down on the table. "I thank you for the offer, but I am fine." She watched as Laurel slowly sank down on the small mattress and gingerly leaned against the footboard. "Are *you* well, my lady?"

Laurel motioned for Adanel to sit and did not answer until Adanel sat down on the other side of the bed as there were no chairs in the small room. "Having the twins was far worse. And while I admit my little Brion picked the worst time to make an appearance, he is healthy, and with exception of being a little tender and wishing I had more energy, I, too, am doing astonishingly well considering I gave birth less than a fortnight ago."

Adanel just stared at the woman, trying to keep her mouth from being agape. No one mentioned that Lady Laurel had been pregnant and just had a babe. Her slight grimace was the only indication that something was amiss. Had Eògan's attack precipitated the birth? Almost assuredly it did, but then why was this woman, who had every right to hate her, being so civil?

"Lady McTiernay, you are scaring me far worse than all those angry lairds trying to flay my skin off with their questions. If you would just tell me what you wish to know, I will do my best to answer."

Laurel took in a deep breath and then slowly exhaled. "I appreciate your candor, Adanel, so you will have mine in return. I brought you here for the same reason you were brought before the lairds in the great hall. I need to understand your role in what happened to my husband."

"I can only tell you what I told them."

Laurel gave her a half smile. "Aye, but they interrupted you countless times, inserting their own opinions. Here is what I know, Adanel. If you and Dugan had never met, my husband would never have had his head smashed and a knife lodged into his chest. I would not have gone into early labor. I would not have almost lost my life and that of my son's. My family would not be in turmoil right now, and I would not have a gaggle of angry lairds hovering about shouting everything they speak."

Adanel swallowed, nodded her understanding, and then began to tell her story once more. At first, she was full of contrition, knowing some of the consequences of what she and Dugan shared. But as she spoke, her voice became more clear and assertive. She was not the reason the McTiernay chief had been attacked. Dugan had been just as present during their liaisons as she. He also could have come after her, and he could have investigated Conan's attack in the fall. Then there was Conan and Laird Conor McTiernay, neither of whom were respectful to her brother when he had told them about her pregnancy. Many people could have done a number of things differently. Aye, she was one of them, but she was not the sole reason, and she certainly was not behind the actual attack. No one was going to come to her defense, and those few who would were being ignored or not allowed to speak. It was up to her to stand up for herself, and by the time she finished telling Laurel about her latest fight with Dugan, including how she revealed the truth about her pregnancy, there was no shame or repentance in Adanel's voice for any of her decisions.

"Why did you not tell Dugan the truth about your fake pregnancy earlier?"

Adanel widened her eyes. "Before we left?"

Laurel nodded.

"Because Nigel had been right. Dugan was offering me a means of escape as well as a promise to keep me and my friends safe and that was mostly because he thought I was carrying his child."

"But you said that taking you ensured your father would follow. Dugan would have brought you with him even if you had told him the truth."

Adanel looked at Laurel for a long moment and then asked, "If you were me, would you have taken the chance that Dugan might understand?"

Laurel did not answer and instead asked another question. "When you and Dugan met, you said that you had first thought to leave the loch and never return or see him again. What changed your mind?"

Adanel sat still for a moment. "I admit that knowing he was a McTiernay soldier gave me hope that maybe I could convince him to take me away from my life. But even if I had learned that Dugan never could or would help me escape my father, I would have still come. I'm not sure I can explain how important those few hours each week were to me. Imagine for years having to be careful of everything you said or did and then suddenly getting the opportunity to be yourself. When I was with Dugan, I did not have to be careful of what I said, where I was, or who saw me. I could laugh, argue, even be silly if I felt like it. Freedom is addictive, Lady McTiernay, and I think Dugan felt similarly. Whatever labels, expectations, and limits we lived with disappeared when we were together. He made me feel safe, and I had not felt that way in a long time. I wanted more. Can you blame me?"

Again, Laurel did not answer. "How much more?"

Adanel licked her lips. "As much as Dugan had been willing to give me," she answered honestly.

"And what about this other man, this Daniel?"

Adanel looked down at her hands. "Daniel was a wonderful man, and I cared for him greatly. He was sweet and kind, and did not deserve to be chopped into pieces with me being forced to watch, unable to stop it from happening just because he made the mistake of falling in love with me."

Laurel pulled her head back and her composed veneer was lost briefly as she looked nauseous from learning exactly what Adanel had meant earlier when she said her father had killed the only man who ever truly loved her. "I . . . I'm sorry."

Adanel swiped a tear. "Because of what my brother did to your husband, you know what it's like to watch the man you love die and not be able to do anything to stop it."

Laurel nodded, her gaze suddenly distant. Adanel knew she had gone back to that awful moment. A second later, Laurel shook her head and became present once more. "And what of your mother? You never mentioned her."

"There is little to tell. My mother was the eldest daughter of Laird MacLeod. When she married my father, the MacLeods got free access to a port they did not have to spend resources to maintain and control. Therefore, Bàgh Fìon became a common stop for those ships carrying the more profitable goods. My mother got pregnant with me almost immediately, my brother a few years later."

"Was it a happy marriage?"

"I have been told that while my Mackbaythe grandfather was alive, my father repressed his proclivities, and they were amicable toward each other. But when my grandfather died, my father became a different man. Two years later, my mother learned she was once again pregnant. Eògan was already acting out, hurting animals, other children—doing anything he could to get our father's acceptance and attention. My mother tried to stop him, but could not. She lost her life with her decision to end her pregnancy. I was mad for a long time at her, but as Eògan grew older I came to understand why she did not want to see another son turn evil," Adanel finished, brushing away tears that began to fall.

Laurel reached out, clasped Adanel's hand, and gave it a squeeze. "I am sure she never meant to abandon you or your brother."

Adanel sniffled and once more attempted to wipe her cheeks dry. "My brother grew up idolizing my father more out of survival than anything else. In the end, though, it did not matter. Eògan became just like him and deserved to die."

"Was your mother's death the reason why your father did not try and terminate your pregnancy?"

Adanel nodded. "He needed me alive. He had been planning his alliance with Laird MacCoinnich for eighteen years. And while another few months of waiting was not ideal, he had rather risk my giving birth, which he knew my mother survived twice, than force me to take juniper."

"I understand why you claimed to be pregnant; you said that you were trying to gain more time." Adanel nodded. "But I find it incredible that no one noticed the truth for eight months."

Adanel snorted. "My guards did. Brùid almost immediately realized that I was faking symptoms. He made sure that only he and Nigel saw me for any length of time. As for keeping others in the dark, it was surprisingly easy. My father had decreed me to be locked away from everyone and ordered that I have no visitors. It was my punishment, but the sequester allowed me to perpetuate the illusion. I just made sure to always walk around with a pillow under my bliaut that periodically got larger."

"And so you were there, in the tower, for eight months just waiting for Dugan," Laurel murmured incredulously.

Adanel shook her head. "Only until I learned that he refused to marry me, despite my being pregnant. Remember, I was told Conan was the man whom I had been meeting." She waited for Laurel's nod in understanding. "After that, Nigel and Brùid planned another escape for me. I was to fake my death during labor and escape on a ship."

"Is Daeron MacCoinnich really that awful? I mean to run away where you knew no one."

"Did you not do the same? Did not Lady Ellenor?" After three days of listening to chambermaids whisper in the halls, Adanel had learned quite a bit about the McTiernay wives.

Laurel opened her mouth and then closed it. "Aye, we did. The idea of marrying someone we did not love, even if they were not completely awful, was not an option either of us would consider." She tapped her chin. "But what I don't understand is what Laird MacCoinnich has to gain from his son marrying you. Eighteen years is a long time to wait. If he really wanted the port badly enough, his army is large enough that he could have just taken it by force."

"My mother's family, the MacLeods," Adanel answered. "They would have blocked the entrance to Upper Loch Torridon and shut down the port. However, my marriage to Daeron would allow him to take over the port without opposition because I am half MacLeod, especially if

Daeron maintained the same agreement my father had. Meanwhile, Laird MacCoinnich had been given many concessions over the years to make it profitable until Daeron came of age."

Laurel took a deep breath, looked Adanel in the eye, and then slowly exhaled. "I have just one more question. Why would your father declare war on the McTiernays? Even if your brother had attacked Conan and not my husband, we would still be where we are now. At the brink of war."

"My father does not have a large army to lose. The MacCoinniches will be doing the fighting, not him. In his mind, they are working for him, though I doubt they realize it."

Laurel pursed her lips in deep thought and after several seconds stood up, opened the door, and called out to the guard waiting to escort Adanel back to her room. As they waited for him to arrive, she said, "Thank you, Adanel. I think I understand better now what happened. I promise you are not a prisoner here, but I do think it is best if you return to your room for now. I will make sure food and drink are sent to you."

Once Adanel left and was no longer in sight, Laurel turned, opened the door to her bedchambers and immediately frowned upon seeing the unrumpled bedcovers. The bed was rarely used for she and Conor always shared the one in his solar. She loved this room though and used it regularly to change, bathe, and prepare for special occasions.

Stepping inside, she closed the door and then walked over to the large man looking out the window to the courtyard. To her, he was just as good-looking as the day they met. His wavy, dark brown hair was slowly graying at the temples, but his gray eyes were the same as they ever were, reserved, strong, and full of warmth and love whenever they looked at her.

Laurel tilted her head so that it rested on his shoulder. "Did you learn what you needed to know?"

"Aye," Conor replied, and kissed his wife on her head. "I did."

"She really is innocent."

He chuckled and gave her a slight squeeze before returning his gaze to the activity below. "At least of trying to wage war against us."

"Adanel has been through so much, and what happened today . . ." Her voice drifted off. "It was not right, Conor. You should have heard your brothers. I cannot imagine what they would have done if you truly *had* died," she murmured, and then shivered at the thought.

"Lady Adanel will be fine. Dugan would not have brought her all this way only to let her come to any harm."

Laurel disagreed. There were a lot of ways to cause a person harm and physical injury was only one of them. Conor should know that after all they had been through, but she uncharacteristically kept her potentially quarrelsome thoughts to herself. When she and Conor argued, they did it fully, vocally, and always passionately. Unfortunately, neither of them were ready for fighting—and the resulting making up—yet.

To the surprise of all, Conor was recovering much quicker than Laurel from the events of that horrendous night. The blade that everyone believed had killed him had not penetrated deeply. She had roused just as Conor was about to be stabbed, startling the attacker and reducing the power behind the strike. The knife that had her screaming had been lodged in his breast bone and had not been his first wound, or his most serious injury.

Most of the blood everyone had seen on Laurel's lap and hands had come from the blow he had taken to the back of the head. A day later, when he finally woke up to the relief of everyone, he was told that he had a new son, but his wife was still in serious danger.

Laurel had named their baby Brion after the MacInnes soldier who had calmly taken over the scene. All focus had been on Conor and safely removing the knife. When they discovered there was also a head wound, Laurel had felt her first pain. It had been sharp and not one that preceded the natural progression of labor.

Her nine months of pregnancy with Brion had been fairly uneventful, but his delivery had been anything but ordinary. Stressed and worried about Conor, Laurel had been unable to relax, causing it to take hours for him to arrive. Then the blood came, and she had lost consciousness.

Shock had taken over the castle, and husband and wife were placed in their beds. The McTiernay brothers and their wives took vigil, waiting and praying for a miracle to happen. And to their shock and profound happiness and relief, it did. Conor had awakened first and, upon learning about the state of his wife, demanded that she join him in the solar. A few said it was coincidence that Laurel roused once she was by his side; some said it was just not their time. But most who knew them believed it was their love for each other that had kept them alive, each refusing to let go, willing the other to stay.

"You promised to rest while you listened," Laurel softly chided.

"I did."

Laurel lifted her head and looked back at the tidy bedcover. "Unless you made the bed for the first time in our marriage, you did *not* rest."

"I don't need to lie down to rest. My head no longer hurts, and the cut on my chest was not deep. If anyone should be resting, it is you. You pretend otherwise, but you are still weak."

"I am not weak. I just tire easily, and unlike you, I do rest when my body tells me I should," she clarified, wrapping her arm around his.

Conor looked down and gave her a small smile. "See that you continue to do so or I will make you. I mean it, Laurel. If I should ever awaken again to find you . . . not with me, you and I *will* have words. And I will win."

Laurel went up on her toes and gave him a soft, lingering kiss that held every bit of meaning and love of the more passionate ones they shared. She again rested her head on his shoulder. "What has you so preoccupied?"

He pointed to a dust cloud in the distance. The Star Tower was one of the tallest in Scotland, allowing guards and watchmen to see far into the distance. "See that?" he asked, pointing to the horizon. "We will soon have company."

Laurel stiffened and raised her eyes to meet his. She knew dread filled them and fought to get a grip on her nerves. She hated fear. Hated reacting to it. Hated knowing what it did to Conor seeing her afraid when he could not afford to worry about her right now. "You come back to me, or it will be *me* having words with *you.*"

Conor turned, and with a groan, he gently grabbed her by the waist and claimed her mouth in a white-hot kiss. Every nerve in her body sprung to life like it had from the first time he had held her in his arms. One simple passionate embrace was all it took for her to feel his never-ending love for her. His tongue invaded her mouth, touched every corner, tasting her, until she was overwhelmed completely.

When their mouths eventually parted, Conor gently

caressed his lips against hers and brought his hand to her face, slowly moving one of the wisps from her forehead. Then, with just the tips of his fingers, he tenderly traced her face, touching every hollow, feeling every curve he had kissed so many times. Finally, he murmured, "Laurel, I need to go."

She blinked and realized someone was knocking on the door. Colin was on the other side saying Laird Mackbaythe had arrived, and as Adanel foretold, the MacCoinniches were riding with him.

Conor went to the door, and as he opened it, Laurel pointed her finger at him. In the most serious voice she could muster, she said, "I mean it, Conor, we *will* have words and heaven is no place for us to fight."

He grinned and gave her a wink. "Can't imagine God would want to deprive us the pleasure of making up, love."

And with that he was gone.

Taking several deep breaths, Laurel smoothed her bliaut, straightened her back, and then went through the door that connected her bedroom to her dayroom. Eleven pairs of eyes immediately locked on to her, each swirling with questions that were barely being contained.

"Well, ladies, did you learn what you needed to know?"

Laurel was not lying when she said she was using the chambermaid's room to keep from being interrupted. But there had been much more behind the location than a simple need for privacy.

It had become clear after the first hour that Adanel's interrogation in the great hall was less about getting information and more for espousing anger on a shared target. Each question had been preceded by a condemning lecture or a small speech of foreboding. The previous week had been filled with mostly shock and fear, but with her and Conor recovering, anger had taken over not just the McTiernay brothers, but their allies. Eògan's death and Laird Mackbaythe being unavailable made Adanel the sole recipient of their ire.

In truth, Laurel had not felt guilty about letting it go on for so long. The Mackbaythes had almost cost her the life of not only her husband, but that of her son as well as her own. It was not an easy thing to just let go. But hearing Adanel's combative comments to Laird Crawford, Laurel had realized that there was much more to the woman's story, and it would never be heard in such a hostile environment. Adanel should have been cowering and weeping under such abuse, and yet with each new verbal slice, the woman's resolve not to cower and accept their judgments became only stronger.

Laurel learned Conor felt a similar frustration when she had gone to check on him and discovered that he had been listening behind the servant's entrance. He had suggested that she bring Adanel to her dayroom and have a private conversation—one that he would secretly listen to and from there make the final judgment to her fate.

Laurel privately decided that more than just Conor needed to hear her and Adanel's conversation. Men thought linearly, not emotionally, and almost every decision Adanel had made was based on emotions. Therefore, Laurel had brought her closest friends and the other McTiernay wives to her dayroom to covertly listen, make a decision, and then formulate a plan.

All had agreed that they needed to know just who Adanel Mackbaythe was—a spy for her father or an innocent who honestly had no idea or part of what happened with the attack on Conor. But what came as a surprise to Laurel was that every single one of her friends also wanted to know exactly what was between Adanel and

Dugan. Because it was clear from the cold looks the two of them had repeatedly shared in the great hall that something was behind the nearly tangible tension between them.

Ellenor and Brighid, who knew Dugan best, without question believed him to be deeply in love. Laurel had not been convinced as he had not asked a single question or said even one word in Adanel's defense. But when she went back in to see if the lairds had made any progress, she had quickly seen exactly what Ellenor and Brighid had. They were right. Dugan was indeed undeniably in love. He had looked like a man being tortured. Every sharp word, every verbal lashing Adanel had taken, he had felt, maybe more so. But what Laurel could not discern was if Adanel felt the same about Dugan. That was why she arranged for all her friends to listen in her dayroom to see if their conclusions aligned.

"Could you hear our conversation adequately?"

A large, robust woman with wild red-and-gray hair slapped her knee and gave Laurel a wink. "Every word. I dinnae think any of us are wondering if the fire has dimmed in the bedroom for ye and the laird any."

Laurel rolled her eyes. She should have known this would happen. "Did you really need to listen to me and Conor to know that, Hagatha? I would have thought you—as a midwife who just helped to deliver my fourth child—knew where babies came from."

"Dinnae get cheeky with me. I'm just saying 'tis good to hear ye two at it again."

Laurel suppressed a groan and sat down in the chair Makenna vacated for her. She knew Hagatha was just trying to lighten the mood. Hearing her talk about Brion had reminded all in the room about the dangers of labor. Out of the twelve of them, half were pregnant. She had just given birth and Hagatha had long ago passed her childbearing years. Her friend Maegan was not even married, Rowena was busy supporting her husband Cyric and his politics at court, and Brighid was just glad that she was for once *not* pregnant with another boy. Mhàiri, who's wedding to Conan two weeks ago had brought them all together, might have been pregnant, but it was too soon to tell.

"Anyone else more interested in my and Adanel's conversation?" Seeing she finally had their attention, Laurel asked once again, "So, ladies, did we learn what we needed to know?"

Ellenor waved her hand conclusively. "It is as I said earlier. Adanel loves him. And what's more, Dugan loves her with everything he is. He was quiet because he was hurting. He truly feels betrayed, and with his family history, that it is a deep wound she tore open. He is just reacting accordingly."

Crevan's wife Raelynd absentmindedly rubbed her stomach with one hand and tapped her chin with the other. "I'm not convinced Adanel does love him though. She cared for him at one time, aye, but she never admitted to loving him then or now. Just this Daniel, and . . . well . . . I mean after seeing his death, it could be she is too afraid to fall in love."

Married to one of the McTiernay twins, Raelynd tended to see the world plainly and was not easily persuaded by nuances and unspoken emotions. Laurel could not wait to see how she adjusted her black-and-white judgmental tendencies after the birth of her first child. And yet, once Raelynd believed in someone, there was no more loyal a friend.

"I don't know how we are sisters sometimes let alone twins," Meriel said with a sigh, shaking her head. "Ellenor is absolutely right. Those two are unquestionably deeply in love."

Makenna, Colin's bold and unpredictable wife, winced. "*And* unquestionably angry with the other. And not the good kind of anger where making up makes it all worthwhile. Their anger is the kind that destroys love."

Laurel nodded. "I saw that as well. Love can only suffer so much pain before it breaks and dies."

"I wouldn't be surprised if that hasn't already happened," Mairead grumbled, and despite being pregnant and promising her husband that she would stay off her feet, began to pace. "I don't care how much I love Hamish. If he sat there like a stone while hateful questions were being launched at me, we would be done." Her hand sliced through the air. "No sweet words or apologies could make me forget that."

"So, is that it? We do nothing to help them get past this despite knowing that we all"—Meriel moved her finger in a circle—"needed a bit of help to come together with our men? Just like us, Dugan and Adanel have strong personalities and—"

"—aye, did you see how Adanel's got stronger with every question?" her sister Raelynd popped in.

"—*and* that makes for strong marriages," Meriel continued. "I say they just need a similar nudge."

"They are going to need a whole lot more than a nudge," Mhàiri cautioned, biting her bottom lip. "I know that I just married Conan and joined this group, but while you were up here talking with Adanel, Dugan was in the great hall *talking*."

Rowena nodded. She and Mhàiri had decided at least a couple of them needed to know what was being said after Adanel had left. Living with her husband Cyric in the middle of King Robert's very political court had taught her that information was always best when learned firsthand. Husbands tended to filter, often unintentionally, the most important points. "After Adanel left, Mhàiri and I heard Dugan's account. He was devoid of emotion and spoke of their relationship as if it was a series of facts."

"Which told us that his feelings were *very* much involved," Mhàiri added. "Only a broken heart can make a person that cold and angry."

Brighid sighed. "I heard him talking with Donald and Cole last night, and while I love Dugan dearly, he is acting as if he is the only one hurting and that his pain in some twisted way supersedes, or even negates, what Adanel has suffered."

"Today, during the questioning, he was so quiet." Maegan, the youngest of the group, had been physically bothered by Dugan's aloofness. "He looked . . . I don't know . . . guilty?"

Makenna began to bob her head along with her finger. "That's *exactly* what he looked like. Guilty. He *knew* what was being said was wrong and did nothing to stop it. I did not pick up on it at first, but by the end, he was so uncomfortable sitting there that watching him made *me* feel uncomfortable."

"I don't think Adanel is going to forgive him for just sitting there like that," Maegan said with a shake to her head. "I don't know that I would."

"Aye," Mairead sighed in agreement. "That woman is not the kind to just take abuse and keep coming back for more. I know I wouldn't. I'd walk away and not look back." She looked at Ellenor and gave her a small shrug. "I'm on Adanel's side."

Ellenor waved her hands and shook her head. "I think we can all agree that Dugan was a *toll-tòine* today, but he *does* love Adanel and everything that I heard her say to

Laurel makes me believe she still loves him as well." She looked around the room. "Can we at least agree on that?"

Aileen sighed. She was Laurel's closest friend and usually the first to give someone the benefit of the doubt, but she was struggling. "All of us are supporters of love and playing the matchmaker of bringing two people together. But loving someone does not give them the right to heedlessly inflict pain. There is *always* a price to pay, and I'm afraid that it might be too large a price for Dugan and Adanel to be together."

"It makes me sad," Rowena said softly. "I wish things could have worked out differently for them for I expect Adanel would have kept Dugan on his toes. He needs someone like that."

"What are you all saying?" Brighid shouted. "We have known Dugan for years, and he has not *once* let a woman in. He even keeps those he is closest with at a distance. I am *not* going to let us consider the option of just walking away. If that happens, he will lose his first and probably only chance at love."

"I have to agree with Brighid," Ellenor piped in. "If Dugan lets Adanel go, he will make the mistake of seeking and marrying her complete opposite. Imagine having someone who is timid and overly amenable in this room."

Hagatha snorted. "She'd get eaten up alive."

"I don't like the idea of a man marrying me just because I'm the opposite of someone he deep down loves," Maegan said, advocating for the potential victim should that happen.

Mairead stopped pacing. "Well, I like Adanel. All she was doing was fighting the best way she knew how— which is something I am *very* familiar with. Aye, she knew she was hurting Dugan by keeping the truth from him, but she honestly thought he would understand in the end. And you know what? If any one of us had been in her position, we probably would have made similar decisions."

"She feels alone," Makenna said. "I don't want her to feel that way. Because she is not."

"So, we have decided they love each other and that we are going to at least try and help them get together." Raelynd looked around the room and saw nodding heads. "The next question then is *how*? Exactly how are we going to persuade those two stubborn people to just let go of their anger and be happy together. Because Mhàiri's right. It's going to take a hell of a lot more than a nudge."

Laurel rose to her feet and went to the window. Down below she could see Conor and his brothers mounting their horses to go meet the laird who had unwittingly ended the future of his clan. She knew Conor would be fine. He had not just the McTiernay army behind him, but the armies of at least a dozen lairds. But upon victory, decisions will be made. Decisions that affected so many lives, most of whom did not live here. A clan was about to cease to exist and its clansmen had no idea. What was to become of them? It was a disturbing question, but it had a potentially interesting answer.

"Ladies, Laird Mackbaythe has arrived and the men are riding out to greet him."

Shocked looks overtook their faces. Makenna's jaw flinched as she stood up and went over to confirm what Laurel had just said. Seeing the back of her husband's head as he rode out the gate, she grumbled a warning. "Be prepared for yelling tonight, ladies, because Colin is going to be reminded that wives do *not* like being told about battles after the fact."

Laurel shook her head. "I don't think there is going to be one. I thought so at first, but Conor acts differently when he is going into battle. I should have realized it days ago after he had spoken with Dugan privately."

"What did Dugan say?" The question had come from Aileen, but it was the one everyone was thinking.

"In essence, not much more than you already know. The only thing Conor did tell me was that there was a well-thought-out reason behind everything Dugan did. I did not think much about it at the time, but I should have. From the moment Dugan left to chase after Conor's attacker, his plan had been to entice Mackbaythe to come down here." Laurel also suspected Dugan had always intended to get Adanel. "He knew what would happen if the McTiernays rode north. An entire clan would be wiped out, but not if Mackbaythe came here."

"What about Laird MacCoinnich?" Brighid asked. Her husband Donald was one of Cole's commanders. If there was going to be fighting, he would be at the front, leading Cole's men. "We all know he is not coming to fight for Mackbaythe, but is coming to bring Adanel back with him so that she can marry his son."

Mairead clucked her tongue. "MacCoinnich certainly did not bring his army all this way just to leave empty-handed."

"He's coming because he doesn't know," Laurel said softly, looking back out the window, imagining what was happening. "Laird MacCoinnich doesn't know why Adanel was taken or even what he is about to face. When he does, he might just turn around and leave."

"Or he could fight," Hagatha cautioned. "Many men have fought over a woman."

Raelynd's brows furrowed. "He's about to face half of Scotland. Does Laird MacCoinnich really think Conor will let Adanel marry his son so he can take over the port? Conor is going to want more than just Mackbaythe's head. I'm thinking Cole is about to be tasked with managing a port and enfolding another leaderless clan into his masses."

Laurel turned around and, with a knowing, mischievous smile, said, "Raelynd, you are a genius. And, ladies, I think I know of a way where we can give Dugan and Adanel the nudge they need."

Chapter Nine

Dugan studied the army-covered valley in front of him. If there was going to be a battle, it would be a large bloody one and it would take place in this normally peaceful valley. Today was a first. No enemy to the McTiernays had ever ridden onto their land with the intent to cause them harm. And Dugan had purposely made it happen.

He urged his horse into a trot and rode silently out to help greet the two men he had driven south. One would meet his death, and the other would discover the real reason why his son would have to find a new bride to marry.

Conor McTiernay was leading the charge with his brothers right behind him. The only McTiernay missing was Clyde, the youngest brother who had been fighting the English all over Scotland since his youth, and though Cole never said so aloud, he feared his little brother was now fighting demons that would prevent him from ever returning home.

Each McTiernay chieftain had their commanders with them, but no one else. Their combined McTiernay armies, their allies, and all their men remained behind, waiting on the other side of the valley for a sign of peace or a sign of war. God help them all if it was the latter. The battle would not be some skirmish discussed anecdotally over dinner. It would affect clans everywhere, changing political balances, alliances, and even Scotland's overall strength to fight against England and be declared independent.

Dugan had gambled much knowing MacCoinnich would ride with Mackbaythe, never knowing that Conor had lived. But even if he had died, today's outcome would be the same for while Mackbaythe was a fool, MacCoinnich was not. The moment he realized that Eògan's attack happened on the evening of Conan's wedding where every ally and friend was present, MacCoinnich would step away and let justice be served. Bringing both lairds south was the surest way to *prevent* a long battle and innocent bloodshed.

The only thing Dugan had not anticipated was Adanel.

Despite what he said or what others thought, he never could reconcile the woman he knew last summer with someone who could help plan and enact such an attack. He had not initially thought to even see Adanel let alone bring her back with him, but once he had made the decision, nothing would have changed his mind. She could have pulled the pillow free from her bliaut in her tower room and he would have still brought her with him. He had needed answers. Why had she betrayed him? Why had she lied? Why had she played him for a fool? And now that he had those answers he was at a loss as to what to do next.

Since he had discovered the truth about her identity, his thinking had been based on a certain set of facts. And while she had added some unexpected context, it was not enough to dismiss all the anger and hurt he had been feeling for months. The fact that she had lied and initially thought to use him remained, and therefore so did the resentment and pain. Unfortunately, seeing and hearing Adanel only added to his agony.

It never occurred to him that she had been hurting as well and that her anger and anguish was every bit as acute as his. And while Dugan understood her every justification, every reason, every *excuse*, he just could not get past that she had intentionally deceived him.

Granted he had mistakenly thought her deceit had been maliciously derived. It had not. He believed that now. But still, Adanel had not trusted him. She was the one who failed to trust him first.

He knew Adanel had expected him to say something during her questioning. He would have had there been a true need or had she been in danger, but it was her decisions that led to her being in that room and those questions being asked. Dugan refused to fight her battles, and in the end he had not needed to. His *aithinne* showed every man and woman in that room she was capable of defending both herself and her friends.

It was not until the very end that he had second thoughts about his staying silent. "*My* guards and *my* people, however, are not to be blamed for his actions," Adanel had said. She had not been just defending herself, but those who she thought were being unjustly judged. He had made her fight her battles alone, but she had not just fought for herself, but also for Faden, her guards, and her entire clan.

At that moment, he knew he had done wrong. Aye, Adanel could speak for herself, but she should not have had to, especially to people he knew were incorrectly prejudiced against her. But it was too late now and the cold look of loathing in her eyes when she had left made it clear that there was nothing he could say she would want to hear. Dugan had had his chance to speak. It was gone, and so was any hope that they might have a future.

"No need to ask which one is Mackbaythe," Cole murmured.

Mackbaythe and MacCoinnich were riding out to meet them, and they, too, were not alone. Dugan counted eight commanders in addition to Mackbaythe, MacCoinnich, and MacCoinnich's son, Daeron. Both lairds were easily spotted among them and stood out.

MacCoinnich held himself as a man with great power and great responsibility. He knew what it meant if war between his clan and the McTiernays broke out today. He did not want it. The cost to Scotland and his people would be enormous, but to not make a stand would have made him appear weak and vulnerable.

Age alone made Daeron MacCoinnich recognizable. At eighteen, it mattered little that next to Conan, he was probably the smartest of all in that valley. But he lacked experience to know what to do with the knowledge, and worse, he lacked control.

They could have been looking at a thousand men all dressed the same, and there would still not have been a doubt as to who was Laird Mackbaythe. He had brown hair, a square jaw, and the same brown eyes as Adanel, but it was his supercilious sneer that gave him away.

Mackbaythe pointed an accusing finger at Conor as he neared. "You killed my son. My only heir. I demand retribution, and if I do not get it, we will go to war."

Conor remained seated on his horse and took on a re-laxed posture. He glanced at MacCoinnich, who gave nothing away about his feelings regarding such demands, and then looked back at Mackbaythe. "And what is this retribution you seek?"

"Land. For the death of my son, all the territory and

clansmen under the McTiernays of Torridon would be given to me and be under my rule."

"And you are to deliver Lady Adanel to me by sundown, unharmed."

Conor's brows shot up in surprise, hearing the haughty demand of a newly turned eighteen-year-old.

"Aye," Mackbaythe interjected, taking back control and attention of the discussion. "And in penance for you taking Adanel, no McTiernay will be allowed to cross Mackbaythe or MacCoinnich land again. Do so and die."

Such a threat was a serious one. Hamish was the chieftain of the McTiernays of Farr, located on Scotland's northern border. The MacCoinniches held a wide stretch of the Highlands that was traversed by many northern clans when journeying south. The path used was sparsely populated and had little to no impact to the large clan so crossing their lands had never been an issue. But to go around both Mackbaythe and MacCoinnich lands and travel along the eastern shoreline would add weeks to anyone's journey.

Conor remained relaxed and just smiled. "Never thought I would see the day you let another laird speak for you, Willemus. Especially a powerless weasel like Mackbaythe."

Dugan had not known Conor and Willemus MacCoinnich knew each other. He probably should have guessed as powerful as they both were, but it was obvious that Mackbaythe had not known that fact either.

"Powerless?" Mackbaythe sneered. "When you are dead, you will see—"

"He doesn't," MacCoinnich said, answering Conor's implied question. "And neither does my son."

Daeron felt his father's admonishment and visibly shook with anger. But he smartly remained silent, letting his father continue. "However, both have grievances that

I will not ignore. One of your men killed Mackbaythe's son and then wrapped him in a McTiernay plaid to be delivered days after his death. And my son's bride was stolen by a McTiernay the week before his wedding. Daeron is understandably angry. Give us Lady Adanel and the man who killed Eògan, and we will leave in peace. Your passage north will be more difficult and longer taking the eastern route, but that is better than unnecessarily losing many good men to a bloody battle."

Conor rubbed his jaw. "Well, when a man orders his son to kill me on my land and on my brother's wedding night, he should expect his son to arrive home dead."

Every inch of Willemus MacCoinnich froze as he looked Conor in the eye. Conor held his gaze with a frigid look of his own. "I see Mackbaythe failed to disclose that part of his story."

Daeron leaned forward and said through gritted teeth, "That has nothing to do with a McTiernay taking Adan—"

"Son, do not say another word," MacCoinnich ordered, his tone cold and deadly. Nothing like the one he had used before.

Daeron clamped his mouth shut, clearly unhappy, but he did not argue.

Conor then returned his attention to Mackbaythe. "Eògan thought to kill Conan. That was what you sent him to do, was it not?"

Mackbaythe's breathing became more rapid, but he did not say a word. Only hatred poured out of his brown eyes.

"Your daughter's pregnancy was ruining all your plans," Conor said in an even, level tone that made it only seem more frightening.

Daeron MacCoinnich flinched upon learning Adanel

was with child. He looked at his father, but Willemus ignored him and kept his focus on Conor.

"You blamed the McTiernays for her being with child," Conor explained, "and you wanted revenge. Understandable, but revenge is a costly endeavor, and you did not want to pay the price. You wanted someone else to."

Conor then looked at MacCoinnich, who remained completely still, contemplating all that was being said and how it would impact his next move.

Conor continued. "Eògan was a fool from the day he was born, but you sent him here anyway. You knew what would happen when he attacked. You knew I would direct my army and those of my brothers to retaliate, and you thought to trick Willemus into fighting for you. But you made two mistakes.

"The first was your timing. You sent your son to attack during Conan's wedding. Every McTiernay ally was here and therefore saw what Eògan did. As a result, not a one returned home. They instead sent for more men." Conor gestured to the large army behind him. MacCoinnich swiftly assessed the view, and Conor noted the moment Willemus realized just how many different tartans he was looking at. It was not war with the McTiernays they were threatening to wage, but with half of Scotland.

"But you made an even bigger mistake. Eògan did not attack my brother Conan. *He attacked me and nearly killed my wife and unborn son.*" Conor let his gaze swerve to meet MacCoinnich's. He then looked back and at a now very agitated Mackbaythe. "But I'm still here, and you can have no doubt what that means."

"I never sent Eògan to kill you."

Laughter filled the air. Conan nudged his horse forward. "Nay, you sent him to kill me."

Mackbaythe glowered. "For what you did to Adanel!"

he shouted in an effort to try and rally MacCoinnich once more to his cause.

It worked with Daeron, who once again looked like he was about to unsheathe his sword and attack.

Conan waved him back. "I never touched your reluctant bride, boy, who, by the way, was never pregnant. That was a ruse she devised until she could figure out another way to avoid marrying you."

Daeron gripped his sword so tightly his knuckles turned white. Once again, his father saved his life. "Unsheathe that weapon, and you will die justly and unavenged." Then upon his signal, MacCoinnich, along with all his commanders, pulled their horses back, wordlessly indicating they had broken with Mackbaythe.

"I accept your terms of retribution," Conor declared. "All your territories and clansmen will now be mine."

Mackbaythe started breathing rapidly. With MacCoinnich abandoning him and the realization that death was upon him, Mackbaythe panicked and yanked on his reins to turn his horse around and ride away, but Conan had anticipated the move. With his foot, he shoved the man off his saddle.

Mackbaythe immediately jumped up and pulled free his sword as each McTiernay brother unhurriedly dismounted. Mackbaythe swung his blade around several times in a pitiful attempt to look like he could protect himself.

"I told your son to leave and never return when he came down and threatened me. You both should have listened while you had the chance," Conan said, and with a flick of his wrist, sliced off his left ear.

Mackbaythe cried out and pressed his left hand against the wound. His right hand began to wave his sword with even more abandon. Unconcerned, Craig stepped forward and took off his other ear.

Unthinking and in agony, Mackbaythe thrust his sword to attack but lost the weapon when Crevan clipped it out of his hands as he sliced him across the chest. Mackbaythe staggered but before he could fall, Colin lunged his own blade through his gut, keeping him upright.

Conor took a moment to stare at the man gurgling blood who had almost cost him his reason for waking up in the morning. Then deciding he was done dealing with the man, Conor raised his sword and said, "This is *my* retribution."

And with a single swing, Mackbaythe's head was severed from his body.

Colin pushed the limp form off his sword and along with the others went back and remounted their horses.

"You got Mackbaythe. Now I want my bride," Daeron shouted, his hand still holding tightly to the handle of his sword.

Conor just stared at the young man for nearly a minute. He glanced at MacCoinnich, who for the first time, was visibly fuming at this son. Returning his attention to Dacron, Conor said, "You are young, brash, and arrogant. Experience will temper the first two qualities and a good thrashing would help with the third. Fortunately for you, my chest still hurts, and I am in no mood to give such a lesson. Prove your father is not raising a fool and do not speak again."

Conor then said to MacCoinnich, who was discernibly curling his fingers around the grip of his sword, "I have no desire to see your son die, but another word from him and he will earn himself a good scar or two."

MacCoinnich released his grip and nodded in agreement.

"Tensions are high, Willemus, and based on the numbers, if our tempers erupted, no one would win."

"The Mackbaythe clan lacks an heir. His daughter was promised to my son. By right, his lands should be ours."

"Lady Adanel refuses to wed your son, and she has the protection of not just me, but all here. But you cannot have me believe your only goal here was to bring together a man who was a boy only yesterday and a much older woman who would make his life a living hell." Conor bobbed his head toward McTiernay Castle. "I suggest we talk someplace where in the course of discussion and compromise, violence is far less likely to occur, which we would both regret."

MacCoinnich raised his hand and signaled to one of his commanders. "Tell the men to make camp here." He paused and looked at Conor for approval. Upon seeing a nod, the commander rode away to see the orders were followed. MacCoinnich then sighed, feeling the weight of what happened and the decisions yet to be made. "I've always wanted to see the famous McTiernay great hall."

Conor gave him a half smile. "Then you shall."

"But I want to hear what *he* is saying," Bonny moaned, and pointed to the young man in the corner.

Brenna tossed her pale, wavy, gold hair she inherited from her mother over her shoulder and swatted at her sister's hand. "That man knows nothing about Lady Adanel and why she and Cole's commander got married this afternoon. They did not look happy and neither did Father Lanaghly. These are her friends who might be talking about why."

Crossing her arms, Bonny furrowed her dark brown eyebrows and glared at her older sister. "They didn't marry. They handfasted," she grumbled.

Being seven years old and having been in similar situations with her older sister before, Bonny knew she would not be able to convince Brenna to go where she wanted anytime soon. Most of the time she did not care and let Brenna, who was three years older, have her way as she was the one who knew where all the best hiding spots were. Such knowledge had enabled her to learn a multitude of secrets throughout the years. But when their mother, Laurel, had started preparing for their uncle's wedding, it was Bonny who had been the one to recognize the best hiding spot in the great hall to both hide and listen to any gossip that might be shared.

Just like Uncle Conan's wedding, night after night there had been activities with a constant flow of people going in and out of the hall. But unlike Uncle Conan's wedding, no one wore jovial expressions. Tonight was the first time in days children had been allowed to join in on the entertainment. But when Bonny heard her mother instruct the dinner tables not to be dismantled and put away but moved against the walls, she had immediately gone and found Brenna. Her sister had quickly agreed the long tablecloths that hung down so low they touched rushes on the floor created not only an ideal place to hide and listen, but the means to stealthily move from one interesting conversation to another.

Some of the things they had learned Bonny was sure would have shocked their mother, her friends, and even their father, who was chief of the McTiernays and rarely surprised by anything. But it was unusual for Brenna to tell any adult what she had overheard, mostly because no one ever asked her. Her sister might be a habitual eavesdropper, but she was not a gossip.

Unfortunately, that did not matter a lot to their mother, who seriously disliked the practice of snooping on adults and had tried almost everything to get Brenna to stop. Bonny was not sure her sister could. Brenna *had* to be in the know and usually dragged her along for company. Bonny usually went without argument, because she found people's reactions to various unexpected pieces of information to be fascinating.

Brenna's blue eyes bore into Bonny's gray ones. "I *know* they only handfasted. Stop being so picky! Now, be quiet. I want to listen," she said, and peeked out between the overlapping tablecloths once more.

Bonny huffed but did as her sister asked despite her being completely wrong. Just because she liked to be accurate did not make her picky. Brenna was also wrong in wanting to eavesdrop here. These people were only talking about gushy emotional stuff like love, who was hurt, and how to find happiness. That last one was easy. Anyone could find happiness if they just concentrated on the things that made them smile. She hoped Brenna got bored soon because she knew that the most interesting conversation was happening between the two angry men across the room.

Her uncle Conan had often said after a little more life experience Bonny would show everyone just who was the true brilliant McTiernay mind. But being only seven, there was so much she did not understand; however, Bonny was certain that she was much better than Brenna at discerning the truth behind a person's look or action. And the man across the room was not just angry, he was plotting revenge. Bonny was itching to learn just whom he was mad at and what he had planned.

"Can you believe what they just said?" Brenna whispered incredulously.

Bonny blinked and shrugged her shoulders, making it clear that she had not been paying attention.

Brenna rolled her eyes. "If you want to know about maps, languages, and boring stuff, look at Uncle Conan's books. But if you want to know about people, Bonny, you are going to have to *listen*."

With an irritated sigh, Bonny tried to focus on what was being said on the other side of the tablecloth.

"I told you they loved each other," Nigel said, rocking back on his heels.

"If they do, it's masked under a lot of anger," Tybalt countered with a shake of his head. "People in love tend to stand close to each other when at the altar and speak occasionally during their wedding feast."

"Adanel would never have married him if she did not love him," Nigel asserted.

"What I witnessed was not love. It was two people being smart. Dugan wisely accepted the offer to become laird knowing there would never be another opportunity like it again, and Lady Adanel wanted a way to keep her people safe from Daeron MacCoinnich. Again, I say their union was based on simple common sense. Nothing more."

"Well, common sense won't keep them together. Only love will and we have only a little time to help them to realize their feelings."

"You only have a year and a day, and I think it would take five times that before either admitted to even liking the other, let alone being in love," Faden commented.

Nigel shook his head. "Not me. Us," he clarified, waving his finger to all in their group. "*We* have a year and a day."

Garrett gave Nigel a dismissive wave. "I agreed to help Dugan grow and prepare his own army over the next year. I did not agree to play matchmaker. And neither did any of you. Besides, none of you are going to have the time. Watching you train with the McTiernays this last week made it clear that each of you need significant improvement. That should be your focus. Not playing cupid between two adults who are more than capable of discovering their feelings on their own."

Faden crossed his arms over his chest and let go a huff in agreement. "I am embarrassingly out of practice."

"At least you spent most of your time on your feet. I can't believe Dugan wants me to continue being Adanel's guard," Brùid grumbled. He knew he was not very good with weapons, but he secretly thought his size and strength gave him an advantage in a fight. He had been proven wrong so many times in the last week he had lost count.

"It's because Dugan knows you would lay down your life for her," Garrett reminded him. "And right now that's more than what he would get from anyone else. Besides, no Mackbaythe knows the truth. You're big and as a guard everyone assumes you know how to use a sword. Before anyone learns any differently, you will be deadly with or without a weapon. You and I will train privately each morning until you become just as lethal as you look."

"So if you are building Dugan's army and training his guards, what are all those McTiernay soldiers going to be doing?" Nigel asked. "And how many are coming?"

"Least a hundred, maybe two," Garrett answered, "and they are coming to give Dugan a chance. They are going to ensure people understand and accept they are no longer Mackbaythes but part of the McTiernays of Gerloch. Trained McTiernay soldiers can't make people be happy about it, but they can quickly quash the inevitable uprisings and let Dugan focus on getting the port not just functioning, but profitable."

"Something that the MacCoinniches have no desire to help see happen," Faden reminded them all.

Tybalt inclined his head, acknowledging the fact. "True. Laird MacCoinnich was not happy about losing the port and he never would have agreed if he thought to have lost it permanently. He fully believes that in a year his son will be running it as planned and the MacCoinnich clan will finally have unfettered access to the western seas."

"I am going to get another drink," Faden said, lifting his empty mug, and the others agreed they could use a refill.

"They were *not* interesting, and we learned nothing," Bonny moaned.

Brenna peeked out between the folds and studied Adanel. She was talking to her mother so eavesdropping on her was not an option. Better than most anyone, her mother had a gift at knowing when her daughters were near, but unseen and listening. "If I were ever to have red hair, I would want it to be like hers," Brenna said with a sigh.

Bonny pulled the cloth back a bit farther. "Not me. Too curly," she said, taking a glimpse and then letting go.

"Mine already is curly," Brenna said, swaying her locks back and forth.

Bonny wrinkled her nose and pushed her sister's blond mass out of her face. "I know."

Brenna stopped and leaned forward with her finger pointing to various women in the crowd. "Men like curly hair. Look at Makenna. Look at Mama and Brighid and Mairead."

"Mairead's hair is wavy, not curly, and Makenna's is only *slightly* curly. Besides, you constantly complain about how it hurts to comb your hair. It doesn't hurt to comb mine."

"You are so annoying!" Brenna hissed.

"I'm also *bored*. We learned nothing from listening to those soldiers, and we still don't know why Dugan and Lady Adanel got married."

Brenna rolled her eyes. "I was not listening to learn that. It's just what he said." Brenna pointed to Nigel's lanky back. "They love each other."

"Nay," Bonny countered, and pointed to Tybalt. "He said they married because they had to."

Brenna's shoulders slumped with frustration. "You just don't understand love. Just think about how much Mama and Papa argue. And Uncle Conan and Mhàiri." She puckered her lips and realized there were a lot more examples. "And Uncle Colin and I heard Hamish arguing quite loudly with Mairead just yesterday. That's proof enough for even you that being mad at someone is a sign of the deepest, most heartfelt type of love."

Bonny wrinkled her nose. "Seems like a painful, loud kind. You can have that if you want. I'm going to look for the happy kind of love where we smile at each other."

Brenna shrugged and turned to watch Dugan. He was stealing glances at Adanel when she was not looking, and Brenna had no doubt that he really did love her. "One day after Mama and Papa had a big fight, Aileen asked why Mama was smiling. She told her that passion was a key ingredient to a great marriage. So I'm going to look for that."

"Maybe," Bonny semi-conceded. "But I still want to be happy at *my* wedding."

Brenna waved her hand. "Shh. Those two men you wanted to listen to are coming this way."

Daeron MacCoinnich blatantly stared at Adanel, uncaring how uncomfortable it made her or how furious it was making her new, though temporary husband. Daeron had known since he was a young child that his father planned for him and Adanel to marry. He had accepted his fate at first because he had no choice. When he was older, however, he had come to view his upcoming marriage as a shrewd strategic move that would significantly strengthen the MacCoinnich clan. It would also be personally advantageous. Nothing else would give him equivalent leadership experience as well as the chance to act as a laird decades before his father's death.

What Daeron had never expected was to actually desire Adanel. And he did. Almost to the point of obsession.

Adanel was more than just beautiful. She had appreciated his memory and admired his intelligence where most women thought him strange and uncomfortable to be around. And yet, he knew she did not love him.

When Adanel had postponed their fall wedding supposedly because she had always longed for a spring wedding, he had been exceedingly unhappy. He had also wondered if it had been really just a ploy for more time. After all, while he very much wanted Adanel to welcome him to their marriage bed, she might not have been as excited about the idea of marrying someone nearly ten years younger than her. So, he had spent the winter in the arms of any woman willing to teach him how to be a good lover. From their moans, he had learned fast and well, and had been ready to enjoy the fruits of his labor with his bride. If only he could learn how to gain people's trust as easily.

No one knew how often Daeron wished to be not as smart as he was. And he was not alone. He had overheard his father admitting to his mother once that Daeron had a gifted mind beyond anyone he had ever met, but that it continually caused problems because it made him incessantly argumentative. That Daeron was right most of the time did not seem to matter. It was the speed he made his decisions that made his father uncomfortable, for he incorrectly believed there was no way anyone could adequately think through the consequences so quickly.

This week had been no different. If his father had allowed him to speak his mind when he had demanded Adanel's return, today's marital outcome would have been a far different one. His father had thought to avert war, but in doing so, the MacCoinnich clan had come across as weak. Now the McTiernays knew they could use his father's reluctance to fight as leverage. A threat Daeron had hoped to use to his own advantage with Adanel.

"Drink this and calm down."

Daeron glanced down at the mug being shoved into his hands before leveling an angry stare at his father.

"You consider yourself to be a brilliant man, Daeron, but you have yet to realize that to have trust, there must first be respect."

"Both of which I constantly need to re-earn with you."

"And you will continue to have to do so until you stop letting yourself be controlled by your emotions."

Daeron tightened the grip on his mug. "If I were controlled by my anger, I would not be here pretending to agree with every concession you have made over the past few days."

"I did not concede. I am proving a point and doing so in a way that will not incur half of Scotland or King Robert's wrath. In a year, the McTiernays will fail, and when they do, they've agreed to turn over control of the port to the western seas to us."

"But meanwhile these McTiernays think they can just take whatever they want without repercussions. They took Mackbaythe's head, his port, his clan, and now they've taken Adanel. She was to be *my* bride, Father, *mine*," Daeron gritted out, and pounded his chest.

Willemus shook his head. "The McTiernays took headaches and nightmares, nothing more. Bàgh Fìon has been poorly run for the last two decades. Both it, the castle, and its defense towers are in need of major, and more importantly *costly*, repairs. Most Mackbaythe clansmen did not care for their laird and many might actually be glad that he is dead, but that does not mean they will welcome another clan's rule. Leading a hostile clan is going to work against the McTiernays, not for them. And remember, all agreed that Dugan had to have the port open and running before the winter months."

"And what about Adanel?" Daeron challenged. "You practically shoved her in Dugan McTiernay's lap when Lady McTiernay suggested that a wedding would be the best way to merge the clans and build immediate loyalty."

Laird MacCoinnich took a deep breath, held it, and then exhaled. "Whether you accept it or not, Adanel was never going to marry you, Daeron. *The woman was going to fake her death.* And if you had married her, she would have made you miserable. Now, she is going to make trouble for her new husband. Who knows? Maybe in a year she will welcome your suit when she shrugs off his. Just have patience, and all that you think is lost will be ours," he finished, and then briefly squeezed Daeron's shoulder before leaving him to continue brooding.

Brenna tugged on Bonny's sleeve and waved for her to follow her. Bonny shifted and was about to join her sister to wherever Brenna wanted to go next when she heard Daeron talking to himself. She stopped in her tracks.

"A year and a day," Daeron murmured. "The moment that Adanel terminates her handfast she will be mine. If not, the McTiernays will learn never to take from a

MacCoinnich again. Even if I have to wait until I am laird, they . . . will . . . pay."

Bonny shivered. The young MacCoinnich meant what he said. And she suspected he was the kind of man who never forgot about such a vow. Even if he had to wait years to get his revenge, he would have it.

Chapter Ten

Dugan floated on his back and stared up into the early morning sky, letting the cool water of the river flow around him. It was the most peace he had felt in what seemed like months. A few weeks ago, he had been clapping Conan on the back telling him that he was glad to take over the soon-to-be vacated role of eternal bachelor. And he had meant those words. And yet, here he was, married to a woman whom he both deeply desired and wished never to see again

He was also a laird—a responsibility he had long ago given up desiring. Being Cole's commander, he knew that being a laird was not just hard, it meant one lived with a constant headache. There was always something or someone demanding attention, pleas from clansmen who lived both near and far, never-ending castle maintenance, the burden of defending decisions with those few who disparaged them out of ignorance, and the financial burden of balancing defense and economic priorities. And those were the easy challenges for they were expected. He was facing all of that as well as much more.

He was essentially conducting a hostile takeover of

a clan where corruption, cruelty, and deceit were commonplace, and most of its tiny army was incompetent. And to make the situation personally more difficult, it was not just any clan, but one in which a seaport was at its heart—something he knew infinitely more about than anyone realized. Only Conor and Cole knew where he came from and how he had come to live in the Highlands.

Because he understood the full scope of what was being asked, it had been insane to agree to become chieftain of the McTiernays of Gerloch. And Dugan might never have done so if it had not been for Adanel—a woman he neither wanted nor could bear to have belonging to someone else.

Dugan held his breath and went under the water and rubbed his scalp brusquely. They had been traveling for four days, mostly in the rain. Yesterday afternoon, when the clouds parted and looked like they were going to stay away, he had ordered everyone to stop and take time to eat well, bathe, and sleep. No one had argued.

Traveling with almost two hundred soldiers was aggravatingly slow through the mountains. Everyone had been filthy when they had boisterously stripped and made their way into the cold water. Mud had swirled in the waist-high deep stream for hours, and Dugan had decided that he would rather endure a few more hours of grime and bathe in the morning, by himself, in clean water.

It had been the right decision. He needed these few minutes alone to think about all that had occurred and mentally ready himself for the rest of the day. By midafternoon, he would enter Bàgh Fìon as its new leader. How he was greeted would tell him a great deal, including if his first decisions as laird had been the right ones.

When it came to the overall fate of the Mackbaythes, Dugan had agreed with Conor, his brothers, and the

McTiernay allies—all of whom had not been shy about voicing their opinion. There was disagreement, however, on how to handle Faden, Nigel, Tybalt, Brùid, and Garrett.

When he had first arrived with them, Dugan had asked Finn, the leader of Conor's elite guard, to ensure their safety during their stay on McTiernay lands. Finn had not been happy about the ballsy request, but with hundreds of angry soldiers camped near and around the training fields, Finn also knew that only under his elite guard's protection they would remain unharmed.

The elite guard had kept them safe, but they had also tested the five Mackbaythes to assess their worth and competency as soldiers. Watching the men train had given Dugan a headache even before he had accepted the role as their laird. All but Garrett seriously lacked fighting skills.

Brùid was big, but he knew nothing about handling a weapon. Tybalt was fast and surprisingly accurate, but lacked knowledge of many defensive techniques that were geared for small, but strong men. Nigel was a novice with potential. Faden, Adanel's uncle, had at one time been probably very good with a sword, but lack of regular training had made him slow and weak. Garrett was the only one who had been able to hold his own and admittedly learned a few new tricks from the McTiernay guards while teaching a couple of his own.

So when it was time to select a commander, Dugan had no qualms about choosing Garrett. Others did, which caused grousing among the McTiernay brothers and their allies. Conor and Cole, thankfully, had recognized his reasons and supported his decision.

Dugan would have considered either of his fellow commanders, Donald or Jaime, as he knew them well and trusted them, but then Cole would have lost two of his three commanders. Something Dugan not only did not want to do, but did not think was necessary. Garrett already knew many of the Mackbaythe guards. He knew which ones to keep and who were corrupt. As a familiar face, Garrett also had the best chance of recruiting clansmen—a high priority as Dugan had only a year to build an army to the size needed to support the clan's lands as well as the port. But most importantly, he trusted Garrett. The man had saved his life numerous times, already knew about Dugan's past, and had proven he could keep it a secret.

The only real problem had been convincing the mercenary to give up his lucrative job for a more noble one. Garrett had a restless soul and a reluctance to set down physical or emotional roots. Plagued by his past, he allowed it to shape his future—something that Dugan understood. Dugan also knew that his friend needed to be part of something that did not involve the constant threat of death. He needed to help build a person's spirit, not end it. In the end, Garrett had reluctantly agreed to be his commander, but only for the same year and a day Dugan was handfasted to Adanel.

Dugan had wished it was for longer, but then he was not even sure if he would still be laird next year. He had no doubts about his ability to eventually gain the clan's support, build an army, or even get the port running with a profit. But his marriage to Adanel? Would he want to remain married to her in a year's time? Would she? And if the answer was no, what would that mean? All were good questions that unfortunately would not have answers for another twelve months.

After the commander issue had been resolved, the next long and heated debate had been about who and how many soldiers should be lent to Dugan so that he could build a trustworthy and capable army of his own. Crawford and MacInnes had cautioned against going in with a massive force, believing it would only cause more resentment and greater resistance. Cole and Hamish disagreed. Both had experience assimilating other clans and believed Dugan would face opposition regardless his approach.

After weighing all the input, Dugan had decided he needed almost two hundred trained soldiers. He also suggested that the men come from not just McTiernay armies, but from their allies. It was a substantial request, but it gave him enough men to guard the towers, the castle, and the port as well as adequately oversee and protect the lands that extended to MacCoinnich borders. More importantly, it meant Dugan would not have to depend on the trustworthiness or skill of a single Mackbaythe guard. In a few months, Dugan hoped to have enough men recruited and trained to start shadowing the McTiernay guards. When his men were ready, they would permanently assume those responsibilities. Hopefully in a year's time, all soldiers from the borrowed army would have returned to their lairds, clans, and homes.

Conor had thought it a brilliant plan for it discouraged MacCoinnich from even considering raising a sword prematurely, for retaliation would come from not just the McTiernays but every ally who had loaned Dugan soldiers. Such a battle would also be bloody, costly, and undoubtedly catch the ire of King Robert, who was in constant need of men to support his campaign in Ireland.

MacCoinnich had also volunteered a dozen of his own guard. When his offer had been quickly and definitively rejected, he had taken the blatant refusal as an insult, and for a while the entire agreement was in jeopardy. MacCoinnich had decided to use the situation to his advantage and gain some additional concessions. Dugan,

however, had called MacCoinnich's bluff by agreeing
to his offer, as he had from all the other McTiernay
allies. Dugan also explained that as a new McTiernay ally,
MacCoinnich would be first expected to exchange a
handful of guards with *every* laird present—a practice
McTiernays and their allies had followed for years.
MacCoinnich quickly clarified that he was not offering
an alliance and that his offer of guards to Dugan had
simply been a gesture of good faith.

Then five grueling days followed discussing and se-
lecting just who would go from each clan. The soldiers
had to be single men who were not leaving any families
behind. They had to be highly capable as well as physically present. Dugan was not waiting for another two or
more weeks for runners to be sent and for ideal soldiers
to arrive.

In the end, it had been a difficult process, but they
had eventually been able to make the selections, one of
which was from Conor's own elite personal guard.
Loman was placed in charge of the motley temporary
army. Dugan knew very little about the elite guardsman,
but those he trusted held Loman in high regard, both as
an honorable man and as a skilled soldier. Dugan never
doubted the latter, but several times over the course of
the trip, he had wondered about the former.

Single, good-humored, and too full of charisma with
his sandy hair and smiling blue eyes, Loman had no
problems beguiling women. And with only one woman
riding with their large group, all that nauseating charm
had fallen solely onto Adanel. Every time Dugan looked
up, the man was helping Adanel saddle her horse, giving
her water, or answering a question. Unfortunately, it was
never enough to enable Dugan to say anything without
sounding like a jealous fool—which he was neither. Still,

Loman's supportive antics were annoying, which were made even more so because they shouldn't be.

When Conor offered Adanel and Dugan the option of marrying, both had looked at the other and after several long seconds, gave a single nod, agreeing to the proposal. Adanel's other option had been to walk away from her life just as she had planned to do a month ago. Adanel had even told Conor and the rest of the lairds that Dugan had been the wise choice. He knew the area, had the right temperament, and already had relationships with Garrett, Tybalt, and her guards.

It should have pacified any qualms Dugan had in agreeing to marry her as none of her reasons had anything to do with an emotional attachment to him. And while it should have eased his mind, it had not. Instead, it had irked him far more than it should have. That was because his true reason for accepting the lairdship had not been based on the challenge, the honor of being chosen, or even the logic that he was the best qualified; it had been almost purely emotionally driven.

Knowing that, Dugan had almost walked away the morning of their wedding. He could have continued to be Cole's commander with no one thinking less of him. Every soul present knew the struggle it was going to be overhauling a decrepit port and overseeing people who had deep-seated trust issues with those in authority. And because the port was physically wedged between three irreconcilable and powerful clans—the MacLeods, MacCoinniches, and McTiernays—whoever took over was going to be tested repeatedly and indirectly over the next several months, if not years.

Success would require a unique combination of perseverance and patience, something most Highland lairds lacked—him included. And yet, after leading men into war and then spending years as a commander of one of the more powerful clans in the region, Dugan believed he could help this small clan regain their pride. It would take time to build confidence in themselves as well as him, enlist their loyalty, and create unity under the name McTiernay, but he firmly believed it *was* possible.

His marriage to Adanel, however, was something altogether different. Dugan only hoped they could find a way to be compatible and forge a partnership founded on the mutual desire to see the clan prosper. But they would have to start talking to each other for any of that to happen.

Dugan could count the words they had exchanged since their wedding and the number was low. More than once he had questioned his decision to marry Adanel and take on the monumental task in front of him, but each time he did, he came back to the one thing that had made him agree in the first place. If he had not, Adanel would have married someone else to take on the roles of laird and husband.

That was something he could not handle. Knowing that she was someone else's wife and what all that entailed would have eaten him alive. So, he had agreed to Conor's proposal.

Dugan had no idea if it was even possible to reconcile what Adanel did with trusting her, but he did need to be free of her. He needed to replace memories of her and him at the loch with ones that he could easily put aside and forget. Aye, marrying her was a gamble, but after a year and a day, he should be finally able to walk away with no regrets. The port would be in good shape, the clan would have made the transition, and most importantly, whatever hold Adanel had over him would be gone. When their handfast was complete, she could marry someone else, have a family—perhaps with Loman—and it would not matter at all to him.

The year could not pass fast enough. For right now, the idea of Adanel in another man's arms sent a frisson of jealousy through him. Suddenly the image of Loman with his hands around Adanel's waist helping her off her horse sprang to mind, and Dugan plunged his head back into the river's cold water, wishing he could just will his wayward feelings into submission.

Standing up, Dugan shook his head to remove the excess water and refocused his thoughts on the day in front of him. The sun had fully crested the horizon, and it was time they left. He made his way up on to the shore to get dressed, mentally listing all the things that he needed to do. He needed to speak to Garrett and Loman about his plan to enter Bàgh Fìon and assume control over the village and port with hopefully no lives lost. He needed to make sure Brùid understood his role as Adanel's guard going forward, and sometime during the next few hours, he needed to talk with Adanel about addressing the clan as a unified couple.

The McTiernays were strong because of good leadership, strong morals, and unwavering loyalty, all of which sprung from the partnership between the laird and his lady. Dugan and Adanel may not share the deep love that existed between the McTiernay brothers and their wives, but he still valued her opinions, ideas, and ability to challenge him when needed. Those qualities may be the only things he trusted when it came to her, but Adanel had all three in abundance.

Dugan leaned down to pick up his léine and slid it on. He then grabbed his plaid, ignoring the coiled gold ties lying on top of it as they fell to the ground. Wrapping the cloth around his waist, he automatically sought out his belt. The belt, however, was nowhere to be seen. Frustrated, Dugan threw the tartan over his shoulder and began to look around, getting more and more livid with each passing second. He had not thought about it when he first came up to his things, but his clothes had not been as he had left them. His shirt and plaid had been neatly stacked in a pile with his shoes on top rather than haphazardly tossed over a rock.

Someone had been here. They had folded his clothes, cleaned the bottom of his shoes, and *taken his belt.* In its stead were some bits of gold string and lace. The joke was not funny. Even if he thought for a moment that the flimsy strings could secure his plaid, Dugan refused to try. He'd rather walk around with just a shirt barely covering his arse and privates—two things that someone was going to find missing once he found the culprit.

The moment Dugan asked himself who had a death wish and the balls to play such a prank, only one name sprang to mind.

"Nigel, *thu Bastard. Na h-uilc 's na h-uirchill ort!*"

Adanel was looking all around for the gold ties to her bliaut and was almost in a panic when she heard Dugan muttering curses, wishing an assortment of evils and diseases upon Nigel. She hoped Kara's brother was far away. If he were wise, Nigel would not show himself until Dugan's ire had calmed down significantly for she was somewhat inclined to join his tirade as she was only able to partially dress herself. Nigel deserved whatever punishment he received.

Adanel bent down, slipped on her shoes, and then scooped up the heavy leather belt and her bag that held her brush and soap.

Dipping into the cool waters this morning had felt like heaven after days of slow travel in the drizzling rain. As the only woman in a sea of men, it would have been impossible to find a spot yesterday afternoon to privately bathe unless she ventured far away from camp, something she was not inclined to do after hearing talk of wildcats in the area. After everyone had finished, Adanel had been even less inclined to bathe seeing the murky water and had opted to wait until this morning.

She and Dugan had barely spoken since they left, exchanging niceties and only when necessary. Loman, however, had been a godsend. Never would she have thought a McTiernay elite guard would be so kind after what her brother and father had done. But she thanked God Loman was willing to help and answer her questions because Dugan's cold demeanor had made it clear that their new marital status had done nothing to lessen his anger toward her.

Adanel vacillated between feeling apologetic for her decision to keep her identity a secret and vexed that Dugan refused to even try and see her point of view. The man was impossible and her frustration with him grew with each mixed signal.

Dugan refused to look at her, yet demanded that she be within arm's reach at night. He barely spoke to her, but if someone else chose to, he always found a way to join the conversation and quickly end it. Why he had agreed to marry her was a mystery.

After he said nothing in support of her actions nor countered some of the nastier accusations he knew were untrue during the laird's harsh interrogation of her, Adanel had truly believed that Dugan felt nothing for her and never had. It had turned her own heart cold, and Adanel was not sure what it would take to rewarm it, despite Laurel's emphatic promises that Dugan actually did love her.

"I can't marry Dugan!" Adanel had protested when

Laurel first mentioned the idea. "He hates me, and after what happened in the great hall I think I am feeling pretty similarly about him."

Laurel had just waved her hand dismissively. "Anger is such a fleeting emotion. You should never make life decisions based on it."

Adanel's brows had shot up, and she quickly retorted, "I am not just angry, Lady McTiernay. That man watched and did *nothing* while I was practically accused of colluding with my father and brother on the attacks against your family. What I am feeling for Dugan goes *far* beyond anger."

Laurel had simply shrugged as if Adanel had a point, but not a serious enough one that changed anything. "So you are angry. I am not saying you shouldn't be nor would I tell Dugan to just dismiss the resentment he holds for you. And while I agree he is acting like a *toll-tòine*, Dugan will eventually realize that he hurt you, too. If you are married when that happens, you can help heal each other and forge a new bond of understanding and trust."

"There are a lot of things I feel for Dugan, and anger is only one of them. I'm sorry, Lady McTiernay, but I think I can 'heal' a lot quicker if I am not married to the source behind my pain!"

At that, every woman in Laurel's dayroom had shaken their head. It was clear that they were all in agreement even if Laurel was the only one doing the talking. "You will definitely not heal faster, and it might not even be possible for you to heal completely, because we"—Laurel opened her arms and gestured to all those in the room—"believe you still love Dugan and *that he still loves you.*"

Adanel had thought Laurel mad for even a blind person could see the hostility between her and Dugan. It was practically tangible. However, the McTiernay wives had been relentless, and eventually they had made two convincing points. Despite her fervent wish for it not to be true, Adanel *did* love Dugan.

"He just needs time," Laurel had promised. "Dugan's past is riddled with betrayals, and while those stories are not mine to tell you, he will learn to trust you again."

"But will I ever trust him?" Adanel pressed back. "After all that has happened, I don't know if it is possible. He let me be verbally crucified in front of several lairds who now have an unfavorable impression of me that will be impossible to erase. But what I don't think I can ever forget is that Dugan himself thought the worst of me. Things that if he truly loved me he would have never believed. At the very least, he should have given me the benefit of the doubt until he could have asked me about them directly. But Dugan never even tried! So now I must ask myself, do I want to marry a man who 'loves' me like that? The answer is I do not."

That was when Laurel offered a second and more compelling reason to marry Dugan. "Ask yourself another question, Adanel. Do you think you will ever be able to love another man the way you loved Dugan?"

Adanel had pressed her lips together and after several seconds shook her head. She wished it were not true, but the Dugan she had met weekly the previous spring and summer had ruined her for all other men.

"Is not the *possibility* that I am right worth the risk?"

Adanel had refused to answer Laurel then, but later, when Conor asked her and Dugan if they would agree to marry, Adanel had nodded yes, believing it would not matter for she never dreamed Dugan would agree to bind himself to her.

But the damn man had gone and said yes. And after a week, he had not changed his mind. Now, the deed was done.

What Adanel needed now was time. Time to help her

clan transition to a situation she honestly felt would improve their lives. Time for her to sort out all of her own feelings, and time to know if Laurel had been right. What Adanel did not want was to be permanently stuck with someone who felt nothing for her and was only using her as a means to becoming laird. So, she had quickly amended her agreement. Their marriage would be a handfast arrangement and last for no more than a year and a day.

Her suggestion had barely been uttered before Dugan had barked out his full support, stating that he thought the idea brilliant and that he, too, would only agree to such an arrangement. Adanel knew at that moment Laurel had been woefully wrong.

"*An duine bu chòir a ghoil ann an cuan.*"

Hearing Dugan's livid vow, Adanel bit her bottom lip and hurried around the bush to where he stood examining the ground. She was not sure how Dugan was going to boil the ocean with Nigel in it, but his threats were getting more creative by the second and in her hands she held the means to calm Dugan's growing ire.

The winding stream, which was just deep and wide enough to bathe in, had several spots where overgrown bushes of thistles were densely nestled in between several of the sharp twists and turns. When Dugan had risen just before dawn, he had bumped Adanel with his foot unawares. Awakened, Adanel had decided to follow him and demand that they talk. But when she had caught up with him, his belt and plaid were already on the ground, and he was in the process of yanking off his léine.

Adanel was emotionally hurt, cross with lack of sleep, and aching from days of slow travel. She was also a woman with two good eyes that could not help themselves as they feasted on his broad back, long legs, and the dimples in his rear cheeks. With each step Dugan took toward the shoreline, his muscles rippled, creating a fire in her blood that warmed her body in places she had thought would never be warm again. No man compared to Dugan. He still was and always would be the most gorgeous man she had ever seen.

Adanel had quietly moved out of sight deciding that Dugan had the right idea. She could always confront him later, and what she really wanted was to clean the grime and dirt that clung to her like a second skin.

Stepping back farther, she saw that on the other side of the bushes the stream had twisted back, providing her a perfect, private spot to bathe, with the bushes between her and Dugan as a barrier. Immediately, she went back to where she had slept, grabbed her small bag, and returned to strip down and enter the waters. As quietly as possible, she had scrubbed the filth out of her hair and off her skin, and when done, Adanel had felt like a new woman.

Still hearing Dugan splash about, she had slipped out and donned her chemise before running a brush through her hair. She had just finished and was pulling on her bliaut when she had heard Dugan's first string of curses, which steadily grew in both volume and savagery.

"Is this what you are looking for?" Adanel asked, stepping around a bush so that he could see her.

Dugan's eyes narrowed as he saw the wide leather belt swinging in her grasp. "Did you take it?" His tone was more surprised than bitter.

Adanel shook her head. "I heard you rise to bathe and thought I would do the same. I was just getting dressed when I heard you threatening Nigel." She flapped the side sections of her bliaut. Without the gold ties to bind the gown to her frame, she felt like she was wearing a dark blue bag with a hole cut out of the top. "I have no need for this belt, but I could use the laces you are crushing in your grasp."

Dugan looked at the string crumpled in his hand and grimaced. He walked over to where she stood, and they traded items. Swiftly, he pleated the plaid around his waist and belted the material in place. Meanwhile, Adanel laced up the sides of her gown as quickly as possible. Seeing her similar need to be fully dressed gave him an odd sense of comfort. He and Adanel may have at one time been at ease to be without clothes in front of the other, but right now his léine and plaid felt like necessary armor—and he needed all the protection he could get.

His fury at her betrayal had done nothing to lessen his desire for her. If anything, the woman was more gorgeous than ever. Adanel was his ideal woman—tall with a tiny waist, full breasts, and a wealth of red hair tumbling down her back that drew attention to her perfectly rounded bottom. But it was her expressive brown eyes he missed the most. He ached to see them sparkle mischievously or darken in the throes of passion.

Dugan wondered what Adanel would do if he were to pull her in his arms and kiss her, ignoring everything and everyone except the feel of her flesh against his. He honestly did not know how she would react, and while he longed to prove she still wanted him just as much as he did her, part of him feared that Adanel would shove him away. A greater part, however, feared that she would not.

"We should reach Bàgh Fìon a few hours before night-fall. Will you be glad to be home?"

Adanel paused tying the last knot on her gown. She had been contemplating how to begin, and if necessary, demand a conversation before he walked away. Then, without warning, Dugan had started one. It was a silly question, almost as inane as asking about the weather, but she felt only relief that he was at least attempting to talk with her. "I . . . um, I will be glad to see my friend Kara and her husband . . . but as for going home, I am more than a bit nervous."

"Your people won't welcome your return?"

Adanel licked her lips and took a deep breath. "They hardly know me," she answered honestly. "I was locked away this past year and before that I limited my interaction because it unwantedly drew my father's attention to not just myself but them."

"How do you think they will react upon seeing us?"

"As you can imagine —with awe and fear. The McTiernay army you are bringing is fearsome. Honestly, I feel nervous around them, and I've been traveling with them for the past few days. My father's soldiers are *nothing* like what you are bringing to our small home."

"In a way, I hope you are right. Fear does not bring about loyalty, but it can be a tool to keep peace and order, allowing the seeds of loyalty to be planted."

"Loman is worried that you will meet nothing but hostility at every turn." Dugan was about to say something caustic about not wanting to hear about the commander's opinions when Adanel said with a little shake to her head, "Loman is wrong."

Dugan smiled, loving the sound of those three words rolling off her lips. "And why is that?"

Adanel tilted her head and studied him for several seconds. Dugan knew she was trying to ascertain if he was seriously asking her opinion, but she must have finally decided that he was. "My clan is fractured and has been for a while. The scant few who enjoyed my father's proclivities have sick minds. Their numbers are not many, but they will seek to destroy whatever you try to build, and nothing you do will dissuade them."

Dugan's smile grew larger. "We are in agreement.

One of Garrett's first duties is to identify those men, and they will be banished. If you see any, tell me or Garrett. I have no desire to win the loyalty of such people over. It would be a fruitless effort. They will have to seek their pleasures elsewhere."

Adanel blinked, shocked that Dugan was listening to her input. Her father never asked, let alone listened, to *anyone* for their opinion, especially not a woman. Laurel had said that the secret to the McTiernays' success was not in their leadership, strength, or power, but the women they were married to, and that she was now part of that unique group. "Outwardly our men appear almost invincible, but we wives are their strength. Without us, they are vulnerable," Laurel had told her. "But remember, without them, we are too."

It was hard for Adanel to believe that she was now married to one of those invincible men. As a McTiernay wife, it would no longer be acceptable to sit and silently observe. It was time for people to learn who she was as well if Adanel intended to be lady of the castle and all that the title entailed.

"I . . . I will," Adanel finally said to Dugan. "But I really do believe those numbers will be few. Most of my clansmen and women just want the opportunity to provide for their families and lead a safe, happy life. They will be hesitant at first, but what you are offering will be accepted once they believe it is real. However, many still will not want to relinquish their name. Mackbaythes can trace their roots back generations, and some take great pride in their ancestry. They are the ones I would be most concerned about. They may like all you have to offer— the protection of the McTiernays, even a good profit, and a more prestigious port—but they will *not* like . . . or agree to be McTiernays. One cannot just demand they change who they are."

Dugan crossed his arms. "I'm not asking them to change families, just clans. And while it may not have been easy, the nomads of Torridon did so, as well as the clans of Farr. Your people will do the same, or they will have to find somewhere else to be Mackbaythes. Only McTiernays will live at Bàgh Fion." He pressed his lips together before asking, "Are you one of the ones struggling with letting go of being a Mackbaythe?"

Adanel's brows slanted down. "Not as much as you might think and not nearly as much as my clansmen expect I would. Ever since I was little I have considered myself a MacLeod, like my uncle and my mother. When I think of Mackbaythes, I think of my brother, father, and to a degree my grandfather, who were driven by greed and power. My struggle is not letting go of who I was. It's becoming a McTiernay that is daunting," she said with a shiver.

Without thought, Dugan reached out and rubbed her arms brusquely. "And why is that? You seemed to get along quite well with the other McTiernay wives."

He had watched Adanel interact with Laurel, Ellenor, Brighid, and the rest. Seeing her being welcomed into their tight-knit group had lifted a weight he had not known he had been carrying. Those women had uncanny insight into others, being able to quickly identify those with suspicious ulterior motives. He had witnessed Ellenor do it multiple times for Cole, and her relaxed posture around Adanel convinced him, more than anything else, his new wife was not typically disloyal or untrustworthy. It was not enough for him to risk his heart again, but it gave him hope that he and Adanel could make this next year work despite their history.

Adanel looked away as she recalled some of the words spoken and looks she had been given. "I may no longer be seen as the enemy by the women, but it will take far more than marrying you to make me a McTiernay to the men."

"It will also take time for me to be truly recognized as laird," Dugan said reassuringly. "But the results of our actions shall win them over."

Seeing he misunderstood, Adanel shook her head. "I'm not talking about proving myself," she clarified, looking him directly in the eye. "I am *disliked*. Hearing the truth did very little to change the minds of the lairds allied to Conor McTiernay. Certainly, none of them trust me and probably never will. I was glad to leave despite meeting Laurel, Ellenor, and the women. They were nice, but their husbands . . ." Adanel shivered. "I hope never to see any of them again."

"As Lady McTiernay, you will."

"Not unless they venture up to Bàgh Fìon they won't, and I doubt a single one will make the effort."

Dugan took a step back. Her tone had been clipped, and the scowl on her face made it clear that Adanel found the McTiernay brothers and their allies distasteful. Instinctively, he went on the defensive. "What did you expect? You are a Mackbaythe."

"I thought I was a McTiernay."

He ignored her quip. "Your father and brother attacked Conan and almost killed Conor!"

"That was not me!"

"They know that!" he yelled back. "What does that have to do with anything? Why do you care?"

"You really don't get it, *do you?*" Adanel asked pointedly. The last bits of her fortitude that had been suppressing her true thoughts and feelings had just broke. "You think *you* were betrayed?" she asked rhetorically. "What I did was *nothing* compared to *your* betrayal of *me*."

"I never *once* deceived you. It was you who manipulated

me by toying with my emotions and making me believe one thing when you knew the truth was altogether different. You lied to get your way, uncaring of the cost to others."

"I did not lie," Adanel denied. "And while my actions were for my benefit, they were *not* to your detriment."

"I did the same thing as you. I stayed quiet when I could have spoken."

Adanel's brown eyes grew even darker. "Your pride might have been injured by what I did, but little else. Nothing about what you do, how people treat you, or how you are perceived by others changed by my little deception." Adanel scowled darkly. "Not like what your betrayal did to me."

"Don't blame me," Dugan declared in a low, savage tone. "It was your decisions and your lies that brought you to this point. Not mine."

"But I had reasons—good ones, even if you disagreed with them. But what you did?" Adanel looked toward the sky and threw her hands up in the air in defeat for she knew Dugan still did not fathom what he had done to her. "That cannot be undone, and it will haunt me forever. Every McTiernay knows me and will remember me from that day. That's when their judgments were made, and first opinions rarely change. I will never be able to meet any of those people again without the memory of being interrogated in that great hall coming back. I will forever be judged guilty for accusations you knew were untrue. You could have changed that. You could have defended me or at least stood up and made it clear that you did not agree with the maliciousness of their charges. You should have known I would never have attacked anyone. But what was worse"—she got up close to him, her anger and pain clear to see—"*you did not even want to give me a chance to defend myself. You wanted them* to attack and judge and presume all just to assuage your wounded pride."

Dugan held her gaze. Her words were well aimed. He could not deny anything she was saying, and while he had regrets, she had yet to acknowledge that it was her own actions that led to that day.

"Even at my own wedding—days later—I was made to feel unwelcomed and distrusted. You once again had the ability to stop the hatred, *and yet you still remained silent.*"

Adanel reached down to grab her bag, which she had dropped when lacing up her gown. Nothing she was saying was making a difference. Dugan had made up his mind to be hurt and resentful. The man actually believed he had a right to his pain more than she had to hers. "You don't love me," she said softly as the truth of the situation sank in. "I'm not sure you can. You want perfection, and that doesn't exist." She threw her bag over her shoulder and added, "For the next year, I'll be your wife and support you however I can, but that is all I can give you. You destroyed the potential for anything more."

Chapter Eleven

Dugan sat on his horse beside Garrett and watched as Loman led the small army into the valley below. Just over a month ago, he had sat at this very spot in hopes that Garrett would agree to help him find and abduct Adanel. This time his arrival did not entail an infiltration scheme with minimal impact and interaction. This time, his arrival meant change at every level, for everyone.

Garrett pointed to the port. "It's empty."

The village around the port Bàgh Fìon looked busy, and there were MacLeod ships he could see in the distant horizon, but Garrett was right. None were docked, and none looked like they were making their way to the port. Those ships were acting as a blockade.

"I suspect the reason is simple," Dugan said. "It's the solution that is going to be intensely complicated."

Garrett grimaced in agreement. "Damn MacLeods. I'm surprised they heard the news and reacted to it so soon."

Dugan was no stranger to ports, having grown up working in one. However, he had never thought to go near one again. It was where his mother and brother taught him the meaning and pain of betrayal. The memories were definitely there and yet, he did not feel the dread and foreboding he had anticipated. Instead, Dugan felt the unexpected excitement of a challenge, and the MacLeods were definitely going to be one.

"It was quick, but predictable. My being declared laird by Conor McTiernay was not going to just be accepted by our northern neighbors. The MacLeods—more than anyone—feel they have a right to not just the port, but the Mackbaythe clan."

"But Adanel is married to you," Garrett countered.

"That is probably the only thing that is keeping them from outright attacking."

Dugan knew the MacLeod embargo was just one of many hurdles he would be facing.

"Do you expect additional trouble?"

"Aye," Dugan answered. "But Adanel will probably bear the brunt at first when she takes over the keep. Her father surrounded himself with those who will not be glad he is gone. I've told Brùid and the guards Loman is assigning to the castle to expect trouble and let me know if it escalates to her being in any danger, but I need to prep for what's to come. The real danger comes from those beyond these hills and waters. Our failure is what MacCoinnich and MacLeod want, and they will both try to exploit any weaknesses within the clan to their advantage."

"Aye, but who? How many?"

Dugan pointed toward the bay. "The docks, more specifically, those in charge of storing, selling, and shipping goods. That is where the money was. It will be the center at the majority of the corruption. Those that believe in honor and strength will have looked elsewhere for a living."

"Not everyone who will be against you will be dishonest," Garrett cautioned. "Many Mackbaythes can trace their roots back generations and will not be willing to just erase the names of their parents, grandparents, and those before them."

Dugan rubbed the back of his neck. "Aye, that is what Adanel said. And while I agree, I'm not sure what to do about it."

Garrett shrugged his shoulders. "Nothing to do. It is done. They just now have to accept it."

"And when they test that notion?"

Garrett grinned at him. "If I knew the answer to that, I'd be laird and you'd be in charge of the recruiting and training."

Dugan smiled back.

"The truth is that these clansmen are like those of any other clan. The people are good intentioned, but ultimately self-interested," Garrett said in a more serious tone. "A select few will applaud your failures, and while their voices will be the loudest and seem like they speak for the masses, they don't. Most will be waiting to see if you bring success or destruction. Only then will they act accordingly."

"Circular logic there, Garrett. I need their trust to succeed, but to succeed, I need to gain their trust."

Garrett chuckled. "Aye. You also need to make sure they understand the alternative is the MacCoinniches, or possibly the MacLeods. Neither of those lairds has a thought for these families. For them, this port is a means to an end. For you to make this work, you need to make it your home."

"Like you, I only agreed to be here for a short while, no longer."

Garrett shifted in his saddle and looked at his friend square in the eye. "And just how are you going to demand their loyalty when you give them none in return?"

Dugan returned his friend's stare with one of his own. "I could say the same to you," he challenged. "You promised to stay while I was here. If I were to stay longer, would you?"

Garrett snorted, threw his head back, and laughed, but there was no joy in the sound. "If you only knew," he sighed. "If you only knew," he repeated softly to himself, and raked a hand along his scalp. With a deep breath, he said, "I'll tell you what I think you have suspected for a long time. Before you joined with Cole, there were a handful of us who fought together. Remember Leith and our small group looking out for each other?"

Dugan nodded.

"We banded together because we each had a past. All different and yet all the same."

Again, Dugan nodded.

"I did not come from a powerful clan, but my father was successful." Garrett pulled out his sword from its sheath and twirled it in his hand. "So successful he ensured I received the best training in the area. And while he was a hard man, I loved him. I respected him, and I'd like to think that he felt the same about me. Our family was close, but when he died I learned that the love my mother and siblings shared for me was all an illusion. I now realize it probably always was. I went through hell after my father passed away. Every decision my mother made was twisted to my brother's favor. Every action and conversation I had was constantly condemned or viewed in the worst way. They brought up anything— even ridiculous and highly distorted things—to justify their stance."

Garrett took a deep breath and then in a casual tone that sounded as if he was unfazed by what he was relating, he continued, "It became intolerable, and one day after once again they had made it blatantly clear I was not wanted, I left." He chuckled. "I don't think they were expecting that, but they should have known it would eventually happen."

Dugan did understand. All too well for his own story was eerily similar. "And is that the reason you want to leave in a year? To return and make amends?"

Garrett shook his head. "I reached out a few times at the very beginning, but they ignored my attempts. Later, I had someone contact my mother to see what would happen. Her rejection, if possible, was even more hate-filled than before. She chooses to listen to my brother and all his maneuverings to ensure I stay away. But she did not just prefer him over me. She chose him *instead* of me. I have resolved myself to her only wanting one child. So I will not be returning. Ever." He could see Dugan was skeptical and added, "I wish them no ill will, but I have been told by mutual acquaintances that my absence has not changed anything. They do not miss my company, and I no longer miss theirs."

"Maybe if they knew what you were doing here, if you were settled and had a family and therefore posed no threat to them, that would change things."

Garrett looked at Dugan as if he had lost his mind. "My having a family would only *add* to the reasons I would stay completely away. No child deserves to have that kind of hate in their lives. And that's what they would have because that is all my family knows. They can't help it. It's what happens to someone who chooses to nurture anger. After a while, it is all they know how to give."

Dugan heard Garrett's clipped words and their double meaning about him and Adanel. "Sounds like you are harboring more than a little resentment yourself."

Garrett shrugged. "Not as much as you would think. I've made my peace about what happened and moved on. But when I do leave here, it won't be because I was running away."

Again, the double entendre. "If you have something to say, then say it," Dugan stated crisply.

"I just did," Garrett retorted, unafraid despite seeing Dugan flexing his fist. "Your anger fuels Adanel's and hers drives yours. One of you needs to let go, and it should be you."

"And just *why* should it be me?"

"Because, my friend, you are going to lose her if you don't. And I know the loss of losing someone you love. I had no choice but to walk away, but you do."

Dugan's back straightened. "I don't love Adanel. I might have loved who I thought she was at one time, but even those feelings are gone."

Garrett snorted. "Adanel is *exactly* who you thought she was, and you know deep down along with everyone else that you love her. Even Conor McTiernay's two little girls—what's their names? Brenna? Bonny? Even *they* know you love Adanel. I heard them whispering about it while they were hiding under the tables in the hall during your wedding feast. If those two wee ones can see it, then denying it is senseless."

Dugan's jaw tensed. "Fine," he barked, "but you can love someone and not want to be around them."

Garrett shook his head. "You remind me of my mother. She prefers to hold on to her anger *and* have someone to blame for it."

Unable to sit any longer, Dugan dismounted his horse and began to pace. Problem was he did not know what he felt. Was he angry at Adanel? Aye, but it did not consume him like it once had. What now plagued his thoughts was her only wanting to handfast with him. She wanted nothing permanent. She agreed to their marriage to help legitimize the McTiernay claim to the clan and Bàgh Fìon, and thereby possibly prevent a rebellion and the deaths of many. Her reasoning had been logical, but it had also been like a punch in the stomach. Instinctively, Dugan had proclaimed that he, too, only wanted to handfast. But that had been a lie.

The following week in preparation to leave had been difficult. Their wedding had been manageable as long as he kept his distance. But seeing Adanel as they journeyed back to her home had been akin to torture. His desire for her was not dissipating, but growing. And while he wanted to grab her and share the physical bliss he knew they would have, it was clear Adanel did not feel the same.

She *loathed* him. Her looks of disgust and betrayal this morning had hurt like hell, and as a result, it rekindled the pain she had caused him over the winter. He had reacted without thought and let the pain renew his simmering anger.

Despite what Garrett thought, Dugan did not want to hold on to his anger, but it was the only thing he had to protect what little was left of his pride and tattered heart. It was the armor he needed to distance himself from Adanel.

"What I'm feeling is not like blowing a candle out, where one moment it is there and with a simple action it's gone," Dugan said, in an attempt to provide an explanation without revealing his true emotions. "You want me to trust someone in a way that I cannot. Like you, I've been betrayed by those I loved and who supposedly loved me. And I ask you, how many times does a person need to learn a lesson before they stop repeating their mistakes?"

Garrett sighed. "I don't know the answer, but I do know that Adanel can only take so much, and you, my friend, will lose her long before your handfast is complete."

Dugan closed his eyes. "I should have realized you would take Adanel's side."

"I'm not. She made a mistake. So did you. You both need to decide if you are going to let your mistakes define who you are, or if you are going to let them go and seek the future you really want and go live it." Garrett tightened his grip on the horse's reins. "On this I speak from experience. If you wait too long before realizing that you want the latter with Adanel, it will be too late."

Before Dugan could ask for clarification about what Garrett meant about him speaking from experience, his commander had dug his heels into the side of his mount and sent his animal galloping to join the slow-moving army. It did not matter. He could ask later, but doubted he would get an answer. Dugan had his secrets and Garrett was entitled to his own.

Dugan stood in the empty great hall of Lasairbhàigh Castle. He named Mackbaythe Castle Lasairbhàigh after Adanel's fiery temper and mane, though he doubted anyone including her realized it. He looked around and sighed. The rushes were old, and he suspected the unpleasant odor came from them. The bin for the firewood was empty, and the hearths had not been cleaned in weeks. The tables were in disarray, and some of the chairs and benches had been recently broken in large brawls or their violent equivalent. The room was, in a word, a disaster—just like the docks.

What was not in need of repair was in desperate need of cleaning. The castle staff upon hearing of the takeover by the McTiernays had done little to no work over the past couple of weeks. Several had made their acrimony for the takeover evident by defecating in places, including in his solar and the laird's day chambers.

Dugan was not sure what kind of reaction they intended to rise out of him, but not a thing that was done had been unexpected. It also was not his problem for he had given complete responsibility to restoring the castle to Adanel. It was a daunting task, and he would help as he could but he had too much to do with the docks, the army, and the rest of the clan to adequately oversee the cleanup, repair, and refurbishment of the castle. While a notable burden, Dugan hoped the challenge—and eventual success—would boost Adanel's confidence, proving to her that she was just as capable as the other Lady McTiernays.

"I know it seems like a lot, but I am sure you can do it." His tone was warm and sincere.

Entering Bàgh Fìon, both he and Adanel had made an effort to put their anger aside. Their ride into the port had been cordial, and their dialogue warmed with each exchange. Their efforts to stop pummeling each other and at least act civil was a welcome reprieve from their recent encounters. The McTiernays may have thought a juicy fight was a good way to express strong emotions, but Dugan far preferred the laughter he and Adanel had shared in their private moments last summer.

Adanel stood next to him, wide eyed and with her heart pounding. "I think you overestimate my abilities to inspire people."

"Nay, I do not. Anyone who can make Laurel McTiernay an advocate like you were able to and as fast as you did is not someone who should be underestimated." He meant it, and soon the castle servants would discover the meek young woman who used to hide from this place was gone. In her stead was the Adanel he had met last summer—a woman who was strong, feisty, and incredibly stubborn. It might take her a while to get her footing, but one thing Dugan was sure of was that when Adanel was pressed too far, she would fight back.

"I have no idea where to begin," she said, waving her hand at the obvious food and bones poking through the rushes. "It is obvious no one has any care or pride in their work. They do not want to be here, Dugan, and without willing servants, how will I get this place fit to use again, let alone entertain and welcome guests?"

"You told me that most of your clansmen were good people who wanted to work. Seek out those people to help you."

Adanel shook her head. "I have no idea who has what skills or even who would be willing."

For almost all her life, her role around the castle had been one of obscurity. Adanel never had dealings with those who worked castle duties, and she had no idea how to cultivate those relationships now. They not only did not want her, they did not trust her. In their minds, by marrying a McTiernay, she had sanctioned all the changes being forced upon them. As such, Adanel feared she actually might be the most hated between the two of them.

"So you will make mistakes," Dugan replied with a lighthearted shrug. "I'm sure I will make many myself over the next few months. Just do me a favor and keep Brùid close." Adanel nodded. She would keep the guard near and not just to pacify Dugan. She was not sure how emboldened the staff were, but they would be less likely to try something with Brùid nearby. "With him around no one will physically go after you. Hopefully, none would even if he were not, but I don't want to find out."

Adanel tilted her head to look at him. For a moment, Dugan sounded as if he cared and was worried about her. It warmed her heart, but she told herself not to read too much into it.

"Meanwhile, don't expect me to be around much for the next few weeks. I'll try to make dinner when I can, but there is a lot to be done at the docks."

Adanel's brow creased with concern. "I saw that the port is empty."

Dugan nodded. "Your uncle's clan is blocking the passageway to and from the inner seas, but it doesn't explain why the fishing ships aren't going out in the bay. I've asked Loman to work with Fearan whenever he can. With all that has happened, the port master is probably doing the job of ten people right now and could use any assistance he can get. Meanwhile, my focus is going to be on the docks and just what is going on with the goods in the storage buildings. This mess is nothing in comparison," he said, gesturing to the filthy rushes.

Adanel swallowed. That was *not* good news. She reached out and grabbed Dugan's arm. "Don't trust him."

"Fearan, the port master?" Dugan asked, surprised.

"Nay, he is a good man." Adanel nervously licked her lips. "Don't trust the *dock*master. He was my father's man, and he will work against you, though he will say otherwise. You would be best to just banish him now."

Dugan looked down at Adanel's fingers clutching his forearm and rested his hand on hers. Her scent had been bothering him since they entered the room and not even the stench of rotting food could dampen its effects on him. "I will but not yet." He gave her a slight smile and a wink. "Trust me. I have worked with thieves before. They always reveal their secrets. Usually without even knowing. Once I know his, I'll send him on his way, but not before."

Adanel sighed and reluctantly withdrew her hand. "What about the other two towers?"

Dugan let her step back and fought the compulsion to pull her into his arms and hold her tight. That was the problem with letting go of his anger. It allowed room for other emotions. "Garrett's using them to house the soldiers guarding the port and the castle when they are not on duty."

"How?" Adanel scoffed. "I am sure there is no bedding, and as for food . . . I'm not even sure how to feed you and me."

Dugan laughed. "We're soldiers. A dry room with a fireplace to heat it is a luxury compared to what we have when we are out patrolling the borders exposed to the weather. There'll be no complaints, especially not if they ever want to eat in this room once you have it ready. Until then, they'll eat whatever they hunt. Do not worry, *aithinne.*"

Upon hearing his nickname for her, Adanel could not suppress a frisson of desire going up her spine. She prayed Dugan only thought she was cold and left soon for he was not behaving like the angry man from that morning. He was acting more like her mystery Highlander from last spring—the one she had lost her heart to. With every passing minute, she was in danger of falling back into the trap of believing Dugan felt more for her than antipathy.

"So Brùid is with me, and Garrett is overseeing the new army and the towers. What about Nigel, Tybalt, and Faden?"

Dugan fought back a small smile. Garrett was wrong. He had not lost Adanel. For a moment, her eyes had darkened and sparkled with luminous desire. Adanel still wanted him, and despite everything he wanted her as well. Like him, she was resisting her feelings, something he was not sure he wanted her to do.

"Dugan?" she pressed, realizing his mind had wandered. "Faden and the others? Where are they?"

With a little shake to his head, Dugan rubbed the back of his neck. "Um, they are training with the McTiernay army. Once we have our army formed, they will join them."

Adanel's lashes fluttered in an effort to stop a sudden spurt of tears, which she quickly brushed away. "I just wish they were around. I could use a friendly face."

Unable to resist, Dugan pulled her to his chest and ran his hand up and down her back in a light caress. "Don't worry, Adanel. I'll make sure they have rotations with you regularly. Those three care not that I'm their laird and would hunt me down if I didn't."

He could feel her lips curve into a smile and resisted the urge to kiss the top of her head when she chuckled against his chest. *This* was the way things were supposed to be between them. And for the first time in a long while, Dugan hoped that maybe they could be. "You are safe, Adanel. I know you never felt that way with your father, but you are now. No one will hurt you. That I promise."

A fortnight later, Adanel sat in Kara's inn, slumped in a chair. She let her head fall onto her crossed arms at the end of her friend's dining table. "Is it just me? Or are *all* of them out to get me?" she moaned to Kara. "Running the castle would be difficult enough with well-trained, supportive servants. I sometimes wonder if they are plotting to kill me in my sleep!"

Adanel had expected resistance, not open hostility. And it came from everywhere—the stables, the kitchens, the chambermaids taking care of their rooms, even the swordsmith. Farmers sent their worst food, and no one was willing to sell their goods to anyone where it might benefit Dugan, Adanel, or any of the McTiernay soldiers. After two weeks of enduring bad food, insolence, blatant disrespect, and a growing stench and filth that had to be intentional, Adanel feared that she should start sleeping with a dagger.

Kara tucked a loose strand of her wavy brown hair behind her ear. Her blue eyes looked hesitant, and she bit her bottom lip not knowing what to say. "I had no idea it was so horrible. I mean hardly anyone is upset that your father and brother are gone. Most are troubled about having to become McTiernays, wearing their plaid, and swearing allegiance to Dugan. But I don't think it's about them wanting to remain Mackbaythes. Our clan name has not meant anything honorable in decades, but—"

"—it's the ultimatum they don't like," Adanel said with a sigh. "Dugan expected that and said they would adjust in time. Honest leadership and being able to provide for their families were supposed to help ease the adjustment. But the ones over there"—Adanel waved her hand in the direction of the castle—"have no interest in a position that pays well and helps their families. They just have one goal. To make my and Dugan's lives, as well as the life of any McTiernay they see, absolutely miserable."

Kara pressed her lips together and nodded. "It's too bad your father never had a steward. He would know how to go to the village and hire a completely new staff."

Adanel sighed again and lifted her head, resting her cheek on her hand. "I've thought about it. Believe me I have," she reiterated, seeing the look of doubt on her friend's face. "But I honestly believe only a handful of the staff are involved in the most egregious acts. The rest are just looking the other way when the few that *are* causing the problems hatch their plans. Problem is that I don't know who those few are."

Kara lightly elbowed Adanel's side. "Probably shouldn't have avoided your father's castle all those years. Then you'd know exactly who they are."

"If only I could find out, but it's not like anyone is going to tell me. That's *another* reason why I need you to take charge of Lasairbhàigh's kitchens! You could tell me who is causing problems!"

Kara leaned back and waved her arms back and forth, rejecting the idea. "This little visit has only convinced me that I was right to turn down your offer. Not only am I sure I would be working alone," she stated without any remorse, "I wouldn't have any decent food with which to cook." She picked up the piece of bread Adanel had brought over and banged it on the table.

Adanel frowned at the example of the poor fare that she and Dugan had been served the night before. She had hoped that by showing Kara just what she was facing, her friend might change her mind. "This is actually good. At least it's not rotten. Last night, Dugan picked up a piece of meat and, after smelling it, cautioned me to stick with the bread. Loman came by with some birds later and that's what you see here." She gave a woeful look at her friend, who poked at the dried, overcooked meat in front of her. "And it's not just the food. Most of the chambers have been untouched, and I am almost positive several of the servants are sleeping in a few. And then last night . . ." Adanel moaned and covered her face with her hands.

Kara winced at the sound of her friend's anguish. "Why? What happened last night?"

"Dugan marched all the way to the Village Tower, entered my chambers, and dumped what had to be every piece of clothing he owned on the floor except that of which he was wearing. This morning I was out washing both our garments, which is why I was late today meeting you. Until they dry"—she waved down the front of her bliaut—"this is all I have to wear."

Kara's blue eyes grew round and large. "What you just said brings to mind so many questions I don't know where to begin. How mad was Dugan? What did he say? And he expected *you* to wash his clothes? Does he not understand how wrong that is and that there are severe problems with the servants? And probably my biggest question is just *why* were you in the Village Tower and not with him in Mackbaythe Castle?"

"Lasairbhàigh Castle," Adanel reminded her as she threw her head back onto her arms. Dugan had changed the name upon their arrival right before he announced that Adanel would be overseeing the changes, improvements, and all staffing matters regarding the castle.

"*Tha mi duilich,*" Kara apologized. "Habit! You know how much I like the new name."

Adanel peeked out from her arms and narrowed her gaze as a warning to say no more. One of the first things she had done upon getting back was to visit her friend as they had much to catch up on. Adanel wanted to discuss all that had happened and the McTiernay wives, but Kara had wanted to talk about Dugan. She was far more interested in her sudden marriage, and all that it meant—or in Adanel's mind did not mean. Kara's romantic heart would not be daunted though, and even saw the castle name as a tribute to Adanel and the color of her hair.

"And Dugan was not mad. He was frustrated . . . but

not with me," Adanel insisted. "Actually, since we arrived, he has been unnervingly supportive."

"Unnervingly supportive?" Kara repeated, wondering at the choice of words.

Adanel nodded as she bit her bottom lip. "I'm wondering when he is going to erupt again, and yet Dugan told me that the castle was my responsibility and when problems occurred, as he expected them to, that I should handle them however I wanted. And despite all the many, *many* problems I've had the past few days, he has not said a word. He just repeats that I should work through the issues as I think best. Last night was not a condemnation . . . it was more like a plea. Dugan just asked if there was something I could do to help out when it came to the laundry until I had the castle under control."

"I must admit to being . . . well, shocked," Kara said, blinking, and then rose to her feet to stir the stew she had been preparing for her and Fearan's supper. When done, she turned back around and with her hands on her hips, said, "So, then answer my last question. Why are you not sleeping together? You are married, are you not?"

"Handfasted," Adanel clarified once again. "And until a few days ago, we could barely stand each other's company."

"So, you are telling me that it's been almost a month and you have not yet consummated your marriage? I mean last year, the way you spoke, you could barely keep your hands off each other."

"I think it's best if I just stay in the Village Tower for now. I'm not even sure Dugan is sleeping in the castle most nights anyway."

Kara threw up her hands in exasperation. "You went

through all the effort to trap him in marriage and now that you are married, you act like it's not what you want!"

Adanel grimaced. She loved that Kara could be direct, but at times—like now—she did not appreciate her candid disposition. "I did not try to *trap* him, Kara. I would never do that. And being married was something neither of us wanted."

"Laird McTiernay forced the two of you to make promises?"

"Not exactly. I agreed, so did Dugan. But what choice did we have? It was the only way I could come home, and this was Dugan's one opportunity to become laird."

Kara waved her hand in a dismissive gesture. "I know how to spot a marriage *trap* when I see one. Without women using them, the human race would have died out long ago. Remember my little plot to get Fearan's attention? If I had waited on him to admit his feelings for me, I would have had gray hair and wrinkled skin before our first kiss." She leaned forward on the table and stared at Adanel. "Now look me in the eye and tell me you had no hand at all in what happened. That this handfast was someone else's idea and that you just agreed to it."

Adanel refused to even glance in Kara's direction. For Kara, that was enough. She slapped the table. "I knew it!"

Adanel refused to admit to *trapping* Dugan. In a way, Laurel and Conor had trapped both of them. Adanel had no idea what Dugan was told or learned, but Laurel McTiernay had not been quiet with her grand scheme or the reasons behind it. She firmly believed Dugan and Adanel were in love and just needed some time to work things out. Until the last couple of days, Adanel thought Laurel completely insane for not recognizing that some angers did not fade with time. But when Dugan had held her in his arms in the great hall, she had prayed for Laurel to be right.

Then Dugan had disappeared, and aside from two very poorly cooked dinners in a great hall whose only improvement was the removal of rotten rushes and his appearance last night with a handful of his very dirty clothes, she had not seen him. Even those three encounters had been brief, with little conversation. Adanel wanted to blame exhaustion, for she could see that, like her, Dugan had been getting little sleep, but that was not why she had been quiet. Fear was her reason. Fear that if he were kind, nice, or even funny—the qualities that had endeared him to her—she would begin to fall for him again, and worse, that he would see it.

Adanel finally looked Kara in the eye and stated, "It was not *my* trap. It was Laurel McTiernay's. Seems she is a hopeless romantic like you."

Kara's brows shot up. "Becoming a McTiernay is looking to be more promising than I thought."

"*Her* plan was to give us time. *My* plan was to return home and help my people."

Kara returned to her seat, sat down, and crossed her arms. "I'll remind you that we've known each other our entire lives, and while for the most part you are a sweet and kind soul, you are not weak. However, you've played that role so much over the past few years you have forgotten that is not who you really are. You may not like to cause trouble, Adanel, but when it smacks you in the face, you fight back. If you had not wanted to marry Dugan, nothing could have made you do so. Or do I need to remind you about how you pretended to be pregnant for eight months and were planning to fake your own death—all just to get out of a marriage you did not want!

The only conclusion I can make is that you married Dugan because you wanted him. You *love* him, Adanel."

"How can you say that?" Adanel asked hotly, pushing away from the table so she could stand and pace. "You know what Dugan said . . . did . . . or *didn't* do. I'm just grateful we are being civil to each other after all that has happened."

"And yet you still love him."

Adanel opened her mouth to deny the accusation and then clapped her mouth shut, knowing she could not lie. Not about this and not to her best friend. "Even if you are right, it does not matter for Dugan does not feel the same about me."

Kara leaned forward. Her blue eyes had lost their levity and had become cold and serious. "The day you returned, I listened to all that you told me. Every argument, every harsh word you two shared. I listened to you recall what those lairds said to you and even what this Laurel McTiernay asked you about afterward. I heard and I hurt for you, knowing that you suffered. But now I need you to listen to me. Dugan McTiernay is not here to be laird. Aye, he is determined to do the job and do it well, but *that is not why he is here.* He is here because you are. That man loves you."

Adanel sank back down into her chair. "Then why doesn't he say so? Why does he act just the opposite?" she posed, ignoring the memory of him holding her close and giving her encouragement. *Kindness is not love,* she told herself.

"He, well . . ." Kara paused and shook her head. "He . . . just doesn't want to. My guess is it's the same reason you won't tell him your feelings. He's afraid that after all that has happened you will never love him back. One of you needs to allow yourself to become vulnerable and I think that is going to have to be you."

Adanel jumped up once again and threw her hands in the air. "Me?" she asked through gritted teeth. "Why is it always up to the woman?" She glared at Kara. "Seriously? I'm asking *why is it up to us* to get a man to admit he is in love? Look at what you had to do. Why do we have to put our hearts out there to be trampled on when men, who are so big and strong, are too afraid to even admit to simple interest?"

Kara rolled her eyes. "That question has been asked by women since the days of the Garden of Eden. There is no answer, but I'll tell you what I figured out last year with Fearan. Those women who demand the man to become vulnerable first end up lonely. I decided I'd rather be happy and in love."

"I cannot do it, Kara," Adanel said, shaking her head. "I cannot just walk up to Dugan and admit that I love him. I have no idea what he would do, but I cannot imagine a single scenario that ends up with us happy in the end."

Kara shook her head. "Even *I* didn't do that," she chided. "God, if I had, Fearan probably would have run out the door, and I would have never seen him again. Men can only handle so much emotional honesty at the very beginning. What you need is to lure Dugan in."

"Lure him in?"

Kara nodded. "Change the pattern. You were in one where you fought all the time, which can only be sustained for so long. Unfortunately, this cordial one you are in now can last forever. Mine lasted twelve years, and you two don't have that long." Kara tapped her finger against her chin. "With Fearan, he needed to feel wanted and I wanted to feel needed, which is why my sham of an unwanted suitor setup worked so well. It allowed Fearan to come in and play the hero and I loved it. Didn't matter if it was not real, it *could* have been. That's what

Fearan realized. So"—she paused and looked at Adanel—
"just what does Dugan want from you?"

Adanel blinked. Kara's logic sometimes was twisted,
but somehow, it usually worked out. Today, however,
Adanel was not so certain. "He wants to be able to trust
me," she finally confessed. "And that is not something I
can just give him."

Kara tilted her head and gave a little shrug. "Maybe
he is already trying to. I mean he *did* put you in charge
of the castle."

"And I'm failing."

Kara rolled her eyes. "You know what you have to do.
You just haven't been willing to do it."

"I honestly don't think a clean castle, good food, and
helpful servants are going to make Dugan trust me."

"Not saying it would. I'm saying that it means he *wants*
to trust you. And the way to get someone to trust you is
to trust them first."

Adanel pursed her lips and was about to ask how when
the door burst open and Fearan walked in grumbling
about his day. "Not even Mackbaythe undermined me
the way this new laird is doing, Kara. Damn man is going
to learn that he is not—"

His eyes landed on Adanel, and he stopped midsentence. Fearan glanced at his wife, who stood with an exasperated expression and then pointed at her friend.
"Oh, uh, *tha mi duilich.*" He offered his apology with
sincere embarrassment. "You know none of what I was
saying was meant for you."

Fearan did not like Dugan McTiernay, but he did not
want Adanel to feel like she was no longer welcome because she had married the man. When she gave him a
smile and rose to let him sit down, he knew all was well.

"Bad day, love?" Kara asked.

Fearan took in a deep breath and then let it go. "Aye. And tomorrow will be worse. The new laird just ordered a third of those who worked on the docks to be escorted off his lands—including the dockmaster. And if he thinks of loading all those duties onto my shoulders, he needs to think again," he grumbled again, forgetting about Adanel.

"Were they dishonest men?" Kara asked, as she went to get a bowl for his dinner.

Fearan nodded. "Every single last one of them would have stabbed him in the back given the chance." He reached over and grabbed a mug and poured himself some ale.

"Then isn't their banishment a good thing?"

"Aye, if done humanely. But a couple fought back, and they are now dead." Fearan looked at Adanel and uncurled one finger around the mug and used it to point at her. "Your father took delight in killing men and it sickened me, but I tell you nothing he ever did was as scary as what I saw your husband do today. That man killed with no emotion whatsoever." Fearan shivered. "It shook my core then and does even now, thinking about it. I honestly think he would have ended the life of every single one of those men if they had fought back and never lose a wink of sleep. You're married to a cold one, Adanel. Cold and heartless." He took a deep gulp. "If he's smart, he'll stay far away from me. I'm not one to be trifled with. You tell him I said that."

Adanel stared at Fearan for several long seconds. "I will," she replied but disagreed wholeheartedly at Fearan's assessment. To take joy in death like her father had was far worse than unemotionally ending one. The cold death of the two men probably saved lives for Adanel suspected any more corrupt men would rather be banished than resisting and dead. She gave Kara a quick hug. "Do me a favor and swing by the castle tomorrow. I've decided to shake things up and could use your help."

Kara pulled back and with a skeptical look, asked, "How?"

Adanel glanced over her shoulder and smiled at Fearan. "I think I'm going to take a lesson from my husband. Emotions kept me from doing what I needed. Starting tomorrow that ends." Leaning in so that she could whisper in Kara's ear, she added, "Tonight I'm going to start earning back my husband's trust."

Chapter Twelve

"Come in."

Dugan paused to take a deep breath, staring at the closed door. He glanced once more down the winding stairwell though he knew Brùid was outside the tower standing guard to ensure they had privacy. Never before had he been so nervous to meet a woman—and this one was his wife! At least she was in all ways but the most important one. But based on the message he just received, that was about to change.

He had been on his way back to the castle when Nigel had found him with a message from Kara. *Adanel wants to see you. Tonight. In her chambers in the Village Tower. Alone.*

Unfortunately, the messenger had been Nigel, and there was no telling if he had been adding in the suggestive breaks or not, but he swore that the message was accurate and verbatim. And even if Dugan ignored Nigel's dramatic inflections, the message's meaning was clear. Adanel was ready to make their marriage a real one.

A week ago, Dugan would have outright rejected the offer, but it was not just the long days that was making him tired. It was sleepless nights thinking of her. He wondered if Adanel was well, safe, how her day was, and a myriad of other things, including if she ever thought about him. He longed for her touch and, after the short embrace they had shared in the great hall, it had been all he could do to leave and not claim her as his body had demanded.

Though they had only seen each other a few times since then, that day had sparked a change between them. He once again found himself enjoying her company and hating the times they were apart. Each time he saw her, especially alone, he was one step closer to caving to his primal desires, uncaring of the consequences. Adanel was his addiction and always would be. Regardless of all that transpired between them, she was the one for him, and there would never be anyone else.

Dugan had thought his desires had been one-sided. Then came this cryptic message and his mind—and body—had been reeling in anticipation for this moment.

"Did you hear me?" Adanel asked with a smile, seeing that she startled him by opening the door. "Come on in."

She waved her arm and Dugan entered woodenly as he saw the dinner for two on the small table. He was not sure what he expected, but he'd visited enough women who were trying to woo him into bed to immediately recognize that was not Adanel's intentions. "I received a message you wanted to see me here? Alone?"

Adanel nodded and gestured for him to sit down. "I hope you are hungry. Kara made this, so trust me when I say it is delicious. She could even challenge Fiona as being the best castle cook if she would only agree to work for me."

Dugan raised a brow but sat down. "She won't? I thought of all people, your best friend would support you."

Adanel poured him some wine and then some in a mug for herself. "She and Fearan only recently married, and she wants to spend her time being a wife and hopefully someday soon a mother. Being a castle cook is hard work and leaves little room for anything else."

Adanel sat down and closed her eyes as she took a bite. Her face was one of pure pleasure. "Ah, Kara, you do know how to cook," Adanel moaned.

Dugan followed her and found himself moaning in agreement. "This *is* good. You need to try harder. We would be the envy of all who visited if they had a bite of this."

Adanel grinned and nodded. "That's an idea. Maybe Kara would come help when we had visitors."

"Is that what you wanted to see me about? Kara? Cooks?"

"In a way, but first, I heard you finally made a move at the docks. Fearan said that nearly a third of those that work the docks have been banished. He also said that two did not make it."

"I doubt that is what he really said." Dugan paused and swallowed some wine. "The man looked positively green when I gutted those two bastards even though they had lunged for me first and I gave them two chances to desist before I ended their misery."

Adanel bit her bottom lip. "Fearan is not a fan of bloodshed, which is kind of a miracle with all the deaths that have surrounded this place for years."

"Well, I don't like unnecessary bloodshed either, but when it is my life or that of another at stake, blood is going to be spilled and I make no apologies for it."

"Nor should you," Adanel agreed. "I just thought you said you were going to wait until you learned all the dockmaster's secrets. When you said that, I thought it would take several weeks."

Dugan scowled and then took another bite, which quickly erased the frustrated look into one of bliss. "*Mo chreach*, this is good. And you were right. I did think to wait longer, but no one has any secrets to tell. At least none that I am interested in. Their only goal was to cause mayhem without thought to themselves or those around them."

"Fearan did say that the ones you exiled were all corrupt."

"Not all of them, but the ones who weren't were weak-willed and afraid to go against those they felt had the power. Their loyalty would always be in question. Maybe in the future, wherever they end up, they'll have gained a little mettle."

"What are you going to do now?"

Dugan leaned back and turned the mug back and forth in his hand. "The docks were overstaffed. We'll eventually need more men once ships start coming in again, but I don't expect recruiting will be a problem. Most of the ones removed were lazy, late to arrive, and early to leave. Those who remain will have to work hard to make up for the smaller numbers, but they will be paid significantly better." He pointed at her with a knowing smile. "That will get the attention of others. But none of that will mean anything with the port blocked and Fearan trying to undermine me at every opportunity. Right now, his antics are playing to my favor, but the day they do not, your friend Fearan and I are going to have a talk. He thinks he has power, and in a way, he is correct, but he's also never served under a real laird. Soon, he is going to learn just what that means."

Adanel's eyes grew wide. This afternoon, she had heard Fearan's frustration, and it was obviously not one-sided. "What is he doing?"

"To get to Bàgh Fìon from the inner seas, ships pass through Loch Torridon, then Loch Shieldaig, and finally Upper Loch Torridon, where our port is on the eastern end. Being able to move so far inland by ship is what makes this port so valuable—that and its deep waters right to the shoreline allow even large ships to dock and not have to ferry their goods."

None of this was new information to Adanel, but she wanted Dugan to keep talking so she just nodded.

"The MacLeods have at least three ships blocking the narrow pass between Loch Shieldaig and the Upper Loch. So shipping and receiving goods via the port is not going to happen until I speak with MacLeod."

Adanel had never met her grandfather, and after he abandoned his youngest son and refused to give her safe harbor when asked, she was not sure she wanted to. "When are you going to talk to him?"

Dugan gave her a small, reassuring smile. "Not anytime soon, in case you are worried about having the castle ready. I won't meet with him until I have something to negotiate with—besides my leaving and letting him take over the port."

"You think that is what he wants?"

"He sent a herald, who was waiting for us when we arrived. Your grandfather made it clear that until I relinquished the port, he had enough ships to have at least two or three blocking our port indefinitely. He also sent a message to your uncle telling him not to plan on returning unless he could make the McTiernays see reason. Didn't Faden tell you?"

Adanel shook her head, but hearing that Faden had heard from his father did explain her uncle's recent surly attitude. With Brùid now as her guard, Faden spent most of his time with Garrett training and recruiting soldiers. Last time they spoke, her uncle had assured her that right now sparring was the best way for him to spend his time. Now she knew why.

"Do you think Laird MacLeod might attack?"

Dugan shook his head. "MacLeod might rule the seas,

but he'd be slaughtered if he tried to attack us via land. Not even Daeron MacCoinnich would be naive enough to make such a bold move. Nay, MacLeod knows that we need the port active and that time is not our friend. But I know something he doesn't expect I do," Dugan ended with a smile.

Adanel leaned forward, her brown eyes wide with interest. "What?"

"That your father had something over the *blaigeard,* and once I learn what that is, MacLeod will be a problem no more. I just need to figure out what it was. First, though, I need to knock some sense into my port master."

Adanel sat up. She had forgotten her original question. "What exactly is Fearan doing?"

Dugan stabbed his fork into a potato and popped it into his mouth. "Your friend Kara may be the best cook in the Torridon mountains, but she's married to a *toll-tòine,*" he finally said.

Adanel leaned back in her chair, stunned. People who worked the docks loved Fearan and to hear Dugan think otherwise shocked her. "Fearan?" she asked, still not quite sure why Dugan thought so little of the man.

"Aye," Dugan affirmed. "The port may be deep enough to allow a ship to come to the shore, but that doesn't mean you can get to the dock from just any direction in the bay. You have to know how to navigate the deeper part of the waterway and that man has not shared his knowledge of the channel with anyone—ever. He is holding the damn information hostage, uncaring of whom he hurts just to make a point that he is important. Unfortunately for him, Conor appointed the one McTiernay who knows quite a bit about ports and channels. So if Fearan wants to have a battle of wills, he is going to have it, and he is going to lose. You may have come home only to lose your best friend after all. For if

Fearan doesn't start cooperating soon, Kara is going to be living somewhere else, for they sure as hell won't be welcome here."

Adanel stopped midbite and slowly let her fork down. "I don't understand," she murmured, realizing just how bad things were going to get. Based on what she had heard from Fearan earlier, he was not going to back down. Kara might think her man was shy, but he also had a streak of pride that ran a mile deep, and it was about to be tested in a way it never had before. Dugan was not her father, and it seemed Fearan's knowledge of the port did not hold the same leverage it had in the past. "Fearan has been running the ports for years without any issues."

"*That's* the problem. He's no longer running the ports! He refuses to support the safe docking of a single ship—including the larger fishing trawlers that bring in food for the clan."

Adanel had not known that. The fishing boats would be unaffected by the MacLeod blockade as they usually just went out in the bay. Many of the families did have someone to go hunt a few times a week, but fish was the primary diet for most of their clansmen. "If that's true, soon there is going to be a problem. Most of what we eat comes from the sea. If people grow hungry, they will blame you."

Dugan sat back and crossed his arms. "Which is exactly what Fearan wants to happen."

Adanel rose to her feet and went to go stand by the window. She looked out and could see the inn in the distance. Somewhere inside were Fearan and Kara, unaware that their future was in jeopardy.

"But why?" she finally asked, turning around. Her face had morphed from bewilderment into one of indignation. "Just *why* would Fearan do that? Doesn't he realize what will happen? That the *clan* will be injured and the only person who *won't* lose will be you?"

A sudden desire to pull her into his lap almost overtook him. Seeing Adanel angry on his behalf made his whole body tighten with need. Rising to his feet, Dugan went to stand next to her. "I have no idea why. I've been focused on the docks and getting a handle on what goods we have to ship. The buildings were looted pretty badly before our arrival, but Garrett helped me with a few unannounced raids, and we were able to secure much of what was taken."

Adanel reached out and grasped his arm. "So there are no issues with the army?"

Dugan briefly closed his eyes, thinking the torment of her lies were nothing compared to the torment of her touch.

Shifting, he broke her light hold and went to go throw a couple of logs onto the fire. He needed something to keep his hands busy or he needed to leave, which would have been the smarter of the two choices. But he had yet to discover why Adanel had wanted him to come and visit her tonight, and in truth, he was not ready to leave her company. It was surprisingly cathartic to talk to her about Fearan and have her not automatically take the port master's side, which he had thought she would do.

"Outside of not a soul knowing anything about fighting or using a weapon, the army has been the least of my worries." When they had ridden up to the port, he, Garrett, and Loman had surrounded Adanel in preparation for an assault. To their surprise, they had not been attacked, but welcomed.

Most of the soldiers serving under Laird Mackbaythe disliked him intensely and hated what he had forced them to do. Those who had local families or businesses joined only to receive necessary protection, but it was at a great personal expense for they had been miserable.

The true power behind Mackbaythe's army was the mercenaries Adanel's father had hired—all of whom with the exception of Garrett—had left the moment word came of Mackbaythe's death. Their absence left those in the army wondering what was to come.

Unlike their fellow clansmen who had felt the brunt of their laird's apathy to their well-being, most of the soldiers had witnessed firsthand Laird Mackbaythe's abhorrent cruelty and the enjoyment he derived from others' pain. Hearing that he had died and that the clan was being taken over, the soldiers had rejoiced. In their mind, the McTiernays offered a chance at true prosperity, and with Dugan as laird, the respect they never had as soldiers would be theirs. Everyone knew McTiernay soldiers were esteemed by every clan in the Highlands. The men were not only eager to train and learn, their attitude was infectious, making recruiting something unexpectedly far easier than Garrett or Dugan had anticipated.

"Training for most of them is hard. Most McTiernays begin at the age of sixteen or even younger to practice basic maneuvers so they have rudimentary skills when they join the army, even as a first year. Most here lack even fundamental skills, but they are willing to learn and they are much better at listening than young boys. We just need to be patient. Skill comes with practice and time."

The latter of which we do not have, Adanel thought to herself. Much could be accomplished in a year, but to have an army skilled enough to defend itself against MacCoinnich when Loman and the loaned soldiers returned back home? No one could accomplish that. Not even Conor McTiernay himself.

Dugan finished stoking the fire and placed the poker next to the hearth. He looked around her chambers. "I wouldn't have thought you would want to return here."

Suddenly nervous, Adanel brushed her palms on the sides of her bliaut. Almost all of their safe topics had been covered. "I didn't think so either, but before it was my prison. Now it is my safe refuge."

Dugan bobbed his head in understanding. "Right now, maybe it's best you stay here until the keep gets cleaned. When it is, you will be eager to live in the castle. The furnishings in the rooms are a luxury I'm surprised a clan this small can afford."

"As I only recently discovered," Adanel huffed with disgust, thinking of how her father must have gotten the money. "But I do plan on moving my chambers to the keep once I can prepare rooms. Here"—she looked up and carefully chose her words—"there's just a lot of people coming and going that I don't know. Brùid is big, but he is only one man."

Dugan frowned at the implication. "Are you saying Garrett has men sleeping *here*," he said, pointing to the floors below them, "while you are staying in the tower?"

Puzzled, Adanel said, "Aye. I'd say at least two dozen men. And I know as soon as I leave he plans on using this floor as well so he can use the bottom floor to store weapons."

"Has anyone bothered you?" Dugan demanded, his tone suddenly chilly.

Dugan had led soldiers for many years and was not naive to their ways. When they were off duty, they liked to drink. Many just passed out, but some got belligerent and others became overly vocal. He fit the latter category and in an inebriated state had a couple of times revealed his whole life story to Cole. It was how Cole knew about his history running a port, and also how

Cole knew that he had at one time been enamored with his wife, Ellenor.

Thinking about it now, Dugan wondered why Cole had not nailed him across the jaw and sent him packing. If one of his commanders—especially Loman—said similar things to him about Adanel, Dugan was not sure he would be so understanding.

"Maybe I should tell Garrett to keep the tower clear until you get the castle ready."

Adanel clasped her hands in front of her. "That's what I wanted to talk to you about."

Dugan's brow furrowed. "Clearing the tower or getting the castle ready?" Seeing her reaction to the latter, he asked, "Did something happen?"

Adanel threw her hands up in the air in mock resignation. "That's the problem. *Nothing* is happening." She began to pace in the small area. "If I'm lucky, my requests only get ignored. Most of the time, if I ask something to be done, like cleaning your solar so that you have a decent place to sleep, I come back and the situation is even worse than how I left it. I've tried being firm. I've tried being nice and everything in between. I've even tried ignoring the insult so whoever did it would not get the satisfaction of knowing how much it bothers me."

Dugan reached out and caught her hand just before she spun around to walk back to the bed. "So what have you decided?"

Adanel blinked. "Decided?" she murmured, having no idea what he was asking.

Her focus was on the soft touch of his thumb as it caressed her wrist. She looked up and the intense heat of his gaze burned her up from the inside out. His face was calm, his body relaxed, but his eyes . . . they were burrowing into her soul saying, *I know you. I know you as no one ever has. I want you. I will have you.*

"Did you make a decision on what you want to do? Or do you need my help?"

"Oh, um, a little of both," Adanel answered as she reminded herself to breathe. That deep attraction they had felt upon first meeting, their instant connection for reasons that could not be explained, definitely still existed. It was almost as if she needed to touch him and be touched by him, like she needed air or water. Something primitive and utterly feminine deep inside her was coming to life and the idea of asking for his help as a first step toward rebuilding his trust was suddenly overwhelming.

Adanel sucked in a quivering breath and took several necessary steps back. She needed to explain her plan and ask for his help. To do that, she needed to think. Instinctively she waved her finger, gesturing for him to remain where he was. "I . . . um . . . aye, I need your help."

"You said that."

"Well, stop looking at me that way and maybe I can tell you why!"

"What way?" Dugan pressed, though he knew already. He was like a wild animal scenting a female in heat, and it took all his concentration to control his basic urges. If she had not moved back, she would be in his arms right now. That may not have been the reason why she called him to meet her here, but it was the reason he had come and the reason he had stayed. The memory of what it felt like to hold her, be with her . . . he was getting hard just thinking about it. Being with Adanel was a pleasure unlike anything he had ever known. He wanted to experience it again . . . and again and again.

Adanel stared into Dugan's blue eyes. There was no mistaking their dark look. Her every nerve ending was responding to their unspoken message. Desperately

Adanel tried to focus on something besides his eyes and wound up staring at his chest. Once again, she momentarily lost composure. Spinning on her heel, she walked to the window and looked outside, praying she could force herself to maintain a respectable distance from him. "What you did today, with the dock workers . . . I think I want to do something similar with the castle staff."

"Bold step. But are you sure you want to banish them? Higher wages will keep men wanting work at the docks, but removal might not achieve what you hope in your case."

"I'm not talking about banishing them, but I am talking about dismissing all of them. No one thinks I will do it because they know that I need staff to help me with the castle just as much as they need their positions." Adanel glanced back over her shoulder and, seeing Dugan still safely across the room, she turned back around. "That would change if they saw someone else doing their responsibilities in their place."

"You want to use the soldiers." Dugan whistled, knowing how much the idea would be disliked. At the moment though, he did not really care. With each look Adanel sent him, he could see her desire and almost taste her on his tongue—hot, wet, and woman sweet. It was taking everything he had to keep from agreeing to whatever she wanted and then charging across the room, ceasing all their talk.

Adanel nodded, trying to look unaffected by the heat of Dugan's gaze. But a few feet of separation were doing nothing to stop her awareness of him. "I need just enough to remove all castle staff as well as those working in any building or nearby jobs connected to the castle and to keep them out. Then with six more to work directly with me I'll be able to make my point. There are three in particular I hope to borrow for I realized on the journey here, they are remarkably good cooks. The kitchens are not dangerous nor are they heroic; however, if people saw that I could get replacements for one of the hardest jobs in the castle, they would realize everyone is vulnerable."

Dugan closed his eyes and forced himself to think through what she was proposing and not on how her rapid breathing was causing her chest to rise and fall. "Might work. What do you need the other three for?"

"One to help me assess the castle and what needs to be repaired first, and the other two just need to be hard workers, regardless of the task given. Until I've gone through each room, I'm hoping your men can prevent anyone from coming near unless you or I approve."

"This is going to take how many days?"

Adanel winced, unaware she had stepped closer to Dugan. "Most likely a few, which is why I needed the guard to keep anyone from returning."

That last bit hinted at the true nature of her plan. "And where are these dismissed servants going to sleep? Don't most of them stay in the castle? I know the blacksmith and the baker live there. When they lose access, won't that mean they lose access to their home? Their beds?"

Adanel's face lit up, and she took another step forward. "That is *exactly* what I'm hoping they realize. As far as places for them to stay and sleep, it is summertime. Soldiers sleep outside all the time. I did it for a week on the way here and survived. They will too, and as far as food?" Her eyes narrowed, and her lips twisted into a cynical smile. "We have yet to be served even one decent, edible meal. They left us to fend for ourselves. It's their turn."

Dugan reached up and tucked a lock of her red hair behind her ear. "I knew you would find a way, Adanel," he said softly, deliberately using his own desire to ignite hers.

Hearing him whisper her name chilled her to the marrow, disabling her ability to retreat. The scorching heat arcing between them was almost palpable and yet she remained frozen, unable to move, even if she wanted to do so. If Dugan touched her in any way she was doomed. Her whole being was already committed. It had been since the first moment she had seen him a year ago.

"Adanel . . ." Her name was a soft growl of swiftly mounting desire as Dugan's hand slid underneath her hair and curled around her neck. His need for her was all-consuming, and she had only seconds to stop an embrace that would not end with a simple kiss.

Adanel caught her breath at the relentless, deep need that etched his mouth and filled the blue pools of his eyes. Dugan was no longer the playful, skilled lover from last spring intended upon seduction and mutual pleasure. He looked at her as if she was his only need, his only desire—his entire world. Looking at him now, she realized Laurel McTiernay had been right. Dugan was just as consumed by her as she was by him, even if he refused to admit it.

"Dugan," she whispered.

His thumb played on her lower lip, halting whatever she was going to say. The caress was soft and teasing. "Inside and out, you are more beautiful than any female I have ever seen. Every time I hear your voice, see you, talk to you, I want to take you into my arms. *Murt*, all I have to do is think about you and I need to feel you, be with you."

Unable to delay another moment, he leaned down and brushed his mouth lightly across hers, urging her to comply. When he heard her soft whimper from deep in her throat, the sensual sound pushed reason aside. His other hand came up to cradle her face, and he drank hungrily from her lips as if she were a drink of the sweetest water and he was a man dying of thirst.

Adanel's hands went to his shoulders and responded in kind. Feeling his tongue sweep across her lower lip, she wrapped her arms around him and opened up to him, moaning as he deepened the kiss.

She had kissed Dugan many times, in many ways. Hungry and demanding; long, soft lingering embraces that seemed to last for hours; hot, all-consuming kisses that drove all thought away but need and desire—but he'd never kissed her like this. Adanel did not even know she could be kissed like this. It both drained her and at the same time refilled her with a love for him that had not diminished at all despite all the pain, the arguments, and the distance.

Blood roared, wild and hot, through Dugan's veins. Balanced on the dangerous edge between joy and agony, one hand palmed her buttocks while the other tunneled into the thick waves of her rich auburn hair. Could he really have forgotten so thoroughly how wonderful it felt to have her in his arms?

Moving, he slowly walked Adanel back until her knees hit the bed. His hands were on a mission. One undid the laces of her bliaut, and the other traced her spine from her slender neck down to her hips until the last of her clothes had fallen to the floor. A gentle shove had her gasping as she fell back. In seconds, he removed his belt and plaid, and then tore his own léine off, the last bit of hindrance separating them. Then he was on her, basking in the feel of her soft naked skin against his own. It was almost more than he could bear.

He wanted to go slow, to savor their reunion, but the moment she stroked his lower back with her fingertips, his willpower shattered. Propping his upper body on his elbows, his mouth once more came down on hers. He invaded, pillaged, ravished her lips, and Adanel returned it all.

She couldn't think if she wanted to. She could only feel the power of her desire pulling at her, stroking and demanding. She fisted her hands in his hair not willing to let him go for a second, terrified she was reopening herself up to him and yet exhilarated at the same time.

Dugan shuddered in response. While his lips embraced hers, his hand caressed her bosom. Kneading her breast, he brushed his thumb across her nipple and found desire had already hardened it into a taut nub. His heart pounded,

He lowered his mouth to her breast and latched on to a pink bud, sucking it deep into his mouth.

"Dugan!" Adanel gripped his biceps, but he ignored her. He was totally focused on the feast before him. His memory had failed him these past few months for he had forgotten how beautiful she was, how soft. Her body was the perfect refuge from the hardships of his life.

Adanel ran her fingers up his arms, sinking them into his hair and pulling him closer. With a pop, he released her nipple and roamed the valley between her breasts until his mouth found her other one. Her groan had him suckling even harder.

Adanel writhed with pleasure, arching her back so that he took more of her in his mouth, relishing the feel of being with him once more. There could never be another. Dugan had spoiled her for anyone else and if she could not be with him, then she would rather be alone.

Adanel could not take anymore. It wasn't enough. She wanted more. If he did not make love to her soon, she would die. "Dugan," she moaned. "Please."

She reached down to touch him, but he caught her hand. "Not yet," he said. "It's still my turn." Then his lips returned to her skin and began to trace a sensuous path to where he would bring her to ecstasy over and over again.

Gripping her thighs, he pushed them apart and settled between them. Her unique scent called to him as his thumbs gently parted her curls. She was plump, pink, and already glistening.

Lowering his head, he tasted her and nearly lost his mind. She was as sweet as honey and as intoxicating as fine wine. Separating her lips, he continued his exploration until he found her berry and latched on to it. Adanel tried to raise her hips, but he wouldn't let her move and held them down as his mouth and tongue lathed the moist heat he had created in her.

"Oh, God, Dugan!" Adanel moaned, her head flipping back and forth. She shuddered again and again as he tasted the heart of her. It had been so long since she had felt like this, and he was only getting started.

One of his hands moved from her hips down to her thigh and began the slow torturous way back up, driving her to the brink of losing control. Then he slipped a finger into her. Her hips bucked, and he added another. Growling, Dugan kept his restraining arm across her hips never breaking off his attack.

Then he felt her first ripple of pleasure as white heat flooded his mouth. She clutched him, her nails digging into his scalp, and she let go a small cry. Instead of letting go, Dugan cupped her hips and lifted her tighter against his mouth, refusing to let the waves of pleasure fade despite her cries and weak struggles.

"Please . . . Dugan . . ." Adanel gasped, only to cry out again in denial when he released her to crawl back up her body.

Dugan's hands shook. Hell, his whole body shook and he had not yet been inside her. He was not sure if he was going to survive their coming together, but he no longer cared.

Knowing his control was about to vanish, he pulled her under him and moved so that he was aligned with the core of her body. She was more than ready for him and he plunged deep inside her, finding bliss in surrounding heat. For a second, he could not move. Adanel shifted a little beneath him. The glide of her silken skin against him nearly ended the matter right then and there. He lifted her hips and thrust into her once again with another powerful surge, sinking into the snug, tight channel of her body.

She cried out in ecstasy, and Dugan pulled back and dove into her again. Adanel dug her nails into his back, and he pressed his face into the curve of her neck, moving harder and faster with each thrust. Her legs wrapped around him, spreading herself wide to bring him further. Then she locked her ankles behind his back to keep him there.

His pace was brutal, the desire unrestrained, but Adanel rode each thrust, hardly aware of the passionate moans she was making. Her own desire was just as unrestrained and wildly erotic. Her body had taken control and had joined his rhythm, making his movements more rapacious. He drove into her again and again, with a fevered urgency, which left him reeling.

Feeling her release approaching, Adanel pulled Dugan's head up. Her tongue mated with his just as her body suddenly splintered.

Dugan held her at the peak, riding the crest until her cries and the heated velvet of her body surrounding his drove him right over the precipice. With his head thrown back, he roared his climax. His eyes tightly shut, a raw shudder tore at him and he could do nothing but pour himself into her.

When sanity returned, Dugan found himself still on top of Adanel, pressing her into the bed. Easing away, he caressed her cheek and found it wet with tears. "*Aithinne*, what . . ."

Her fingers on his lips silenced him. Curling into his side, she laid her head over his heart.

They lay like that, basking in each other's arms, for a long while. Dugan knew they needed to talk about what happened and what it meant, but he was not sure the answer to that himself. Ignoring their past was not the solution for it would only return in a way and at a time that would resurrect all their doubt and pain with it. For them to truly move forward, they needed to talk, but the right words refused to come to mind.

They had made love, and it had been tumultuous and explosive. Their past had done nothing to dampen their desire for each other, but carnal need was one thing. Emotional commitment was another and he was not ready to vocally commit to the latter until after they spoke. Falling in love with Adanel had nearly destroyed him once, and he was not going to make such a leap until he was absolutely certain he could trust her with his heart.

He was wondering if Adanel's thoughts were similar in nature when she suddenly sprang up onto one elbow and looked down at Dugan. Her eyes were sparkling. God, he missed how beautiful they were when she was happy. "I have a *great* idea concerning the docks."

His brows popped up in surprise. The direction of her thoughts had definitely not been the same as his, but infinitely preferable. He swung his free arm around and crooked his elbow behind his head. "Let me guess. Your uncle Faden?"

Her forehead furrowed in disappointed confusion. "How did you know?"

"I had the same idea myself and asked him to be the dockmaster. He turned me down."

She pulled her chin back. "Well, did you try?"

Dugan cocked his head and narrowed his gaze. "What do you mean 'did I try'? I wasn't going to plead with him. Faden's a grown man. He can make up his mind."

Adanel quirked a single brow. "Not in my experience. Most men need a nudge now and then," she said as she gave a slight push to his thigh with her knee.

"You think *you* were responsible for this?" He pointed at her and then him. "*I* kissed you. You wanted to talk about the castle, about which I might have a great idea."

"Tybalt?" Adanel smiled upon seeing his grimace. "I was going to ask him to be the one to help assess the rooms and prioritize what needs to be done."

"He'd make a great steward . . . if he agrees. But he seems to like training with Loman's men."

"Oh, he'll agree," Adanel promised, then rolled onto his stomach and placed a lingering kiss on his chest. "Just like Faden will agree after you talk to him again and *convince* him why you really want him for the job."

Dugan flipped her on her back. The feel of her soft lips against his skin was making him grow hard again. "First, I need to convince you of something."

Adanel's breathing quickened as she felt his length press against her upper leg. Her heart began to beat faster. "Such as?" she asked, hoping Dugan would say what she now knew was true. That he loved her still and wanted them to be together forever.

"As this," he groaned, and surged forward, penetrating her, letting her body, still slick, wet, and hot, coil around his tightly. Once again, he found heaven in the unrestrained enthusiasm of her arms before they both collapsed into much needed sleep.

In the middle of the night, he woke and made love to her once more, this time slowly, reverently, until they found themselves completely depleted, lying side by side on the soft rug in front of her hearth.

Dugan leaned on one elbow, his free hand resting lightly on the curve of her waist. Adanel raised a finger and ran it slowly down the dark trail of hair on his taut abdomen. With a soft laugh that was a half groan, he caught her hand and caressed her fingertips with his lips.

Their eyes locked, and Adanel once again felt an over-whelming warmth in her heart. "I love you, Dugan."

Immediately she felt him stiffen, and his expression became cold and distant. Her heart seized, and she knew she had made a mistake. Not in proclaiming her love, but for even allowing herself to feel that way about him.

She wiggled away from his side and sat up. "You don't feel the same," she stated without emotion.

"I don't know what I feel," Dugan said woodenly. For months, he had focused solely on his anger, letting it fester and grow. He had used it to protect his heart, and with it gone, he was vulnerable to her proclamation in a way he had not expected.

Adanel stared at him, her eyes large, dark, and pene-trating. "What is that supposed to mean?"

"It means whatever you want," Dugan said, getting to his feet.

Quickly he yanked on his léine. Grabbing his belt, plaid, and shoes, he then headed for the door, not taking the time to put anything else on.

"Wait! Dugan, we need to talk—"

He heard nothing else as the door swung shut. He closed his eyes for a second and then rushed down the stairs in case she tried to follow him. On the bottom floor, he ducked into a corner and quickly dressed. He left the tower with a brief nod at the two men guarding the entrance who had come to relieve Brùid earlier that night. "No one goes in this tower until Lady Adanel has given her permission."

Without waiting for affirmation that he had been heard and understood, Dugan pivoted and headed to the coldest river he could find.

He had just hurt Adanel again. He had seen the anguish in her eyes and yet, the turmoil of emotions rolling through him kept him walking in the opposite direction of where she was.

He needed time to think. And to do that he needed to be alone.

Chapter Thirteen

With a steady gaze, Faden studied Dugan, who sat across from him. "I already turned you down once," Faden said. "Unless you can get Fearan to listen to reason, there are no ships. And without ships, you have no need for a dockmaster."

Dugan smiled but his expression held no mirth, only anticipation of a long overdue challenge. "Once you agree, then we will talk to Fearan together."

Faden crossed his arms. "What makes you think I'm going to agree this time when I didn't before?"

"Adanel," Dugan replied simply, and then leaned over the table to refill Faden's mug with more ale. Like the rest of the rooms in Lasairbhàigh, the laird's dayroom was both spacious and opulent compared to most castles he had seen. Even Conor McTiernay's dayroom was not as extravagant, though Dugan preferred it to what he had here. The ornate table and overly stuffed chairs with filigree on all the exposed wood spoke of wealth that small clans did not have. The hardships others had to endure so that Mackbaythe could pretend otherwise was repellant.

Faden took the refilled mug and slugged back half the contents. "Why am I not surprised," he murmured.

"But she was right to ask me to try again."

Faden popped a brow.

"She told me that all men needed a nudge."

At that, Faden laughed. He could not help it. "And this is your version of a nudge?" he asked, wiping the mirth from his eyes.

"You know you should have the job. Plus, you are a MacLeod and can help me break the blockade."

Faden rubbed his face. "That is precisely why I should *not* be your dockmaster. I am a MacLeod, and I *should* be able to help find a solution. But my father is only interested in one thing, and it is *not* this port or your lairdship." He placed his elbows on the table and leaned forward. "Like my brothers before me, I was sent here, not to guard my niece as everyone was told, but to steal back the leverage Mackbaythe had on my father. Did you know that?"

Dugan shook his head. "Nay, but I am not surprised. You obviously were not successful."

"No." Faden snorted. "Which is why I was never allowed to return home."

Dugan narrowed his gaze and finally said, "But you are home." He waved his hand around the room. "These people have been family to you for what? Nearly fourteen years?" Faden nodded. "That makes Adanel your family and *these* clansmen your kin."

Faden shook his head. "Unfortunately for me, you can't choose family."

Dugan stood up and went to look out in the courtyard. There was a flurry of activity happening. Almost a week ago, Adanel had announced the removal of all staff working in or near the castle to the shock of every single person affected.

Adanel had gathered them all together in front of the castle. She had acknowledged their anger at being forced into becoming McTiernays, and then she had reminded them that the Mackbaythes of Gerloch had been viewed with contempt by neighboring clans for at least the past two generations and for good reason. Her grandfather had been greedy, and her father and brother had been evil men. Because of their actions, other clans believed *all* Mackbaythe clansmen and women were the same.

Adanel had declared she knew that was not true, but she also had made it clear that she knew her father and brother were not the only Mackbaythes who enjoyed in cruelty. Some had grown to relish such events, and those that did had no place working in what was now Lasairbhàigh Castle or even remaining on McTiernay land. However, she believed most of them to be good and hardworking people who loved their families and just wanted to provide for them and give them a good life. As McTiernays, they could have all those things. They just needed to accept recent changes and do their jobs well.

Unfortunately, it was clear to Adanel that the majority of those supporting the castle sought to resist change. And while she could wait until they grew to accept the new laird as their own, she was no longer willing to sleep in the Village Tower or eat poor food. And with the raise of her hand, McTiernay guards started ordering people away from the castle and all the surrounding buildings. All were cast out, from the baker to the blacksmith to the stable master. Even those who knew their jobs were essential to running the castle had been forced to leave. The resulting resentment and fury had been almost instant, but with Loman's help, Adanel had already stationed McTiernay soldiers everywhere in anticipation of their resistance.

As shock turned into anger followed by understanding that their jobs and in some cases, homes, were truly gone and there was little they could do, fear invaded both expressions and voices. Shouts about needing food and shelter were sprinkled in between threats and promises of retaliation. Unfazed, Adanel told them that they were lucky it was a warm summer's day as the outside would be their home until decisions were made about their future.

The curses thrown at her had been vicious, plentiful, and loud. Adanel must have felt Dugan's eyes upon her and had looked up to the window where he stood only to give him a sharp shake of her head, making it clear she did not want him to intercede. She had been resolute in her decision. They had pushed her too far, and she was no longer sympathetic to anything they had to say.

It was then Dugan began to fear that in his leaving so abruptly last night, he had done the same to Adanel. He had pushed the thought aside this morning but it kept returning. He was still not ready to talk about his feelings, but when he was, would she be willing to listen?

"You're wrong," Dugan said, countering Loman's assertion, "you can choose family. I was persecuted by the one I was born into and chose to walk away rather than endure the pain they callously inflicted. I also chose to accept a new family when I agreed to become a McTiernay."

Faden shifted in his seat and rested his right ankle on his left knee. "You weren't always a McTiernay?"

Dugan let go a halfhearted chuckle and turned away from the window. "I'm not even a Highlander by birth."

Surprised, Faden took in a deep breath. "And here I thought nothing was more important to you than loyalty."

In one swift fluid movement, Dugan unsheathed the

dagger at his waist and threw it at Faden's head. Its tip dug deep into the wood as the blade rested against the man's cheek. "Challenge my loyalty to the McTiernays again and you won't have anything left to worry about. You'll be dead."

Faden slowly reached up, pulled the knife out, and handed the dirk back to Dugan. "Why?"

"Why did I not kill you just now? Or why would I kill you over something so important to me that it would cause me to walk away from the only woman I'll ever love?" Dugan demanded, his voice ruthless and bitter.

Faden exhaled, realizing just how close to death he had actually come. "Both."

"The reason you aren't dead is Adanel. The reason I asked you to be dockmaster is not because of who your father is, but because of who you are to her. My trust is an extension of hers. And I never would have asked if I did not think you could do the job."

"And the other?" Faden asked, wondering if Dugan would answer him or just leave him to wonder.

Dugan leveled his blue eyes on him, trying to see if the man was in earnest. "Without loyalty, nothing has value. Friendships become undependable, alliances are pointless . . . even a parent's love for their child can be rendered meaningless."

Faden's brows rose.

With a sigh, Dugan went back to the table, but instead of sitting down he stood behind his chair and gripped the back. He had never told his story to anyone for it was none of their business. But he really did want Faden to be his dockmaster. Maybe it had not been intentional, but the man had told him about his own difficulties with his father. Maybe by reciprocating Dugan could build Faden's trust in him.

"I was born near the waist of Scotland on the coast

where Highlanders and Lowlanders mingle daily. As a result, I grew up learning both Scots and Gaelic. I did not come from wealth, but my father had a steady job working on the docks, and when I came of age, I worked alongside him until he passed away. But a hard, tedious life on the docks was not what I wanted nor did I have a desire to become a seaman. I desired something different for my life. At that time, William Wallace was fighting for Scotland's freedom and I wanted to join his men. I trained whenever I was not working, fighting anyone who would spar with me. Then, one day the dockmaster was murdered. Rumors flew about that I had done it for my dislike of the man was well known. My own mother was one of the first to believe all the vile gossip. Of course, I had not killed the man nor was there proof that I did. Still, my mother never stopped reminding me of the emotional damage *I* caused her "

Faden let go a low whistle of disbelief. "I'm not sure what to say," he said softly. He had issues with his father, but there was a difference between callousness and utter betrayal.

Dugan gave a single nod in agreement. "The one person who should've known the truth, who should have never doubted me, chose to believe the worst without even asking me if it were true."

"What did you do?"

Dugan bobbed his shoulders. "One day, I made it clear how I felt about her still holding resentment; she yelled and slammed the door on my face and refused to speak with me. So I left and joined Wallace's force. Years later, I lost the chance at lairdship of the Torridon nomads to Cole McTiernay, learned my best friend had thought I made a mistake in accepting the decision, and killed him when he tried to take the life of Cole's wife."

"Lady Ellenor?" Faden asked in disbelief. He had

been in the region for years, and yet this was news to him. Betrayed twice in such a way . . . things that had never made sense suddenly did. At first, Dugan came off easygoing and unnaturally calm. He was quick to crack a joke and often wore a smile, but it was rare it reached his eyes. Faden had known since their first meeting Dugan's laidback attitude was a mask to hide the darkness within him. Everybody wore some type of facade for everybody had something to hide. Faden hid his failure to his father, and Dugan hid the part of him that found it hard to trust another soul.

Dugan looked at him. "So be my dockmaster."

"You can trust me after what I just told you about why I'm here? Because you may not be Laird Mackbaythe, but my father still has the same demands of me."

"I'm betting that you are your own man. Your loyalty may not yet be with me, but it is with your niece, whom you have protected for years."

Dugan moved to swing his chair out and sit down again. When he did so, the chair leg clipped his ankle causing him to lose his balance. Dugan began to fall. Instinctively, he reached out and grabbed a nearby wall sconce, knocking off the candle, to regain his footing. But upon bearing nearly all of his weight, the sconce moved downward, making it clear the candle holder also served as a lever that lifted a portion of the wall hidden behind a tapestry just below it.

Dugan let go and immediately heard a *thunk* as the stone wall fell back into place. He flung back the wall-hanging and could barely see where part of the wall had moved. If he had not seen the sconce move and heard the wall shift, he would have not thought twice about the odd divot.

Curious, Faden jumped out of his chair. He came up and gave a quick tug on the sconce. When nothing happened, he yanked it once more, this time with significant force, and once again a portion of the wall moved. The opening was narrow and not quite waist high.

Dugan leaned down. "It's not a passageway, but it is deep," he said, and reached in to drag out a large, very heavy chest from where it had been hidden. Behind it were two other similarly sized chests. Faden let go of the candleholder and the wall fell back into place.

"Did you know about this?" Dugan asked.

Faden shook his head, his heart pounding. "Nay. I'm not sure anyone did."

Dugan opened the lid and knew immediately Faden was right. Mackbaythe would have never told anyone about its contents. It also explained how Mackbaythe was able to afford a large mercenary force and probably bribe MacCoinnich so that he would not take over the small port. The chest was full of gold coins, on top of which was a bulky velvet bag.

Dugan picked it up and peered inside. What he saw caused him to rock back on his heels in shock. He handed the bag to Faden. "Do you know what this is?"

Faden fingered the crest on the outside. He knew *exactly* what the bag contained without even looking inside. For three decades, he and each of his brothers had been searching for this bag and its contents. Having found it, Faden was faced with the improbable decision of having to choose which family had his loyalty. Dugan was right. Family was a choice, and surprisingly, in his case was a simple one. Adanel and her clan were his family, and he was going to help protect it the best way he could.

"It belongs to Adanel. It was her mother's and should go to her," Faden said, handing the bag back to Dugan. "Before we start talking about what that represents and what you intend to do with it, you should know, I'm accepting your offer of dockmaster."

Dugan looked up, his brows arched high in surprise. Then with a wicked smile, he said, "If that's true, let's put this back where it will be safe and go see Fearan. I've been looking forward to this conversation for some time."

Fearan looked at each man around the table—the new laird, his McTiernay commander Loman, and Dugan's recently appointed dockmaster, Faden. One by one each man returned his stare with a cold one of their own. Fearan snarled. If they thought to intimidate him, they should have picked another location. Here, overlooking the port, was where he felt most comfortable. In this room, he ran Bàgh Fìon. This was his world more than it was any others'. He knew the waters, the channels, and the hidden death traps. No one else did. What the new laird failed to understand, but soon would, was that Fearan did not need them. It was they who needed him.

For more than two weeks now he had kept the ports closed to both outgoing and incoming ships, and that included fishing vessels. He did not like doing it, but it had been necessary for him to make his point. Captains and their crews would only navigate the channel if *he* brought their ships safely into dock. Otherwise they would be risking their boats and potentially their lives.

Fearan had not made the decision to shut down local fishing lightly. It was a key food source for the village and many were feeling the effects. No one was starving yet, but disgruntlement was growing as hunting was becoming more difficult with the McTiernay army also hunting for their food. Fearan hoped their voices would become loud enough to persuade the new laird to see reason. All he wanted was to be left alone to do things the way they always had been done, which was his way and *only* his way. It had taken a similar strong stand to make Laird Mackbaythe understand his power, and just like him, this McTiernay would eventually have to acquiesce or fail.

Kara, however, was worried. His wife agreed with him in principle—he knew the port best and should be allowed to run it. He was an honest and good man whom all knew and trusted. Dugan should have trusted him as well instead of sending in his McTiernay commander Loman to oversee everything he did and ask questions at every turn. But all Kara's conversations with Adanel had his young wife concerned about his approach. Those who challenged the McTiernays supposedly lost . . . every time.

If the McTiernays were a seafaring clan like the MacLeods, Fearan might have been a little concerned. But the clan only boasted of two small harbors, neither in key locations, and both were only used in support of local fishing.

One of the few captains who secretly did a little trade with Cole McTiernay had met Dugan a few years ago and had sent a message warning Fearan against shutting down the port altogether. But when Fearan had witnessed Dugan slay two men the day he banished a third of the dock workers, he had feared their clan's new laird was no better than the one he replaced. Learning that Dugan wanted to give Faden the job as dockmaster only confirmed his original opinion.

Adanel loved the MacLeod soldier, but she did not know her uncle the way he did. Years ago, Fearan had caught him sneaking in and out of buildings, rummaging through items that were not his. Fearan had given him a warning, but Faden had continued. Never hearing of anything stolen, Fearan was forced to remain silent.

Without anything to substantiate his claims, he would look the fool.

Fearan bristled at the memory. Faden, a corrupt man in a corrupt position, was the one who should have someone overseeing his every move, not him. But Dugan had sent Loman to look over *his* shoulder. *He*, someone who knew everyone and was respected by all, was being followed around by a McTiernay soldier who knew nothing about ports, boats, or even the difference between sea and brackish water.

Dugan may have wanted Fearan to prove his trustworthiness, but by the end of their talk, the new laird would learn that it was *he* who needed to earn *his* trust, not the other way around.

Fearan drummed his fingers against the table. "Did you come here to persuade me to reopen the docks?" he finally asked, breaking the silence. "I will as soon as he"—Fearan pointed to Faden and then at Loman—"and he are gone. Leave me to do my job as I see fit. The harbor men trust me. They'll work for me. If I trusted you, they would work for you, but I don't so they won't."

A slow smile curved Dugan's mouth. "You seem to think that I need to earn your trust, Fearan. But let me remind you that I, not you, am laird of this clan, and it will be I, not you, who will run Bàgh Fìon."

Fearan paused his fingers at the implied threat and then began to tap them once more in a steady rhythm. "Do you know the real reason why the MacLeods or the MacCoinniches never tried to seize this port?" he questioned, not expecting an answer. "Two reasons. Both lairds hate each other, but they also need each other. MacLeod only makes money when his ships are hauling goods, and MacCoinnich needs ships to sell his clan's goods at a profit to the Lowlands. Mackbaythe understood that and acted as buffer. But that was not the only reason they left this port alone." He leaned forward and stared Dugan in the eye as he jabbed a thumb toward his chest. "It was because of me."

Fearan sat back and continued. "I brought the boats safely in. Every one of them. This is the only port for a hundred miles in which heavy goods can be loaded on and off from shore. Bàgh Fìon saves weeks of travel through the mountains and months if the destination is in the south. This port offers death to any ship trying to dock alone. Only one family has ever known the safe way to move up the channel, and with my father being dead, I am the only one left with the knowledge."

"For now," Dugan replied, his tone, body posture, and facial expression all unfazed by the port master's speech.

Fearan swallowed. It was not the response he was expecting. He had thought to see a growing understanding cross the man's face as he spoke, but either Dugan still did not understand the situation or nothing Fearan stated had been a revelation.

"And," Dugan calmly added, "there was a third and primary reason Mackbaythe had escaped attack. He paid them, just like he paid his mercenaries and his corrupt dockmaster. There's something else you have failed to realize," Dugan said in a tone pitched low and intense, brooking no argument. "We McTiernays don't take well to threats."

Fearan sat very still. He had threatened Dugan. Not with physical harm, but with his power. And after weeks of no boats coming in or out of the docks, Dugan had to know the threat was not an empty one. Right now, Dugan was posturing for he needed Fearan and the power he wielded.

"As far as you being the only one able to direct the boats in and out of the dock, Loman told me of the situation. He also explained that the passable channels were not mapped and their location was something you never shared. Interesting for a man whose actions are supposedly for the good of his clan."

"It *is* good for them!" Fearan barked. "That knowledge was the only thing allowing me to do what I needed to protect them from Mackbaythe and before him, his father."

"And what about now? Aren't you using your knowledge to starve your own clansmen? All I ask is that you share this critical knowledge with others and yet you refuse? Do you not care about the impact it would have on this clan if you were to suddenly perish?"

Fearan's jaw tensed. He was far from dead and had decades left to live, but the port was a dangerous place. Accidents did happen. But it was a necessary risk that he, like his father, had taken.

"Despite what you think, I do care for this clan," Dugan continued, "and soon I won't need you to direct the boats into the docks for I'll have a new port master to do the job."

Fearan was incensed. He forced himself to speak slowly and deliberately to ensure Dugan understood just what would happen. "Adanel's grandfather tried what you threaten. They watched my father and thought they knew the route, but days later ships sank from holes created by the rocky sandbars that litter this bay."

Dugan shrugged dismissively. "Those men were guessing. Mine won't be."

Fearan's bulging eyes studied Dugan's expression, trying to gauge if he was bluffing or if the new laird actually meant what he had said.

"I grew up near Dumbarton," Dugan offered casually. "I spent my youth working every position there was around the docks. I've seen channels change after massive storm surges, and I know how port masters found them again. It takes time to send out boats with ropes testing the depths but, Fearan, *I will do it,*" he promised, his voice suddenly low and pitiless. "And I will find every sandbar, every deep path, and every crevice. I will know everything there is to know about that bay. It might take me all year, but I will have my men map every navigable sector of these waters, just like your family did many years ago. So think twice if you think you have power over me. Because you don't. You hold no magic, just knowledge. And that knowledge can and will be gained by other means if necessary."

Fearan began to breathe deeper and quicker. This new laird was not making an idle threat. He was delivering a promise.

"What's more," Dugan added while leaning forward to rest his elbows on the table so that he could form a steeple with his fingers, "if I'm sending men out to find and mark that channel, that means you decided it was not in your best interest to see this port thrive. When you and your wife leave these lands, I suggest heading south. Seek out a large port in the Lowlands like Urewin. They are always in need of those comfortable working around the docks. But whatever you do, don't go north. The MacLeods will not be happy with the port down, and our ally the Mackays will definitely not welcome you as I plan to make every Highlander aware of your role in this port's status."

"The MacLeods have shut down this port more than I. It's of little use to you," Fearan reminded Dugan, trying to remain calm and failing.

"Only for now. The MacLeods are currently flexing their muscle. Soon though, it will be my turn."

Fearan knew he had made a mistake in underestimating Dugan. "I don't take well to threats either."

"Good. Then stop making them, and I will do the same." Fearan's brown eyes locked on Dugan's blue ones and suddenly widened in shock as he realized what Dugan had said. "The last several generations of Mackbaythe lairds have been either highly foolish or mad. Your grandfather did what he did to survive. Your father followed in his footsteps and, wisely, so did you. But I'm not a Mackbaythe laird and those tactics will not work on me."

"Just what do you want?" Fearan asked.

Dugan raked a hand through his hair and in an exasperated tone, said, "I only want to help, Fearan. I sent Loman to assist you, not undermine what you were doing. He asked questions to learn and came to me when you refused to tell him anything. He realized you being the only one with knowledge of the channels was too large of a risk to be acceptable, but more importantly, he recognized that your job is too much of a burden for one man to bear. For years, your role as port master has been limited to that of guiding ships in and out of port, giving you little time to handle maintenance issues. But repairs desperately need to be made. After that, we need to expand the docks to allow smaller ships to load and unload on the northern side of the port near the Fortress. And this part of the dock needs to be doubled, if not tripled, in size. Right now, only one large ship can come in at a time and be docked."

Fearan blinked, no longer caring if the shock he felt could be seen clearly across his face. He leaned and pressed his finger down on the table. "If you are serious, then my knowledge is insufficient. The bay will need to be remapped for the current channel won't support such an expansion."

"But I'm guessing you think you might know a way where we could expedite a mapping endeavor."

Fearan sat still for a moment before sitting back and crossing his arms. "I've wanted to do just what you have described for years, but I lacked the manpower or support to do it. I am almost positive there is another deep conduit just off the main channel, which could easily enable us to double our capacity. But there is a sandbar blocking the way. Mackbaythe ignored the possibilities."

"Do you have any ideas about how to break through?"

Fearan gave Dugan a grudging nod and began to outline his plan, something he never dreamed of doing—especially with a man who less than an hour ago threatened to send him packing.

When he was done, Dugan looked at Loman and rose out of his chair. "Find the men to make this happen, Fearan. Determine what needs to be done and then run the operation with Loman's support. Oh, and find a couple of apprentices and start teaching them everything you already know."

Fearan stood up as well. "So am I still your port master?"

Dugan arched a single brow. "You talked, I listened. I talked, you listened. We both learned a lot. I know you are smart and are willing to take a stand for something you believe in, even if it is a foolish one. You learned that I am not nearly as naive as you thought me to be, and that maybe, just maybe, I might be worthy of your support. And because Adanel loves your wife, I have no desire to uproot her. So aye, you are going to remain port master and help me make Bàgh Fìon the finest port along Scotland's northwestern shores."

At that, Loman and Faden, who had not said a single word, also rose to their feet and the three men left the small room, giving Fearan much to think about.

Chapter Fourteen

Adanel waved to Kara and then waited patiently for her friend to weave through the throngs of people and tables to cross the room. "Quite the crowd!" she said with a large smile after arriving.

The corner Adanel had staked out was at the far end of the giant great hall where the main hearth was. The rectangular room had been built to be intentionally massive to allow for various spectator events to take place and be seen by visitors and preferred clansmen. Outside of being large, there was little else to boast about the boxlike hall. It had three hearths—one large one at the end where the laird and dignitaries sat and two on the southern wall. In the center of the northern wall was the main entrance and on each side of the double doors were three large square windows. The kitchens were connected to the doors situated opposite to that of the main hearth. The room's decor was scant compared to the massive, intricate tapestries that hung in the McTiernay great hall. Instead of wall hangings, weapons hung between the two smaller hearths. But the room was at least now clean and the new rushes on the floor gave off a pleasant scent.

Adanel smiled at Kara, but it did not reach her eyes. If she had not been so busy for the past three weeks, she would have probably retreated back into her room and shut out the world. "Aye, there are a lot of people," she agreed. "A month ago, I would not have thought tonight ever possible. Tybalt and I are far from getting this castle truly where it ought to be, but thankfully we made enough progress in time to celebrate."

Kara grinned and linked elbows with Adanel. "Amazing what a little motivation can do."

She had sat with Adanel as her friend had brought in and spoke with each staff member individually before deciding whether they would continue working in the castle, and if so, in what capacity. Adanel's frustration finally had gotten to the point where she could make the hard decisions, and once there, she had proved herself to be a very capable lady of the castle. If Adanel determined a person needed to look elsewhere for a living, she did not even let them retrieve their things. Instead, she had one of the guards bring their items outside for them to collect. Anyone hostile to her cause was not going to be given another opportunity to deface her home.

Kara tore a piece of the warm bread she had snatched from one of the tables. She popped it into her mouth and grinned. "The cooks I suggested are even better than I thought," she said in between chews. "I stopped by the kitchens and took a peek, and I must admit, part of me wondered what it would be like to prepare a feast."

"You want it, the job is still yours," Adanel said, glancing around the room.

Kara shook her head definitively, glad she was not going to be pressed anymore on the subject. Seeing Adanel's shifting eyes, she tried to follow her friend's gaze. "I love celebrating Midsummer, and I cannot remember when the clan was welcomed to enjoy St. John's Eve at the castle. Even the dockworkers and harbor men have come," she said, pointing at a group of men openly gawking at the large room.

Adanel glanced their way. "MacLeod still has his ships in place but at least they are letting Cole's ships in and out. It gives them work, but it's minimal."

Fearan as an enemy had made life difficult, but the man as an ally had been unbelievable. It was as if he had a new lease on life as every dream he had ever had and suppressed was finally possible. "The dockworkers may not be very busy, but now that my husband is not grousing about, he is working the harbor men almost nonstop. I keep telling him to relax at least for one night, but he refuses."

"Does Dugan need to know? Just tell one of the guards and—"

"Nay, it's not like that," Kara reassured her. "Fearan loves what he is doing. You should see him. He practically bubbles with excitement whenever he tries to explain what is going on. Aye, the man is overworked, but it is by choice and I cannot be the one to dampen his enthusiasm. Soon he will slow down, but until then, you'll have to put up with me grumbling."

Adanel's face warmed and she gave Kara's arm a squeeze before freeing it. She was happy for her friend and hoped Fearan realized how lucky he was to have a spouse who believed in him and supported him unreservedly. "Well, any time you feel the need for company, you are welcome to join Tybalt and me. We may not bubble with excitement, but not a day passes that something unexpected does not happen."

Once the castle had been emptied of staff, she and Tybalt had toured the castle. Everything had needed to be cleaned, but more than that, few rooms had been regularly maintained, so most were in disrepair. The great hall, the keep, and the rooms guests frequented were the only ones that needed minor work. In the rooms that had not been used for years, she and Tybalt were constantly finding a wide assortment of items. A few were valuable, and many were alarming. Just today she had thrown a phallic-shaped wooden statue of the pagan god of fertility into the fire.

"How is your steward liking his new position?" Kara asked, unfazed that Adanel was still scanning the room.

Adanel wrinkled her nose but then gave Kara a brief, but genuine smile. "He grumbles a *lot*," she said, resuming her search. "He is always finding something else we missed during our initial assessment of the castle's state, but deep down I think Tybalt loves every aspect of being a steward. He loves planning what needs to be done, overseeing the work, paying the salaries, and especially ordering people around." Adanel leaned over and whispered, "I'd worry about him liking it too much, but he is good at it! The man is a genius at getting people to listen and do what he says."

Kara gave Adanel a look of disbelief remembering the interviews. Not a soul had been happy, even the ones Adanel had rehired. "After everything that happened? I would have thought there would be constant acts of retaliation based on the looks some of them gave you."

Adanel did not say anything. There had been some resistance at first. When the staff realized they could and would be replaced, most had said what they needed to in order to keep their positions. However, some believed incorrectly that being rehired meant they could return to their shoddy ways. The blacksmith was the first to learn that would not be tolerated and had been sent to look elsewhere for work. The candle maker made splendid candles, but he had not been able to hide his seething hatred of the McTiernays. As a result, the junior candle maker and the apprentice got promoted and the candle maker was now working on the docks, learning the hard way that everyone was replaceable. He was still fortunate for he at least got to remain with the clan.

The baker was another one who was very capable at his job, able to reliably produce decent breads and pastries, but Adanel had seen him cheering in the crowd when her father had forced her to be present during some of his more horrific shows. The man had enjoyed watching animals rip at each other almost as much as her father had. He was not only removed from the castle, but Dugan had agreed to permanently banish him from all McTiernay lands.

Adanel had worked with the remaining castle staff finding in many circumstances poor work quality had been due to lack of instruction, lack of equipment, or just plain fear. Some she hired back though they made it clear they were very angry about becoming McTiernays, but Adanel felt that given time they would grow to appreciate just what it meant to be part of a clan that others respected.

"If all is going well, then why are you so nervous?"

Adanel continued to scan the room but spared a second to glower at her friend. "You know why."

Kara winced and joined Adanel in looking for Dugan. Tables filled the great hall to allow for as many people as possible to join the feast. Earlier she had signaled for the servants to begin bringing out the food, when she had spotted Kara come in. People were beginning to take their seats along the benches but until Dugan decided to appear, the celebration would not go forward.

"You both are still not talking?"

Adanel answered with a shrug. "It was his choice to shut me out."

"Aye, but now it is *you* who refuses to say anything."

Adanel straightened her back at the light rebuke. "And what should I have done, Kara? Continued to stand by and do nothing when someone so cruelly continues to inflict pain? If someone hit me, the next time they raised their fist I would duck. Well, that is what I am doing—ducking."

"But for how long?"

"Until I no longer feel I need to." Adanel craned her head to see in the back. More people were coming in, but Dugan was still not in sight. Would the man really not show just to avoid sitting next to her? Tybalt affirmed that Dugan knew what she had been planning, but they had not actually spoken. She just assumed Dugan would know to come. But then, she had also just assumed after making love for hours that they were both ready to move forward and not hold on to the mistakes of the past. She had been wrong then, and she could be wrong now.

"And what about the laird? Has he tried reaching out to you?"

"Don't be coy. You already know Dugan did. I'm sure Faden told Fearan who told you. I think it worked better in my favor when those two men did not like each other."

Kara looked sheepish and guilty, but not apologetic. "Oh, Fearan still wonders about Faden, but he did admit to a growing respect for him and his abilities to run the docks and manage the men around him. Don't tell either of them I said this, but they do work well together," she whispered. "Both have similar gruff personalities and prefer direct talk over vagaries. But enough about them and Dugan. I want to know what was in the box Faden gave you."

Adanel kept her eyes on the crowd. "I have no idea. I didn't open it."

Kara's jaw dropped. "Fearan said that Dugan had ordered Faden to bring it to you. I've been itching with curiosity ever since he told me, and *you haven't opened it?*"

"I don't want to know."

"Whatever it is, it might be Dugan's way of apologizing, or at the least making an attempt to try and get you to talk to him again. You need to open it."

Adanel shook her head, her face set in implacable lines. "Dugan thinks he did nothing wrong, so it is definitely not an apology. And I have no doubt that its contents are something to encourage me to be more accommodating to the whiplash of the emotional blows he likes to throw my way. Dugan can try to bribe me, but I am simply uninterested in what he has to offer any longer."

Kara let go a soft snort. "The two of you *really* need to just admit that you love each other and let the past go."

"I tried, and I don't intend to do so again."

"So that's it then? You will just finish out the year and then what?"

Adanel pressed her lips together and frowned. "I don't know, Kara. I have not thought that far ahead. All I know is that at this time I have nothing to say to the man and am uninterested in anything he has to say to me."

"I hope you aren't talking about me."

Adanel and Kara spun around at the interruption, knowing instantly the owner of the friendly, upbeat voice. Seeing the handsome McTiernay commander, Adanel reached out and gave him a hug. "Loman! Thank you so much for helping with the bonfires outside. Everyone is eager to light them for it has been years since we have had anything like this around here."

Loman grinned and tossed his sand-colored hair back behind his shoulder. It was longer than most men's and he almost always had it tied back, but tonight it was free of its constraints and the change looked well on him. "It was my pleasure, and I thank you for your patience. When I agreed to come to Bàgh Fìon and help Dugan, I honestly had no idea how much work there would be. It's a nice change from being an elite guard, but there are never enough hours in the day it seems. I must say I have been looking forward to tonight and just taking time to relax and enjoy the festivities. Midsummer's Eve has always been one of my favorite holidays."

Adanel nodded in agreement, her smiling brown eyes reflecting the flames from the fireplace. "Mine too. I love it when the old ones retell the legends of St. George and the dragons."

"Aye, the stories are good, but I love the dancing. Please tell me you ladies intend to participate."

Kara clapped her hands enthusiastically. "I love the quadrille and the Scottish reel. But Adanel here," she said with a nudge of her elbow, "is a master at the jig. No one is better."

Loman threw his head back and laughed at Kara, who was practically jumping with excitement. "Well, Lady Adanel, if you are good at the jig, then you will be a contender to win the sword dance."

Puzzled by what he meant, Adanel asked, "Did you say contender?"

"Aye," Loman answered with a nod. "The dance turned into something of a unique rivalry for us McTiernays when Lady McTiernay decided to join the men one year."

Adanel's jaw dropped for a second and she slowly closed it as she could just see Laurel being bold enough to do such a thing. "She actually did the sword dance with the men?"

"Not only did she dance, she won. For we never stop until only one man—"

"—or woman," Kara piped in.

"Or woman," Loman added with a smile, "remains standing."

Adanel could just imagine Laurel smiling and jumping around with her blond curls bouncing everywhere. Sword dance music was infectious as soldiers pounded the floor, deftly hopping between the quarters made by crossed broadswords to the quick beat of the music. "And you say other McTiernay women now do this dance? Not just the soldiers?"

"Aye, and not just soldiers either. A McTiernay farmer won at Conan's wedding. Though I suspect he had been practicing for weeks." He could see the twinkle in her eye. "So can I lay a set of swords next to mine? I could use the encouragement in front of your clansmen."

Adanel rolled her eyes, but laughed, feeling once again excited about the night. "I absolutely would love to join, but I've never done the sword dance before, and it has been years since I've seen it done. I'm afraid I don't know how."

"It's simple." Loman took her hand in his and showed her the first move. "Now just hop out and then back, make the cross, and now back again. You can make any pattern you like but you just cannot touch the blade *or* stop moving."

"Like this?" Adanel asked, using his arm for support with one hand as she pulled up her bliaut with her other hand to practice the steps.

"Aye, now faster."

Adanel repeated the steps but inadvertently caught the hem of her chemise with her toe causing her to fall into Loman's arms. He easily caught her and was about to help Adanel back to her feet when he froze.

Adanel turned her head to see what had caused him to suddenly tense up and then froze herself. Sometime during her conversation with Loman, Dugan had arrived and made his way to their corner.

After all the arguments she had had with the man, Adanel honestly believed she knew what her husband looked like when he was mad. She could not have been more wrong. Nothing she had ever seen compared to the fury staring at her and Loman. His blue eyes had darkened dangerously and the pent-up anger that had been building for weeks looked like it was about to explode.

With carefully controlled self-discipline, Dugan put out his hand and said, "I believe, my lady, it is time we address the clan."

Adanel raised her chin with a cool stare in his direction, righted herself, and then deliberately placed only her fingertips in his palm. "Whatever you wish, my lord. I am yours to command."

His to command, Dugan huffed to himself as he led her to the main table. If only that were true, he would order her back to her chambers to wait for his arrival, which would not be anytime soon. He had a lot to say and it would take more than a few hours for him to calm down enough to say it. Damn woman was a nightmare and while he knew a lot of the hell he'd been in the past few weeks was of his making, it was not *all* his doing.

What had Adanel expected from him with her impulsive declaration of love? Had she wanted him to return the sentiment even if he had not been sure he meant it just to spare her feelings? Why had she not spared his and let things continue as they were?

That night had been the best he had had in almost a year, and with three heavy words, it had changed. And because he had not responded quick enough with his own affirmation of love, she had declared he did not feel the same. He had not said that, *she* had. Dugan was not sure what he felt and that had not been acceptable. He could still see the critical look in her eye as if he had physically slapped her. He had had no choice but to leave, think, and figure it all out without questions, accusations, and most of all judgments. He had to know that what they had was real. For if it was not, pretending otherwise would hurt her far more than anything he could have said. So he had left.

Maybe he should have expected Adanel to block him out after leaving her the way he did, but he had *not* expected her reaction to be so final or so complete. According to the maids, the locked box Faden had brought to her had yet to be opened.

Garrett had been right. One could only endure so much pain, and Adanel had reached her limit. She was through trying and had made it abundantly clear the past few weeks. That was when he had decided Adanel was right. There would never be another for him, but that did not mean he and Adanel were meant to be. They caused each other too much pain to try and make it work.

It had been difficult to acknowledge, and he had not fully reconciled his mind to accept where they were now, but Dugan had thought he could act the role as laird with her by his side without incident. Then he walked into the hall.

Adanel's red hair made her easy to spot despite the crowd. Dugan thought she would have been looking for him, eagerly waiting for his arrival, but based on what he saw, he was not even on her mind. Loman was.

His stomach rolled as he had observed the scene. Her hand on Loman's arm, her laughter, the commander's enjoyment as he taught her how to do the sword dance. If Loman thought his wife was going to be dancing next to him tonight, he would soon be on his way back south. Loman was a hard worker, likeable, and in general a godsend with all that needed to be done, but Dugan refused to spend the next year watching the man win over the affections of his wife. Adanel was *his*.

Even if pain, hurt, and misunderstanding made her lost to him forever, she would always be his. Nothing would change that.

With a brief tug, Adanel freed her hand and moved around the large chairs to stand next to Dugan in front of the main table. She listened as he spoke to the crowd, but she barely heard a word.

The blinding fury that had been rolling off him when he found her laughing with Loman had been palpable. Dugan had the nerve to act like he was jealous!

She had no interest in Loman or any other man, but after the way Dugan had discarded her, he had no right to interfere even if she did. After the deadly stare he had issued Loman, she doubted the jovial commander would come within twenty feet of her again, let alone share a conversation . . . or do the sword dance next to her. And she couldn't blame him for Dugan looked like he was ready to kill Loman just for keeping her from falling.

"Let the feast begin!" she heard Dugan shout. The hall was full of happy cheers and hails as everyone began to dig in to the plates before them.

Dugan glanced to his side and leveled a stare on Adanel, which she coolly returned. Then at the same time, they sat down, both with the intentions of ignoring the other for the rest of the night.

"*Daingead*!" Dugan shouted, leaping to his feet only a second before Adanel joined him. "*Cò ann an ifrinn seo a chur air mo chathair*?" he bellowed, pointing at his seat.

Adanel wanted answers as well as her backside was in a similar state as Dugan's, completely sodden with some sort of pie or stew. Someone had put a plate of food in both their seats while Dugan had been talking to the crowd. It was an impossible feat. No one nearby would dare do such a thing. Except perhaps one man. There was only one person she knew who could have slipped by without capturing her attention.

Adanel looked around for Kara's brother. "Nigel!" she whispered through gritted teeth. "This time I won't wait for Dugan to kill you, I'm going to do it!"

Suddenly, the laughter of the hall permeated their stunned states. Adanel realized that to study their seats, she and Dugan had turned around. Therefore, their wet, food-dripping backsides had been on display to everyone in the hall. It was too much to ask for them not to laugh, but it only added to Adanel's humiliation.

"*Murt*, you are coming with me," Dugan barked. He grabbed her hand and started marching toward the doors ignoring all the shouts and laughter.

Once again, Adanel realized she had only *thought* she had seen Dugan mad. The man was inventing new levels of anger with every passing moment.

Dugan headed straight for his solar in the keep. He wanted no interruptions. He wanted no comments. He needed to calm down.

When he entered his chambers, he tugged Adanel

inside and then slammed the door closed. When he turned around and saw her standing there looking at him as if it was his fault their backsides were sticky with stew, he snapped.

Dugan had not really thought about why he was bringing Adanel with him. It had been instinct. She was in a similar state of disarray, and he did not want the crowd to continue jeering at her, even if it was in good spirit and fun. But now that she was here, in front of him, in his bedroom, where they could finally clear any misunderstandings, the last thing he wanted to do was talk.

With a fierce gaze, he started walking toward her. Adanel's eyes grew large, and she instinctively began walking backward until her back hit the stone wall.

Dugan's arms went to her sides, and he came in close. "Can't sleep. Can't eat. Can't think. Everything I do, my mind comes back to you." His face came in so close that if she tilted her chin even a little, they would touch. "I tried to stay away, but I can't anymore. I hear you when you aren't around. I see you in my dreams. I can taste your mouth, feel your skin . . . you haunt my every move, *aithinne*. You have since the moment I first saw you and no amount of time, distance, or anger is ever going to stop that."

Adanel swallowed. Dugan desired her, aye, but she already knew that. She wanted more and until he was ready to give her his all, they were not going to work. "You and I? It isn't going to happen. You need to let me go," she declared softly but with firm resolve. Fear was in her eyes. She had been hurt too many times.

"*Cha dèan mo chas!* Aye, *aithinne*, this absolutely *is* going to happen. I'm done with avoiding you and you avoiding me," Dugan growled. "Weeks of nothing but you on my mind. Weeks of going to bed alone when you should be in my arms. When I saw Loman talking with you, attempting to see if he had any chance, I almost lost it and killed the man. All my life I wanted what I've got here in this room, and I'm not going to lose it now because you and I can't figure out how to talk to one another."

"You won't lose it," Adanel whispered, afraid to assume more into what he was saying. "I'll leave. The castle still needs improvement, but you'll have Tybalt and every day you are winning over more and more of the clan. I'm sure—"

"—do you honestly think I'm going to let the first woman who makes me happy, makes me think about the future, of a life I never thought possible, just walk away from me?"

"We only handfasted, Dugan, you have no obligations—"

"—I'm not going to," he stated in a voice so deadly serious it scared her, but it also gave her the first tiny bit of real hope.

"Dugan—"

"Listen to me, Adanel. *I'm not going to let you go.*" And before she could say another word, he caught her face between his hands and invaded the sweet, vulnerable warmth behind her lips with an intimate aggression that seared her senses. Adanel had no choice but to respond and clenched her fingers around his shoulders. The light encouragement was all Dugan needed to deepen the kiss that was going to end only one way. Adanel no longer cared.

The past few weeks had been hell. Dugan could not sleep or think? It had been the same for her. She knew she should stop him, demand an explanation for what happened last time, and get him to admit his feelings for her, but in his arms, she had no willpower. Her mind always lost to the sensations in her body.

Dugan could feel the tension in Adanel's body dissipate as their kiss melted away rational thought. His head was reeling with the feel of her and he craved more. His hot, slick tongue glided against hers, tasting the faint tang of ale. He broke off the kiss, lifted his head slightly, and sucked in air.

"Dugan," she whispered, rocking against him; and then going up on tiptoe, Adanel sought his lips again.

"*Dia,*" he murmured, and crushed her mouth once more against his, needing each stroke of her tongue.

He explored her mouth with an expertise that never failed to make her dizzy. His hands had moved from her face to her back, pulling her to him so that she was tight against his body. Her pulse raced and hot little ripples of pleasure slid down her thighs as she felt the hard bulge beneath his plaid. Sensuously, she moved against it.

The tease was not enough. She wanted to feel him, and his clothes were obstacles. Pulling, ripping, Adanel yanked them off as Dugan did the same with her gown in a desperate effort. When free, he swept her in his arms and carried her to his bed. Laying her down, he covered her with his massive body, pushing her legs open for his touch.

Adanel moaned and began to writhe as his fingers penetrated deep. Dugan dropped his head and took a nipple in his mouth. Her body arched toward him, and he groaned to the sound of her mewling as his tongue lathed and his fingers teased, pinched, massaged, and stroked her into a delirious wetness.

His mouth broke free and began to attack her neck, moving upward. "You're mine, Adanel," he decreed.

"There'll never be another for me and there'll never be another for you."

Adanel groaned her agreement, but Dugan was not satisfied and his free hand gave her neck a squeeze. "Say it," he demanded huskily.

"I'm yours," she breathed, her words ragged from passion.

"Forever, Adanel. Say it."

Adanel nodded. "Forever. I always have been yours, Dugan, and I always will be."

With a guttural groan of need and possession, Dugan slanted his mouth over Adanel's again, searing her lips to his. Then his fingers began to increase their rhythm until Adanel could not hold back any longer and cried out, begging for more while claiming it was too much.

Dugan flipped her over and, pulling up her backside, he thrust into her. Feeling her body respond to his, her hips pushed back to meet him as he pulled back before thrusting hard once again. Adanel shouted cries of satisfaction and need. She wanted him harder, deeper, and Dugan quickened his movements.

Adanel pressed her cheek into the pillow as she let herself be consumed by the pounding strokes and the feel of him owning her again and again. Pleasure mixed with sensations that felt too good to be pain.

"*Murt*, I missed you—how you feel, how you sound, every last damn thing about you I missed," Dugan murmured against her back, never slowing as he drove her to the edge.

Adanel screamed as wave after wave of intense pleasure assaulted her. Dugan smiled in triumph and then hollered her name as he thrust deep one last time. Not a soul in the vicinity could have mistaken the shout for anything but what it was—pure, indescribable pleasure.

Dugan collapsed next to her with his body half sprawled over hers. He felt like he weighed three times his normal weight and he could barely lift his head to speak.

Feeling Adanel wiggle, he removed his leg and let her roll to her side. Reaching up to run fingers through his hair, Adanel whispered, "I love you, Dugan, with all that I am, I love you. Never doubt it."

Once again his body stiffened. But instead of pulling away, his gaze locked with her luminous brown eyes. "Do you have any idea how much that means to me?"

Adanel blinked and felt tears begin to form and fall down her cheeks. She shook her head.

"Every battle I have ever fought, every friend I have ever lost, every hard decision I have ever faced, I would make again because they brought me to you. *You*, Adanel, made all the *cac* I've ever done or put up with worth it." He held her gaze. "I was afraid I lost you."

Adanel shook her head. "Not possible."

Dugan wiped away a tear. "If I haven't driven you away yet, I don't think anything can."

"I'm going nowhere."

Dugan cradled her face in his hands. "You are the love of my life, Adanel. And I will never give you cause to doubt that again."

Adanel swallowed and then flung her arms around him to hold him close so that she could whisper in his ear, "You're everything I ever dreamed of, Dugan. I love you with every beat of my heart, every breath of my body. Now and forever."

Chapter Fifteen

Wrapped in a blanket, Adanel stood at the solar window and smiled. The revelry from the feast could be heard through the windows and in the halls. She had never seen her clansmen celebrate as freely or with as much joy. The bonfires had been lit. Tybalt, Garrett, or Loman had seen to it. Most likely all three in some way.

At the time, she gave no thought to leaving the great hall full of clansmen with her backside soaked in some type of meat stew. She still had no idea exactly what she and Dugan had sat on or who put it there, but suspected it had been Nigel. The man had constantly played practical jokes on her and Kara when they were growing up. Also, he was the only one who had the nerve—and was senseless enough—to actually follow through with such an insane idea. And though she would never tell him, Adanel was glad he did. It had forced her and Dugan to speak to each other. Without something so unexpected and jolting, she was not sure they would have come together until too much time had passed.

Hearing the door scrape open, Adanel twisted her neck to see Dugan come in with a tray of miscellaneous food items and a pitcher of ale or water. He gave her a wink and, angling his foot awkwardly, he closed the door. After placing the tray down on the table, he sauntered over to where she stood and pulled her back against his chest.

Nuzzling his mouth against her neck, he said, "I brought food, my lady."

Adanel tilted her head, simply enjoying the sensation of being in his arms and the feeling of being loved without secrets or constraints. No matter what happened with the future of the clan, the port, or his lairdship, nothing would change this. They had claimed each other multiple times in the past few hours and no doubt would do so again and again in the weeks and months to come just to reassure each other they were still there and would remain at each other's side.

Adanel's stomach rumbled, and Dugan chuckled before lifting his head. "You, *uithinne*, are hungry."

Her smile lit up her face. "I am. It is not helping smelling our clothes covered in stew."

"Good point." Dugan walked over to the corner where their clothes lay in a heap. "The odor of these will turn to a stench soon." He then picked them up and walked over to open the door.

"I need those!" Adanel exclaimed, but without enmity. "*You* have other things to wear in this room. I do not!"

Dugan returned to her side and playfully looked underneath the blanket she had wrapped around her confirming what he already knew. Adanel had not a stitch on her. "We will fix that later. I'll have someone fetch all your things from the Village Tower and bring them here."

Adanel arched a brow. "First, my things have not been in the Village Tower for over a week. Seems *someone*"— she elbowed his side—"ordered for no one to be there when I was in my chambers."

Dugan gave an unapologetic shrug. "Of course I gave that order. The idea of single men so close to you while you were sleeping or bathing . . . you were far too accessible for one guard to protect."

"Well, it was making things miserable for Garrett."

"I knew that, and I did not care."

"Well, I *didn't* know that and I *did* care, which is why I moved out last week and into the chambers on the second floor."

Dugan's brow furrowed. "That's two floors down. I want you here."

"And I will sleep here, but I am not bathing and preparing for the day in this room. You need your chambers and I have found that having my own dayroom is quite convenient."

"Fine, as long as your nights are here with me," Dugan conceded, and put his chin on her shoulder. He studied all the commotion outside. The bonfires lit up the sky and the dancing had commenced. More people were gathering, and in general, the activity was growing. "Everyone seems to be having a good time. They were clearing the tables and starting to dismantle them to make room for singing and dancing when I went to find us some food."

"Were they laying out the swords?" she asked.

He crinkled his brow. "Aye."

"Loman was telling me all about the sword dance. It's what he was showing me when you glowered at him."

Dugan gave her a possessive squeeze. "He won't make that mistake again."

Adanel giggled. "I don't think any man who saw you tonight will ever talk to me again. Still, I was looking forward to trying the McTiernay's test of endurance."

"That it is."

"Have you ever won?"

"I've come close, but I can only go so long before I start losing my balance and dancing on the blades instead of between them. Nimble my feet aren't." Dugan gave her nose a quick kiss. "No dancing tonight, but I did bring food," he said, using his chin to gesture toward the table. "I was surprised to find servants still at their duty and they quickly came to my rescue."

"I'm just glad you were still able to find us something to eat," she said with a twinkle in her eye.

He gave her a single nod. "You have no idea how right you are. I went down just in time. In another hour, I doubt anything will be left. Those working will then have the onerous job of cleaning up."

Adanel rested her cheek against his chest. "They won't be. Those making merry will do it in the morning. With the exception of the kitchens, those who are working tonight have the next two days off."

"That's a shame."

Adanel furrowed her brow and pulled away slightly to look at him. "What is? Because they were much appreciative. Out of everything, I think that offer has endeared me to them the most. Well, that and the pay."

It was Dugan's turn to look confused. "I was talking about the kitchens. The food was actually very good and I have a feeling that we are going to suffer the consequences for not letting them also have time off."

Adanel's brown eyes widened in understanding. "Oh, there will be no retaliation," she stated without doubt. "First, everyone is well aware of what would happen if they did. They would be gone, no matter how important they were."

Dugan gave her a crooked smile and a small chuckle. "Aye, I think everyone has figured that out."

Adanel playfully elbowed him in the side. "Kara was furious with me about your little stunt with Fearan. The man was truly shaken at the prospects of losing his job and having to move and start all over."

"As he should have been because I was in earnest."

"He knew that. I think that is what rattled him so. But I told Kara that while I love Fearan, he had not been acting in the best interest of himself or the clan. Of course, she claimed he had been."

"And what did you say?" Dugan asked, warmed that even when they were not speaking, Adanel had been defending his position and decisions.

Adanel blinked. "That Fearan was acting as he had always done. He was treating you as if you were like my father or my grandfather before him, and that was a mistake. While hard to admit because I *am* related to them, both were cowards. It's why they liked to use fear as a weapon and shrank when someone stood up to them. Fearan's whole approach was based on the assumption that you would react the same way they did. And it was a mistake."

"I'm just glad Fearan realized I was not bluffing because I would have hated to lose him. He really does know what he is doing and is full of new ideas. Some fairly radical, but I am going to let him try many of them."

Adanel giggled. "I know. Kara says Fearan is so happy that it is like living with a little boy during Christmastide." She reached up on her toes and kissed him on his cheek. "Thank you. Because as partial as Kara is to me, she loves Fearan more and I fear that our relationship might have been in jeopardy if the man was still brooding."

"Well, anything I can do to save the friendship of my wife and her best friend." Dugan laughed and gave her a light squeeze. "And you have yet to explain what you meant about the pay."

"Nothing really," Adanel said with a shrug. "When I sent everyone away and started bringing them back individually to talk about what they did, what they wanted to do, their frustrations working under my father, one of the most illuminating answers I received was to the one Tybalt asked: Why did you work for Laird Mackbaythe when he was so cruel and changeable?"

"What was the answer?"

"Money," Adanel answered simply, with a shake of her head. "It seemed my father paid them well and they believed that with the port down and the MacLeods blocking ships coming in and out of the upper loch, you would not have the funds to pay hardly anyone, especially those who directly served my father."

Dugan bobbed his head, seeing why they might have thought that. "Most lairds probably would not have the funds to continue paying staff until coin started regularly coming in."

Adanel turned back to look out the window. "I'm embarrassed to admit that I had never before considered the idea of pay and money. So when it first came up during our interviews, I was uncomfortably worried. I could not promise them what they wanted or needed to hear. And without that promise, I knew that staffing the castle at all would be impossible, let alone with those who would be willing to do the hard work to make this place what it could be. But Tybalt said not to concern myself with payment. You had enough to cover whatever was agreed."

"I do and it was worth it." Dugan rubbed her arms encouragingly. "The change has been remarkable."

"But how?" Adanel asked. "When Tybalt said, quite convincingly, that there were plenty of funds and that all who deserved to be paid would be, I was sure he was just stalling for time. But I've seen him meet with the staff and pay them. *Where* did he get all that coin?"

Dugan studied her expression and knew that simple platitudes and evasiveness were not going to work. Her eyes swirled with curiosity. Adanel was going to prod until she discovered the answer. "I have money, Adanel," he finally stated. "Quite a bit for I was not always a commander. Remember, I was almost named laird of the Torridon region instead of Cole McTiernay."

"You were almost a McTiernay laird?" she asked incredulously.

He shook his head. "I was born a Conanach. I'm not a Highlander by birth; I just spent the majority of my adult years in this region. I knew the language, and with my size and skill with the blade, people in the north assumed that I was one of them. But I grew up on the mouth of the River Clyde working the docks."

Adanel's jaw dropped in shock. How could she not know this about him?

He grinned. "I suspect there is a great deal we don't know about each other, love. We will learn all our secrets in time," he said, and tugged her hand toward the table.

Adanel blinked, realizing she had spoken her question aloud, and then followed him, plopping down on his lap when he pulled her toward him.

"So"—he paused to pull off a piece of bread and give it to her—"if I had been named laird, the clan would have probably become Conanach. But, it was a good thing I was not named laird."

"Why?" Adanel asked, covering her mouth as she chewed.

"Lots of reasons. Mostly I would not have made a good one at the time. I had led a small group of men, but that is not the same as a clan. Working for Cole, I not only got leadership experience, but I also learned what it took to be a good laird."

"And the money?"

"Well, as I said, I led a small group of men—one of whom was Garrett—" Adanel's eyes popped open and then she rolled them as if she should have realized their relationship was anchored in his past. "—and if you were good at fighting, something we all were, it could be very lucrative at times. Some of the men liked to spend their money on women and drink; I saved mine."

"What were you saving it for?"

He shook his head. "I'm not really sure, actually. I guess I just didn't want the lack of coin to keep me from going after an opportunity I wanted to pursue."

"Then is Tybalt paying the staff using your savings?" she whispered. "*Faireachdainn.*"

"That *would* have been the case, but my savings are still ours to use as we want," he said, pulling off a piece of meat and eating it. He moaned with pleasure. "This is *very* good. I was told Kara refused the position of the head cook in the kitchens."

"She did," Adanel affirmed, and opened her mouth to take the piece of meat Dugan was offering. She closed her eyes and enjoyed the succulent flavor. "You're right. This is good. Kara did not cook it, but she is the one who helped me find the ones who did. Most had never worked in a large kitchen, they were just women she had known for years in the village. She also taught them some of her tricks to bring out the flavor."

"She did a good job, but I am surprised Kara was able to get so many."

"We would not have if not for the coin Tybalt is paying them . . . which you just implied is *not* yours?"

"Oh, it *is* mine," he reassured her. "It just did not come from my savings. Seems your father had quite a large stash of gold he had kept hidden away. Based on the little I could glean from the corrupt dockmaster before I banished him, your father had quite the scheme going. Through lies and manipulation, he got both sellers and buyers to agree to only minimal markups, while telling the other something quite different."

"Goods going through our docks were marked up *twice*?"

Dugan nodded. "And your father reaped the benefits for years. *That* is the coin I found and that is what I am using to make all the repairs and support Fearan in his expansion endeavors. Without it, we would have been doing the minimum until the port was running again."

Adanel stared at the food on the table, flummoxed by what Dugan had just told her. "I cannot believe they did not know it was happening."

"They would have if MacCoinnich and MacLeod ever spoke to each other. But they don't and your father took advantage. Still, they had to have suspected something, though not the degree to which it was happening. It was probably the reason MacCoinnich agreed to your father's marriage idea. I am also sure that the deception is partly behind MacLeod's reason to blockade the port."

"I thought that was because my grandfather believed he should have Bàgh Fìon because I am half MacLeod."

"Speaking of which, what did you think of my gift?"

Adanel looked away, knowing a sheepish look had overtaken her expression. Until now, she had not felt the slightest bit of guilt in refusing to open the box he had sent. "I haven't looked at it."

Dugan ran his tongue along his teeth. "It was not a bribe. Faden and I found it with your father's stash and he said it belonged to your mother. That makes it yours."

Adanel's mouth dropped. "I did not know."

"Where is it?" he asked, grabbing her waist and lifting her to her feet so he could stand.

"It's next to my chest on the floor," she mumbled, feeling very foolish as she watched him leave the room and go to her chambers. Less than two minutes later he had returned, box in hand.

"I could not find the key."

Adanel swallowed. "I did not want to be tempted so I put it in here, on that table over there." Dugan gave her a look. Adanel shrugged. "I did not want the servants to find it."

Dugan got the key and handed it to her. "Open it. I think you will be both surprised and pleased."

Nudging the tray out of the way, Adanel took the box and placed it on the table. She then pushed in the key and opened the lid. Inside was a velvet bag with the MacLeod crest embroidered on it. She glanced up at Dugan, who nodded encouragingly for her to continue. Carefully, she stretched the bag's opening and slid out the contents. Adanel knew immediately what she was looking at.

The MacLeod jewels. Necklaces, brooches, bracelets, hair clips—all items purchased from abroad and coveted by the Highland clans. Only the queen had jewels to rival those that were shining before her.

Adanel fingered a large emerald on one of the necklaces and then looked up. Her face blanched. "And you said that *Faden* saw these? He *knew* what was in this bag? Are you certain?"

Dugan's brow furrowed seeing her grave countenance. It reminded him of the look he saw Faden had upon seeing them. "Aye," he answered.

"*A thighearna!*" she murmured, so softly he barely heard her. Adanel slunk down into a chair. "These," she said, pointing at the fortune, "are the famous MacLeod jewels. I have never seen them, but my mother told me about them several times when I was little."

"Well, I don't have to ask why your father did not give them to you, but you seem surprised that they even exist."

Adanel grimaced. "I was not sure they did, or um . . . that they were *here*. You see, my grandmother gave them to my mother in order to convince her to marry my father. She was about to back out, afraid that she was going to make a mistake she would have to live with for the rest of her life. These jewels were to ensure that she would be respected, but if necessary, they were also the means for my mother to escape. She foolishly left them out one night and my father took them. Of course, she sent word to my grandmother of what happened, who had then told my grandfather. From what I was told, he was furious. He had no idea of what my grandmother had done."

"Laird MacLeod wants the jewels back." Dugan sat down next to her.

Adanel nodded. "It was the real reason my grandfather sent all his sons down here to guard the 'interests of the MacLeod' because it was certainly not me or my mother. Faden is the youngest of my uncles and it was shortly after he arrived when rumors started to fly that my grandfather was going to stop MacLeod ships from coming to Bàgh Fìon. It was said that my father made a threat and it worked for MacLeod ships returned to our port. I don't remember much. I was only twelve at the time."

"You remember enough," Dugan said, leaning forward with his elbows upon his knees.

"But what is so surprising is that *this* is what Faden has been looking for all these years. These jewels are his way back home."

"He told you this?"

She nodded. "It was right after Daniel"—she paused and looked at Dugan, relieved to see no animosity that she had almost married someone before him—"was killed," she finished. "It was horrible and Faden sent word to my grandfather asking to return home and provide refuge for me. Faden was told that he knew the price to come home and until he could pay it, he—nor I—would be welcomed. Angry, Faden told me everything. By that time, he had been searching for years. I, of course, joined the hunt and we looked *everywhere*, Dugan—stairwells, passageways, even the docks themselves."

"They were well hidden. It was by accident I came upon them. If I had not literally stumbled, it is possible that they—and all your father's gold—would never have been found."

The blood drained out of Adanel's face. "Faden will be leaving us now that we have found these."

"He was the one who told me to give them to you." Dugan slid the bag in her direction, somewhat in awe of what he was looking at. He had only glanced at the jewels before. If he had known exactly what they were, he would have done something more to keep them safe. For if anyone had known what was in that box on her floor, the locked box would have been destroyed and the MacLeod jewels would be missing again. "I don't think he plans on using them."

Her face lit up and Adanel shoved the bag and the jewels in his direction. "But *you* could. You could do just what my father did and coerce my grandfather into ending the blockade and restarting trade with us. These jewels could be the key, Dugan, to everything. You already have won over the docks and the soldiers." She waved her hand to the revelry taking place outside.

"The rest of the clan will soon be just as supportive, and with the port active, no one could argue your claim to being laird here."

"They are your jewels, Adanel. They belonged to your mother and now you."

Adanel looked down and picked up a hair clip. Small amethysts lined its border, each surrounded tiny diamonds. Above them lay three rows of pearls with amethysts finishing the look in a simple swirl design of gold. "I want this one," she said softly, and put it aside.

She then gathered the rest of the jewels and put them back into the velvet bag. Once more she slid it toward Dugan. Picking up the hairpin, she said, "I *am* part MacLeod and our children will be as well. I want our daughter and our daughter's daughter to have something that leaves her heritage in no doubt. The MacLeods are powerful, and having this hairpin as proof of our lineage could be helpful to our great-grandchildren one day. Besides I, well, like it," she said with a smile. "But use the rest. They are the MacLeod jewels. I am a McTiernay. And after all that my uncle did for me over the years, I want to give Faden a chance to go home."

Dugan was almost positive that Faden would go home, but only to visit. The man's family, his friends, the ones he trusted, were all here. And now that he had a position that was both challenging and rewarding, Dugan could not see Faden giving it all up to once again be the youngest of five brothers. "If you are certain about not keeping them," Dugan murmured, still slightly amazed that Adanel could so easily push them away.

"I am."

"Then I think first, we will put these, including this"— he picked up the clip and put it back in the box alongside the bag—"in a safe place until I can send word to MacLeod to come and get them."

Adanel looked puzzled. "You are just going to *give* the jewels back to my grandfather?"

"It's like you said. They are the MacLeod jewels. They were given to your mother but they should remain with the MacLeod clan. They should be worn and enjoyed by your grandmother, not collecting dust."

"But what about the blockade?"

Dugan reached over, tenderly gripped her chin to tilt her head toward him, and gave her a light kiss on her lips. "Remember what you told your friend Kara? I am not your father and only a fool would have done as he did."

"You are not a fool," Adanel said with a smile, gliding off her chair, leaving the blanket behind. "You are chieftain of the McTiernays of Gerloch, my husband, and most importantly, the keeper of my heart."

"Aye, I am definitely that," he said, and scorched her to his soul with a kiss.

Chapter Sixteen

Laird MacLeod continued to study the brash new McTiernay laird who had summoned him to Bàgh Fìon. MacLeod was an old man. His once flaming red hair was nearly all gray. His stomach protruded far more than he liked and his energy waned in the afternoons. But what had not lessened with time was his ability to read men, negotiate, and strike a spark of fear in a man's eye upon will.

His cold stare normally made men quiver with fear. Coupled with the drumming of his fingers on the table for long minutes without stopping, he never failed to make even the most arrogant of men begin to have doubts. But this McTiernay laird—this *Dugan*—was an enigma. He was calm, powerful, and had a quiet strength that could be just as inflexible as his own.

Dugan was brown-haired, blue-eyed, and muscular; MacLeod could see why his granddaughter had fallen for the new laird. When Adanel had come to the dock to welcome him as he got off his ship, MacLeod had been shocked to see just how much she looked like her mother. Faia had been the eldest of his two daughters and had captured his heart the day she was born. Her red hair had curled around her face and bounced whenever she smiled. It had never occurred to him that he had been giving her over to a madman or that Faia's wedding would be the last time he would ever see her. He had never dreamed a lot of things that had happened. But seeing Adanel was like looking into the past with a chance to make up for past mistakes.

Something he was willing to do, but not at any price. Somewhere around this port were jewels that could practically buy all of Scotland. The sparkly baubles themselves meant little to him, but they did represent power. Their loss had made him look weak and that was something he despised.

He had made the MacLeod name into something powerful and it was not by giving in to emotional whims. And yet, the McTiernay had surprised him with presenting a business plan that might prove to be very profitable.

The trade over the years from the small port was of little consequence to him, his captains, or his clan, but with what Dugan was proposing, that could change. Bàgh Fìon could grow to be a central area of commerce. However, the young laird needed ships—he did not have . . . but MacLeod did. Unfortunately for the McTiernay, he did not do business with those he did not trust. He had done it once, at this very port, and after his daughter had paid the price, he vowed never to do it again.

"The expansion would indeed allow three times what the port can currently handle. And I agree that you can even handle a greater variety and amount of merchandise," he said, giving a cold glare to his youngest son, Faden. He was no longer a boy, but a man, and by his cool, unwavering countenance, more like him than any of his brothers.

Faden had *not* been at the dock to meet him. He had joined the meeting along with the port master after Dugan had called them in. At first, MacLeod had

believed it had been Dugan's idea for the delay, but
quickly corrected that assumption as soon as Faden
looked him directly in the eye. There was no familial
warmth there. MacLeod had privately wondered if it had
been a mistake to reject Faden's request to come home
six years ago but dismissed the thought. To have accepted
meant he agreed to give up the chance of recovering
the MacLeod jewels, something Mackbaythe had sworn
he did not have, always claiming one of the soldiers or
servants had stolen them and disappeared never to
return.

"And I agree expanding the routes south to the new
McTiernay markets will increase not only traffic but in-
troduce a whole new set of buyers. That could make
things very lucrative, especially as those routes will be
protected now that one clan controls both Torridon and
Gerloch lands."

"But?"

MacLeod raised a bushy red brow. Dugan just returned the stare, waiting for him to answer his question.
Suddenly, MacLeod found himself with the urge to twitch.
"*But*," he snarled, giving away some of his frustration, "I
am not inclined to give you my ships." He waited for
Dugan to ask why and when the seconds stretched into
minutes, his impatience got the better of him. "I am not
inclined to give you my ships because I don't know you
and therefore I don't trust you. I scarcely trade with Cole
McTiernay and his reputation for being fair and honest
is well known. You may have slapped the name McTiernay
on everything around here, but these were Mackbaythe
lands and men for too long. I know their ways."

"And yet you chose to do business with him."

MacLeod's face turned red. "And I am choosing *not*
to do business now."

Dugan pursed his lips together and then let go a sigh

as he placed his palms flat down on the table to rise. Faden and Dugan's port master, Fearan, rose as well. "Then I am sorry I requested you make this trip."

MacLeod let go a loud snort. The herald the McTiernay had sent had not relayed a *request*, but a carefully worded demand. *Laird of the McTiernays of Gerloch highly recommends you immediately sail for Bàgh Fìon before next steps are taken to end the blockade.*

That was a threat. Dugan knew it. MacLeod knew it. And he had almost called his bluff. The only reason he had come was because of the man's chief. Malcolm MacLeod was not friends with Conor McTiernay, but he had met the man on a few occasions and learned enough about him to know that the McTiernay chief did *not* bluff. And if Conor had appointed Dugan to be one of his chieftains, it was likely he had put someone there of similar mind and personality. MacLeod had needed to hear for himself what *next steps* meant, but from what he could see, they were just empty words.

"I would like to offer you accommodations for the evening, and I believe my wife has planned a banquet feast in your honor as your granddaughter."

MacLeod rolled his eyes and rose to his feet. He should have known. Dugan was planning on using Adanel. He was married to her and she was a MacLeod—or at least half one. "Tell my granddaughter her gesture is appreciated, but that I must return immediately. Besides, you need to spend the next several months worrying about how you are going to make this port run without any ships to trade your goods."

MacLeod gestured to the barrels stacked in the corner of the meeting room. It was a spacious area on the top floor of a building right off the docks where the port master probably conducted most of his business. The stairs he had climbed were on the outside of the building and led to an open deck area that one could stand on and see into the bay for miles. In the distance, he could make out two small dark dots—the MacLeod ships he had sent to prevent any others from coming through. So far none had tried.

Dugan backed away from the large table but instead of going to the door, he went to the other side of the room alongside which were numerous crates and various materials, including signal flags. "I will give Adanel your message. I am sure she will be sorry to hear of your early departure, but she will understand. As far as running this port without MacLeod ships, I have already taken measures to do just that."

Dugan went to a small crate underneath the window and opened it. Then, he paused and turned around. With a smile, he said, "I find it fascinating how many people assume I am a Highlander by birth. Conor knew, of course, that I had grown up near Dumbarton when he asked me to be laird." Dugan's smile grew and MacLeod knew his face had given away his shock. "And while the MacGhille and the Caimbeul clans cannot boast having the number of ships that you can, they do have them *and* they have large armies to protect them if need be."

MacLeod just stood there. He was both furious and impressed. He could not help but think that the rumors were true: *McTiernays never bluff.*

"Both clans have always wanted an inroad into the northern waterways," Dugan continued. "I sent a herald down to meet with them when I sent my request to you. I must admit that is why I added some urgency to your message, because I wanted to give you first chance to agree to my proposal and let me know the space you required and how often to expect your ships. And while we could not come to an arrangement, I do appreciate you coming so quickly."

MacLeod refused to show his ire or how close he was to caving. But he knew, just as Dugan did, that the MacLeods would not interfere with either MacGhille and the Caimbeul ships. To do so would mean war and not with the McTiernays, but the western half of Scotland. They could make it so that he could never leave the inner seas.

Dugan had won, but he had not won *him*.

MacLeod walked to the door, but just before he opened it Dugan stopped him. "MacLeod, one last thing," he said, pulling out a bag. "A month ago, I found this by sheer accident in, well, let's just say an *incredibly* hidden location."

Dugan dropped the bag on the table. "Of course, seeing its contents, I offered them to my wife thinking I might surprise her. As you can imagine, they did, but she also told me what they were. Her mother's jewels given to her by her grandmother. She had never seen them before, but her mother had told her about them, it seems." He pointed at the bag. "She doesn't feel it is right to keep them as this is now a McTiernay clan and they are MacLeod jewels. She asked me to return them to you." When MacLeod reached for the bag, Dugan added, "She did take one amethyst hair clip as an heirloom to wear as a reminder of her mother. Of course, she planned to tell you all this later tonight and was hoping to return them to you herself, but I feared you might not be inclined to stay so I brought them with me just in case I was right."

MacLeod looked inside the bag and then back at Dugan. They were all there. Emeralds, diamonds, rubies. No longer caring if Dugan saw his shock or not, MacLeod said, "These . . . these . . . they mean a lot to our clan. When my wife . . ." He choked up, still unable to believe not just what he was holding, but also that Dugan McTiernay had just *handed* them to him.

MacLeod would have done anything to get these back. He had given up his youngest son. He had forced his favorite daughter to remain here and eventually die all to get them back. Were they worth it? He had long ago stopped asking the question in fear of the answer.

MacLeod squeezed the bag and then straightened his shoulders. Looking Dugan in the eye, he acknowledged, "I said I did not know you. Five minutes ago, I did not. Sometimes it takes years to get to know a man and even then he can fool you."

Dugan nodded, having experienced that very thing when his best friend, Leith, had tried to kill him as well as Cole's wife, Ellenor. They both survived, but they both had scars from the event.

"And sometimes," MacLeod continued, "a single action can give you so much insight into the internal workings of a man, that you have no doubt as to who he is. This"—he shook the bag—"is such an action. The MacLeods will be pleased to use Bàgh Fìon as one of its main ports going forward." He snapped his fingers to the captain, who had been sitting quietly. "Work with the port master and my son," he said, to Faden's surprise. "I have a feast to join and a granddaughter that I would like to get to know a little better."

For the first time that day, MacLeod saw Dugan smile. It was not a large one, but it warmed his blue eyes, which had previously looked cold and impassive. That single action was another insight the new laird probably had no idea he had revealed. Dugan and Adanel's marriage, as unlikely as it was, was based on love, not circumstance.

"I hope you have a buttery," MacLeod announced, tapping his belly, "and that it is full!"

Dugan chuckled. "I do and it is," he replied, opening the door just as a frazzled soldier entered.

"Laird! You are needed immediately at the castle.

Daeron MacCoinnich has arrived with several men and he is making demands to Lady Adanel and—"

Dugan heard no more as he dashed down the stairs and ran to the great hall where he had last seen Adanel.

Dugan watched the man squirm underneath his sword. "You *dare* to threaten my *wife*," he hissed.

Daeron's eyes darkened with fury. "She should have been *mine*."

Dugan pressed forward so that blood began to drip down Daeron's throat. "Want me to end your suffering? Say another word and I will."

Adanel's trembling hand on Dugan's arm stayed him from making the cut final, but it did not cause him to drop his sword. "Don't kill him," she whispered. "At least not here." When he did not move, she added, "Please, Dugan, I just replaced all the rushes," hoping her ridiculous comment gave him pause.

It worked. Her words surprised him enough that it broke through his anger and got him to take a step back so that his guards could restrain Daeron. "Take him to Daingneach and throw him in the dungeons. I have no doubt that his father will be here shortly to get him. The boy is a fool, but his father's not."

Garrett nodded and dragged an unprotesting but unrepentant Daeron away. Thank God, Tybalt and Brùid had reacted quickly and that the castle guards had hustled to their call. By the time Dugan had arrived, every one of the two dozen men Daeron had brought with him had been disarmed and were kneeling on the ground in front of the great hall. But during the commotion, Daeron had slipped inside where Adanel and Kara were with a couple of servants discussing the menu.

Daeron had surprised them and had just grabbed

Adanel's arm and was about to plunge a dagger into her chest when Dugan had burst in, sword in hand, ready to do battle. MacLeod, Faden, and Fearan were right behind. Fearan immediately headed for his wife, but Dugan only had eyes for Adanel.

Without a word, Dugan had charged Daeron, giving him no time to think. Dugan had flipped Daeron's sword out of his grip and spun the man until his back was against the stone wall and his neck was under his blade.

Once Daeron was out of sight, Dugan gathered Adanel in his arms, shaking. The fear of seeing her so close to death still coursed in his veins. Never had he been so close to losing control. In battle, he was always completely calm and focused. It was why he had lived when so many others did not, but seeing Adanel in danger made him realize that there was no end to the deaths he would cause if something ever happened to her.

"I'm well, Dugan," she assured him, rubbing his back in an effort to calm his shaking body. "You got here in time. I promise you, I am well."

He gripped her head between his hands and claimed her lips, plundering her accepting mouth, needing proof that she was still there with him, that he had not lost her. Adanel met him fully, her kiss as insistent as his. Only when Dugan was thoroughly convinced she was indeed well, living and still by his side, did he let her go and release a deep breath that he had not realized he had been holding.

"Laird," Loman asked, standing behind him. "Word just came in that Laird MacCoinnich is approaching and he has at least another three dozen men with him. He should be here within the hour."

Keeping Adanel tucked next to his side, Dugan ordered, "Call every available McTiernay soldier to duty. We will meet them with our full strength."

"Already done, laird," Loman replied, and turned to leave.

"Do not engage first. I doubt MacCoinnich is here to shed blood. He just wants his son, who is *very* lucky to still be alive."

"Aye, laird."

"And, Loman," Dugan said, "you can escort MacCoinnich in here and see that he has food and drink until I arrive." He looked back down at Adanel. "I might be a while."

"My son is brash," MacCoinnich conceded.

"He's a fool," Garrett muttered, "and he's lucky not to be a dead fool."

Daeron, released from the dungeon after being there only a few hours, muttered, "I wish you had killed me, then there would be war and the McTiernays would be erased from existence."

MacCoinnich jumped to his feet. "*Cease!* If he had killed you, I would be here simply to collect your carcass and drag it back home. God, you may be brilliant, son, and you may remember everything, but *murt!* I sometimes think you are the densest man to ever live! If I had just one more son, I would have sent you away long ago, never to walk MacCoinnich lands again."

Dugan's eyes popped wide open as did those belonging to every single soul sitting at the table, including Daeron's.

Dugan had requested MacLeod and his captain to join them. MacLeod had not been part of the discussions that led to Dugan being named laird, but he was going to be included going forward. MacCoinnich and the McTiernays had hopes of retaining a civil relationship, but with MacLeod there was a real chance for more. Dugan wanted to explore that possibility, and including MacLeod on strategic discussions concerning MacCoinnich was a step in that direction.

Daeron did not cower. Dugan gave him that. But he did stop talking.

"*Now*," MacCoinnich said with a huff, retaking his seat, "my son was telling me that his intentions were honorable and that he had brought goods to trade. Rumors were that a MacLeod ship was sailing in today and he wanted to be here when it was at the dock in hopes to meet with their captain. There *is* a cart full of goods as *proof*."

Dugan looked at each of his leaders in turn—Loman, Garrett, Faden, and then Fearan. For Daeron to know that MacLeod had come in to port so soon meant there was a MacCoinnich spy in their midst, and that was not acceptable.

MacLeod sat forward and with his elbows on the great hall table, he clasped his hands. "I was there, MacCoinnich. Your son almost killed my granddaughter and you think I am going to trade with you?" He scoffed, sat back, and glared at the powerful laird. He fought back a smile when MacCoinnich shifted in his seat. At least someone was still affected by his stare.

"The MacCoinniches have access to Scotland's eastern shores," Dugan said, knowing that Bàgh Fìon was far closer to their larger villages. It was also only a day's ride from the MacCoinnich's tower keep. Hit hard by the English, Laird MacCoinnich lacked the funds to build a castle and it was one of the reasons he had his mind on Bàgh Fìon, its castle, and the two towers.

"It might be more profitable for you to seek trade in that direction. We are opening up negotiations with MacGhille and the Caimbeul clans as well as the Mackays and McTiernays of Farr, and of course the McTiernays and Schellden clans just to the south. Bàgh Fìon might no longer have the capacity to meet your needs."

MacCoinnich narrowed his eyes. "That was not the agreement. You were—"

Dugan cut him off. "To have the port running within a year so that it was self-supported. I was to have the Mackbaythe clansmen accept McTiernay rule and name, and train my own army within a year. There was no talk about limiting those I would have to do business with. You assumed I needed you. I don't."

MacLeod chuckled. "If it makes you feel better, MacCoinnich, I made the same mistake of underestimating him."

The old laird sent him a scathing look. "It doesn't."

"That doesn't mean I *won't* trade with you though. If you're amicable to some changes. Starting with *that* man never stepping onto McTiernay soil again," he said, pointing to Daeron. "He does, he dies, and all trade ends."

"You touch my son, and we will go to war."

Dugan leaned forward. "*Then we are at war now, MacCoinnich.*" His voice, though quiet, had an ominous quality. "He held a blade to my wife's chest. For that alone I should kill him, you, and every man you brought with you, without mercy."

Daeron was lucky to be alive but his reprieve wouldn't necessarily last long. If MacCoinnich wanted war, he would have one. Massive casualties would result, but if there was any clan in danger of being wiped from existence, it was that of MacCoinnich—not McTiernay.

War, however, was not what Dugan wanted. He also knew that while Conor did not desire it either, he would, without a doubt, support him. If any men knew what it was to love their wives, the McTiernays did. There was nothing they would not do for them and that included going to war if one of their own was threatened.

"I demand a cut of every good and item we sell," MacCoinnich said through gritted teeth.

"As you should. *And* if I agree to do business with you, I'll give you the same cut I'm giving the MacLeods and what I will be offering any others that go through my port." Dugan sat back in his chair and crossed his legs, putting an ankle on his knee. "If we were to trade, you can only come through our lands using the main route, the one that hugs the mountain path. No more coming through our farmlands and grazing areas. Not even once."

MacCoinnich gave a single nod. "My goods will be escorted by my guards."

"As long as their numbers are no greater than a half dozen that won't be a problem."

"That's not enough to fend off an attack."

Dugan waved a hand. "My men will ensure there won't be one." He paused and then said, "You weren't inferring that *I* would be attacking, were you?"

MacCoinnich ignored him. "And I want a building for just our goods. No others, manned, by my men."

"If I agree to do business with you, I'll agree to the building but not the men."

"Four men."

"Two who are approved by Faden," Dugan countered, wiggling two fingers. "And again, only if I agree to do business with you."

MacCoinnich threw his hands up in the air. "And what will it take for you to do that!" he demanded.

Dugan slowly turned his head so that his gaze was solely on the man who tried to end his wife's life. "I want the names of every MacCoinnich spy in my port. And if I find out you missed one, all agreements will cease and I will burn all the goods in your building. I will then slice open your guards and leave their guts at your border."

The silence in the room was deafening. "And I want

those names, MacCoinnich, even if we don't come to an agreement."

MacCoinnich's eye twitched.

MacLeod coughed into his hand and said, "Agree, MacCoinnich. McTiernays don't bluff."

MacCoinnich knew that to be true. He also knew who his spies were. "There are three. My commander knows their names." They had infiltrated three years ago to see if the port was in such disrepair that it was worth the cost of taking over. Whether it was or not had quickly become moot. Adanel had been promised to his son, and while he would have easily ended that arrangement if Daeron had resisted, the boy had gone and fallen in love with the bewitching woman. The port was going to be theirs regardless.

MacCoinnich had ordered his men to remain and learn all they could about the port, its dealings, and the men who ran it. It was how he had learned that Dugan had routed out the corruption and had started making changes to expand the port that would allow more ships to dock. If true, this little port would evolve into a thriving one, which would make McTiernay rich the honest way. But that coin Dugan was using to repair this hall and his port was *his* gold and there was nothing MacCoinnich could do about it. It was nearly enough to provoke him into declaring the war nobody thought would happen.

Dugan looked at Garrett and Faden. "Please find those men and tell them that they will be going home today with their laird. And you might want to remind them that they will not be welcomed back."

Garrett and Faden left and the small group became even smaller and far quieter. MacLeod took a deep breath and smacked his fist on the table. "McTiernay, you promised me ale and I suspect MacCoinnich could use a large mug himself."

MacCoinnich grimaced but gave a single nod.

"MacCoinnich, my wife has planned a welcome celebration for her father this evening. You are welcome to attend."

MacCoinnich took in several deep breaths and looked around. The great hall was the same and yet vastly different than the last few times he had been there. The windows had been washed allowing for a lot more light, and the stench was wonderfully missing. Death no longer lingered in the air. The servants, the few that he saw, did not scamper about in fear, trying to do their job and yet not be seen. The smells wafting in from the kitchens adjacent to the hall were more than pleasing. They were making him hungry.

Fact was, he wanted to stay but he also knew that his son should never be in a room with Adanel McTiernay again.

MacCoinnich glanced over his shoulder to his sullen son. "Daeron cannot stay. He has many, *many* things to do when he gets home. Including packing. I think it is time you visit your aunt for a while. Maybe time with Laird Stuart will teach you how to curb that temper of yours." He did not add that the Stuart's southern border was that of England and about as far away from MacCoinnich lands as he could send him.

Daeron rose and stomped out of the room, but smartly remained quiet until he was outside. Then he shouted for a horse.

Dugan was not concerned about the immediate actions of the young man. Daeron was a fool and easily spoke about dying, but he did not have a death wish. Dugan could only hope that when Daeron returned, he would be more mature and in control of his temper. Hopefully that was possible.

MacLeod was right. There were some actions that defined a man and he had witnessed enough from Daeron to know that the young MacCoinnich did not like to lose. A few months ago that had happened when Adanel married Dugan. Daeron had lost again today and then again with his father. These events would forever be etched in the man's memory, of which all knew was everlasting.

The young MacCoinnich was dangerous and impetuous and did not fear crossing a line that others would never dare. That was proven when he almost thrust a knife into Dugan's wife's chest. Mackbaythe had died for almost killing Conor, and Dugan hoped he did not live to regret not ending Daeron for attempting to kill his wife. He feared he might. Daeron now viewed the McTiernays as his enemy. Someday he *was* going to be chief of the MacCoinniches, and when that happened, his long memory might come back to haunt all of them.

"I, however," MacCoinnich said, recapturing Dugan's attention, "am *not* needed immediately back home." He looked around again and said, "I'm interested in seeing what this place looks like when not steeped knee deep in muck, mayhem, and atrocities."

Epilogue

Dugan lay languidly on the bed, unable to move, completely drained of any energy. Adanel had collapsed on top of him, her breathing still heavy from their love-making. He doubted he would ever grow weary of their passion, or if he would ever desire her less than he did in that moment.

After six months, life at Bàgh Fìon was busier than ever. The expansion of the port was coming along, but it would be at least another couple of years until the initial dock expansion was done. He also wanted to erect a curtain wall around the keep and the main buildings supporting the castle, but that would have to wait until there were people available. Between the building of the dock and the additional storage buildings as well as running the port and overseeing basic clan needs, too many things had a higher priority and there were barely enough workers to support already active projects. The clan was almost too small to do all that was being envisioned.

Even now, they were having to curtail those wanting to join the guard. They had doubled their original goal. Granted, they were still learning one end of a sword from the other, but Loman was gifted in the ways of training men. He and Garrett often switched duties, Loman placing the ex-mercenary in charge of the seasoned McTiernay soldiers. At first, Dugan had been concerned, but he need not have been. They all respected Garrett and followed his lead just as if he had been a McTiernay all his life. But he wasn't one. And though his friend had accepted the label of commander, Dugan knew that it was only temporary. When the year was over, Garrett would be leaving, regardless of how much Dugan hoped otherwise. The man was plagued by something. Dugan could only pray Garrett would quickly find a way to release his burden and return someday.

Loman was aware Garrett would be leaving when the year was out and had already spoken to Dugan about him—a handful of others wanting to remain when the other McTiernay and allied soldiers left to return back to their homes and clans. Dugan had quickly made Loman the commander of his own elite guard for the man was a skilled and capable leader, uncannily and accurately anticipating orders before they were given. Dugan then had the task of sending word to Conor that another of his prized soldiers had permanently left the nest.

If someone had told Dugan six months ago that he and Loman would grow to be close friends, he would have thought them mad. But the man had proven himself not just capable and loyal, but a trusted confidant who always gave an honest, direct answer.

As for Adanel, she had been just as busy. Most of the castle had been in poor condition when she and Tybalt had started, even more so than they had first thought. Some rooms had been declared dangerous as rot had eaten through the wooden floors in multiple spots. But the buildings and rooms the servants used had been even worse.

Deciding the kitchens were the priority, Adanel had them overhauled first, which meant a lot of cold meals for two months. Tonight had been the first meal prepared in them since the doors reopened and Dugan had to admit that it was worth the wait. And that was just the beginning. Adanel had plans to bring Lasairbhàigh Castle to its full potential glory, and those aspirations also included the two towers—Baile Tùr and Daingneach.

Dugan sighed and let his hand glide up and down Adanel's spine, hoping nothing interrupted this moment. The love they shared was deep and profound. He still could not quite believe that he had found a soul mate, someone whom he trusted absolutely and completely with everything he was. He knew Adanel felt the same, and while he was still learning more and more about her each day, he had no doubts about the authenticity of her spirit and her love for him.

Dugan lowered his head as she raised hers. He loved that she looked drowsy, sexy, thoroughly loved, and gave her a brief, hard kiss before she rolled over and cuddled into the crux of his arm.

"I love you," she murmured with a sigh against his chest.

"And I love you, *aithinne*," he said huskily, his hands stroking her hair, his mouth brushing her temple. Then with a stretch, he rolled to his side so that he could look at her and watch the firelight play on her features.

Adanel raised a finger and ran it slowly down his chest and along the dark trail of hair on his taut abdomen. With a soft laugh that was a half groan, he stopped her, caught her hand, and caressed her finger with his lips. "Do that and you know where it will lead."

Adanel wiggled her brows. "To a family," she teased.

He shook his head and leaned down to nuzzle her

neck. "Nay, I've been careful. I want you all to myself for a little while longer."

Adanel giggled. "How much longer?"

"I don't know," he mumbled against her shoulder, peppering her with kisses. "In five or six years, I'll probably be able to let you go long enough for you to birth my son."

She swatted his shoulder. "Birth your son! Aye, we will wait until *you* can be patient enough for me to feed our *daughter*."

"Nay," he said, moving lower. "These are all mine," he whispered just before claiming a taut pebble with his mouth.

Adanel groaned and arched her back. It did not matter how many times they came together, how many times he touched her in just this same way, it always caused her blood to run in her veins and her body to come alive.

"See," he said, coming back to claim her mouth, "I cannot get enough of you."

Adanel nodded. "I think we need to find someone for Nigel and Brùid."

"Nigel is too young. It would be cruel to foist him upon a woman, even if she was willing."

"You're probably right about that," Adanel giggled.

"And I'm pretty sure Brùid scares women."

Adanel winced. "Again, I think you are right. Imagine a woman underneath him. . . . He would crush her."

Dugan groaned and rested his forehead against hers. "I do *not* want to think about Brùid with a woman."

"Then think about Faden and how alone he looked at dinner tonight."

Dugan rolled his eyes. "I love your uncle, *aithinne*, and

he is a superb dockmaster, but the man simply repels females. How many times have you tried?"

"Well, there must be someone out there for him."

"A woman who loves crazy hair, large ears, and a crooked nose?"

"If someone could love Laurel's midwife Hagatha, someone could love Faden," Adanel huffed.

Dugan raised his head and peered down at her, his face one of utter shock. "That woman is married?"

"Was," Adanel corrected. "Very happily too. And her temperament matches her looks, so if *she* could find someone, so can Faden."

"Then let the man do his own looking," Dugan groaned, and then furrowed his brows. "What about that widow he used to see when we were meeting at the loch?"

The sparkle in Adanel's brown eyes dimmed. "She is getting married to someone else. She claimed that all Faden cared about was work."

"I'm sorry, love. I know you want your uncle to be happy."

Adanel shook her head. "She wasn't the one for him. If she had been, Faden would not have let her go. He didn't even blink an eye when I told him about her wedding. So his soul mate is still out there, waiting for him to find her."

"Again, I'm telling you to stay out of it. Men don't like it when women meddle in their affairs."

Adanel scoffed and gave him a slight shove. "You liked it well enough when Laurel and the McTiernay women interfered in *yours,* or do you still believe it was Conor's idea for us to wed and you to become laird?"

Dugan froze above her. Seeing that she was serious, he rolled to his back and flopped an arm across his forehead. "*An truaighe mura.*"

"Don't worry. Laurel says all the husbands get it eventually."

"Get what?" he asked hesitantly, giving her a quick glance.

"Why McTiernays are so successful. Because while you all are incredibly good-looking, smart, and undeniably great leaders, you also have us," Adanel said, crawling onto his chest. She gave him a quick peck. "You need us wives by your side. We are each a McTiernay husband's secret weapon. So trust me, Highlander. I'll never let you down."

"Oh, I do, *aithinne*. Forever."

"Forever," she agreed, just before his lips hit hers and they gave each other what they always wanted and could never have too much of—true, undeniable, endless, passionate love.

Three months later, Brùid put the last small block of wood down and stretched his back from side to side. He then laced his fingers and stretched his arms, feeling the tension release all the way down. He had just finished chiseling the last block that afternoon and had rushed to get them up here before Adanel and Dugan came up to change for dinner.

He looked around at the two dozen small toys and wondered if there were enough of them. Aye, they were everywhere, but would Dugan get the message? Was it too subtle? All of his other practical jokes had been designed to force the two to talk to each other when they could not figure out a way to do so themselves. Today they spoke plenty, just not about the right things. These toys were supposed to fix that, but looking at them, Brùid wondered if they would work.

It had taken him three weeks to carve the blocks. Three weeks, in which *he* had known that Adanel was pregnant while Dugan had remained ignorant.

The only reason Brùid knew was because he was Adanel's guard. Dugan rose so early in the morning that he did not hear her rush to the chamber pot to expel last night's meal. Brùid knew very little about pregnancies but he remembered her pretending to do that when faking her last one. But this time her retching had been in earnest. What he did not understand was why Dugan still did not know.

At first, Brùid had thought Dugan was aware and the couple was just waiting to make the announcement. But when the laird had called Adanel to climb a steep ladder and join him on top of a building to take a look at something they were doing on the docks, Brùid realized Dugan was clueless. He could not imagine the smitten laird making such a request if he knew she was not eating for just one anymore.

Brùid sighed and slowly closed the door, hoping that what he had done was enough. Never had two people needed more help talking to each other than Adanel and Dugan. Even when they were happy, it seemed they still needed help. He was not sure where they would be without him.

They had to be goaded into every one of their arguments, major admissions, and even declarations of love. Some of his little tricks had been quite clever, too. Shortening Adanel's reins right after they had rescued her had been subtle, but leaving Dugan only laces to secure his plaid that morning at the river had been a stroke of genius. Sitting in the meat stew, however, was by far the best. People still broke out into hysterics when it came up in conversation. Little did they know who was behind it all. And it had all worked, just like Brùid knew it would.

The toys will, too, he promised himself. *The laird will figure out their meaning.* And in a few months, the blocks would be put to good use.

Ayc, his ideas always worked. But the best thing of all about them was that Nigel always got the blame.

Connect with U s

Visit us online at
KensingtonBooks.com
to read more from your favorite authors, see books
by series, view reading group guides, and more.

Join us on social media

for sneak peeks, chances to win books and prize packs,
and to share your thoughts with other readers.

facebook.com/kensingtonpublishing
twitter.com/kensingtonbooks

Tell us what you think!

To share your thoughts, submit a review,
or sign up for our eNewsletters, please visit:
KensingtonBooks.com/TellUs.